JEFF ABBOTT'S
SAM CAPRA THRILLERS

DOWNFALL

"Abbott packs a lifetime of thrills and suspense into a mere five days...Abbott excels at spinning complex webs of intrigue combining psychological twists and abundant action...Sam is both pawn and knight in an exciting chess game."　　　*—Publishers Weekly*

"Action-packed, never-stop-for-a-breath storytelling."
—Dallas Morning News

"Filled with action, intrigue, twists, and a variety of locales...It's perfect for a summer weekend's reading pleasure."
—Fort Worth Star-Telegram

"[A] whirlwind ride...*Downfall* moves like a juggernaut out of control and is impossible to put down...a torrid read that grabs the reader by the throat and never lets up."　　　*—BookReporter.com*

"Often wildly entertaining...a ton of action."
—Austin American-Statesman

THE LAST MINUTE

"An explosive cocktail."　　　　　　　　　*—Washington Post*

"[An] adrenaline rush that won't stop."
—San Antonio Express-News

"Abbott is one of the best thriller writers in the business, and he delivers action and complex characters...The next Capra novel cannot come fast enough."　　　*—Associated Press*

"This is the second in the Capra series, and he hasn't slowed down. It has killings, betrayals, big-time conspiracies, and action galore."
—Oklahoman

"Gripping...edgy...a breathless suspense novel...As a writer [Abbott] is fluid, smart, witty, and easy to take."

—*Dallas Morning News*

"Like *Adrenaline*, this is a fast-paced thriller with a likable, morally conflicted hero...Let's hope Abbott isn't through with Sam. He's a very well-drawn character, and it would be nice to see him again."

—*Booklist*

ADRENALINE

"Twisty, turny, and terrific."

—*USA Today*

"Outstanding...genuinely moving...Abbott hits full stride early on and never lets up. Readers who thrive on a relentless narrative pace and a straight line to the finish won't be disappointed."

—*Publishers Weekly* (starred review)

"Breathless fun...You really do keep turning page after page."

—*Cleveland Plain Dealer*

"Deliciously crafty...heart-pounding thrills...a stunner...It should launch him into the Michael Connelly or Dennis Lehane stratosphere...Glorious sensory acumen...with just the right amount of snarky wit."

—*Dallas Morning News*

"Extremely compelling...a thriller that will get even the most jaded reader's pulse racing...a grand slam home run...Everyone will want to see what Abbott, and Capra, have up their sleeve next."

—Associated Press

"Thrilling."

—*New York Daily News*

"Exhilarating...Confirms Abbott as one of the best thriller writers of our time...I think Jeff Abbott's the next Robert Ludlum. And I think Sam Capra is the heir apparent to Jason Bourne...The most gripping spy story I've read in years...Great read!"

—Harlan Coben

"This is a wonderful book and the start of one of the most exciting new series I've had the privilege to read...Sam Capra is now on my short list of characters I would follow anywhere. *Adrenaline* provides the high-octane pace one expects from a spy thriller, while grounding the action with a protagonist that anyone can root for."

—Laura Lippman

"*Adrenaline* lives up to its name. It's pure thriller in pace, but Abbott manages to keep the book's heart anchored in the right place. The characters aren't cardboard action figures, but people under incredible stresses and strains. I read it in a big gulp."

—Charlaine Harris

"A white-knuckle opening leads into undoubtedly the best thriller I've read so far this year...*Adrenaline* will surely vault Abbott to the top of must-read authors. The relentless action will hook you from the heart-stopping opening to a conclusion that was as shocking as it was heart-rending."

—*Ventura County Star* (CA)

"*Adrenaline*, like its namesake hormone, is all about pace, and a high-speed pace at that. A word of caution: Don't start reading [it] just before bedtime!"

—*BookPage*

"Sam Capra is the perfect hero—tough, smart, pure of heart, and hard to kill. And *Adrenaline* is the perfect thriller. Taut and edgy, with breakneck pacing and perfect plotting, it's a breathless race from the shocking, heart-wrenching opening sequence to the stunning conclusion."

—Lisa Unger

"Hero Sam Capra likes to unwind with parkour, leaping from building to building, clambering up walls and hurtling through space across the urban landscape...The sport's a fitting metaphor for Abbott's style, tumbling from page to page with the frantic inevitability of Robert Ludlum...It all works beautifully."

—*Booklist*

BLACK JACK POINT

JEFF ABBOTT

GRAND CENTRAL
PUBLISHING

NEW YORK   BOSTON

Copyright © 2002 by Jeff Abbott

Grand Central Publishing
Hachette Book Group
237 Park Avenue
New York, NY 10017

www.HachetteBookGroup.com

Printed in the United States of America

OPM

Originally published in 2002 by Dutton

First Grand Central Publishing Edition: April 2014

10 9 8 7 6 5 4 3 2 1

Grand Central Publishing is a division of Hachette Book Group, Inc. The Grand Central Publishing name and logo is a trademark of Hachette Book Group, Inc.

The Hachette Speakers Bureau provides a wide range of authors for speaking events. To find out more, go to www.hachettespeakersbureau.com or call (866) 376-6591.

The publisher is not responsible for websites (or their content) that are not owned by the publisher.

ATTENTION CORPORATIONS AND ORGANIZATIONS:
Most HACHETTE BOOK GROUP books are available at quantity discounts with bulk purchase for educational, business, or sales promotional use. For information, please call or write:
Special Markets Department, Hachette Book Group
237 Park Avenue, New York, NY 10017
Telephone: 1-800-222-6747 Fax: 1-800-477-5925

For Charles

PART ONE

PART ONE

THE DEVIL'S EYE

There comes a time in every rightly constructed boy's life that he has a raging desire to go somewhere and dig for hidden treasure.
—MARK TWAIN

1

---◆◆◆---

IN SHIMMERING HEAT, Jimmy Bird smoked a cigarette and paced off a rectangle of dirt. About the size of a grave, a little wider, a little longer. Jimmy wasn't good at math—that algebra in high school where they mixed letters and numbers together had been his undoing—but he could eye a piece of ground and calculate how long it took to clear and dig to a certain depth. Ditches. Garden beds. Graves. The earth on Black Jack Point fed salt grass and waist-high bluestems and Jimmy pictured a hole six feet across, six feet down. He figured it would take him and his partners three hours of steady digging, being a little slower in the dark. Then an hour or so to sort through the loot, load the valuables on the truck, and good-bye poverty. In a few days he'd be poolside in the Caribbean, chatting up coffee-colored girls in bikinis, fishing in water bluer than blue, buying a boat and lazing on its warm deck and watching the world not go by.

But he felt uneasy even with millions in the dirt under his feet. *What if somebody sees us?* he'd asked this morning.

Then we take care of them, Jimmy, Alex had said.

What do you mean take care of them?

I mean just what you think. Alex said it with that odd

half smile, caused by the little crescent-moon scar at the corner of his mouth. Like he was talking to a child.

I don't want none of that, Jimmy Bird said, and as soon as he said it he knew he'd made a big mistake. It showed a lack of drive, a complaint he'd heard about himself from his wife, his mama, his daddy, even his little girl.

Alex had kept smiling like he hadn't heard. That smile made Jimmy's bladder feel loose.

I mean we shouldn't leave a mess, Jimmy quickly amended. *That's all I meant.*

Alex smiled, patted Jimmy's back. *No messes. I promise.*

Jimmy Bird took a stake with a little flutter of fluorescent orange plastic ribbon topping it and drove it into the middle of the ground. Make it easier for them to see in the dark. He felt relief that old man Gilbert wasn't going to be up at his house tonight. He couldn't see the Gilbert place through the density of oaks, but that was for the best. No one to see them. No one to get hurt.

No messes. I promise.

Jimmy Bird didn't like those four words the more he considered them—maybe *he* had gotten demoted to *mess*—and he patted the pistol wedged in the back of his work pants for reassurance. Patted the gun three times and he realized it was just the bop-be-bop rhythm of his little girl patting the top of her teddy bear's head. He'd miss her most of all once he left the country. He'd send her some money later, anonymous like, for her schooling. She might get that math with the letters and numbers mixed together way better than he had.

By his reckoning he would go from ditchdigger to multimillionaire in about twelve hours. Jimmy Bird slung the metal detector back over his shoulder and moved through the heavy growth of twisted oaks.

* * *

They drove home early because the bedsprings squeaked.

Patch Gilbert was a romantic but a bed-and-breakfast full of artsy-fartsy bric-a-brac was not his idea of a love nest. But his lady friend, Thuy Linh Tran, had wanted to go to Port Aransas, even though it wasn't terribly far from Port Leo and could hardly count as a real getaway. Thuy thought Port Aransas romantic because it was actually on an island; you rode a little ferry to get there, and you could watch the porpoises darting in the ferry's wake. They'd had a nice dinner and red vino at an Italian place, Patch had taken his pill to rev his engine, they'd snuggled into bed, and he didn't even have Thuy's modest gown off before they discovered the bedsprings on the genuine antique bed screamed like banshees every time they moved.

"We're not making love in this bed, Patch," Thuy said.

"But I took a pill." At seventy he felt no erection should be wasted.

"No."

"It's Monday night. This place is mostly empty. Ain't nobody gonna hear us, angel." He started nibbling on her ear.

"No." She was sixty-nine and more stubborn than he was. So they had quarreled—the trip was her idea but it was for his birthday, and he wasn't happy with this squeaking turn of events—and in a fit, they got dressed and checked out and just drove back to Port Leo, to Patch's old house on Black Jack Point. The drive was mostly awkward silences. It was midnight and they were both in sour moods and Patch suddenly worried that Thuy needed a little courting. She wanted to go straight home when they got back to his house but he convinced her to come in and make up and drink a little wine.

She wasn't sleepy. Arguing had riled her up, made her more talkative; so he was hopeful she'd spend the night.

"How long's it been, baby, since you walked on a beach late at night?" Patch Gilbert poured Thuy another glass of pinot noir. "Now that's romance, a beach real late at night."

Thuy smiled. "I ran across a beach at midnight, with three children in tow, hoping not to get shot and to find a spot on the boat. When I left Vietnam, Patch. It wasn't romantic." She leaned over and kissed him, a chaste little peck against his wine-wet mouth. "I should go. I haven't been up this late in years."

He felt their time slipping away. Her kiss gave him that shivery energy of being twenty-five. At least inside. "Come down to the beach with me."

"I thought you retired from sales."

"Well, honey, if I have to *sell* you on the idea—"

"You didn't sneak another one of those pills, did you?"

"Don't need 'em."

"Shameless."

"We don't have time for shame. Listen, we'll just get the sand in between our toes." His voice went husky and he took the wineglass from her hands. "It feels good, the wet sand against your skin."

"Patch."

"Baby." He kissed her gently, almost shyly. He felt the neediness in his own kiss, the hopeful wondering—not felt since high school, before the marines, before selling drilling equipment for so many years, before cancer took Martha and left him alone—if there was going to be any dessert on his plate. He loved Thuy but had never broken the habit of lovemaking as careful conquest.

"I'm too old for anyone to call baby," Thuy said.

"Never too young," Patch said. "Let's go." He took her hands in both of his and stood. Gentle insistence worked wonders. After a moment, she stood with him.

The night was clear but the moon was an ill-lit curve. Patch frowned, because he loved the moonlight on the bay, on the sands, on the high grasses. It silvered the world, made it lovely as a dream. Tonight was too dark. He and Thuy walked down the long path, a line of gravel threading through the salt grass, down to a small curve of beach. The blackjack oaks were gnarled and bent from the constant wind from St. Leo Bay. He and Thuy slipped off their shoes—boots and socks for him, espadrilles for her—and they walked to the edge of the surf, the summer-warm water tickling their toes.

"The Milky Way." Thuy pointed at the wash of stars. "We call it *vãi ngan há*."

"What do you call kissing?"

"Hôn nhau." She ran a finger down his spine and he grinned at her. "I counted those same stars as a little girl. I wanted to know exactly how many there were. I wanted them all. Like most children I was a little greedy."

"I'm greedy for you," Patch said.

They kissed, and she leaned into him, the surf wetting the cuffs on his jeans. He was sliding a worn hand under the silk of her blouse when he heard a motor rev steadily, then purr and die. He leaned back from her.

"Patch?"

"Listen."

He heard it again, a truck motor, the engine rumbling, a door slamming, down the beach and over to the west, deep in the grasslands, in a thick growth of oaks, from the southern end of Black Jack Point.

"Damn it," he said.

"What is it?"

"Kids joyriding on my land." He walked up the beach, smacked sand off the bottom of his feet, hopped, pulled on socks, yanked on his cowboy boots.

"Let them be. Let's count the stars."

"They're trespassing," he said. "Digging ruts in my land."

"Maybe they're looking for a makeout spot."

"Not here. This is *our* spot."

"Just call the police," she said.

"Naw. I'm gonna go talk to them. You go on back to the house."

"No." She slipped on her flats. "I'll go with you."

"Might be snakes out there."

"I'm not afraid." She took his hand. "I'll show you how to lecture kids."

They walked up the beach, into the grasslands, into the darkness.

2

―――――⟪◉⟫―――――

As Stoney Vaughn wiped the smear of blood and brains from his hands, a sick fluttering twist in his guts announced: *You just screwed up your life forever, buddy.* It was an unusual feeling. Failure. Shock. The loss of control that flooded his heart. He glanced up at Jimmy Bird, loading the newly boxed coins into the dark hollow of the storage unit. Intent on his work, Jimmy wasn't looking at him, or at Alex either. Alex was watching along the corridor of storage units, a gun in his hand, making sure that no one saw them. The only light was from the truck's headlights.

Stoney wadded up the hand wipe Alex had thoughtfully offered, threw it on the floor, reconsidered the wisdom of that act, and tucked the bloody wipe into his backpack. Against the hard heavy lump of stone he kept wrapped inside. He had to be careful now. He swallowed the dryness in his throat, kept the shudder out of his voice. "Alex. This changes everything."

Alex Black didn't even glance his way. "Not really. I planned for this."

"How, exactly, did you do that?"

"We lay low for a while. We can't buy the land right away, obviously."

"Obviously."

"So we wait a bit. One of those nieces will be wanting to sell soon, and then you can unfold the wallet and play your little get-famous game." Alex stepped back inside the storage unit, unclipped a flashlight from his belt, played it over the boxes. "Which one's got the Eye?"

"There. Small box on the top," Jimmy Bird said.

Stoney forgot to breathe. He felt the heavy weight of the emerald in his knapsack, feeling bigger than a fist, bigger than a heart. Oh, Alex would kill him. Alex pried open the box, played the light over the big fake green chunk of rock Stoney had slipped into the emerald's place. He'd been so careful, going through the loot, finding the stone first, replacing it with the fake before the others even spotted the emerald. He waited, watched Alex glance over the stone.

Then Alex shut the box.

"Gentlemen," he said, his head down, his round wire-rim glasses catching the glow from his flashlight, "here's the plan. We double lock the doors. Stoney, you got the key to one lock, I got the key to the other. Alibis, those are your own problem. But none of us knows the others, none of us ever heard the others' names." He glanced over at Jimmy. "You come with me. We'll clean up your truck, get rid of the evidence."

"The bodies—" Stoney started.

"Aren't going to be found for a long time," Alex said. "If ever."

"I knew him. The cops'll come talk to me," Jimmy Bird said. His voice was hoarse, trembling.

"Maybe not."

"I don't want to sit around. I want my cut now."

Alex stared at him.

"I'm just asking for what's fair," Jimmy Bird said.

"Sure. I understand. But first, man, we got to get your truck cleaned up. We'll give you your cut tomorrow, help you redeem it for cash, get you out of the country."

"Thanks. I just want what's fair."

"Fine."

After the three men stepped out of the storage unit, Alex slid down the door, fastened a lock onto one side. Stoney, his hands steadier than he thought possible, fastened the other. *Click. Click.* Locked.

"Now," Alex said. "Mr. Bird. Mr. Vaughn. I know you'll both behave. Now that you're accessories." He turned the flashlight's beam up into his boyish face.

"Don't threaten me, Alex," Stoney said. "You don't have a dig without me. You wouldn't have any of this without me."

"That's right, Stone Man," Alex said. "I also killed two people for you tonight. So maybe you owe me more than I owe you right now."

Stoney kept his mouth shut.

"Let's go, Jimmy. Stoney, we'll talk in a week. Not before. Calm down. I just made all your wishes come true." Alex smiled, slapped him hard on the shoulder. "Go home, sleep tight, don't let the bedbugs bite."

Stoney forced a smile. He watched Alex and Jimmy Bird climb into the winch truck. Stoney got into his Porsche. He followed the truck out of the storage lot; it turned right, heading south back to Port Leo. Stoney turned left, heading up toward Copano Flats and the comfortable sprawl of his bayside mansion. He jabbed at the radio and head banger rock—*Nirvana, great,* he thought, *the voice of a dead guy*—turned up too loud, blasted the car.

He kept one hand on the steering wheel, the other hand in the knapsack where he'd placed the emerald. It felt hot in his hand, which was crazy; buried in the ground for nearly two hundred years, it should be cool.

You just stole a couple million dollars from a homicidal maniac, he thought.

Stoney Vaughn made it a half mile down the road before he had to pull over and throw up.

3

———◆———

FOUR O'CLOCK TUESDAY AFTERNOON, court done, justice dispensed, and the Honorable Whit Mosley wanted nothing more than to swim twenty hard minutes with his girlfriend in the warm Gulf off Port Leo Beach, eat a big steak at the Shell Inn, cuddle with Lucy on the couch, watch the Astros raise his hopes again, make love at the end of the game, right there on the couch like they'd done night before last while the postgame show droned. Lucy liked baseball as much as he did. But now Lucy was standing in his office door, frowning, not looking in the mood for a steak or a swim or a ninth-inning delight.

"I think Uncle Patch is missing," Lucy said.

Whit shrugged out of his judge's robe, let the black silk fall to the floor, glad to be just in his regular Hawaiian shirt and old khakis and Birkenstocks again. The air conditioner in the courtroom sputtered with signs of age, and this July in Port Leo had been blister-hot, everyone in traffic court cranky, and his robe smelled a little stale. He'd have to wash it tonight. Judicial laundry. Not listed in the job description.

"He's not down here at the jail," Whit said. "No senior citizen discount."

"Don't joke, Whit," Lucy said. "He's not at his house. His car is there—he's not."

"I thought he and Thuy went to Port A."

"I called the B and B I booked for them and they checked out last night. Didn't even stay a few hours."

"Maybe they went to another hotel."

"But his car is *here,* Whit."

"What about his fishing boat?"

"Still here. His doors were unlocked. And there's wine-glasses out on the table. Two of them, one with wine still in it."

"So they came home and didn't clean up. Maybe he's just out with Thuy in her car."

"I called Thuy's daughter. They haven't spoken to her today either, which is unusual. They said she calls them every day. Whit, really, I'm worried. They're old."

"They sure don't need chaperons."

"You're not listening," Lucy said. "I have a bad vibe about this." She fingered the little amber crystal around her throat. "Something has happened to them. Call your friends at the sheriff's department, or help me go look for them."

"The police won't do much of anything for twenty-four hours," he said, not thinking, and she burst into tears.

He had never seen Lucy cry before. He took her in his arms, let her rest her face against his shoulder. "Okay, Lucy, okay. I'll call the sheriff's office, all right? And we'll start making phone calls. We'll find them. But when Patch finds out you've made all this fuss, you got to take the blame for it."

She sniffled. "I will. Okay, thanks, baby. My aura's feeling calmer already."

"Sure, Lucy." He didn't pay much heed to her talk of auras and vibes, but it was part and parcel of Lucy and part of loving her. He kissed her forehead, wiped away her tears with the ball of his thumb.

He dialed the Encina County sheriff's office, figuring that within an hour or so Patch and Thuy would be found out fishing along a stretch of Black Jack Point, and all would be good and fine.

It didn't happen.

The sheriff's office, once called, found a broken window at the back of Patch Gilbert's house. Lucy noticed certain items missing: a silver candelabra, a cookie jar in which Patch kept ample cash, a jewelry box that was a family heirloom. The search began.

Patch Gilbert owned over two hundred acres on Black Jack Point, and on late Wednesday morning, the searchers found the turned earth along the edge of his property. The disturbed soil was a hundred yards up from the beach, a rectangle of torn loam hidden among the thick fingers of the oaks, broken grasses draped over the ground like a shroud.

The deputies and volunteers started digging and Whit made Lucy wait up at Patch's house.

"Wait here with me," she said. "Please." She was shaking, her freckled arms folded over each other, her hair a mess from having dragged her fingers through it nervously.

"I can't, sweetie. I got to be down there." He was justice of the peace, and because Encina County didn't have its own medical examiner, he also served as coroner. If there were bodies he'd order the autopsies, rule on cause of death, conduct the inquest if it was needed. His chest felt sucked dry at the thought of Patch and Thuy murdered and buried. But he didn't like the vacant, broken look in Lucy's eyes.

He put an arm around her and turned to Deputy David Power. "Maybe I should wait with Lucy."

David made a dismissive noise. "You're supposed to be down there," he said, as though comforting relatives of the dead was second-class duty compared to forensic investigation.

"You don't need me until you find bodies," he said, and he felt Lucy's skin prickle under his fingertips.

"Sure, Judge, whatever." David Power turned and headed down toward the thick copse of oaks.

Lucy watched him leave. "Well, he's got lots of negativity."

"He doesn't like me," Whit said. "I'm friends with his ex-wife."

"Maybe you should go down there," she said. "I'll be okay."

"I'll stay here as long as I can."

He and Lucy sat in Patch's den, a dark room covered with thick brown paneling in turn covered with fishing trophies and a fake muscled marlin. He held her hand and watched *All My Children* to avoid thinking about what the shovels might be unearthing.

Lucy stared at the screen. "I cooked dinner for the two of them last week. Meatloaf. I burned it a little 'cause we got to talking and I was drinking too much beer. It tasted like a shingle. They didn't complain, ate it with a smile."

Whit squeezed her hand.

"I should call Suzanne," she said. Her cousin, her only family other than Patch.

"Let's just wait and see."

They watched a commercial offering tarot card readings

for a call-per-minute charge while an energetic woman with a doubtful Caribbean accent proclaimed the future to amazed callers.

"That approach is so misleading," Lucy said. "Look at her. She's hardly listening to that caller—she's just slapping those cards down." Her voice was flat as she pretended the searchers weren't tearing up her uncle's land.

"I'm sure your psychics do a better job, sweetie." Lucy owned the Coastal Psychics Network, which, as she put it, served the needy and the bored across Texas.

"At two bucks ninety-nine a minute, that is robbery." She fingered the amber crystal on her necklace. "I at least run a clean ship. Maybe I ought to advertise more. I'm cheaper than Madam Not-Reading-the-Cards-Right."

He hugged her a little closer, gave her a tissue for her nose. "Need to tell you something about Patch."

"What?"

"He was the one suggested I call you for a date."

She laughed but it was half tears. "Did he now?"

"Called me up after you were in my court. Said I had given you too heavy a sentence for those unpaid tickets."

"Not unpaid. Ignored on principle." Same argument she'd used in court. A little more effective with him now. Patch had settled her five hundred dollars' worth of fines. She'd done her community service, Whit checking on her a little more than needed.

"He said I ought to even it out by taking you to dinner."

"Old men playing matchmaker is a bad idea." Lucy wiped at her eyes. "Because they won the war they think they know everything."

A deputy—young, sunburned, blond buzz cut bright with sweat—appeared in the doorway. "Judge Mosley?

Could I speak with you?" His mouth barely moved as he spoke.

"Are they dead?" Lucy asked. "Is it them?"

"Yes, ma'am. It looks like it's them. I'm real sorry."

Lucy put her face in her palms. "Well. It was a bad vibe," she finally said from between her hands.

4

∞◆∞

CLAUDIA SALAZAR LET the sun warm her closed eyes. She had dozed on the pool lounge chair, the water evaporating off her skin, thinking, *I could get to like this.*

Claudia's past few days had been busy: finally closing out a series of burglaries on Port Leo's south side, aimed squarely at the tourist condos, by arresting a repeat offender who sadly had three kids and was bound back to jail; covering two extra late shifts for a patrol officer friend who was down with a bad summer cold, because the whole Port Leo police department was shorthanded; and then the terrible Gilbert/Tran murders, which were beyond Port Leo's jurisdiction but the sheriff's office and the police department helped each other with high-profile cases. David Power, her ex-husband, had politely declined the police department's help and her thought had been: *Pride goeth before a fall.* It was the most biblical thing she had thought in years. She wondered, without ego, if he was too irritated with her to want the department's help.

She decided not to care. As of today, she was officially on vacation.

She opened her eyes, sat up on the lounge chair, watched Ben standing by a table between the pool and the French doors, fiddling with a stubborn cork on a wine bottle.

"What a rotten guest I am," she said. "I fell asleep."

Ben Vaughn pried the cork out and grinned. "You're exhausted. Don't worry about it."

She smiled. If she'd gone swimming with David, drunk wine in the early afternoon, then dozed, he would have used it as a basis for analysis: *Did I bore you? What's wrong with me?* Ben just let her be, and she was grateful for that.

Claudia stood, feeling self-conscious in a new purple bikini a bit too adventurous for her, pulled a long T-shirt over her head, and smoothed it out along her hips. "No more wine. Two glasses is my limit."

"You're on vacation," Ben said. "I made lunch. Hope that's okay."

"I'll find it in my heart to forgive you. So what can I do to help?"

"Just sit. You're my guest." Ben disappeared back into the house.

The deck for the pool ran along the edge of St. Leo Bay, and in the summer heat the bay water looked green as old glass, the waves like white lips rising to the surface for a kiss, then vanishing. She put on her sunglasses. Vacation. Well, a few days off and then back to the grind. But sitting on a multilevel deck, with a private dock, backed by the house that had to be approaching seven thousand square feet... well, it was better than eating takeout and watching old movies on video, which was how she'd spent her last vacation.

Ben returned, carrying a tray. Two huge shrimp salads, the shrimp firm and pink, perfect crescent-morsels, slices of avocado, a small crystal pitcher filled with a homemade dressing, rolls steaming. He set the lunch down in front of her.

"Where's the chocolate?"

"Ingrate." He poured them each wine again, held his glass aloft in a toast. "To a great vacation for you. And to old friends."

"To old friends," she said, clinking her glass against his. *Friends. Funny word,* she thought. *It could cover too much ground.* They'd been lovers long ago but she couldn't look at him and think *ex-lover.* He was too different now from the shy, gangly boy she'd known.

"And we didn't even have to catch the shrimp," Ben said.

"Sometimes I'm relieved by that. Other times I think it's a shame. My dad's the last Salazar who's still shrimping." The smile dimmed slightly on Ben's face and she set down her fork. "I'm sorry. I didn't mean to bring up an unpleasant memory..."

Ben smiled again. She liked his smile, warm and happy, with a front tooth slightly crooked. "It's okay. My folks have been gone a long time, Claudia. I miss them but you keep going on." His parents had been lost in a sudden storm on the bay's edge, their shrimp boat swamped. Ben had been sixteen at the time, his brother, Stoney, just starting college. "I might have made a good shrimper."

"You would have gotten bored."

"But you're your own boss." Ben took a small sip of white wine. "Out on the water, out in the sun. Now Stoney, he would have sucked at shrimping."

Claudia glanced around the deck, the private dock, the too-big-for-her-taste house. "It wouldn't have paid the mortgage on this place." She liked the pool, the lunch, being with Ben, but felt an awkward consciousness of being in his brother's house, as though she were trespassing. She had kept glancing at Ben, trim in his modest swimsuit, with his nice hands and his smile, and wanting to kiss him, but she wouldn't. Not here. If she kissed him she might not stop and his brother might walk in at any moment. "What exactly does your brother do? You said investments?"

"I can never quite figure it out. He did venture capital work out in California for a while, got a little singed in the dot-com meltdown, decided he wanted to come home. He does a lot of consulting for financial services firms in Dallas and Houston. He's trying to get me into his business." He shook his head. "Stoney used to steal my allowance, set up a lemonade stand with our money, give me a cut. We'd make more than our allowances put together. I think he's still following that business model."

"It seems to be working."

"He has expensive hobbies. Cars. Boats. Treasure hunts."

"Treasure hunts?"

"He's financed some treasure dives in the Florida Keys—you know, galleons that wrecked in shallow water, got buried by the sands on the bottom. Takes a team to recover them. It's his obsession. Crazy way to risk your money. You got to make the big bucks to play that game." His tone went wry.

"And you're not interested in the big bucks?"

Ben grinned again. "Me in finance? I'd be doomed. The clients would be doomed." He shook his head. "I like teaching, but the pay sucks, and too many of the kids are unmotivated and the parents care even less. I'm starting to think you seriously got to have a call to teach, like being a priest."

"Or a cop," she said.

"Or a cop," he agreed. "You ever think of giving it up?"

"Last year, briefly. But no, not seriously."

"Living here with my brother—well, Stoney's spoiled me." Ben speared the last fat shrimp in his salad, pushed it through the little pool of dressing in his bowl. "But I don't have a talent for making money."

"Money's not everything."

"It can sure buy a whole lot of it."

"Still."

"You're right. And Stoney's not what you'd call happy. He's nervous. Jumpy. I don't want to think what he was like when he worked in a high-stress job."

"Let's talk about something other than your brother," Claudia said. The three glasses of wine and lazing in the summer sun made her suddenly feel a little playful. "That was a delicious lunch. Thank you. I didn't know you could cook."

"I knew you'd had a hard week," Ben said. "Least I could do. Citizens should support their officers in blue every way they can."

A tease colored his tone and she skimmed her toe-tips along the muscle of his calf, just to flirt back a little. She stopped as the French doors opened. A man came out, tall and brown-haired like Ben, but a little thicker in the shoulders and the stomach, dressed in a summer khaki business suit, but no tie, the shirt buttoned to the throat. His hair was gelled, combed to Ken-doll perfection, and he didn't smile until Ben turned toward him.

"Hi, bro," Ben said. "Come on out."

"Don't want to interrupt," the man said.

"It's your house," Ben said. "You can't interrupt. Claudia, this is my brother, Stoney. Stoney, Claudia Salazar."

Stoney Vaughn offered Claudia a hand with nails manicured as smooth as pearl. His grip was firm but the flesh of his palm was soft. "Claudia. I remember you from school. I was a few years ahead of you. Nice to see you again." His gaze went quickly down her, to her breasts, her hips, back to her face, quicker than a blink but she saw it and was glad she had on the T-shirt.

"Hello," she said. "You have a lovely home."

"It's comfortable."

His modesty was so false she almost laughed. Instead she said, "Will you join us?"

"I can't today. I've got to do some work up in my office. But you two enjoy yourselves."

"Claudia's taking some time off from work," Ben said. "She's an investigator with the Port Leo police."

Two beats of silence. "Really. That must be fascinating," Stoney said.

"If you find burglaries riveting."

"Claudia likes to fish," Ben said. "Maybe tomorrow morning we could take the *Jupiter* out into the Gulf, have some fun. Why don't you take the day off, come along? Bring one of your girlfriends. Who's on the A list this week?"

"None of them. I'm in the doghouse. I've been too busy to call. Work's just been nonstop lately. Y'all go, though."

"Please, do come," Claudia said.

"Yeah," Ben agreed.

"Sure," Stoney said. "That sounds great. Claudia, lovely to see you. Enjoy the pool. Have fun."

They shook hands and Claudia watched him hurry back in. She had the oddest feeling he wished her and Ben gone, out of his sight, out of his house.

5

---•◦◦•---

WHIT GRABBED HIS forensics kit and followed the young deputy down past the manicured lawn, through the thick growths of wildflowers and the high grass. Ahead was the wide bowl of St. Leo Bay; Black Jack Point occupied the northernmost stretch of the bay's reach, with Port Leo south and at the middle of the curve. The bay breeze shuffled the hot, sticky air, and on the wind Whit heard the murmuring voices of the deputies, of the Department of Public Safety crime scene crew. For a moment, the crowd out of sight, the voices sounded ghostly, even in the eye-aching sunlight. He remembered being here as a boy, Patch telling the local kids he let fish and swim off his little dock, *You know, Black Jack Point's haunted by old Black Jack himself, and by pirates and Indians and settlers that got scalped, got their throats cut. Be sure nothin' don't grab your foot while you're swimmin'. It won't let go. They like a young soul best. Taste goooood.* And the safe thrill of being scared and being fairly sure that Patch was joking. Mostly sure.

They hadn't moved the bodies. The hole was deep, nearly six feet, the soil threaded with torn grass. He knelt at its edge while the DPS crime scene tech snapped off photos. The group was silent now, the buzz of the mosquitoes the loudest sound.

Patch Gilbert lay on his back, arms spread, dirt still covering most of him, his mouth open wide and loam pooling between broken teeth. His face was ruined, beaten into pulp, a plane of graying hair askew on his scalp, little broken tiles of bone peeking through his forehead. Thuy Linh Tran lay atop one of Patch's arms, as though he cradled her in a comforting hug. Dirt was scattered on her bloodshot irises. A bullet hole marred her forehead.

Whit slipped plastic bags over his shoes, carefully stepped down into the grave, touched Patch's throat, then Thuy's. He wrote down the time on his death scene form. For the record. Suddenly the promise of tears burned at the back of his eyes and he wanted to cry for this funny, good old man and this generous woman, but he didn't want to lose it. Not in front of this crowd. He felt David's stare against his back.

Whit stepped back out of the grave. He began his work of detailing the scene for the inquest report and the autopsy orders, keeping his eyes on the papers. It was easier that way.

David knelt down by Whit. "I think the man got hit with a shovel. Hard. Repeatedly. Probably even after he was dead. Wonder why the killer shot her, though. Maybe broke the shovel on him, couldn't use it on her."

"Patch would have fought hard," Whit said.

"He's an old man," David said.

With about ten times the heart and guts you'll ever have, Whit thought.

"Makes me think of a case I read," David said. "Up in Oklahoma, '65 or '66, old couple got killed while out walking, buried right off a hiking trail..."

Whit tuned him out. David loved to recite old police cases from true crime collections as though they held all the beauty of love sonnets. All the details and none of the context. Whit bit his lip. When David paused for breath, Whit asked one of the techs to take extra photos of their faces, of their wounds. The techs did, and measured the depth of the bodies, carefully clearing more dirt back from the corpses when one of them gave a little cry of shock.

"What is that?" The tech stepped back from where Thuy's feet still lay partly buried and Whit saw two curves of brownish skull exposed.

"Look here," another tech said, clearing away dirt next to Patch's knee. A crooked brown bone of finger, bent as if to beckon. "Old bone. Real old."

"Don't touch it," Whit said. "Stop the digging."

"Why?" David asked.

"There's other remains buried with them. I got to call the guy in San Marcos. This closes down everything."

"We're not stopping. This is a serious crime scene—" David began.

"They talked about site analysis in JP training. You have to stop the dig."

David took a breath of infinite patience. "What guy in San Marcos?"

"Forensic anthropologist. I don't remember his name. But he's got to check out the site. They must've gotten buried in old unmarked graves." Whit wiped the sweat from his brow. "You can't move 'em until the FA's here with his team."

"Judge Mosley's right, David," one of the DPS techs said quietly. "He's talking about Dr. Parker. He can be here in forty minutes. DPS sticks him on a chopper and rushes him down here."

"Fine," David said. His lips went thin as wire. "Get this guy here, then, quick." He turned away from Whit to confer with the DPS team.

Whit took out the notepad he used at death scenes, jotted down descriptions of the bodies, talked in a low voice with the DPS photographer while she snapped footage, told her what angles would help him at inquest. He tried not to look at Patch and Thuy's broken faces.

Instead, he kept glancing at the old, worn bones.

The forensic anthropologist—a banty rooster of a man named Parker, a fortyish fellow with a shaved bald head and sporting a Yankees cap—arrived by DPS chopper within an hour, accompanied by a team of graduate students armed with dental picks, brushes, trowels, string, and stakes.

Whit left them to their work, spoke words of comfort to Lucy and her cousin Suzanne and the Tran family, all waiting up at Patch's house. He came back down as the afternoon began to melt into night. The Port Leo fire department set up lights so the work could continue. Parker and David talked a lot, David losing patience and getting it back. The team sifted dirt from the site, carefully, and found more bone fragments, little pebbles of teeth. When Parker got up from his digging to gulp a cup of water, Whit cornered him at the jug on the back of a DPS truck.

"So what is this looking like, Dr. Parker?"

"Off the record, Judge?"

"Yeah."

"Because I don't like to commit before all the data's gathered."

"So don't commit."

"We haven't removed bones yet but there's at least two skeletons in there, more likely three. They're badly disarticulated—they're not laid out as if they were buried and then not disturbed again."

"Why would the new bodies be on top of them?"

"I think these old bones were dug up, dumped back in the dirt, and your murder victims dumped on top of them. The whole site's a jumble. I mean, bones that look that old, you expect it. Ground settles over time, bodies sink. But these seem, well, shuffled."

"Anything other than the bones?"

"Latches. Nails. Locks. A few slivers of wood."

"Locks?"

"Locks."

That was freaky, Whit thought. Why would you put a lock on a coffin? "You said wood. From a casket?"

"Possibly."

"Wouldn't a casket have kept the bones better organized?"

"Apparently not these." Parker finished his water. "Don't think they were buried in caskets. Coffins would have mostly rotted away by now, anyway."

"These bones . . . how old are they?"

"The wetter the soil, the browner the bones get over time. These are pretty brown. We'll assemble the skeletons as much as we can tonight and tomorrow. We'll probably remove the bones in the next few hours, once we've cleaned away the dirt, gotten samples, sifted, photographed, and mapped the site. If we can identify the make of the nails and latches, that can help us date the bones."

"The family of the murder victims are friends of mine," Whit said. "We'd like to get Mr. Gilbert's and Mrs. Tran's bodies out of there as soon as possible."

"We'll hurry," Parker said, a softening in his tone for the first time. "You'll need to transfer the old bones to my custody for examination, Judge." Whit nodded and Parker headed back to the dig, flush with light from the fire trucks.

The diggers worked tenderly, quietly around Patch and Thuy, as though the couple slept and the techs were gentle spirits, come to grant them sweet dreams. Finally they were done. The bodies were lifted out slowly, placed on clean sheets. Whit filled out an authorization for autopsy, had David countersign it. He watched the bodies taken away by the mortuary service for autopsy in nearby Nueces County. The service people carried the bodies carefully on their stretchers. The forensic anthropologists continued their work around the old bones, industrious and steady as ants.

By midnight, Wednesday fading into Thursday, the FA team had put an astonishing assortment of bones—including three human skulls, brown as walnuts—into paper bags. Whit signed over the bones to Parker and the FA team headed to Corpus Christi to sleep and finish their work. Lucy slept upstairs. Whit had showered and lain with her until she dozed off, then come down to Patch Gilbert's empty den at two a.m., unable to sleep. He watched an old *Perry Mason* rerun. Perry's was a perfect world for you, one where justice ticked along sure as clockwork.

Whit let the TV mumble along and sat in front of the bay window. He cracked open the window so he could hear the murmur of St. Leo Bay. The night was dark, the moon shy behind clouds, the fireflies glowing and vanishing like candlewick embers, just snuffed out between wet finger and thumb. The fire truck lights still blazed over the now-canopied site, an officer standing watch.

The old house was full of the old man, his laughter, his teasing. On a side table there was a bottle of Glenfiddich that Whit had seen Patch open only last week. He found two shot glasses and picked up the bottle. He poured the shots of fine Scotch, one for him, one for Patch.

He didn't touch either drink for a long moment, then downed both. The Scotch burned his throat a little, made his eyes water. Closest to tears he would get.

Patch. Thuy. Promise you. Whoever did this won't walk.

He went to bed, curling next to Lucy, shielding her from the night.

6

━━◉━━

PATCH GILBERT WANTED a hundred thousand dollars. Raised real quietly," Gooch said. "You know how I feel about publicity. I'm not talking to the police, but I'll tell you about the deal."

Gooch opened a Shiner Bock. He and Whit watched the noontime sun play along the ripples in the Golden Gulf Marina. The summer live aboards were gearing up for lunch, the inescapable Jimmy Buffett tunes drifting across the waters, lunchtime beers popping open, hungover throats clearing and gearing up for another half day of lazy life.

"Am I supposed to be grateful?" Whit pulled a soda from the cooler. "Gooch, don't you do this to me." Thursday morning court had been full—traffic and small claims—but Whit was distracted, bug-eyed from lack of sleep and anxious to hear back from Parker on the bones and the Nueces County ME's office on the autopsies.

"I don't know that I was the first or only person Patch approached." Gooch leaned back in the lounge chair, took off his T-shirt in the bright sun, closed his eyes. His chest was big and broad, dark with tan but white where the scars lay. One, small and blossom-shaped, looked like a bullet wound, another like a healed slash across his abdomen, another like a long-ago stab in his shoulder. He never talked about the scars.

"Why would he ask you for a hundred thousand bucks?"

Gooch opened one eye to stare at Whit.

It was strange to have your closest friend stay an enigma. Gooch could stare down hired killers, practice the intricacies of hand-to-hand combat, and make troublesome people disappear into federal custody. He was a fishing guide, captain of a premier boat named *Don't Ask,* and yet something far more. He was one of the ugliest men Whit had ever seen, with a face a mother might reluctantly love, but he had charisma that drew certain people like moths to flame. Gooch had saved Whit's life several months ago, disposing of drug dealers with all the ease of a priest dealing with tardy schoolgirls. And Gooch had made it clear that explanations as to the *how* would not be forthcoming. Whit had sensed that Gooch waited then, to see if the friendship would survive, if Whit would respect his obsessive need for privacy. Whit was glad to be alive and pretended like nothing had happened.

"People consider me resourceful and discreet," Gooch said.

"Ah," Whit said. A heavy sailboat crawled into the marina; on it, three women in bikinis turned their faces and flat bellies toward the warm sun. Whit watched them lean against the rails in glorious idleness.

"So what level of detail you want?" Gooch asked.

"Go deep."

"Fine. Patch was a steady client of mine. Took him and some of his old army friends fishing. He knows I know a lot of people. People with money. So he asked me if I knew of folks who might be interested in a very quiet, private investment. People who could part with a hundred thou and not blink."

"Patch could have sold some of his land if he needed money."

"Apparently not an option he considered," Gooch said. "I told him I would need to know more. He said he'd tell me more if I got an investor or two willing to talk to him. I told him I couldn't waste the time of wealthy people, that I had to consider these folks were my clients and if this was some harebrained scheme it was going to make me look bad. Maybe he was selling life-size Chia pets, you know?"

"He gave you no indication why he needed this money?"

"Just asked me to line up some multimillionaires. Which, frankly, represents a very narrow slice of my client pie."

"And you think he approached other people?"

"He struck me as being in a hurry. I asked why he couldn't go to a bank; he said he wanted it quiet. But fast. I believe the term he used was 'hot and big enough to blow this town off the map.'"

"So he wanted no attention now, but whatever he was working on would create a great deal of attention later."

Gooch sipped beer. "So there's your anonymous tip. Was it good for you?"

"Maybe he was blowing smoke, Gooch. Maybe he owed someone a big chunk of money. Someone decided to collect."

"Possibility," Gooch said. "You knew him better than I did. Was he a gambler?"

"No. He was always just the nice guy who'd let you swim and fish off his land. I've never heard of him having debt problems."

"Blackmail?"

"Patch? He bragged about taking Viagra. He was incapable of being embarrassed."

"An old man bragging about medicated hard-ons is one thing," Gooch said. "Maybe he had a deep dark secret that had finally grabbed him by the throat. Or someone close to him was in trouble and needed the money."

"Not Lucy."

Gooch clicked tongue against teeth, cleared his throat, watched a little red sailboat putter out into the bay.

"Don't start dumping on Lucy again," Whit said.

"Lucy is lovely. Charming in a giddy, goofy sort of way. Impeccable derriere."

"But."

"I'm not sure she can read a book, much less a mind on the other end of a phone."

"Why can't you like my girlfriend?"

"I don't want to see you conned."

"She's not a con artist."

"Yes, telephone psychics are known for their high ethical standards."

"You haven't really gotten to know her."

"That's true. If you're happy, I'm happy. Deliriously happy."

Whit stood. "I've got to get back to the courthouse. I'll let David know what you said."

"But you'll keep my name out of it?"

"Yes. I'll try."

"Patch wasn't a quitter," Gooch said. "I'd look hard to see if he found that money someplace else."

"Found his wallet and her purse." David sat in the one straight-back chair in Whit's small office. It was shortly after one o'clock on Thursday afternoon. "Dumped in beneath the bodies. Cash and credit cards gone."

"So this was a robbery gone wrong?"

"Burglary, Judge," David said. "You know the difference."

Maybe it was a robbery turned burglary, or the other way around, but Whit decided to be rock-solid polite. Act like a judge for once. Let David be acid; acid was just asshole with a different final syllable. "A burglary, then?"

"Yeah. Tran and Gilbert cut short their stay in Port A, head home two days earlier than expected, catch a perp breaking in the house. Perp kills them both, buries them on a remote stretch of the Point where they're not likely to be found for a while."

"The killer laid Patch's head open. There's no sign of that attack having taken place in the house," Whit said.

"Then it didn't. Maybe they took the old folks from the house, hauled them down into the oaks, killed them there."

"They. Sounds like more than one person. And for all this effort they got a little cash and silver? They don't bother with the electronics?"

"Look, Your Honor. You spend a little more time in this business, you'll see things usually aren't too complicated. Criminals are dumb as stumps. If they were smart they could go be investment bankers. Or judges." A hint of amusement surfaced in his tone. "Killer or killers got surprised, they kill the old folks, they take off."

"Why bury the bodies? Why not just dump them in the bay?"

"They'd float up faster."

"It's quicker to tie weights to someone's feet than to dig down deep enough to hit old graves," Whit said. He started to mention the anonymous tip from Gooch, but David raised a hand.

"Listen, Judge. You pretty sure you gonna rule these deaths as homicides?"

"Of course, yes."

"Then that's all you need to worry about, Your Honor. Anything beyond that, you're stepping on my toes. And my toes, they're real tender. They get hurt real easy. And my feet hurt, I'm in a bad mood. We're clear?"

"Yes," Whit said. "I'm going in to Corpus, to meet with the ME and with Parker and his people around four. They have to sign custody of the old bones back to me. You want to go?" He'd mention the tip then, let David squirm the whole thirty miles into Corpus. Better than listening to talk radio.

"Sure. That's fine. I got a suspect to go question this afternoon."

"You do? Who?"

"Pick me up around three. We'll head into Corpus." David winked, put on his Stetson, stepped out of Whit's office, said a hearty hey to Edith Gregory, Whit's secretary, then headed out down the courthouse hallway with a strut. "I'll tell you about my suspect then if the mood hits me."

"Oh, you're gonna be in the mood," said Whit.

Alex Black closed the door to his room at the Sandspot Motel and flicked on the light. With its overzealous air conditioner and an ongoing next-door groan-a-thon from a couple he dubbed the Honeymooners, this temporary home held few charms. He wanted to leave. He wanted to go to the storage unit and run his hands over the coins, feel the heft of the Devil's Eye, say a silent *screw you* to every archaeologist and bureaucrat who had ever crossed his path. Instead he sat down and called his father on his cell phone.

"Bert Exton's room, please." He waited for the hospice receptionist to connect him, endured bad Muzak for a few moments.

"H'lo?" Tired, weak-sounding.

"Dad. How's today been?" Alex said.

"Only about a three. Yesterday was a nine. Felt great. You shoulda called yesterday."

"Well, soon as I finish up this dig, Dad, I'm coming to Miami. See you for a spell." *And get you out of that death trap, and we'll go to Costa Rica. Let you die peaceful under a beautiful sky. Maybe near some ruins, just for old times' sake,* Alex thought. "How's that sound?"

"That'd be great." Weak cough. "You liking Michigan?"

"Sure." What Dad didn't know couldn't hurt him. Dad thought he was on an Ojibwa artifacts dig. "Good place to spend the summer."

"Bureaucrats giving you hell?" A little rally in Bert's voice.

"No, sir. No one's giving me hell."

"That's good. Proud of you, boy."

What Dad didn't know. "So tomorrow's gonna be, what, at least a six? You keeping a good attitude?"

"Screw optimism. Yeah. We'll aim for a six. You get here, maybe you sneak me in a six-pack, okay?"

"Sure, Dad." He'd sneak in freaking Moet for the old guy. Alex said his good-byes, hung up. He had buyers lined up for the coins—dealing strictly in cash, no questions asked. And he could find a buyer—probably a Colombian trader—for the Devil's Eye, but a big emerald like that he'd have to move carefully. Even getting it appraised would draw unwanted attention. He could be in Miami in a week, any loose ends wrapped up.

Stoney was the one remaining problem.

He lay back down on the bed and began to imagine various deaths for Stoney Vaughn. Quick ones. You didn't want to spend any extra time with Stoney if you could help it.

7

In the clear sunshine of the Gulf of Mexico, the blood and gore painted sparkles across the green waves. Filmy scales glistened like jewel dust. Torn shrimp pin-wheeled down from the surface, pink and brown and white, a kaleidoscope of flesh. Slivers of fish guts bobbed, the light shifting their colors from red to green to gray as they sank beneath the water.

"Beautiful," Claudia said.

"Gross," Ben Vaughn said. "But I mean that in a real manly way."

Thursday morning Claudia stood at the open back of *Jupiter,* a 48-foot luxury craft, fishing rod in hand. She usually preferred fishing on the open deck of a boat, but *Jupiter* offered the cool shade of the cabin, a cushioned wicker chair, a glass of grapefruit juice at her elbow. She watched a heavy Gulf shrimper chug away from them, its wake now colored with the pool of chum Ben had poured overboard.

Ben hoisted himself up the ladder from the swim platform. He washed his hands of brownish film at the sink. "You ready to fish the buffet?"

Claudia smiled. "Am I ever."

"Sort of glad my brother didn't tag along." Ben sat down next to her, relaxed, grinning. "I'm not sure what a third wheel is on a boat."

"Sweet of him to let us use the boat."

"Stoney's too busy to play with his toys. I'm glad I'm not. Summer vacation." Ben leaned over and kissed her, easy. "That's for luck."

She cast her line into the spreading heart of gore, nailing its center. He cast after her, his line hitting the edges of the chum smear.

"You don't need any coaching."

"I just need someone to vouch for my unbelievable fish stories if I end up not catching a thing," she said.

"We each caught a whale, right?" Ben sipped at his soda.

Claudia watched sleek figures dart and turn beneath the bloody cloud. Within seconds a thick-bodied yellowfin hit her line. She jerked once, setting the hook, and then let the monofilament line spin out as the yellowfin raced away, revving along for a hundred and fifty feet. The tug and play went on for ten minutes, and soon the strength at the other end of the line faded. Claudia reeled her prize in and carefully held the bullet-shaped yellowfin aloft for inspection.

"A real beauty. You're gonna outfish me, aren't you?"

"The day is young." Claudia eased the heavy yellowfin into the customized live well in the salon's corner and cast her line out again.

But her luck didn't hold. Her next cast caught a fight-filled bonito that tired after ten minutes. As Claudia reeled the bonito toward the boat a dark shape flashed beneath the faded slick of chum and her line went slack.

Ben pointed into the murk. "Shark. Grabbed your fish for lunch."

Claudia watched a ten-foot silky rocket underneath the boat. Sharks. An odd tickle touched the base of her spine. "I hope he enjoys the lunch I caught him."

"Let's find less crowded waters." Ben went up to the flying bridge and steered *Jupiter* away from the shrimpers' wakes, moving far out past a weather buoy marking seventy-five miles from the Texas coast. They spent the next hour or so hooking king mackerel and ling.

Ben pulled up a big ling, inspected it, let it go. The fish hit the water and dove down into the hard blue dark. "Best catches I've had lately. That kiss worked."

"All mine do," she said. "So I got a question. Why'd you call me, Ben, after all these years?"

He cast his line again, let it settle. "You aren't with David anymore."

"It's funny. Now I actually never feel I was with him."

"You didn't love him?"

"I did. But not the way you're supposed to."

"There's a recipe?"

"There's a minimum requirement. He and I were comfortable together. But comfort wasn't quite enough."

"Did you ever think of me when you were married?"

"Yes," she said. "A few times. But if you had shown up on my doorstep all you would have gotten was a friendly hug and a cup of coffee. I took my marriage seriously, Ben."

"I'm sure you did." Ben took her hand. "I never told you this, but you were my first, Claudia." He grinned. "I had to get you out in the middle of the Gulf to confess that. No danger of anyone overhearing."

"I suspected as much, if I remember."

"Couldn't admit it to you. The guy can never be the virgin."

She squeezed his hand. "Well, I forgive you, Ben."

He leaned over, kissed her, soft and gentle but not tentative. Not the lips of the boy she had kissed at seventeen, not the boy she had given her own virginity to, but a man surer and wiser with his touch. He broke the kiss first, kissed her closed eyelids.

"Now I'm really glad Stoney didn't come. Plus his girlfriends are all idiots."

She wondered what it would be like to make love on the deck of the boat, out here in the middle of nowhere, the sun their only blanket.

"I'll fix us sandwiches, open a nice wine," he said.

"You made lunch yesterday. I'll do it."

"Naw. You're my guest. Just relax. I'll be back in a sec."

Claudia nestled deeper in the lounge chair, letting the breeze of the Gulf hum over her. Really happy to be with Ben. And, she thought with a degree of rationality about love she rarely allowed, Ben Vaughn was a known quantity. The kind of guy her family would embrace even though they had adored David. Her mother, who considered being over twenty-five and single a sign of social leprosy, would surgically attach Claudia to Ben to bolster the chances of marriage.

But do you like Ben or just the idea of Ben? Are you just lonely and he's familiar, someone you know won't hurt you?

Ben brought homemade chicken salad sandwiches on thick sourdough bread, potato chips, and sliced fruit.

"You slaved over this," she said.

"Yeah, opening containers. Stoney's housekeeper stocks the boat when we take it out. I was thinking maybe we could cruise over into Port Aransas later, eat at the Tarpon

Inn if you like." But Ben didn't give her a chance to answer the invitation, his gaze going past her, his eyes crinkling.

"That boat's in trouble," he said.

Along the wave-broken cobalt of the waters Claudia spotted a Bertram sportfisher in the distance, a single man at the bow, waving a red blanket like a flag.

"Moron," Ben said. "Seventy-five miles out and he doesn't bother with enough fuel."

"Maybe that's not the problem." Claudia waved back at the man. He was now hoisting a baseball cap, bright red.

"We'll see." Ben hurried up to the flying bridge, tried to call the boat on standard Channel 16. No response. Ben whipped the wheel about hard and closed the distance between *Jupiter* and the drifting boat. Claudia stood on the deck in front of the bridge as Ben steered toward the Bertram.

Within minutes they pulled close to the sportfisher; its name, *Miss Catherine,* was written in faded blue script on its stern, with *New Orleans LA* beneath in smaller letters. Claudia moved up to the bow, smoothing her wind-whipped hair.

The man standing at the bow of *Miss Catherine* was in his forties, a little heavy and rosy-cheeked, his skin tanned. He wore dark sunglasses and a baggy white T-shirt with a Tampa Bay Buccaneers logo on the front and faded orange shorts. He gave Claudia a sun-squinted smile full of straight teeth.

"Hello the boat," Claudia called. "You in trouble?"

"My alternator's busted. Lost power for the engines and the radio."

"You're a ways from New Orleans," Ben called.

"Oh, that's old. I live in Copano now," the man said.

"This is what I get for hauling around my mother. She's down in the galley yelling a blue streak at me." He shrugged, tossed the red blanket down. "I'm Danny."

"I suppose you need a tow?" Ben sounded polite but unenthusiastic. Copano was ten miles up coast from Port Leo and Claudia knew giving a tow would mean no candlelit dinner in Port Aransas.

"We'd be happy to take you in," Claudia said.

"If I could just borrow your radio, I can summon my tow service." Danny gave Claudia another apologetic smile. "And maybe my mom can borrow your head."

Ben came down from the flying bridge, squeezed along the narrowness between the rail and the cabin on the deck. "Sure, not a problem." He tossed one end of a docking rope to Danny. "I'm Ben. This is Claudia."

"Thank you so much. Y'all are lifesavers. You've got a beautiful boat."

"Thanks," Ben said. "You fish today?"

"Some ling." Danny shrugged toward the empty reel mount on his boat. "Sharks nabbed the tuna I got."

"Yeah, they'll rob you," Claudia said.

Danny gave her an agreeing grin. He slid bumpers over the edge of his boat, finished fastening the rope tethering *Jupiter* to *Miss Catherine,* vaulted lightly over both railings, and pulled a Sig Sauer pistol from under his T-shirt, from the band of his baggy shorts.

The smile stayed in place, the gun aimed at Ben. "Sharks sure do rob, don't they? Just be calm, and no one gets hurt."

Ben paled under his sunburn and took two steps back. "Man, you want cash? I've got maybe a hundred in my wallet…"

"What I want," Danny said, "is for you to be cool and

hush." He blasted a sharp, two-fingered whistle and two men bolted out onto the deck of *Miss Catherine,* guns in hand, beading them on Claudia and Ben. Nylon stockings stretched over their faces, contorting their features into doughy lumps.

"Oh, hell," Ben said.

"Let's just put those guns down," Claudia said, stern.

Danny stared at her. "Don't we have big balls for a—" he began and Ben charged. Ben barreled into Danny and the Sig barked, splinters erupting from *Jupiter*'s deck as the two men slammed into the railing.

The two other men from *Miss Catherine* jumped aboard *Jupiter.* Claudia swung at the first one, a thin rail of a guy, surprising him, her fist connecting with his cheek, knocking him down. But the other attacker, built big and brawny, hammered her on the jaw. She hit the deck, landing on her side, and the barrel of an automatic pistol gouged into her temple.

"Cool it," the thin one—with what appeared to be electric-red hair underneath his nylon mask—screamed. "Stay still or we see if your brains match your pretty little outfit."

Ben was down, too, a gun pressed to the back of his head, eyes wide with shock.

Don't tell them I'm a cop, she mouthed, unsure if he could read her lips.

Ben barely nodded, the big bruiser frisking him with all the gentleness of a wrestler.

"I got some cash, just take it. Okay?" Ben's voice steadied. "No need to get rough, okay? No need for trouble."

Danny came and knelt by Claudia. "You okay, miss?" In a gentle tone, like he cared.

"Yeah," Claudia said.

The thin kid said, "Love boat's over, babe."

Danny leaned over Ben. "Now where's our buddy Stoney?"

"What?" Ben said. "He's at home."

Danny stared down at him. He glanced at the bigger of the two thugs. "Gar, go below. Find Stoney. Don't kill him."

"He's not aboard. He canceled coming with us," Claudia said.

The skinny redhead jabbed his gun barrel into the small of her neck. "Don't contribute to class discussion unless you're called upon, sweetness."

"Stoney's not here," Ben said. "We're not lying to you."

Danny didn't look at him. They waited. Gar—the big guy—returned. "No one else is aboard, man."

"Well," said Danny. "Then I guess I better come up with a new plan, shouldn't I?" He leaned down close to Ben and Claudia. "Let's start with your names, kids. Just who are you and why are you on Stoney Vaughn's boat?"

"I'm Stoney's brother, Ben. This is my friend Claudia." Ben's voice remained steady.

"Ah. A brother. Poetic justice." Claudia saw Danny lean close to Ben's face, pivot the gun barrel against Ben's forehead. "Stoney stole from me. Killed to do it. I want what's mine, and you're gonna help me." He smiled at Ben, smiled at Claudia with a grin that said his mouth wasn't quite moored to the brain. "A brother is something I can use."

8

THURSDAY AFTERNOON, Whit drove out to Black Jack Point. The police dig was done, but an officer remained parked near the tented site and another officer—looking bored out of her mind—sat in a patrol car up where the private road met the highway. Maybe to keep the curious or the indiscreet away. She waved Whit through.

The house reflected the Gilbert fortunes over the years. In the center was the old house, built in the 1820s, fashioned from sturdy oaks, its clear craftsmanship designed to defy the bay's cruel moments. Over the years prosperity dictated which additions had been made: a room on the east side; a new garage bright with white paint; a work shed, its foundation blanketed with a yellow explosion of wild lantana. Patch built the work shed himself, stone by quarried stone. Whit remembered helping him mix the mortar, the teenage boys who fished off the Point all helping out, a thank-you note to the man who'd let them use his land.

Lucy sat alone at the kitchen table, drinking a glass of iced tea. Funeral arrangement papers were spread in a fan before her. He saw Patch in her now: the same clear blue eyes, the determined jaw. But Lucy, for all her brass, had a delicacy in her mouth, her chin, her hands, and a gentleness—like Patch's—that was well concealed. She had not cried again since the bodies were found, showing the steel Whit knew was at her core.

"I don't want to shop for a casket again anytime soon," she said.

"God forbid."

She rattled the ice cubes in her tea. "They won't be able to fix his face right, will they? He's all broke, Whit. They broke him."

He sat down next to her.

"Have they arrested someone?"

"No. But David says he has a suspect." He took her hand. "I don't know who."

She drank her tea. "The sheriff's office took Patch's answering machine, his computer yesterday. I wrote down his messages. I thought maybe there were more people I should call. But what do I say, Whit? He can't meet you for lunch—he's been murdered?"

Whit glanced at the messages: An exterminator was due to spray the house tomorrow—they'd need to cancel that; three notes to return phone calls from Suzanne; the Port Leo library calling about an overdue book. All the daily doodlings of a life moving steadily along its course when fate got mean and reared up and smacked his nose back into his brain.

Whit called the Port Leo library, asked about the overdue book. Lucy watched him with a frown.

"Whit, who cares about a book right now?" she said when he hung up.

"Was he a regular library user?"

"Lord, no. He didn't want to look at it unless it swam,

batted baseballs, or might kiss him." She sat back down next to him. "What's this book he checked out?"

"Jean Laffite, Pirate King."

Lucy shrugged. "I never saw him reading anything but the newspaper and *Sports Illustrated*." She paused. "You haven't talked to Suzanne yet, have you?"

"No. I told her I'd visit her later, get a statement for the inquest."

Lucy tore at her paper napkin under her tea glass. She ripped it into thin shreds. "You said they've got a suspect."

"You making a bet?"

"I'm unforgivable," Lucy said. "Yes."

"Who, honey?"

"Suzanne's boyfriend, Roy Krantz. He and Patch didn't get along too well."

"You never mentioned that."

"They never saw each other more than once a month," Lucy said. "Fangs shouldn't be bared that often."

"Lucy. This is serious. You point at him, it's going to be taken pretty seriously. At least by me and probably by David."

Lucy's voice went small. "You don't want to believe you know a person who could kill two people in cold blood."

"But you think Roy could."

"Bad vibes fairly explode from him," Lucy said. "And I know what you think of my vibes. But I'm even being logical. He was in prison once. For drugs. Not a fact Miss Suzanne advertises."

"Drugs don't necessarily involve violent crime," he said and she frowned. "But why would Roy hurt Patch and Thuy?"

"Suzanne's in the will. She gets half of this land, the money in Patch's accounts. I'm sure it's a fair amount."

"Can't she say the same about you?"

"But I don't have a bad relationship with money like Suzy Q does." Lucy cleared her throat. "Gambling problems. Patch told me and I'm not supposed to know, but he wanted to be sure I didn't give her any money, not like I got more than two bucks anyway."

"How deep is she in?" he asked.

"Real deep. Patch said nearly a hundred thousand in debt, Whit."

A hundred thousand. The lucky number.

Lucy kept on. "Suzanne and Roy drive up to Bossier City or fly over to Biloxi every few weeks. Or gamble on the casino boats out of Rockport or Galveston. She's pissed away her money, and Patch wouldn't give her two cents to rub together. I told David Power this morning."

"And how did David take your suggestion, Lucy?"

"He furrowed his brow. Very insightful aura. He's a deep thinker."

"Maybe if he's thinking about wells and water, and even then I wouldn't be too sure."

"I know that Suzanne won't be happy if she thinks I'm accusing her boyfriend."

"Clearly."

"But don't I have a responsibility, Whit?"

"Yes."

Lucy took his hands in hers. "I should have stayed here to house-sit for him. I've done that before. Roy—or anyone—wouldn't have tried to break in if I was here."

"You don't know that, Lucy."

"I'm playing the what ifs. It's the worst game in the world. It's like a terminal game. You second-guess yourself to death." She wiped the back of her hand along her mouth. "If you're gonna break up with me, this'd be a real bad time."

"Why on earth do you think I'd break up with you?"

"I'm just saying," Lucy said. "Don't you break up with me for at least three months."

"I don't want to break up with you."

"Because you love me, right?" Lucy stared at him. "I'm not trying to paint you into a corner, Whit. Trust me. I feel a love vibe from you but you're not saying it, and if you're feeling it, this'd be a real good time to let me know."

"That I love you? Oh, Lucy, sure I love you."

"You don't have a future in greeting cards."

"I love you, Lucy. I'm not going anywhere." There. Said. Not so hard once the words bit into the air.

"I love you, too, Whit. I do. I've never loved anyone like I love you. I want you to know that, and this is all going to be all right, isn't it?"

"Baby. Yes. It's okay." He got up, kissed her. She kissed shy at first and then she kissed him hard, eagerly, her palms pressing against his back. The phone rang; she broke the kiss.

"Bad timing," she said. She answered the phone. He could tell by her tone it was a relative or a family friend calling, distant somewhere, who had just heard. Lucy sank into a chair by the phone, started mumbling thanks, a brief explanation of the tragedy. Whit put her tea by her. She patted his hand in thanks, and he went into the study.

The Glenfiddich bottle he'd poured from last night was still there. He picked up the whiskey and noticed, for the first time, the tag entwined with a thin gold ribbon along the bottle's neck. Handwritten.

To celebrate days of old. Stoney.

Whit tucked the bottle back into the bar. Seeing Suzanne Gilbert wasn't going to be pleasant now, and he decided he might as well get it over with.

I love you, Lucy had said. He felt a little shiver of happiness, of nervousness, of new possibility opening before him.

Lucy stood in the doorway. Pale again, the flush from their kiss gone. "The sheriff's office called while I was getting off the phone with one of Patch's army buddies. They want me to come in. For questioning."

9

━━◉━━

THE KIDNAPPERS SLIPPED over Claudia's eyes a blindfold, heavy chamois cloth, reeking of boat polish. Hands
clamped on her arms and yanked her to her feet, steered
her belowdecks. She heard Ben stumbling, gasping next to
her.

The air in the cabin lay hot and still against her skin.
Hands pushed her to the main salon's carpet. They tied
Claudia's hands in front of her, the rope laced down to
her feet and bound again. The knots were thick as doughnuts. She heard Ben's wet breathing, like that of a tired,
heavy dog.

"You're going to be so busted," Ben said.

"Doubtful," Danny answered, a decided coldness in his
voice that hadn't been there when he spoke to Claudia. She
heard him pacing back and forth near their heads, perhaps
inspecting them like prize tarpon.

"Where's the journal?" Danny asked. "Where's the
emerald?"

"I don't know what you're talking about," Ben said.

"Let me cut her," Gar said, his mouth close to Claudia's
ear. "Maybe an inch at a time, start with the ring finger."

"Why don't you just calm down?" Danny said, tension

edging his voice. "We're not at that stage quite yet. Search the boat."

They ransacked *Jupiter*. Cabinets torn open, leather cushions ripped, mattresses gutted. This went on for at least a half hour, the boat searched from stem to stern.

Claudia pegged their positions from their voices. She had already labeled them: Danny, Redhead (a throaty, giggling tenor), and Gar (a low baritone). She heard fabric rustle as one of the men dropped to his knees between her and Ben. Then fingertips, gentle, against her shoulder.

"The wrong place. The wrong time." Danny touched her gently. "I want to be a better person than that. Truly. I'm sorry for you, miss..."

"Leave her alone! You touch her I'll kill you!" Ben screamed.

"Shut up, brother. I'm not like some people I could name who slaughter the innocent. We are gentlemen here, aren't we?"

His partners made no answer. Lips smacked to her left, juicy-kissy, and the taste of copper tinged her mouth.

"Listen, we'll be expected back within a couple of hours," Ben said. "We go missing, my brother will have the coast guard looking for us. They'll hunt you down."

"Texas is a long swim away. Let me tell you what you're going to do," Redhead said. His voice held the hard brightness of a game show host. "You're going to get onto the lovely, fancy onboard phone system here, call your brother. He wants to see you again, he's going to transfer five million dollars into a series of offshore numbered accounts. In the Cayman Islands. The Bahamas. Anguilla. When all that's done, we're going to let you and your girl go home to your families. Sound good?" He laughed.

"You're nuts," Ben said.

"Five million's not a lot to him," Danny said. "We could get greedy. Take all of it."

"Kill you if we wanted," Gar said.

"Don't be rude," Danny said.

"Stoney doesn't have a liquid five million just hanging around. It's in stocks, funds, real estate."

"It's happening, baby, *hap-pa-NING*!" The redhead, giddy with putting the screws to people.

"Ben," Danny said. "It's easy. I want three things from your brother. What he stole from me, which is a document, a journal. A valuable artifact connected to that journal, which is an emerald. And five million, to compensate me for killing my cousin, who was a nice guy. There. Isn't that simple?"

"You're crazy. My brother doesn't have what you're looking for, and he wouldn't hurt your cousin or anybody else."

"Isn't your brother a little interested in treasure hunting? Hasn't he filled a library full of books on it?"

"Just as a hobby."

"Hobby. It's gone past that. Time for Stoney to pay the piper. C'mon." Claudia heard Ben yanked to his feet, his shoes scuffing the carpet near her knees. Wetness landed on the back of her neck. Ben's blood.

"Gar, put Claudia in the stateroom," Danny ordered.

Hands hoisted Claudia up in the air, crushing against her breasts and her hips, hurried her like a battering ram down the small flight of stairs and through the stateroom's entrance, heaved her onto the torn mattress. She twisted as she fell, rolling, facing the ceiling.

"Give me a moment, Gar," Danny said. The stateroom

door closed. But she heard gentle breathing nearby, near her face.

"Claudia." It was Danny. "I am truly sorry."

"You sound like a reasonable man," Claudia lied. "Stop this. Let us go. Please."

"If you and Ben are innocent in all this, well, then I'm sorry. But how much do you know of Stoney Vaughn's life?"

"I don't understand."

"Day-to-day living. Does Stoney help old ladies across the street or knock them out of his way? Pet dogs or kick them?"

"I really don't know him," she said.

"Do you think Stoney could commit murder? Kill a man in cold blood?"

Her throat dried. "He's a respected businessman..."

"Ah. His money makes him a saint?" A sarcasm she didn't like at all tightened his voice.

"No," she said. "Just as this mistake you're making doesn't make you a bad person, Danny. Please. Stop this."

Long silence again, the only sound the slap of waves against the hull. "What's done is done. Life doesn't offer erasers."

"No. It offers choices. You can choose to let us go. Piracy is a federal offense."

"*Piracy?*" Danny giggled, a short, sharp laugh. "Tell me, do you think of us as *pirates*? Because I love it, Claudia. You've made my day."

"Let us go, right now, and—"

The door opened again.

"She behaving?" Gar's voice, low. "Or you just copping a feel?"

"Save your crudity for your friend," Danny said.

"I want to have a private chat with her," Gar said.

"Private about what?"

"Don't get in a knot, man. I'm not gonna hurt her. Go on."

Claudia stayed very still.

"You don't tell me what to do," Danny said. "You work for me."

"You want to know where these goods are, right? I can get her to tell without hurting a hair on her head. If she knows. Just give me a minute. You need to go help with Ben talking to Stoney."

The bedsprings creaked as Danny stood up. "I'll be back later, Claudia. You'll be fine," he said. And then she heard the door shut.

A thick fingertip cruised along her scalp, parting her hair. The fingernail, hard and uneven, gouged into the tender nape of her neck.

"You fought us," Gar cooed. "A little fishy like you. That pisses me off."

"Sorry."

Gar daubed his finger at the blood drop on her neck, smearing it along her flesh like finger paint. Slow. Gentle. Suddenly he tangled his fist in her hair, slamming her head hard against the bed's headboard. Her teeth knocked together, her jaw, already bruised, throbbed. She winced but didn't cry out.

"You don't mess with us, okay, fishy? You don't fight us. You don't talk unless you're talked to. Understand?"

"Yes," Claudia said.

The end of the bed creaked under his weight. He took hold of her bare foot—she'd lost her sandals during the fight—and put a pincer grip on her little toe. "I don't like your answers, I break it. Where'd you learn to fight?"

"A defense class at the community center," Claudia lied. She suspected the correct answer—the Corpus Christi Police Academy—might land her over the railing with a bullet in her head.

Gar squeezed her toe. She held her breath. "Where's your purse?"

Oh, no. Her police department ID. She didn't have her gun in her purse—she was on vacation and hadn't felt the need to carry today while fishing—but her badge and ID were in the purse, in a separate wallet from her driver's license, credit cards, and cash.

"I don't know. Around. I don't think I've got five bucks in my wallet."

She heard him stand and walk around the stateroom. She couldn't remember where she had put her purse. When Ben had given her a tour of the boat, she'd set it down along the way. They were in the larger master stateroom. Outside it was a short hall leading to a small guest stateroom with bunk beds and a head, then the small stairs leading to the main salon. At the forward end of the *Jupiter,* more steps leading down to the small galley, then a stateroom, also with bunk beds, a head, and a separate shower. She figured the purse was either in this stateroom or in the salon where they kept Ben.

Drawers opened and closed; she heard an unzipping that filled her mouth with sour-tasting fear until she realized it was the zipper on her purse. Keys jingled—the keys ringed to her wallet.

Did he see the ID? He'd kill her if he knew she was a cop, she had no doubt.

A wallet snapped open. "Claudia Marisol Salazar of 55 Mimosa Street, apartment 23, Port Leo, Texas," Gar said. He'd found her driver's license. She waited for him to spot and open her police ID wallet, say, *Oh, too bad,* and close his fingers around her throat.

Instead Gar pressed his thick, wide hand into the small of her back. "So this nice fancy boat, it stays at Stoney's house?"

"Yes."

"Anyone else there besides Stoney? Staff for the rich man?"

"I think there's a housekeeper who comes when asked. No one living there but Stoney and Ben."

He grabbed her little toe again, gave it a hard twist. "Lying's gonna cost you."

"I'm not lying," she said. "Look, piracy is a federal offense. Adding homicide to it isn't going to help you."

He snapped the bone of her little toe and she screamed into the pillow.

"Did I ask for a lecture from you?"

"I'm sorry," she managed to say, the pain sharp as a blade.

He released the broken toe, tickled and kissed the bottom of her foot, took hold of the fourth toe. "I tell my buddy maybe I like you real good, maybe I want to spend a little quality time with you, he'll stop laughing so much. He'll go green with envy. He gets real jealous if I take an interest in a pretty girl like you. He'll break every bone in your body, starting with the rest of your toes and then the fingers and working up to ribs, collarbone, major organs. And no one out here to hear you scream. So don't lecture me."

Claudia bit the pillow. The stateroom door opened again.

Danny said, "I told you to leave her alone." Sounding a little uncertain, trying to be in command.

"I didn't do nothing," Gar said.

"Her nose is bleeding. I won't tolerate you hurting her."

"I got something for you to tolerate. She's no smarter than he is."

"Did he hurt you, Claudia?" Danny asked.

Claudia hesitated for a moment before choosing her answer. "I tried to kick him and he dissuaded me."

"You're not to hurt her," Danny said, "unless she tries to escape. And by escape, I don't mean she mouths off at you or you feel like dishing out fists. You understand?"

"I don't see no captain's hat on your head," Gar said. His weight pressed against her ribs, his erection poking into her thigh.

"Be a good girl," Gar whispered in her ear, "and I'll keep myself on a leash. Be bad, and I'll play with you. For hours on end." Gar made a wet kiss against her ear. Then he left the room and shut the door.

Silence. Danny must have walked out with him.

Claudia lay in blindfolded darkness, shivering. *They're not gonna let us go. They're not. Even if Stoney pays this ransom. They knew this is Stoney's boat. Knew he was supposed to be out on the water today. Didn't know he canceled. How?*

A journal. A jewel. Treasure hunters. Crazy, but she could not worry about that now. The only thing that mattered was getting help or getting the hell out of here.

So how are you going to get you and Ben out of this?

The kidnappers had the guns but they quarreled among themselves, improvising since Stoney wasn't here, no backup plan in place. So they were being stupid and she would be smart.

Claudia twisted around on the mattress and managed,

by dragging her head down the bedding, to nudge the chamois-cloth blindfold a hairbreadth off her eyes. Again. Again. She could see below the blindfold's edge. The state-room was dark. Thin light filtered in from the oblong port-holes above the bed, cut into rods of black and white by half-opened shutters. On the walls were reproductions of old sailing maps and a framed set of antique coins. Next to the closet hung another yellowed print—a portrait of a man with flowing black locks, wearing a rakish hat and a blue nautical jacket, in an arrogant stance. The print was vaguely familiar, something she'd seen in a tourist bar in Port Leo, but she couldn't place it. She looked at the picture as a focus point, took calm, steadying breaths.

First get loose.

She rolled across the bed. Her hands were bound in front of her and by lying on the bed's very edge and inch-ing forward, she was able to reach and slide open a side table drawer. No gun, no pocketknife, nothing inside but a weathered paperback and a self-winding watch. The bookshelf, a small one, didn't even hold a heavy bookend. A closet stood on the opposite wall but she remembered it only held clothes and hangers. She rolled up to kneel and look out the rectangular portholes above the bed; the state-room was directly beneath the salon, where she and Ben had fished in luxury, and below the portholes was a small swim platform.

Smash the glass in the frames, cut the ropes? They'd hear her, and she wouldn't have time to free herself.

If she could ease out the porthole—no guarantee she'd fit—she could wriggle onto the swim platform. And then what? More than seventy-five miles out at sea, no way to call for help, roasting in the sun until they found her. Or she fell off and drowned. Bound foot and hand as she was, she could hardly wriggle up and across the main deck without them hearing her. Maybe she could ease into the water and slice her ropes on the propellers. *Yeah, just like a movie action hero.* One flick of the propeller switch and she'd shred like cabbage, assuming she didn't drown first. She remembered the silky sharks, plowing through the yellow-fin school. She might be too big for the silkies but sharks didn't measure their meals. They just ate. They would still take her, make her a five-course meal, a leisurely limb at a time.

She listened. In the quiet roll of the waters she heard them threatening Ben, shoving him into a chair, Ben protesting. She lay very still, breathing through her mouth.

She heard a phone ring. Ring. Click on. "Good afternoon, this is Stoney Vaughn."

"Good afternoon, Stoney." Danny's voice was creamy as butter. "This is your friend Danny, from New Orleans."

A pause, then Stoney, annoyed, "I told you to quit calling me, you nut."

"We've got your brother and his girlfriend."

Silence.

"You weren't on your little boat today. Were you too busy killing people, stealing, ruining lives?"

"Stoney," Ben said. "He says you took something of theirs?"

Silence again. "They're lying. Is this some sort of sick joke?"

"The Devil's Eye, Stoney. Give it to me—along with the journal you stole and a big freaking wad of cash, just to make up for all the grief you've caused me—and we'll be even. And I'll let Ben and his friend go."

Then Stoney's voice, not much more than a whisper, "I don't know what you're talking about..."

Claudia struggled to a kneeling position, fumbled for the handle, started cranking open the porthole. *See if you can slide through the porthole. Get up to the deck. Radio for help. Now while they're occupied.*

Slowly, the pane of glass began to rise.

10

━━━◆◆◆━━━

So you haven't seen Jimmy since Monday?" David Power asked Linda Bird. He didn't like to sit during questionings; he liked to stand. Pace around the room a little like a lawyer. Because the interviewee was always nervous talking to the police, guaranteed nervous, even if they were as pure and innocent as a half dozen saints, and him standing made them a little smaller. That was the goal, make them feel small and they'd crack. The Encina County sheriff, Randy Hollis, sat across from Linda Bird, doodling interlocking circles on a legal pad.

Jimmy Bird's wife looked up at David. Her hair was cut in a style last fashionable ten years ago, frazzled from home dye jobs. A small patch of acne scars, badly camouflaged with makeup, dimpled her cheeks. "Yes. I told you that already."

She wasn't feeling small enough yet. He crossed his arms. "No need to get upset, if you don't got anything to hide, Linda."

"You either believe me or you don't," Linda Bird said. "If he's gonna keep asking me the same things again and again, like a parrot, I'm getting me a lawyer, because then he's just trying to trick me." She glared over at Sheriff Hollis.

"I'll call you a lawyer right now, Mrs. Bird," Sheriff Hollis said. He had a low, pleasant voice, the kind that made for good radio. "But no one is accusing you of anything except being Jimmy's wife, and we just want to know where he might have gone to."

"Jimmy mention any places he might like to go? Where's he got family?" David asked.

"All his family's either in the cemetery or Tivoli, and none of 'em like him."

"Names of his family in Tivoli?"

She gave them, an aunt and two male cousins.

"Patch fired Jimmy, what, a year ago?"

"Right before Labor Day."

"Why?"

"Jimmy got mad that Patch wanted him to work on a Saturday and called him a bad word under his voice. Patch heard him and fired him on the spot. Jimmy begged him for another chance, but Patch said he'd crossed a line and he wasn't getting even a toe back over it." Linda Bird lit a cigarette without asking permission; David glanced at Sheriff Hollis, who let it slide.

"Did Jimmy hold a grudge?"

"He really wanted that job back—Patch was a good man, easy to work for most of the time, and doing the odd jobs for him wasn't too much hard work—but Jimmy's pride got the best of him. He talked about screwing Patch over."

"How?"

"Flattening a tire, sugaring his tank. Kid stuff." She tapped ashes into a coffee cup. "He sure didn't mention murder. Jimmy don't even like to spank our four-year-old. I've never been afraid of him and if he could go off and kill two people just like that"—here she snapped her fingers—"then I don't know him. And if he's gone dangerous, I want police protection for me and my little girl."

A patrol officer stuck his head into the interrogation room. "David? Your other appointment's here." David nodded and the dispatcher shut the door.

"You got a suspect?" Linda asked.

"It's on another case," David said.

"Aren't you the busy bee?"

"How's the marriage?" Sheriff Hollis set down his pen.

A pause. "I filed for divorce last week. He knew it was coming."

"So he might have reason to leave town."

"He might. Although he'd hate to leave our girl, Britni. He does love her—I give him that, even if he don't got the sense the good Lord gave a goose."

"Why'd you file?" David asked.

"Irreconcilable boredom."

Randy Hollis leaned forward. "If Jimmy calls you, Linda, what do you do?"

"Tell him to stay the hell away. If he's innocent in this, then he should come forward. If he's guilty, give up. For Britni's sake. Is this all?"

"Judge Mosley's conducting an inquest. He may call you for a statement."

"He's okay," she said with a contemptuous glance at David. "A judge's robe ain't the same as a uniform, doesn't make a man turn mean."

David felt his temper rise. "You be clear on this, Linda. Your husband calls you, you don't offer him any help. You don't want to be an accessory. I don't want to be charging you. Putting your little girl through that grief."

"Try it without proof," she said. "This ain't Red China."

David asked Linda Bird a few more questions he already knew the answers to and dismissed her. She left and David had his hand on the door when Sheriff Hollis said, "David. About Lucy Gilbert."

"What?"

"Are you just taking another statement or questioning her as a suspect?" Asked like he didn't know the answer, and David could tell he did.

"Questioning her."

"Why?"

"She and Suzanne Gilbert are Patch Gilbert's only relatives. They stand to benefit from his death."

"That aside, what you got on her?"

"She runs a disreputable business."

"You talking about that psychic hotline thing?" Hollis said. "How's that disreputable? My mother calls it, says the girls on the phones are real nice and insightful."

"You like your mother pissing away her Social Security on phone psychics?"

"She can piss her money how she pleases. I heard Lucy Gilbert's dating Whit Mosley."

"So?"

"His Honor's not a big friend of yours, is he?" Hollis capped his pen, gave David an unexpected frown.

"We get along fine."

"No, you don't. You've never gotten along with him. Never made the effort, far as I can see." Hollis stood, wadded up his page of doodles. "You got a reason to suspect Lucy Gilbert, a solid lead, you go for it. You questioning her because she's the girlfriend of a guy who's a pain in your neck, forget it. I won't have an officer of mine abusing his position."

"I resent that. Deeply."

"I wouldn't want you to resent it shallowly, David," Hollis said. "We clear?"

"Crystal." David kept his voice steady. "I need clarification on some items in her statement. That's all. In fact, my friend Judge Mosley and I are supposed to drive in together to Corpus for the autopsy results and to meet with the forensic anth team."

"Good. Keep playing nice." Hollis left.

David Power unclenched his fingers. Odd. Hollis and Whit Mosley had been elected from differing parties. Why would Hollis take Whit's side? But he saw it then: both of them from old Port Leo families, the old moneyed families of the coast that didn't include the Powers. Old family allegiances meant more than political party lines.

It wouldn't buy you an inch with him.

He stepped out into the hallway. Lucy Gilbert stood there, along with an older woman he presumed was her attorney. The lawyer gave David a predatory glare like a barracuda who'd missed breakfast, lunch, and dinner.

No sign of Whit. It surprised him; he thought Whit would be here, steam pouring from his ears. Perhaps, David decided, that was best for the moment. But he turned his friendliest smile toward Lucy Gilbert. *You just make one teeny misstep, you had a thing to do with these murders, you're mine.*

"Miss Gilbert? Thanks for coming in. I just had a few questions on your statement you gave the police. If y'all will just step this way..."

Patch Gilbert's older niece, Suzanne, lived in a grand development called Castaway Key, a series of streets and private docks that few born and raised in Port Leo called home. Her house sat facing St. Leo Bay, and in the summer afternoon the bay hummed with craft: sailboats slicing the waves; jet skis buzzing like maddened bees; a pleasure boat loaded with urban weekenders cutting near the shore, extra-bad eighties dance music drifting from its deck. Whit rolled up the window.

Castaway Key was not aptly named. Many houses went for a quarter million and higher. Whit supposed anyone dressed like Robinson Crusoe, ambling along Castaway Key's resort-named streets—such as Hilton Head Road or Cozumel Way—would be summarily brought to him on charges of vagrancy.

Suzanne Gilbert's house was white and modern, and it glittered with windows large enough to drive a car through. Delicate palms and sprawling bougainvillea filled the beds near the curved stone driveway. Brightly painted Mexican tiles spelled out the house number. Suzanne, an artist, seemed flush rather than starving. Or maybe Suzanne was house-poor, and this mansion was a symptom of her supposed financial woes.

His cell phone beeped as he parked. "This is Judge Mosley."

"Judge. Hi. This is Linda Bird. I'm Jimmy Bird's wife. I think you know who he is."

"I know we want to talk to him, ma'am."

"Well, I just talked with that idiot David Power. I don't want to talk to him no more, and the sheriff said I might have to talk to you. So I'm talking because"—she paused—"I find the deputy to be irritating."

"Yes, ma'am."

"New Orleans. I think if Jimmy has run off he's gone

there. Couple of times last month I hear him, late at night on the phone, talking, saying, *Alex.* I thought it was some drunk friend of his. They love to get tight and phone each other. Like gossipy teenagers."

"I see."

"Then the phone bill comes. We don't know people in New Orleans but there's three calls there, late at night. I pay the bills, as I have the job. I ask him about who he's calling, he says it's a mistake. He's a bad liar. I can tell he's lying." She paused. "So then I think maybe Alex is a girl. In New Orleans. How he got a girlfriend in New Orleans is beyond me, but I'm telling you because I sure ain't telling David Power. You want the number he called?"

"Yes, ma'am, I do." She gave it to him and he jotted it down.

"You tell David Power he better treat me nicer next time he sees me, or I'm filing a complaint. I got a lawyer now, what with getting the divorce, and I am in a filing mood."

"I sense your resolve, Mrs. Bird. Thank you."

"You set bond on my brother last year," she said. "An amount we could handle. We appreciated it. I'm voting for you next time."

He thanked her, stared at the phone number, nearly laughed.

Suzanne Gilbert opened the front door as he headed up the stairs. She wore black jeans, a black T-shirt, black sandals. *Idiotic in this heat,* Whit thought. Artist mourning clothes. She was very fair, attractive, a good five or six years older than Lucy. Her cheekbones and chin and nose were all precise and perfect, as measured as an architect's drawing.

She greeted Whit with a brief hug, so quick he wondered

why she'd bothered. Whit suspected that Suzanne wanted to pat his blondish hair flat or put him in a suit, tidy him up for Lucy. He saw her eyes take in his clothes with disapproval: the faded polo shirt, the rumpled khakis, the sandals.

"How are you holding up?" he asked.

"Barely am," she said in a tone that meant anything but.

Whit followed her into a high-ceilinged foyer and then to a living room. The furniture was modern and expensive, imported teak, leather surfaces of tan and black, the carpet a creamy white, brave for a beachside house. Abstract art filled the walls, lined the bookshelves. But all painted with the same crude hand, no eye to detail or form. Savagely mixed, the colors selected to hurt the eye. Jackson Pollock without the restraint. Whit sensed a sudden meanness in the pictures. They were ugliness disguising themselves as talent. He hated the pictures on first sight.

He followed her to an immaculate, steel-dominated kitchen. A man who looked like he might drag his knuckles when he walked stood by the granite kitchen counter, drinking a bottle of Dos Equis. Big, thick-necked, with a shaved-bald head and wearing a black T-shirt and faded denim overalls. A bracelet of intertwining tattoos whirled around one melon-shaped bicep.

"I don't think you've met my boyfriend, Roy Krantz. Hon, this is Whit Mosley. He's the coroner and the JP here and he's conducting the inquest into Uncle Patch's death." No, he hadn't met Roy. The few parties and events where Lucy and Suzanne crossed paths, Roy was always at home or sleeping or working on a sculpture. Roy shunned limelight, it seemed to Whit. Perhaps he had trouble fitting through the front door.

Whit offered a hand; Roy shook it and didn't try to squeeze Whit's fingers into pulp.

The phone rang. "Excuse me," Suzanne said. "News has spread, and people want to bring over casseroles and cakes. You know how it is when you have a death in the family. Everyone swarms over with comfort foods and you gain ten pounds."

As though weight gain were her biggest worry. Whit thought she needed a cheeseburger. But he gave his solemn, conducting-the-inquest nod. "Of course." She left the kitchen, scooped up a phone in the living room, spoke in a low voice.

"You're Lucy's guy," Roy Krantz said. His voice was low and flat and sounded like it had been honed in a prison yard.

"Yes."

"How's she holding up?"

"She's talking to the police right now."

Roy raised an eyebrow. "And what's she saying?"

"Family secrets, probably."

Roy made a noise of thick beer-swallow, kept staring at him.

Suzanne returned. "Something to drink, Whit?" Her voice glimmered a little too cheery, a little too hostess-bright.

"No, thank you. May we talk now? Privately?"

"Sure." Suzanne glanced at Roy, then led Whit down a hall thankfully empty of abstract art-pukings. Two doors opened off the hall: one to a concrete-floored room cluttered with small iron sculptures of gulls, palm trees, flamingos, and assorted equipment; the other to another studio, bright windows framing the view of the bay.

A huge canvas leaned near one window, covered with a stained dropcloth. A worktable stood nearby, dotted with oil paint in blues, mustards, venomous greens, as though poison dripped on its surface. Finished paintings—more of the obnoxious scribblings that hung in the living room—decorated the walls.

In one corner a huge roll of paper lay unfurled, with smears of bright acrylic paint dried on the paper. Whit glanced at it, then glanced again. Two round magenta globes looked like they'd been pressed on the paper from small, pert breasts. A roll of lime paint looked like a hip; multiple handprints lay in blue and pink. Other blobs resembled knee-prints, footprints, and one squat figure eight looked like apple-green testicles. Suzanne wore a bent little smile on her architectural face.

"You're very prolific." Whit nodded toward the calmer paintings on the wall. It was the only compliment he could think of.

"I get bored working on a painting too long, so I paint quickly. But they sell quickly, too." An offhand shrug.

"They're very interesting."

Interesting apparently didn't cut it; she frowned. She sat on a paint-splattered stool and he settled on its twin across from her.

"You're probably wondering why I don't paint the bay, with a wonderful view." Suzanne crossed her legs, dangled a black sandal off one alabaster foot.

"No. But you want to tell me."

She gave a solemn smile. "*Everyone* here paints the bay. Every stupid little dabbler who can barely hold a brush between their fingers. And the required frisky gulls, little boats, swaying palms. Tiresome." She pointed at one small painting, framed in silver, a violent swirl of purple spirals, gray crosses, and white froth that looked like nothing more than idle slapping of paint by an angry child. "That's the bay. My interpretation of it. No adorable dinghies, no fishing grannies, no endangered whooping cranes winging back to the refuge. The bay as it is. Hard. Cruel. Like life is."

He didn't think she knew diddly about hard life in this grand house. Maybe he should have her call Linda Bird. "I'd like to know about your relationship with Patch."

"Are you asking as a judge or because Lucy's said an unkind word or two?"

Now that was interesting. "As a judge."

"I loved Patch. Who didn't?" She tucked her sandal back on her foot. "Artists live up to our stereotype now and then, get moody and mean when the work sucks. Patch always pulled me out of the blues, gave me a slap on the fanny when I needed it." She spoke with the air of the artist, playing out each nuance until it wasn't a nuance anymore. But he saw in the dusky light how brittle her eyes and mouth looked under the fresh makeup. She had cried and cried hard.

"Did he ever help you in other ways? Say financially?"

"You ask that like you know the answer already."

Whit shrugged.

"You know, Lucy doesn't make it easy to love her sometimes, does she? She does have a mouth." She lit a cigarette, a thin, ladylike coffin nail pulled from a pink pack, then offered him one. He declined.

"She told you garbage about me with great reluctance, right? Much wringing of hands? She got a vibe, right?"

Whit said nothing.

"Lucy was born with a finger pointing at someone else. Artists see patterns, honey, and I've seen plenty of this one."

"She said you asked Patch for a large loan."

"I was a little short on cash between paintings and asked Patch for help. He said no, I said fine, we were fine. He's not a bank. I understood."

"You asked for a hundred thousand?"

Her eyes went wide. "Good Lord, no. I asked for ten thousand. I got it from a friend. It's being paid off, no problems." She tapped ashes into a crystal ashtray on the worktable, her mouth thinned. "A hundred thousand. She ought to use that imagination for noble causes."

"She said it's what Patch told her."

"She's dead wrong."

"She and Patch seemed to have a good relationship."

"Lucy likes people who have things and will give them to her. I'm not one of those people. Patch was. He doted on Lucy, just a bit too much."

"Can you think of anyone who'd want Patch or Thuy dead?"

"He only dated widows, and he was successful at it. I could see he might make another man jealous. Thuy, Lord, no. Gentle and kind as a lamb. Retired teacher, loaded with patience. I adored her."

"You and Roy were here in town on Monday night."

"Yes. I already gave a statement to the police. We were here, watched the news, turned in." She paused, tilted her head, gave him a melty smile. "We made love. Twice. So we were awake until midnight or so. That's not in the police statement but I don't mind total honesty with you." Her smile shifted; his skin prickled.

"In a bed or on the canvas?"

The smile widened. "You have a good eye."

Yeah, it's real tough to make out painted, squashed boobs. He saw the perfection of her face created a sense of emptiness—like a house with no curtains in the windows. "Roy's what to you, social engineering?"

"Radio Lucy strikes again." She shrugged. "It was a minor drug conviction, ten years ago. He's clean." She exhaled a cool little stream of smoke. "He was here all Monday and Tuesday with me, okay? Working. He's an artist, too. His studio's across the hall. Sculptures in metal. Gulls, lighthouses, coastal art for the gift shop crowd. He's not an artist at my level but he has potential."

Whit glanced at the body prints on the paper on the floor and thought he saw Roy's rather limited potential at work.

"It's a lot of land at stake. With Patch gone."

She frowned, as though he had dragged a dirty finger across one of her artworks. "Well, the Gilberts have owned most of Black Jack Point since before Texas was Texas. It totals about three hundred acres. Fifty acres is mine. Fifty is Lucy's. Uncle Patch owns another two hundred." She shrugged again. "I've no idea of the details of Uncle Patch's will. I would suppose Lucy and I inherit. But we never discussed it."

"But if you needed ten thousand dollars, why not sell some of your land?"

"We've always had an unspoken agreement not to sell, except as a group. Patch wanted to hold on to the family land, even when solid offers came in. Lucy and I always deferred to him."

"Have you gotten many offers on the land?" Considering the value of waterfront property in parts of Texas, Whit wondered if the land provided a hard motive.

"One, oh, a month ago. I got a phone call from a real estate investor in Corpus. I wasn't interested, but I did refer him to Patch because he was so persistent."

"Who was that?"

"Stoney Vaughn. He's got a montrosity of a house up on Copano Flats. Tedious type. I met him once at a Port Leo Art Center function. And another offer, about a year ago, from a company in Houston. We just say no. We don't want to sell. I don't know if that will change now, with Patch gone."

The bottle of Glenfiddich had been from a Stoney. Maybe interesting, maybe not.

He thought of the skeletons. "Patch ever mention any archaeological value to the land?"

Suzanne didn't answer for a second and he wondered if she knew about the bones. David and the DPS team had kept it out of the papers thus far. But a freakish detail like that was hard to muzzle with so many people now involved. She stubbed out her cigarette, glanced up at him through the trail of smoke. "An archaeologist wouldn't find anything except old dead Gilberts and their junk."

"No earlier settlement on the land?"

"Indians must have passed through or hunted there, I guess. Black Jack Point's always been wild country, though. I don't think anyone else ever built there but us crazy Gilberts." She lit another cigarette. "Speaking of crazy Gilberts, what do you see in Lucy? Do you mind me asking? Yes, she's very pretty but she's very contrary and a bit too high-maintenance."

"She drives me nuts. She makes me laugh. She makes me think. For me that's pretty good."

"Laughing is good. Sexy." Her voice went a little lower.

"I bet Roy's a real giggle factory."

"He can be very sweet," she said, letting her smile grow. "But I do bore easily."

"I'm allergic to paint," he said. "I'd like to talk to Roy now."

Her smile—more carefully crafted than her paintings—went flat. "Sure."

They returned to the den. Roy lay sprawled on the couch, drinking a fresh bottle of Dos Equis, watching *Jeopardy!* He didn't look up at Whit.

"Roy, Whit needs to talk to you," Suzanne said.

"I barely knew Patch. What is the Tower of Pisa?" he said to the television, playing Architecture for $200. He was right.

"It took a lot of strength to beat a man like Patch to death," Whit said.

Roy Krantz didn't take his eyes off the screen. "Probably not. What is photosynthesis?"

Whit leaned down, grabbed the remote, cut off the television in the middle of Botany for $600. "Pardon me. I'm speaking to you. As part of a death inquest. If you don't want to answer questions here, you do it in a courtroom."

Roy stood. Whit was tall but this guy was an oak. "I told you, I don't know anything. And I don't like to miss my program."

"Roy." Suzanne shook her head.

"I'm sorry, baby." For the first time Whit saw tenderness in Roy's sun-hardened face. "Sorry. Okay." He crossed his arms. "I never got to know him, Judge. He decided in the first ten seconds of our acquaintance I was trash. So we declined to occupy the same place at the same time."

"Let's talk prison records."

Roy walked into the kitchen, got another beer, offered a bottle to Whit. Whit shook his head. "I ran some dope for a school buddy, I got caught, I cut a little deal, school buddy didn't. I did a short stint and I've been spotless. Now I got my life back together here with Suze, doing my art, and people just want to piss in my beer."

"Y'all do much gambling?" Whit asked.

Roy glanced at Suzanne and she said, "Lucy." He glanced back at Whit with a smirk. "Actually, we do, and we have the means to and we're not in over our heads. I don't suppose it's occurred to anyone that maybe Mrs. Tran was the target, not Patch. You grilling her family like this?"

"I couldn't say."

"You come after me just because I got a record, that's the easy thing to do. Just as easy to get yourself sued for false arrest. For reporters to get a call to say some poor ex-con who's become a model citizen is getting hassled. You can't bully people, man."

"I didn't realize you felt bullied by me," Whit said. "Please don't cry."

Roy took a step forward. Suzanne put a hand on his thick forearm. "Roy. Don't let him bait you."

"I'm not baiting anyone," Whit said. "Thanks for your time. I can see myself out. I'll let you know if you're needed to testify at the inquest."

Whit drove out of Castaway Key. He remembered the time the land had been developed, this thin sliver of near-island, when he was a teenager. Once this was rough country, not too different from the Gilbert land, thick with salt grass, jutting out into shallow water with a handpainted sign that read PLEASE DON'T PET THE RATTLERS. *And how much is this land worth now?* Whit wondered. *Millions. So how much is that family land really worth to Suzanne Gilbert? Or maybe to her way-smarter-than-he-looks boyfriend?*

He didn't want to think about how much it might be worth to Lucy.

11

CLAUDIA WRIGGLED HER head through the open porthole, attempted to snake her body through. She eased one shoulder out. She turned, trying to navigate her head and the other shoulder out, but the opening was too narrow and the ropes, tight already, chafed hard, gouged her legs. She was angry enough to cry hot tears, and she hated to cry.

The heavy blindfold slipped around her neck like a loose scarf. *No getting that back over my eyes. That's probably worth a whole foot of broken toes.*

She pulled herself back in. A knot of rope caught on the porthole crank. Not good, not good. She caught her breath, eased herself free, and fell back against the bed. She tried to maneuver the blindfold back into place but she couldn't; her hands couldn't push it up far enough to cover her eyes and all her wriggling had loosened the knot too much.

She heard Stoney's shocked drawl over the speakerphone. "I'll give you the money. Okay? But these other items you're asking for, I don't have, please."

Gar said, "Number one," and Ben screamed.

"That was finger number one," Gar said. "Broke it. A pinky. You keep arguing I'll cut it off."

"I don't have what you want!" Stoney said.

"Let's accelerate. I vote to cut off something more important," Redhead said with a giggle. "Where did I put those scissors ... ?"

"No, leave him alone!" Stoney yelled.

"We will," Danny said. Claudia could hear the distaste in his voice. "If you play along. First the five million."

Stoney moaned.

"Got your pen ready, sunshine?" Redhead said. "Put a half million in this account in Grand Cayman." He read off an account number. "That's at the Great Commerce Bank of Grand Cayman. Move that first, will you?"

Stoney made a noise of unhappy agreement.

"Don't whine," Redhead said. "Then another half million in this bank in Anguilla. Here's the account number ..."

More accounts, more banks, the slow carving of Stoney's fortune. Claudia gritted her teeth.

"Now. The journal and the Devil's Eye," Danny said. "You're going to take them to Staples Mall in Corpus. Tomorrow at eight a.m., when the mall opens for the elderly mall walkers. Go to the carousel at the middle of the mall. Leave the journal and the emerald in a Sears bag, each wrapped in plain brown paper and covered with a couple of paperbacks. You'll put the bag underneath the gray horse with the white mane, the red saddle, and the bright blue ribbons. If the police are there, or I don't like how anything looks, your brother and his girlfriend die and I report the murder you committed to the New Orleans police. We get to that point, I don't care what happens to me. But you, you're finished."

There was a long silence. Stoney Vaughn finally said, "I don't know how long this transfer will take. After it goes through the banks in Houston we may not have immediate confirmation, and I'm not at my office right now..."

"We check with Grand Cayman here shortly, and you better hope that money's streaming in," Redhead said.

"We can't control how long the transfer takes once it leaves my bank. You know that," Stoney said. "Let's say I do what you want. How do I get my brother back?"

"We'll drop off Ben and Claudia in a safe place after we've got the journal and the emerald," Danny said. "We'll call you, let you know where they're at."

"That's not good enough," Stoney said.

"Our beef's not with them. It's with you. We're not into killing innocent people. And don't call the police or the coast guard or the navy or anybody. We see choppers coming, we see boats coming looking for us, they're dead in two seconds." Danny didn't seem to notice the contradiction in his words, which made Claudia cold all over.

"You jerk," Stoney said.

"Yes, but I'm the jerk in charge," Danny said.

"Okay. Okay. Please, I want to talk to my brother."

"Here he is. You got five seconds."

"Stoney?" Ben said. He didn't sound scared or hurt to Claudia, more mad.

"Yeah."

"Do what they say."

"How did they get you? I don't understand."

"Boarded us. Please, Sto—"

"Five seconds up, no more talk," Danny said. "Start the money transfers. We'll be checking on you. I'm calling you back in fifteen minutes."

"That's not enough—" Stoney started and then his voice was gone. Cut off.

"Progress," said Redhead. "But I'll just keep these scissors handy, okay, Ben?"

Claudia heard footfalls on the steps outside the master stateroom.

The porthole's still open. She hadn't shut it.

The stateroom door flew open, hard, slammed against the wall.

Gar, with the stocking off his head. A heavy round face, brown eyes, dirty-blond hair askew from the stocking, full mouth. He noticed her blindfold was off.

He yanked the chamois cloth back over her eyes with angry roughness. "That better not come off again, you understand? We'll play this little piggy if it does." He grabbed at her foot, twanged her broken toe. A bolt of fire shot up her leg.

She kept her voice steady. "I'm sorry. It slipped off while I was trying to get comfortable."

"Comfort's not in your immediate future." He leaned down close to her, licked her ear with a pizza-greasy tongue. "I'm not like Danny Boy, who plays nice with you. I don't believe in being in the wrong place at the wrong time. I think fate brought us together so we could have us a little fun."

He picked Claudia up, threw her over his shoulder, and carried her out the door.

Stoney Vaughn sat in dismal shock in his home office overlooking St. Leo Bay, staring at the banks and account numbers Danny had given him.

He lit a cigarette, fired up his computer, and tried to order his thoughts.

Danny had his idiot brother and that girlfriend of his,

somehow. On *his* boat. And that lunatic wanted the journal that had led Stoney and Alex to the treasure, and the Devil's Eye. And five million in pain money.

Forget that.

He abandoned thinking *how did this happen,* because he quickly decided that was pointless. He started thinking of how the cards might play out.

Bad hand number one: He transferred the money, turned over the goods, got his brother back. Wouldn't work. No way he could surrender the Eye—even the fake one in the storage unit—without Alex going nuclear. No way they could let Danny walk free. That went for Ben and his girl-friend, too, especially because she was a cop and God only knew what Danny had told her. Alex wouldn't stand for it.

And if he even tried to cut a separate deal with Danny, Alex would kill him.

Bad hand number two: He transferred the money but didn't turn over the journal or the Eye. Fool Danny, make him think they'd give up the goods and let Alex eliminate Danny during or after the drop. But then he was out five million bucks, and he didn't have that much sitting around. He had maybe a million, and then he had clients who were generous but didn't know it. He sometimes borrowed money and moved it back in when he got new clients. Most of his clients—carefully selected—were elderly, rich from birth, and patient regarding small losses. This creative accounting had bought him the boat and helped with the house, but he couldn't swing five million, not all at once, moved overseas. No way to cover that up.

Bad hand number three: He picked up the phone and called the police, and Danny turned him in for murder. Hell. A murder he didn't do but Danny didn't know different. Too much death—the guy in New Orleans, the old couple in Port Leo. He wasn't a killer but he was an accessory. Prison. No more golf, no more deals, no more treasure hunts, no more luscious coastal social climbers in his bed. Or Alex would kill him to keep him quiet.

Ben's dead no matter what I do, he thought. *If Danny doesn't kill him, Alex will.*

He got up, paced in front of the plate glass. They would be calling back in fifteen minutes, and he had a decision to make.

Danny thought Stoney had stolen the journal from him, killed his cousin in Louisiana. That meant he didn't know about Alex. Didn't know Alex existed. But Alex couldn't do much about Danny while Danny sailed freely in the Gulf.

So he had to get Alex and Danny both there and let Alex solve it. But first he'd cover his bases.

Stoney accessed the Internet, opened up a connection to his network management software that monitored and controlled the investment counselors' activities in his Corpus Christi office. He typed an administrator's code, entered some commands, pressed OK. He'd had this as a time-buyer, a backup plan in case his clients—or the police—got too curious about his records.

Stoney dialed the phone; Alex answered on the first ring. "We have a problem."

"Yes, we sure do," Alex said.

"I need you, um, at my house. Now?"

"That would be my pleasure." Clicked off.

Stoney decided, a boulder in his throat, he didn't like the sound of that at all.

12

WHIT HAD CALLED the Tran family from his cell phone—reluctantly acknowledging that Roy had a point about Thuy being a possible target more than Patch—and Dat, Thuy's son, had suggested meeting him behind the family restaurant. The Tran family worked close to Old Leo Harbor, the older and smaller shrimping harbor. Whit waited on the dock, watching one shrimper hosing down his boat, a flock of hungry gulls swarming above the decks, inspecting it for morsels.

Cong Ly, the Trans' restaurant, was only a hundred feet from the harbor and hustling from the back of the restaurant was Dat Tran, irritated and looking sick and puffing away on a cigarette as though it were his only solace.

"You don't mind if I smoke while we talk?" Dat said, the cigarette merrily burning away.

"Of course not," Whit said. "Again, I'm sorry for your loss." He had visited the Trans briefly the day after the bodies were found. Thuy's two daughters and son knew nothing, they said. This was beyond imagining for them. The talk had been quiet, factual, and brief. "I just came from Suzanne Gilbert's house."

Dat answered this with a stream of smoke.

"You're having to work today?" Whit asked. Given the family tragedy, he thought the restaurant might be closed.

Dat licked his lower lip. "Tourist season. We can't afford to close. Other families, they're running it for us. I'm just here for the dinner rush."

"I wanted to ask you how your mother and Mr. Gilbert met."

"Introduced by my nephew Sam."

"How?"

"Sam was working on an oral history of the county, prepping for his senior thesis. He's at Rice, double-majoring in history and economics. Wants an MBA. Never wants to see shrimp again." Dat blew out smoke. "You know what the kids are like these days. He interviewed Patch for this county history, said he was funny and charming. Invited him to Sunday lunch at the restaurant. Patch met Mother there. Called her, asked her out for coffee." He frowned, and Whit wondered if Dat was gripped by that insidious illness of grief, the if onlies. If only Sam hadn't chosen that history topic...if only he hadn't called Patch Gilbert...if only his mother had said no to coffee. *It could drive you mad,* Whit thought.

"Did you approve of them dating?" he asked.

"Usually it's the other way around," Dat said, his voice tense. "The Anglo disapproves of the Vietnamese."

"I'm not asking from a racial standpoint," Whit said. "I'm just asking what you thought of them seeing each other."

Dat flicked his cigarette into the harbor. It fizzed for a moment, was gone. "Patch was a nice man. But not a serious man. Everything a joke, everything a party. My mother was a teacher, very serious about life. She took his interest seriously. I expected her to be hurt by him." He lit another cigarette, his hands shaking. "You're dating his niece, right? So I heard."

"Yes."

"Maybe Patch's family didn't like him dating a Vietnamese."

"They've said nothing but fond and respectful words about your mother."

Dat glared at him through the veil of smoke. "Of course. She's dead now. Being nice costs nothing." He stared out for a moment over the flat of the harbor. "That investigator, Mr. Power, he said maybe it was a racial killing."

Whit chewed his lip. Of course David would like the racial angle. He was politically minded, hungry for the sheriff's office, and solving a racially motivated crime would stick him firmly on the white steed of morals and justice. But there was no reason yet to think that race played a role, and he felt annoyed with David, perhaps needlessly putting the Trans through this subtle mental torture.

"I don't believe they were killed because they were dating."

"I can. Why not? Most people are blind-stupid. No other reason yet. You give us another reason and I'll listen to it." His faith in humanity seemed badly shaken, another by-product of violent death.

"Did your mom ever mention Patch needing money, Dat?" Whit asked. "A large amount of money, raised quietly?"

Dat looked surprised. "No. Never. My mother was a very discreet woman, Judge. If Patch needed money and told her, she never would have betrayed his confidence. Was he in some sort of trouble?"

"I don't know. Perhaps."

"He wasn't good enough for her." Dat's voice trailed off and for an instant the mask of polite calm fell and Whit saw the man's grief, naked and cruel in its intensity. "Sorry. I know you like the Gilberts. But that family. Their charms escape me. My mother made a poor choice."

There was nothing to say to that, but Whit tried. "We're all so sorry for your loss. I know Lucy and Suzanne grieve for your mother, too."

Dat thumbed his second cigarette into the water. "That's just so enormously comforting to me." He stared at Whit. "Why does a woman nearly seventy need to date, huh? Why couldn't she just stay home and watch TV like other old ladies?"

"I suppose, having survived so much hardship," Whit said carefully, "she valued life. Each day of it."

"Yeah, well, look where that got her. People said we were lucky to have survived the fall of Saigon, survived the boats, gotten to Texas. Lucky. Lucky. That's us." He turned away from Whit, heading back to the restaurant, his luck all gone.

"This is the plan," Whit said. "Can you go to New Orleans, find this Alex that Jimmy Bird was calling?"

"I can leave tonight. Be back tomorrow or the next day," Gooch said. He and Whit stood in the shade of the courthouse, Whit waiting for David to come out so they could go to Corpus Christi.

"I tried the number," Whit said. "It's a motel. Bayou Mee. I also gave the number to the sheriff's office. Hollis or David will probably call the motel but they're not going to send someone to check it out."

"Ooh, let me," Gooch said. He stretched, popped his knuckles. "It's been a boring summer."

"Because David is targeting Lucy, and I want to find out where Jimmy Bird is. He's a disgruntled employee of Patch's."

"So this is actually more about protecting Lucy than about justice."

"Don't go if you don't want," Whit said.

"No need to snap," Gooch said.

"Sorry, Gooch. Be careful."

"I almost hope Jimmy Boy's hiding out there," Gooch said. "The flip side of hiding is that someone might find you and keep you where you're at."

"You don't hurt him, Gooch."

"I can't arrest him. Can't bring him home. I just dispense justice as I see fit?"

That was a scary thought. "No. You make another anonymous tip," Whit said. "No vigilante stuff, Gooch."

"How'm I ever supposed to have interesting memoirs someday, you keep cramping my style?"

Gooch turned and left and a moment later David emerged from the courthouse. He straightened his Stetson, watched Gooch's retreating back.

"Your friend always looks guilty of something," David said.

"So do you," Whit said. They walked along the grass of the courthouse yard. Two news vans, from Corpus Christi affiliates, sat like squat little vultures on the opposite side of the square. Whit hardly gave them a glance, grateful that his ever-casual attire made him look more like a latecomer paying an overdue fine than the county's JP/coroner. David slowed, as though wanting to stop and linger and talk to them. Already baking in the heat were two competing journalists, electrifying their audiences with overwrought prose: *Port Leo remains rocked by the brutal double homicide...A tragic end for elderly lovers...leaves unanswered questions.* Horror neatly filed into worn phrases to boost ratings. Those reporters had never heard Patch's booming laugh, watched Thuy's delicate hands move while she told a story, smelled the soft jasmine of her perfume.

"Big story," David said as he started the engine. "What we do is going to be watched. Carefully."

"You should bone up on your preening," Whit said.

"You might want to get a white shirt and tie," David said. He pulled the car past the reporters, giving them a friendly little wave. Whit saw him wince as he powered up the window, favoring the shoulder that had been shot months ago, as he always did. Whit wondered if the shoulder still troubled him or if David used it as a merit badge.

"You're not going to ask me about how my questioning of your girlfriend went?" David asked as they headed out of Port Leo, along Highway 35.

"No," Whit said. "I'm not worried."

"Did you know she inherits the whole shebang?" David changed lanes, whipped around a slow-moving pickup. He said it as easily as asking if Whit wanted the radio on.

Whit was silent a moment too long.

"All of Patch's money, land, all of it. He cut out his other niece. I just talked with his attorney in Corpus. Patch made the changes less than a month ago."

"I don't think Lucy knows. She told me they'd each get half."

"So she said. She looked like she pissed her pants when I told her," David said. "Man, I love driving. Even in this traffic. Wish I had a BMW, something sweet to point down the road. Lucy can afford one now. That estate, with the land, it's gonna be many pretty pennies." He glanced over at Whit. "Maybe she can spring for that shirt and tie, Your Honor."

13

ALL RIGHT, HERE's the skinny on your bones." Dr. Parker sat across from David and Whit in a borrowed office at the morgue, where the forensic anthropology team had set up temporary shop. "When I'm looking at bones I can only tell you so much. I don't have a way, from visual inspection, to tell you this man died in 1800 or 1900 or what have you unless maybe it was in the past three years. And these boys been dead way longer than three years. You want more specific, you call UT and get in the long line for carbon-14 dating, but that's real expensive and you don't need it."

He cleared his throat, moved aside a stack of photos from the dig. "You got three skeletons at the site. Three skulls, three partial rib cages, six tibia, and an odd number of finger bones and teeth. All died of bullet wounds. Sam got shot between the eyes, Tom and Uriah got shot in the back of the head. The fracture patterns..."

"You name them?" David asked.

"Sure, I name 'em," Parker said. "Helps me to remember they were once breathing people, happy, sad, hauling all the same baggage we carry around right now. Rotate through the alphabet like hurricanes. Up to S now. Let's see." He shuffled papers. "Now I can look at the skeletal remains and tell quite a bit. But because the disarticulation was so severe, we're making some guesses here. Sam was male, five six, European ancestry, about twenty-two at his death, right-handed. Tom was male, five five, European ancestry, about twenty-eight at his death, left-handed. Uriah was male, five eight, European ancestry, about thirty at his death, right-handed. I could be off, in that we might have matched the wrong long bones to the wrong skulls. But you got to start somewhere."

"So they weren't Karankawas or Comanches," Whit said. His own voice sounded too quiet, still processing what David had told him about Lucy.

"No." Parker opened another file. "Now these other relics: the nails, iron latches, and locks. I sent those to my friend Iris Dominguez over at A&M-Corpus. She has books to help identify historical implements. Lots of latches were distinctive, being handmade back then, used to mark the work of a craftsman. Dr. Dominguez says two of the latches come from a Spanish furniture-builder, Olivarez in Barcelona, active from 1770 until the late 1820s. The latches date from a design made around 1818. Another latch comes from a New Orleans furniture-making concern, LaBorde, active from 1800 until the American Civil War. The nails and the locks don't offer so much, less room for distinction."

"This Olivarez and LaBorde, they made coffins?" Whit said.

"Not to our knowledge. They made chests, containers, furniture."

Chests, Whit thought.

"So some point after 1818 is a reasonable guess? If our

three boys have been dead so long, no one should have known about them being there," David said.

"Maybe not. We even found a smaller bone chip in the grass near the surface. The bones therefore have to have been dug up first, then dumped back into the hole, covered some, then your murder victims were dumped on top. It really is strange."

"What if...Sam and Tom and Uriah had been buried with something else?" Whit said slowly. *The latches. The locks,* he thought.

Dr. Parker was quiet for a moment. "I don't know what you mean."

"You said these latches and locks could have come from chests. What do buried chests suggest to you?"

David gave a short little laugh. "What, buried treasure? That's ridiculous."

"Dr. Parker?" Whit asked. "Is it?"

Parker gave a thin smile under his Yankees cap. "I don't know if there's a historical basis for it. I'm an anthropologist, not an archaeologist."

"Your Honor," David said, with great patience in his tone. "Don't go off on a wild-goose—"

"I'm just saying. How do you explain these relics? David, you grew up on the coast, too. You've heard the legends. Sunken treasures off the coasts from Spanish ships caught in storms. Or Jean Laffite. He pirated in the Gulf. Patch used to tell stories about him and buried treasure. That crazy old hermit, Black Jack, that lived out on the Point and claimed to be one of Laffite's men." He thought then of the book Patch had borrowed from the library: *Jean Laffite, Pirate King.*

"But they're just stories," David said. "Nothing more.

Maybe these guys got buried with their belongings. That seems far more reasonable to me."

"They weren't pharaohs," Whit said. "If they were killed and robbed, the robbers would have taken the chests with them."

David rubbed his face. "These men could have been buried in the chests themselves. We didn't find anything that suggested buried treasure at the site. I mean, honestly, do you hear yourself?"

"I'll send you a complete report when I'm done," Dr. Parker said. He seemed eager to be away from this argument. "What do you want done with the boys when I'm finished?"

"The county will bury them properly," Whit said. "You can send them all back to my office."

David stood, shook hands with Parker. Parker clapped a hand on Whit's shoulder.

"Buried treasure," Parker said. "Wouldn't that be something?"

"Wouldn't it, though?" Whit said.

"I've got your autopsies." Dr. Elizabeth Contreras gestured them to seats across from her metal-topped desk. She looked tired as she tucked a lock of hair behind her ear.

"Thanks for the fast turnaround," Whit said.

"Their times of death were between midnight and four a.m. on Tuesday morning. Mr. Gilbert's wound patterns are consistent with your typical garden-use shovel."

"I thought as much," David said.

"His nose, both cheekbones, and his jaw had multiple breaks, his collarbone and skull badly fractured. He would have died quickly. There are a number of postmortem injuries to the body, including four broken ribs and a hard, shovel-point blow to the forehead. The killer kept whaling on him after he was dead."

"Did he suffer?" Whit asked.

"I think not. Did you know him?"

"Yes. He was a family friend. A good one."

"I'm so sorry, Judge."

"Thanks. Anything else of note with Mr. Gilbert?"

"No—just that it was a very brutal attack. Mrs. Tran was shot to death, a .45-caliber. I think they shot her because the shovel broke, so she probably died after Mr. Gilbert. She has defensive wounds on her hands and arms. Splinters from the handle. DPS can probably identify the handle manufacturer from the wood traces, the resins." She cleared her throat. "DPS also did fingernail swipes on them both—you may bear fruit with Mrs. Tran. More likely that she scratched or grabbed at the killers during the assault."

"Killers? Plural?"

Liz Contreras steepled her fingers. "It just seems more likely. Let's say Gilbert gets attacked first and it's a surprise. Whoever killed him either didn't have the gun or didn't have time to draw before deciding to attack Mr. Gilbert. Mrs. Tran's got bruising on her upper arms. Maybe one attacker held her while another attacker killed Mr. Gilbert. Then, with the shovel broken and their composure regained, they shot her."

"So they were digging, one might assume"—Whit gave David a stare—"and Patch and Thuy surprised them?"

"Maybe the killers were camping?" Liz said. "Camping illegally. Campers sometimes carry shovels."

"No signs of a campsite, but there were heavy truck tracks," Whit said. "So let's say there's noise from the truck, and they don't hear Patch and Thuy approach until it's too late. The two of them were supposed to be over in Port Aransas."

"But they weren't. So maybe the killers knew their plans, expected them to be gone," Liz said.

Knew their plans. So who knew about them going to Port Aransas? Patch might have told any of a thousand people in town what his plans were. Not a shy man. Or maybe not. Assume not. So Whit knew. Lucy. Suzanne and therefore Roy. Thuy's family. "If you're right, the killers wouldn't have been worried about making noise."

"Noise?" Liz said. "I mean, you're saying noise above and beyond a regular truck, right?"

"Maybe the truck was doing more than revving its engines. Maybe it was loading something," Whit said.

"Loading what? Out in the middle of nowhere?" Liz asked.

"Judge," David said.

Liz glanced at the two of them, gauging the tension. Whit stayed quiet. "I won't ask. You've got my report. The families can have the bodies back tomorrow."

They walked into the parking lot, got into David's police cruiser. David started the engine but didn't shift into drive. "The treasure idea. It's interesting, but until I see something more it's not relevant."

"You can't ignore those relics."

"I'm more interested in modern-day motives."

"The killers had shovels and trucks, David. Do you think they were digging for oil?"

"I'm not jumping to a whacked-out conclusion, Judge. The skeletons could be old Gilbert family members. That seems far more likely than buried treasure in my mind.

Surely you see that." David eased out into Corpus Christi traffic, headed for the Harbor Bridge. "I mean, I understand this treasure idea's interesting to you because it takes Lucy out of the equation. She's got the prime motive for the murder. She benefits the most." He clicked his tongue against his teeth.

"Lucy had nothing to do with this. She didn't even know about the will."

"You one hundred percent sure she didn't?"

"I am."

"Certainty's a nice thing. You don't see it often. You want to grab dinner?" The unexpected olive branch made Whit suspicious.

"Why?"

"That's nice. We work together. I'm making an effort here."

"Make the effort by not accusing Lucy."

"We'll talk about it. You eat barbecue?"

There was a nasty calculation, Whit thought, in the smile, and he wanted to know what was behind it. "Sure I do. Let's go."

14

GAR CARRIED CLAUDIA out onto *Jupiter*'s deck. She was still blindfolded, and the heat of the sun touched her face and legs. He lurched and for a freezing moment she thought he was throwing her overboard. But then he settled her feet on deck, held her by her shoulders, and she realized he'd crossed the railing to the *Miss Catherine. We haven't really moved,* Claudia realized. She wondered how cold a watery grave would feel, the sky forever denied, your flesh drifting off your bones over the weeks, your leg bones and hipbones and ribs settling into the ooze, like artifacts, for the slow dissolve into muck itself.

"Don't do this," she said. "Please." She balled her hands into fists, but she knew with a sick sinking feeling he was much stronger than she was. She needed a weapon to even the odds.

"He's not going to hurt you." Danny's voice came from behind her. "I just want to talk to you a minute."

So this wasn't about rape, at least for the next five minutes.

Gar steered her—walking made her broken toe throb even worse—into a galley that reeked of burned pizza, with a thin odor of rum and sweat souring the air. He steered Claudia into a vinyl booth and pushed her into the seat.

"Now, Claudia," Danny said. "We can talk for a few minutes. While we wait to be sure Stoney's cooperating."

Breath tickled Claudia's ear. "If this deal sours," Gar whispered, "I'm gonna have fun with you. Pour some cooking oil between your legs and have us a little marathon."

Her heart struck her ribs like a hammer hitting piano wire.

"Let her be," Danny said. "Go back to the other boat."

"Behave," Gar said, presumably to her. Claudia heard a door close, the smell of the rum moved closer, vinyl crackled as Danny slid into the booth's other side. She put her hands—still bound in front of her—on the table. The linoleum was sticky.

"Don't be afraid," Danny said.

"Yeah, right." Gar's threat wriggled in her ear like a worm.

"I don't think he'll rape you. He's all talk. Those two boys, well, they slept in the same stateroom last night and I heard groaning. Don't think they had upset stomachs." The barest hint of moral outrage colored his voice.

"He broke my toe because he didn't like what I said. And frankly, you're not in control of him or what he does."

"I am."

"You're not," she said. "I can hear it in their voices. Those two freaks are just using you to get at this cash. You're too gentle. You don't have the stomach for this or what it might take. You're as dead as me and Ben if this doesn't work out."

"I'm sorry you're in this mess, but you picked your friends badly. You thirsty, hon? Want some water?"

"Please."

A tap gurgled. Then he pushed a glass into her hands. She drank. He moved against the vinyl, making it squeak, trying to get comfortable. "Tell me what you know about Stoney."

"Nothing. I know Ben. I barely knew Stoney in high school."

"High school. Before he was a millionaire."

"Yes."

"He much different now?"

"He has more lunch money."

A match scratched, she smelled the flash of fire. Cigarette paper crackled its whisper and silky smoke brushed her nostrils. "So in high school did he run roughshod over people? Kill anyone who got in his way?"

"Talk is cheap," she said. "What proof do you have he killed anybody?"

"Because only he knew about the journal," Danny said. "I told him about it, he decided he wanted it, and he killed to get it."

The journal. The emerald. She'd heard him refer to both before. But this was about more, about stealing millions of Stoney's cash. "Forget that for a minute, since he says he doesn't have it. Y'all can't get away with stealing his money electronically. Transactions leave electronic trails. You'll get caught within days." She leaned a little toward Danny and smelled rum. "Having a little liquid courage?" she asked.

"You want some?"

"Sure. For medicinal purposes. I get seasick when I'm uncomfortable. These ropes really hurt and my foot's aching." Let him think she was delicate and helpless.

A dribble of rum trickled into her glass. "Where you

work, Claudia?" Danny asked, as though he were a bartender making conversation.

"I'm a secretary," she lied. "I work for a justice of the peace in Port Leo. Judge Whit Mosley."

"You didn't work today?"

Today was Thursday. She had taken Wednesday, today, and Friday off. She would not be missed at the police department until Monday. But the pirates didn't know that.

"I took off today," she said. "Just today because Fridays we have juvenile court. It's always a zoo."

"Damned kids." She heard the soft puff of his cigarette. "How about I call this judge? Tell him y'all ran into motor trouble down near Padre. You'll be out another day. I'll say I'm the mechanic fixing it. I'm sure he'll understand."

She prayed, silently, that if Danny made the call Whit would have the presence of mind not to blurt, *What are you talking about? She doesn't work for me.* Maybe this wasn't a good idea. "He won't accept a stranger calling and making excuses for me. I'd have to talk with him."

"We'll discuss that with my colleagues."

"Colleagues. That's generous."

Ten seconds of silence. She couldn't see his face. Frown of anger, smile of indulgence, scowl of disbelief? Or maybe ready to stub that cigarette out on her forehead.

"They breaking a deal with you?" she asked. "They care about the money, not about punishing Stoney or this emerald or whatever it is you care about."

"Hush now."

"Maybe I can help you."

"Why would you help me, honey?"

"Because I want to live. I'll get you what you want, if you'll get us out of this alive."

She heard only the hard rasp of his breathing.

"You're not like those guys, are you? You're a little older, a little wiser. They're in this for the money. You're in it because you want the money *and* you hate Stoney. That's a big *and*."

Now the silence stretched for half a minute. She couldn't stand it, so her words came out in a flood. "Look. All I know about Stoney is he's got a big house full of security. And I can get you past that security. Ben showed me the codes for the house last night, 'cause I might do some house-sitting for him and his brother when they go out of town. But I'll only help you if you don't hurt me or Ben or Stoney." She wished she could tear the blindfold off, see his reaction to this lie. How did the blind navigate the emotions of the world, gauge human reaction? She listened for the quickening of his breath, for nervous tapping fingers against the table, for uneasy shifts in posture. But there was only the silence.

Then he said, "Do you know why Stoney Vaughn's boat is called the *Jupiter*?"

"Because he thinks he's a god?" She spiced a little bitterness into her tone, figuring she might as well play into his resentment of Stoney by faking anger.

She heard him tap ashes. She sensed him leaning his head close to hers, his breath smelling of garlic, rum, tobacco. "What do you know about Jean Laffite?"

"Who?"

"Laffite. The pirate Laffite."

The words were so unexpected she didn't answer for a moment. "Well, uh, he was a famous pirate in the Gulf a long time ago. I guess the last of the great pirates. There's all sorts of legends that he buried a lot of gold along the coast."

"Jean Laffite had a schooner in his fleet called *Jupiter*. Stoney named his boat after Laffite's. He even has that picture of Laffite in his stateroom. Not nearly as good as the paintings I have, but still an okay one."

She remembered the print. Yes. Laffite the pirate, confident and cocky.

"And do you know why this boat is the *Miss Catherine*?"

"Tell me."

"Laffite's great love was a woman named Catherine Villars. She was a New Orleans quadroon—part black, mostly white—a legendary beauty. Skin like yours, Claudia, perhaps a bit darker." He ran a finger along her hand but it didn't scare her.

"So you and Stoney are pirate wanna-bes," Claudia said. "Rent an Errol Flynn movie and get it out of your system." This talk of pirates made her nervous. Pirates cut throats. Pirates made victims walk planks. Pirates raped and killed.

"Do you know what happened to Jean Laffite?"

"I don't imagine he ended up in a rest home."

"No one knows. Terrible and beautiful, the not knowing." His voice took a strange tone, one of slow, sickened anger that goose pimpled her skin. "Here's the basics. Laffite used Barataria Bay in Louisiana as a base. Made his fortune attacking Spanish shipping. He sold his booty—mostly slaves and luxury goods—in New Orleans. His pirating kept New Orleans fat and happy in black-market merchandise, except Laffite didn't pay taxes."

"They had IRS agents then?"

"Laffite's the social god of New Orleans, but he's an outlaw to the American government. So during the War of 1812, the British navy makes Laffite an offer: Help the English capture New Orleans, and they'll give him gold, land, a high commission in their navy. Think how different our history might have been if the British had taken Louisiana."

"Yorkshire pudding with jambalaya."

"But Laffite tricks the British. He warns the governor about the British plans. Know what the Americans did to repay him?"

"What?"

"The Americans attacked Laffite's base, burned his operations to the ground. All for warning them. There's a sweet thank-you note."

"Well, that wasn't very nice," Claudia said.

"But Laffite's a patriot. A man of honor." The heat in his voice rose. "When Andrew Jackson arrived to defend New Orleans, Laffite offered his pirates to help defend the city. Jackson badly needed experienced fighters and weapons. So Laffite armed New Orleans—he still had more guns than the government, even after they destroyed his camp. With Jackson's blessing, Laffite and his pirates took charge of key positions as the British attacked."

"And Laffite helped win the day," Claudia guessed.

"He dominated the day for them," Danny corrected, battle in his own voice. "His cannons shredded an overwhelming British force. The pirates became national heroes. President Madison pardoned Laffite and his men of their past crimes."

Maybe Laffite just didn't want to lose his market, Claudia thought, but instead she said, "And they all retired to Club Med."

"Well, he wasn't gonna take a nine-to-five job. Once a pirate, you know. Eventually he left New Orleans for Texas."

"And ended up on Galveston Island." This part of the history Claudia knew—standard lore of growing up on the Texas coast.

"Imagine. A thousand pirates on Galveston, working all the waters of the Gulf, bringing Laffite their booty, funneling the goods to Louisiana. But one of his ships attacked an American merchantman. Laffite hanged the captain responsible on a beach gallows so that the American navy, from their ships off Galveston, could see the body dangling—but the U.S. government wasn't appeased. They ordered Laffite out of Texas, out of the Gulf."

Laffite sounded like ninety-percent jerk to her, barely a hero, but Claudia sensed Jean Laffite burned as real as the sun for Danny.

"The man had saved New Orleans but they forgot about that. Typical American arrogance. But Laffite obeyed. In spring of 1820, he sailed away, leaving Galveston burning to the ground." He stopped, as though picturing the scene, a fading shot of an old black-and-white movie in which the cutthroats were the gallant heroes.

"Then what?" Claudia asked, wanting to slap him, to shake him, to say, *This happened almost two hundred years ago. Why am I gonna get killed over this?*

"The stories vary. Some say he went to Yucatán and died of fever. Some say he went to Cuba and died in a sea battle. Some claim he tried to rescue Napoleon from Saint Helena. One man, a supposed descendant of Laffite's, claimed Laffite returned to America under an assumed name, and lived out his life in small-town Missouri." This last option was pronounced with sarcasm dripping from every word. "But no one knows. Of course, so many say that he buried a treasure, worth millions, somewhere in Texas or Louisiana."

"Treasure," she repeated, thinking of Ben talking yesterday at lunch about Stoney. *He's financed some treasure dives in the Florida Keys... Crazy way to risk your money.*

"Imagine the scene, Claudia. The government Laffite served so well in a time of need has completely betrayed him. He left as he promised, but the American navy shadowed and harassed him all the way down the coast. He would have had reason to believe the navy might board or attack him at any time. Or the British or the Spanish might attack him. Remember, he was being evicted, leaving his base, leaving nothing behind. Nothing." A pause. "His only option to keep his treasure from falling into others' hands would have been to bury it so he could return when the heat died down and retrieve it."

"It seems risky," she said.

"Laffite knew the shallows and reefs in getting through the barrier islands and the bays. The American navy couldn't follow him there." Danny cleared his throat. "The proof was in the journal—real, actual documentation— that Laffite buried a fortune near St. Leo Bay. Before Stoney stole it from me. Like you said, you help me, maybe I help you?"

He's inviting you in. The trickle of sweat began between her breasts, down her ribs. It was the only chance she saw; Stoney knew who Danny was, which meant a trail could be followed back to Gar and Redhead. She and Ben were guaranteed dead, unless she could make herself valuable.

Make it good. "Tell me more about this journal. Maybe I can figure out where Stoney hid it. I'm pretty familiar with his house."

"Looks like an old diary, brown, leather-bound, small pages. Written in the 1820s by Dr. John Fanning. He was the ship's surgeon on the navy schooner *Lynx*. According to Fanning, *Lynx* detained Laffite after he left Galveston, boarded his ship outside St. Leo Bay, searched it for traces of loot from a Spanish treasure ship, *Santa Barbara,* which had been lost barely a week before. *Lynx* escorted Laffite to Mexico, dumped him there penniless, pardoned his crew. One of Laffite's crew, a drunk, told Fanning Laffite went ashore with a few other men and buried a trove from *Santa Barbara* at Black Jack Point—but that only Laffite returned. Of course the historians have it wrong, the Fanning journal rewrites Laffite's history. And I had it. It was *mine*."

Claudia bit her lip.

"If the journal's right, the treasure might be worth several million now, on today's market. The historical value alone would be astonishing. Actual, provable buried pirate treasure. Think what the museums would offer, Claudia. The Smithsonian, for instance. Millions. And there was supposedly a great emerald aboard *Santa Barbara*—a huge Colombian gem called the Devil's Eye. It would be of…particular value."

"So you approached Stoney about helping you find this treasure? And Stoney stole this journal from you so he could locate this treasure himself?"

"Yes." He sounded completely serious, for a moment completely sane. If you ignored the words.

"But Stoney has money. He doesn't need a bunch of old gold that might not even exist."

"He has money that anyone else can have. But a treasure, that's one of a kind. His ego can't resist it. And I don't think it's buried anymore. I think he's got it."

"You think he dug it up?"

"I don't think he's been waiting around," Danny said. "He came to New Orleans, where I live, when I was out of town, and he took the journal. He killed my cousin, who was house-sitting for me. A bullet to the brain. A cowardly way to kill."

"I'm sorry your cousin was killed," she said. "Truly. But what happens to me if I help you? If I can get you this journal? Or this treasure?"

"Well, Claudia, I'll let you go." Easy, like he was suggesting they grab an ice cream cone down at the beach.

Right. But she pretended to believe him. "What about Ben?"

"Oh, I'll let him go, too. I don't have a quarrel with either of you. I have a sense of honor."

"Yes," she snapped. "Your sense of honor's why I'm tied up and blindfolded with a broken toe."

A silent minute passed. Then there was a gentle downward tug on the chamois blindfold. It slipped down to her shoulders, like a scarf. The light in the cabin was dim, and she blinked, but now she saw Danny sitting across from her. Thick dark hair was shot with salt, combed back from his temples, his eyes an earthy brown but feverish and bloodshot, a drunkard's eyes. Crazy-man eyes.

In his hand—aimed at her heart—he held an automatic pistol.

"If we're gonna help each other, I gotta trust you, you gotta trust me, right?" he said.

"That's true. And I would like to trust you, which is hard for me if I think you're going to kill me or Ben or even Stoney. Even if he's a killer and a thief."

"I'm not the monster Stoney is, Claudia. I won't kill him. I just don't want him to have the treasure. It's mine.

It belongs to me, in every moral way." Heat colored his voice, his hand slapped down on the tabletop, emphasizing the last three words. "I'll let him live if I get the treasure. I swear on my family's name."

Then that makes it all just fine, buddy. "You don't know me. Why would you trust me?"

"I don't trust you. You don't trust me either, I know. But I don't want to have to kill you. I want the treasure, I want to be shed of these two jerks now, and I don't want to go to jail. You get me into Stoney's house, you live. It's your choice."

She said nothing for a minute. The hunger in his eyes made her skin crawl. *Fine. It's his weakness. Use it against him to save you and Ben.*

"So we got us a deal?" he asked.

Claudia nodded.

15

---◆━━◆◉◆━━◆---

I'M BEGGING YOU NOT TO HURT MY BROTHER,"
Stoney Vaughn said over the speakerphone. "Please. Let
me explain."

"We just called the banks. Ain't no money streaming in,"
Redhead said. No giggle now. "Where're those scissors?"

"Stoney, please!" Ben yelled. "Give them what they
want!"

Stoney's throat cleared. "I can't. The transfers couldn't
go through. The computer systems at my investment firm
are down. We got a virus. They aren't going to be up until
tomorrow."

A moment's silence. "Stoney..." Ben said, his voice
barely above a whisper.

"A virus, you know. Like that Anna Kournikova picture
that got e-mailed around. It wasn't a picture, it was a virus.
Our servers are down."

Gar sprang up from the couch, pacing, angry little hums
coming from him. "So move it via another bank."

"I can't. This server's got to work first. My accounts are
all locked and accessed through here. Please, you got to
give me more time."

"Wrong answer," Redhead said.

Ben felt the tickle of scissors moving along his jaw, his throat, downward along his chest. "Stoney, please, they're gonna kill us! Give them what they want."

"Stoney," Gar said quietly. "You understand our position. It's not negotiable."

"Let me talk to Danny," Stoney said. "Let me suggest an alternative."

"He's not here right now," Redhead said. "You can talk to us. We're all partners."

"Oh. Well. I don't have this journal or this emerald he's talking about, okay? That whole idea, that's just crazy, man. I don't have it. I'll give you the money. But you got to give me time." He paused. "As a sign of good faith, I raise the pot."

"We're listening," Redhead said. The scissors stopped their wandering, poised above Ben's stomach.

"Get Danny to forget about this imaginary jewel he's asking for. Eliminate it as a condition. Let my brother and his friend go. I'll pay you an extra half million."

"Wait a minute," Redhead said. He jabbed the speakerphone's mute button. "What do you think?"

Ben heard Gar let out a long breath. "I'll take a half mil in cash over legends. But he still ain't wired no money yet. So that could be a lie, too."

Redhead jabbed the button again. "How do you get us the extra money?"

"Is Danny there?"

"No," Redhead said.

"I've got a half mil in a separate account." A pause. "But you get rid of Danny. You can have the money. But not him."

"We can't access the accounts without him," Gar said.

"That's your problem. I'll send it when he's done and gone, you understand? And then the rest."

"Stoney, what the hell are you doing?" Ben said. "Holy hell—"

"I'm saving you," Stoney said. "Now just hush, Ben."

"And you just take our word we've gotten rid of him?" Redhead said after a moment's hesitation.

"No. You bring him to me. At my dock at my house at Copano Flats. I'll give you the money as cash when you turn over his body and my brother. His girlfriend, whatever. She's a cop. Do whatever you think is best."

"Hell," Gar said.

"Stoney, for God's sake!" Ben screamed.

"Shut up, Ben," Stoney said.

"Leave Claudia alone. Don't you dare hurt her," Ben said in a low voice. "Please..."

"You could have the place swarming with cops," Gar said.

"But I won't," Stoney said, "because I've just asked you to kill Danny for me. I have no reason to invite the cops to our meeting. Take the money and forget you ever heard of Danny, okay?"

"We'll call you back in five," Redhead said. "Be there." He clicked off the phone. "Interesting turn of events."

"She a cop?" Gar grabbed Ben's arms, brought him off the couch.

"Screw you," Ben said.

"I'll take that as a yes," Gar said.

"This could be a delaying tactic. I don't buy that about the computers being down," Redhead said.

"But he wants Danny dead," Gar said. "And we get a half million as a bonus for what we're gonna have to do anyway."

"Play it this way. Get rid of the woman. Don't take the risk she's a cop," Redhead said. His voice was cool and firm. "I'll set up new overseas accounts for us. Then let Stoney hear Danny die. Strangle him, you're strong enough. Make Stoney move the money then. Then we just see about whether or not he gets his brother back. Little brother might be mad about girlfriend getting offed and might talk to cops. Huh? You gonna talk, little brother?"

Ben made no answer.

"I'll take care of the girlfriend," Gar said. "Have a little fun first, though. I always wanted to do a cop."

"No, you're not," Redhead said. His tone went peevish, hurt.

"Don't worry. You're my favorite. Stay here. Just watch him."

Ben heard Gar move heavily up the steps. "Claudia!" Ben yelled. "No!"

A gun barrel jabbed hard into his testicles. "One more word," Redhead said, "and I shoot them off."

"You—" Ben started but he didn't finish.

"There, you happy?" Stoney's hands shook as he set down the phone.

"Wasn't so hard, now, was it?" Alex sat on the corner of the desk. Pissed as hell when he got here, but then he'd calmed when Stoney explained. It made Stoney nervous.

"My brother—"

"We'll worry about him later. First we got to make sure Danny can't tell what all he knows. You see that now. He put two and two together, he can't live to testify."

"You screwed up," Stoney said. "You should have killed him."

"Our paths didn't cross in New Orleans," Alex said. "Is that my fault?"

"But my brother..." Stoney's voice faded.

"Hey, man, you could have done what they said. Sent the money flying along the cables. You didn't. Don't lay this on me." Alex stood, looked out over the bay. "They ought to be here soon, assuming they call back and all's well."

Stoney leaned over and vomited into a wastebasket.

"That's nasty. Yuck." Alex handed Stoney a tissue. "Now. Problem number two. The emerald that's in the storage unit's a fake, Stoney. Can you explain that to me?"

"So we gonna kill them," Danny whispered.

"No killing anybody," Claudia said. "Not if we don't have to."

"If you're gonna chicken out if push comes to shove, I need to know right now."

She raised one eyebrow. "Don't worry about me."

"Fine, then. I got a plan."

"Let's hear it," she said. He had loosened the rope on her wrists a little and her hands prickled with returning sensation.

"I got chloroform on the boat, thought we might need it to subdue Stoney," he said. "When one of 'em comes back over here, you distract him, mouth off to him, and I slap 'im with the chloroform cloth."

"Maybe something simpler," Claudia said. "Maybe you putting your gun at the back of his head and making him drop his gun."

"What if he don't surrender? What if he shoots you or me?"

"He's not likely to do that with a gun at the base of his skull. And if you're behind him he can't shoot you."

"He might shoot you," Danny said.

"Then you need to press that gun hard against him so he knows you mean business."

"If I shoot one, the other will hear."

"You got a fire extinguisher here in the galley?" she asked. Danny nodded toward the cabinet under the sink. "You put the gun on him, get him to freeze, I'll belt him in the head with the extinguisher. Knock him out."

"That means you got to be untied."

"Yes."

Danny chewed his lip. Now that she could see his face clearly, study it, she didn't like the flat shine in his eyes. Not clever but cagey.

"You begged me to trust you, you got to trust me," Claudia said. "I can't be much help to you tied up."

"You punched me," he said. "You're the toughest little cookie in the jar. You might try to take the gun from me."

"Well, I won't," Claudia said. "You can trust me. It's your call."

He put his gun down and loosened the ropes from around her hands. She kept her hands very still. "If I take the ropes off all the way he'll notice."

"I'll tuck my hands under the table."

"What about your blindfold?" he asked. "He'll be suspicious if it's off you."

"Leave it off," she said. "If we lose, he'll kill me anyway."

Danny took his Sig and got up from the galley booth.

"Do you have any other guns?" Claudia asked.

"No," Danny said. "I'm for gun control, actually."

"Then give me the gun."

"You'll shoot me," Danny said.

Yes, I will, she decided then. *But later and in the leg.*
"This is ridiculous. I'm not going to shoot you."

He still seemed to think, working the inside of his cheek.

She played a cautious card. "Yes, you're just like your
hero, Laffite. Heart of a warrior. You can't make the sim-
plest decision."

His eyes narrowed. "You don't understand. I'm this
close...after what all I've lost...I can't lose the Devil's
Eye. Or the journal. It's what I've lived for, honey."

His stare and his sad confession made her queasy. "You
gonna trust me or Gar and the redhead more?"

"I got a plan. You get down in the stateroom, lie down on
the bed like you're sleeping. He comes down there to check
on you, he's got to go down those narrow stairs. I put the
gun behind his ear then, make him drop his."

"In a stateroom there's not much cover," she said.
"You're nice and safe behind him and I'm not."

"It's just a variant on your original idea." He sounded
peeved.

"With all due respect, I don't think you have the nerve
for this." She kept her voice calm. "I was in the army right
out of school. Give me the gun and let me handle him."

"I'm not giving you the advantage, Claudia. If I were you
I'd shoot me—maybe not kill me, because you seem like a
real nice lady—then get on the radio and call for help."

"Where's your radio?"

"Up on the bridge."

"It doesn't make sense for me to shoot you and then try
to call for help. Your buddies might spot me up on the deck
and open fire."

He didn't say anything, rubbing his thumb along the
Sig's handle.

"But they won't think anything of you being up there, Danny. Can you go up there, call the coast guard on Channel 16?" Sixteen was the regular monitoring channel, on which boats hailed each other in short order before moving their communications to another channel. A lifeline connecting all sorts of boats on the water, Channel 16 was monitored by the coast guard. "Call a Mayday, tell them it's a kidnapping situation, request help."

"And then I get arrested. No way."

"You're going to get caught anyway. My plan's the only safe way out for you. I promise."

Danny stared at her. "But Gar'll have *Jupiter's* radio tuned to 16. They'll hear us. Or they'll see me using the radio and they'll go nuts."

"Then call on 22A. That's the coasties' liaison channel. Go up there, crouch down low, and get us some help."

He shook his head. "If they see me, they'll kill me."

"They're going to kill you anyway and you're a moron if you don't see that."

He suddenly—but gently—pressed the barrel underneath her chin. "Listen. You're not the boss here."

"If you kill me, Stoney won't give you what you want." She felt calmer than she could have imagined with a gun held to her head by a clearly unstable man. But his finger wasn't on the trigger. He was playing with her and the idea of death, and she stared back at him.

"Get down to the stateroom." Danny pulled her to her feet, gave her a little push. "Lie down like you're sleeping or crying. My plan'll work."

She didn't argue. The stateroom on *Miss Catherine* was tiny, the bedspread worn, smelling of Cheetos and beer, like a cheap motel room. On a side table was a stack of books. All about Jean Laffite and early Texas history, little bits of neon-colored paper sticking out from the pages like bright plumage. Clothes lay in an untidy heap on the floor. Danny prodded her with the gun, grazing the back of her head, and she clambered onto the bed, her foot throbbing.

"At least untie me so I can fight him if I have to," she said.

He hesitated.

"So am I help or just bait?" she snapped.

"I'm deciding," he said.

"I thought you were a gentleman."

"Shut up."

"No," she said. "I won't. You want my help, you better start helping me. Untie me. Or you're going to have to shoot me, because I'm not cooperating with you anymore."

He made a sigh of exasperation. "This is why they didn't have women on ships of old."

"You told me before I picked my friends badly. You picked yours worse. You get to pick again, at least for now."

"Danny!" Gar's voice rumbled from the deck.

Danny shoved her onto the bed. "Pretend. We don't got time for your plan." And he hurried back up the stairs. She heard the galley door smack open, heard Gar demand in a low voice, *Where's she at?* heard Danny answer in a mumble that Claudia was scared, downstairs, he'd let her try to take a nap, keep her out of the way.

She tried to wriggle her hands free from the rest of the rope. The rope gouged her skin. She heard Danny saying, "I don't think so."

Claudia yanked her right hand free. Forget being bait. She jumped up from the bed, huddled in the closet. Wire hangers jangled above her head, tangled in her hair. She needed a weapon; she clawed the hangers free from her head.

The hanger. Make it into a loop of wire, a garrote, grab him from behind, choke the air out of him.

She grabbed one, twisted it hard, unraveling the spiral of wire at the top. Another twist. Another. Heavy footsteps pounding on the stairs, Danny screaming to wait a minute. Fists hitting flesh, hard, the unmistakable pop of knuckle against jaw.

Not enough time. She dropped the hanger, looped her hand around the length of rope hanging down from her wrist. Maybe not long enough. Nothing, she had nothing.

The stateroom door flew open, smacked against the closet door. She saw Gar, shirtless, his back a scrimshaw of gaudy tattoos, a mass of muscle moving underneath the faded inks. "You ready for—" He stopped for a second, seeing the empty bed. But she couldn't spring out at him, the open stateroom door jamming up against the closet door.

She was trapped.

Gar glanced around, saw the sliver of her in the closet, smiled with half his mouth. "Hidin' don't help."

Claudia took a step sideways in the closet. Nothing in here, nothing to help her. Her fear tasted like smoke in her mouth.

"Change of plan, Officer. But you'll like it." Gar slid the closet door open, grabbed Claudia by the hair, yanked her out of the dark narrow space. Shoved her to the bed. His pale chest looked wide as a door, his arms like pile drivers. She wriggled away from him. "You don't fight me, you make it nice, I'll protect you from my boy. He's not gonna be happy, you gettin' what he likes. Oh, no. He might cut your eyes out when we're done. So you be a good girl and be nice and I'll—"

Claudia punched him, hard, across the jaw. He blinked, frowned, and blood welled up in the corner of his mouth. He cussed and backhanded her, the knuckles of his hand like rocks against her jaw. Little black flowers blossomed in front of her; he held down her throat, pressed his weight into her legs.

"I'm gonna work all the fight out of you, honey." He grabbed her head and started pulling her up from the bed when the shot rang and she heard a sound like a hard thump on a melon. Blood exploded from Gar's nose, his mouth, spraying Claudia. She screamed. He fell on her, and she kicked out from under him, wriggling along the headboard, tumbling to the floor off the bed.

Danny kept the gun pressed to the back of Gar's head. He stared at Claudia.

"Oh," he said. "Oh. That's done." Then he grinned at her, proud of himself, the dragon slayer. "Are you all right?"

Her vocal cords turned to ice. "You killed him."

Danny pulled the gun away from the blasted back of Gar's head. "Sure I did." Danny seemed to not quite believe his new tough-guy status, staring at Gar, as though the big man's shoulders would suddenly hitch with breath.

She stood, her jaw aching, her foot hurting from the broken toe. "The redhead will come. Or maybe he heard the shot." *He'll kill Ben.*

Danny turned the gun toward her. "You could at least thank me."

"Thank you," she said. "Don't shoot me."

He tilted his head at her and she didn't like the dead, flat look in his eyes. No shuddering shakes over having just killed a man. The fact was done, filed, out of mind.

"I won't leave Ben at his mercy," she said. She moved toward the door; he followed her with the gun.

"Stop, Claudia."

She stopped.

"What are you doing?" he asked.

"I'm going to radio for help."

She expected him to argue with her, order her to stop, but there was only the silence of the waves brushing the hulls of the boats. Then the rev of an engine. Not theirs. *Jupiter*'s.

"Oh, no," Claudia said.

"Stay," Danny said.

She heard *Jupiter*'s motor rev again, and *Miss Catherine* swayed.

"If we're still roped to them..." she started and he lowered the gun.

She ran up the stairs, through the galley, and peered through the galley door's window out onto the deck. *Jupiter* was free from them, the lines cut. Gunning away from them. She could see Redhead in the flying bridge, hunkered down low, steering.

"He's running, he's taking Ben," she said.

Claudia turned to face Danny and the foam hit the side of her face hard, cold and sharp, and pain knocked her down with an iron slap. She moaned, then liquid dribbled onto her face, smelling of stale air and medicine, and she was gone.

16

Dinner was the "Vengeance Is Ours" special: grilled hammerhead, with little plastic cups of melted butter for dipping, drippy corn on the cob, and French fries thick as a finger. Whit Mosley and David Power sat in the canopied shade of the oaks bending over Stubby's. The food was excellent but the locale was not gourmet; rather, Stubby's was a trailer, with a walkup window and a barbecue in the back that offered up pork ribs and brisket, except this morning Stubby's son snagged a hammerhead on the edge of St. Leo Bay and the unlucky shark debuted on today's menu. The tables were old cable spools, upended, each one surrounded by stumps weathered smooth from the rubbing of a thousand butts. Clouds filled the evening sky and it was still too warm and sticky for comfortable outside eating, but David wanted Stubby's. Plus fewer people meant it was less likely they would be overheard.

David bit into his shark, which made Whit think it was truly a dog-eat-dog world.

"Let's get one thing clear. I'm not gunning for Lucy because you're involved with her. You could give me some credit. I can't not consider Lucy. You understand that."

"But you do have this other suspect. Jimmy Bird."

"How'd you know?"

"His wife hates your guts. She called me. I called Hollis about it. She got an idea that Jimmy ran off to New Orleans." Let him talk to Sheriff Hollis about it, Whit decided.

"Well, why didn't you tell me?"

"You were too busy telling me about Lucy," he said. "And Mrs. Bird asked me not to talk to you."

"She's just a drunk."

"I got an anonymous tip today."

David lowered his corn, butter dripping from his mouth. "Aren't you popular?"

"I heard Patch Gilbert asked around town about quietly raising a hundred thousand dollars."

"For what?"

"That I don't know."

"I assume the tip didn't come from a loan officer at a bank?"

"No. Hence the anonymous," Whit said with a thin smile. "But don't you think it would be wise to check Patch's finances? Maybe see if he owed debts, gambling, I don't know what, but this had to be big."

"We're already on that," David said. "Wow, a hundred thou."

"According to Lucy, his other niece, Suzanne, asked for a loan in that amount. Suzanne denied it to me. Said she asked for ten thou, Patch said no, she got the money from a friend. Lucy claims she and her ex-con boyfriend have gambling problems."

"Lucy's sure well-informed."

"Patch had money," Whit said, ignoring the jab. "At least he was land-rich. I don't see why he would need to be trying to get a private loan."

"You sure you don't know who this tip came from? Was this a phone call?"

"It's just anonymous, okay?" Whit said. He owed Gooch his life; if Gooch wanted anonymity, Whit gave it to him. The lie felt slick and unpleasant on his tongue but he didn't change his mind.

"You know who it is, don't you?" David wadded up the wax paper that had held his grilled shark. "That's all right. I'm not going to bust your chops over it, Judge. I mean, you're an officer of the court. A public official. You sure don't owe anything to law and order, no, sir."

"Treat it like any other tip."

"You sure this didn't come from Lucy?"

"It wasn't Lucy."

David mopped at his mouth with a napkin, picked shark from between his front teeth. "Uh-huh."

"It wasn't Lucy."

"I mean, it's one family member pointing the finger at another, right, maybe just a little. A little?" David held up his forefinger and thumb a centimeter apart.

"I know you don't actually suspect Lucy," Whit said and made his tone sure.

"Was she with you Monday night?"

"Yes."

"What did y'all do Monday night?"

"You already questioned her."

"I'm asking you, Your Honor." Stress on the final two words. "As an officer of the court."

Whit tore a French fry in two. "We had dinner at my place. Watched a movie."

"What for dinner, what movie?"

"Gazpacho. Grilled trout. A salad. Some Australian white

wine she brought. I cooked the fish. The movie was *Shakespeare in Love*. She rented it."

"Didn't think you did. And she didn't spend the night?"

He could argue but decided not to. They had nothing to hide. "We both had busy mornings scheduled. She went home about eleven."

"And you?"

"I went to bed."

"When did you see Lucy next, Judge?"

"When she showed up at the courthouse to tell me Patch was missing."

"She's in big debt. That psychic network thing? Well, you got lots of kids calling it. Parents complain, charges get cut. Or the folks that charge up their credit cards, they default, don't pay. But that don't mean Lucy's staff, her expenses, get cut, too. She's gotten in deep financially. She tell you about getting sued by a couple of creditors in the past month?"

Whit was silent.

"I thought not," David said after a moment. He licked butter and shark from his fingers.

"That is still a real long road from murdering people the way Patch and Thuy died."

"I found your button, now, didn't I?" The smile was coldly amused. Miffed, Whit saw, over the tips, over Mrs. Bird calling him, over the idea of Whit having an advantage.

"I suppose Claudia was the same button for you," Whit said, knowing as soon as the words were fired they'd hit like bullets.

David didn't blink. "I'm over Claudia. You can tell her that the next time you see her."

"You want to make trouble for Lucy? Fine. But watch where you step. Be very careful, David, because you take a misstep, I'm going to be on you like white on rice. I think I'll have a talk with your boss about these skeletons, since you don't seem to think they matter very much."

"I didn't say that." David stood. "I'm keeping every angle open. That's what an investigator does. But I'll give you a piece of advice, Judge. I don't think you can afford Lucy Gilbert. The press won't be kind, and they love a little funky twist like her maybe killing two old folks to get the money to salvage her psychic hotline business."

"I think you love the funky little twist more than finding out the truth."

"Whatever," David said. "But you keep telling me to lay off Lucy Gilbert, I'm telling the press. I got the perfect phrases already in mind. And you're gonna be in front of a judicial review board or facing a recall election in two seconds flat."

"Don't threaten me."

"Don't worry. If she did it, I won't ask you to sign her arrest warrant."

After David dropped him off at the courthouse, Whit drove home, to the guest house behind his family's grand Victorian, to do chores on his computer and gather some clean clothes before heading back over to Patch's to stay the night with Lucy. His father, Babe, and his Russian mail-order stepmother, Irina, weren't at home and he felt a tickle of relief. He didn't feel like talking to anyone. In his small kitchen, Whit poured himself a glass of ice water, then flopped on the couch, wanting to get back to Lucy but grateful for the peaceful quiet of the moment. He propped his feet up on the table. He'd head over to Lucy's in a few, get to bed early if Lucy let him. Tomorrow was Friday, the long, annoying haul of juvenile court, his least favorite judicial chore, and then he'd . . .

His bedroom door was shut.

He never left it shut; in the little house in the summer, the window units froze a closed room into a miniature Antarctica and left the other rooms sticky-warm. You had to be careful; sometimes the door, old and a little warped, closed on its own if he brushed past it the wrong way.

Whit went to the door and listened to the rattle and hum of the overtaxed window unit. He opened the door. His bedroom was as he'd left it when he'd last slept in it, the night Patch died: books stacked next to the bedside phone, bed made in haste, dirty clothes in a tidy pile, ready for his Saturday laundry duty, closet door shut. He went to the closet, opened it. Clothes hung in neat lines, a cavalcade of ugly-bright tropical print shirts. In the corner was his computer and a small desk he used for work at home, with a few file folders and the *Texas Civil Practice* books. Nothing gone.

But the room felt subtly shifted, as though every item was just a hair out of place. He went through his files, his drawers, glanced under the bed. Nothing was missing. But the files on his desk were in two stacks instead of one, the books on his desk were leaning, and he hated that.

The room had been searched. He felt the odd tingly linger of an intruder in his space.

He went back to his front door. The lock appeared whole and unscratched. He checked his spare key—still hidden under the porch's neglected potted fern. He inspected the windows. A back window wasn't locked and he couldn't remember when—if—he had unlocked it. He locked the window, went back to the den, refilled his water glass.

He tried calling Claudia Salazar at home, wanting a shoulder to cry on about David Power. No answer. He tried Gooch's cell phone. No answer either; Gooch was still presumably en route to New Orleans.

So who was in your house?

He checked every room. Maybe he had bumped the door the last time he left and it had shut on its own. Maybe David talking to him about Lucy—about what he didn't know, her inheritance, her debts—made him paranoid. What else about her life didn't he know?

Maybe she was embarrassed. Maybe she was ashamed.

It was time to get David off Lucy, time to find evidence that would point elsewhere. David was competent but not imaginative. He might dismiss Patch wanting secret funding of a hundred thousand or the skeletons found with the bodies. They could be little fringe elements that had nothing to do with the heart of the case. And Gooch looking for this Alex in New Orleans might lead nowhere fast.

So what else did he have? The name on the bottle, the guy Suzanne mentioned as interested in buying Black Jack Point.

Whit took his drink and sat down at his computer. He logged onto the Internet, opened a search engine, and did a search for *Stoney Vaughn*.

Results were few—a couple of articles in the Corpus paper, an article in some highflier financial magazine Whit had never heard of. He'd risen fast in the investment world, the kind of quotable grandstander the press loved. Scrappy son of shrimpers killed when he was at the University of Texas—where he'd gone on a full scholarship. Economics

and history degree, MBA from Stanford. Worked for a venture capital firm in Silicon Valley for a while, took a hit
in the dot-com bust, came back to Texas, and apparently
started phoning the Social Register to get clients. The newspaper article included a picture. Average-looking, confident,
hair a shade too glossy, a hint of gut, cool, confident, the
kind of young man the numerous wealthy old ladies of the
coast liked to have handle their money.

Not much else. Another link on the *Corpus Christi
Caller-Times* site when he'd opened his office, another
when he'd built that mansion out on the Copano Flats, a
link to something called the Laffite League. He clicked on
the link.

A simple Web site opened, with an old portrait of a rakish man who wore a broad mustache and looked every inch
the gentleman robber. Underneath the portrait was the text:

> The Laffite League explores and celebrates Jean Laffite,
> the great pirate of the Gulf, one of the most unusual and
> mysterious figures in American history. Membership
> is open to all at dues of $50/year. We have chapters in
> New Orleans, Galveston, and Corpus Christi with a total
> membership over 100. We are academics, historians,
> teachers, students, businesspeople, jet pilots, nurses,
> retirees—anyone interested in the days of old. We spon-
> sor trips to Galveston, Grande Terre, and other sites to
> explore Laffite history and also offer a quarterly news-
> letter on all matters Laffite-related.

Below the statement were links to newsletter archives,
an on-line forum for Laffite discussion, and sites for historical research. And below that, a list of officers of the

League, with Stoney Vaughn as president of the Corpus
Christi chapter. He searched through the rest of the site. No
mention of Patch Gilbert.

A fan club for a dead pirate. An overdue book about
Laffite. Skeletons. And Stoney Vaughn, giver of whiskey,
buyer of land, whose name kept sidling into view.

Whit clicked back to the newsletter articles, wondering if there was much discussion about buried treasure. He
found none—this was all straight, well-footnoted history.
The articles ranged from detailed analyses of the Battle of
New Orleans during the War of 1812, where Laffite played
a key role, to speculation of Laffite's ultimate fate. Several of the articles were attributed to a writer named Jason
Salinger, and the short bio at the end of each minutely
researched piece indicated Jason was a freelance writer
working in Port Leo, Texas.

He looked up Jason Salinger in the phone book. Not
listed. He could track him down tomorrow.

He saw, through his window, his father moving in the
soft glow of the kitchen lights in the big house and headed
up there.

"You want me to change the locks?" Babe Mosley said
after Whit explained.

"Just as a precaution, Daddy."

"Why on earth would anyone be breaking in and then
not taking anything?" Babe sipped from a cup of decaf,
still a big man at sixty, his face creased and handsome.

"I don't know. But I'd feel better if you changed the
locks."

"I'll call the locksmith tomorrow." He lowered his cup.
"You staying out with Lucy again?"

"Yes."

"Come stay here."

"She wants to be at Patch's house, and I don't want her to be alone."

"I wish y'all would just stay here," Babe said. "I'd sure sleep better."

"We're fine."

Halfway up toward Black Jack Point, he thought, *Why wait? See if Stoney Vaughn's at home tonight. Ask him about the Gilberts.*

He drove past the Point, toward Copano Flats, looking for a big mansion.

17

———◦◉◦———

STONEY HAD ONLY managed to keep Alex from shooting him outright by saying, "I don't know what you're talking about with the emerald, but these guys are going to be here soon and we got to deal with them first."

"I looked at it. Closely. It's not real." Alex's voice was low and precise and getting impatient. "The Eye's looking a little bloodshot."

"I didn't know you were an emerald expert."

"Where is it?"

"You're not supposed to have a key for both locks. We agreed."

"You stole from me and you're going to chide me?" Alex, his tone disbelieving, shook his head, the gun in his hand pointing at the carpet for the moment.

"I didn't steal from you." Stoney glanced back out at the bay. "Here they come." But it wasn't *Jupiter*. It was a smaller fishing trawler, idling along the near edge of the bay.

"The Eye, please. I'm not helping you with Danny and his boys if you don't cough it up."

"Listen, I took it to protect it."

"Really. How's that?" Like he couldn't wait to hear the details.

"Danny. Look, he knows we've done the dig, he's in the area, he's seen the papers about Black Jack Point and the murders. He knows we've got the Eye. He might find out where we'd hidden it." He took refuge in outrage. "Listen. You had a key I didn't know about. We're even."

"We are so not even!" Alex's gun came up, centered on Stoney's chest.

"If anything happens to me," Stoney said, "there are tape recordings of our conversations over the past couple of months. About Patch Gilbert. About the Laffite treasure, the Devil's Eye, your little mess in New Orleans. Multiple copies, hidden in multiple places. In multiple forms. Tape. Sound file. A couple of ways you might never guess. But sure to be found if I go missing or die, Alex. I'm not Jimmy. I'm not dumb."

"You're bluffing. You wouldn't take that chance of screwing yourself over."

"I might. For insurance. I've always been over-insured."

Alex put the gun down, turned, and walked out of the office.

"Where you going?" Stoney said. He followed Alex down into the big white living room, full of old nautical maps on the walls, thick leather-bound tomes of history. Alex knelt by the stone fireplace, opened a decorative cylinder of long matches next to the equally decorative stone fireplace. The match was about nine inches long; it could burn for a while and you wouldn't singe your fingertips. He took the cylinder back to where Stoney stood at the bottom of the steps, punched him hard in the mouth. Stoney's lip split. He fell back, a little dribble of blood and snot smearing on his chin.

"Uhhhng," Stoney said.

Alex grabbed the front of his shirt, shoved him back onto the stairs.

"Insurance," Alex said, "can be terribly expensive."

Stoney spat blood. "I can't believe you hit me." But a little quaver in his voice gave him away.

Alex slapped Stoney, lightly, almost playfully. "You steal the Eye from me. You call me, tell me Danny's got your brother and wants to make a trade. For the Eye. So, what, we give them the fake Eye to save your brother? And I never know the real Eye's gone? It's sort of half clever."

"Like you'd let me give Danny the Eye. I'm not that stupid. You never would." He mopped at his nose. "You heard Danny's friends on the phone."

"I did. I'm not impressed. You could have friends I don't know about, Stoney. Playing a phone prank of sorts. All designed to fool me." He grabbed Stoney by the throat. "Where's the Eye?"

"I won't—"

Alex ran the match tip—unlit—underneath Stoney's eyebrows, along the rim of his ear. "Does it tickle?"

"Oh, God, no," Stoney said. "Please."

"I don't want to burn you." Alex struck the match along the wall; it flamed into life. "But I will. Start with this. Then I'll drag you down to your dock. Get some gasoline worked in good on you. Kick it up a notch."

"No, no," Stoney sobbed.

"Where is it?"

Stoney watched the fire. "The Eye's on the boat. My boat. That's where I hid it. Danny's got it. He don't even know it."

"And they're coming here?"

"Yes. Please, you can get it then."

Alex blew out the match.

                    *   *   *

It was now close to eight.

"I don't think the bad guys are showing up, Stoney."
Alex watched the empty dock from the kitchen's bay window. The stars had begun to glimmer in the dying summer
twilight. "I think we've been stood up."

"They said they would bring my brother...for the
money after they killed Danny..."

"You don't look good, man."

Stoney reached for the whiskey bottle, took a tiny sip.
Alex watched. Tiny sips didn't hurt until you'd taken a hundred of them.

"I think, Stone Man, you need to prepare yourself for
bad news. I think these guys killed your brother and this
girl of his. That's why they're not showing up. Can't get the
cash for a corpse."

Stoney let out a blubbery sigh.

"Now. Danny. He's out there somewhere."

Stoney looked up at him, his face as blank as a new
blackboard.

"Let's say Danny's still alive. But he's lost his bargain-
ing chips, 'cause maybe these idiots killed your brother and
his girl. So he's got to go somewhere. He's gonna try to get
at you again—he'd rather have the treasure than you in jail,
if it's one or the other. He can hardly accuse you of murder
if he's done the same now. So where would Danny go?"

"I don't know."

"He's got friends around here. You know him, Stoney."

"No...no one I can think of."

"Other folks in the Laffite League?"

"Some in Corpus, maybe. He's not well-liked; people
think he's nuts."

"Ah. You start making some phone calls."

The doorbell rang. Stoney froze by the phone.

"Not a word"—Alex pulled his gun from the back of his pants, pressed the barrel beneath Stoney's eye—"or I will kill you and whoever's on the porch. You understand?"

"Not—not a word," Stoney said in a broken voice.

Alex hurried to the front door, quietly. He peered through the peephole.

Some guy, blondish, tall, standing on the porch, looking around. His head a little rounder from the distortion of the glass. Wearing a bright orange tropical shirt.

Alex moved back from the peephole. The doorbell rang again, a knock followed.

Alex waited. He peeked through a living room window, barely edging back the closed curtain, and saw the guy in the driveway, talking on his cell phone. Then clicking off the phone.

A knock again on the door, doorbell ringing.

"Mr. Vaughn? Whit Mosley. I'm the JP here. I can tell you're home. Would you please open up?"

Alex waited. A few more knocks. After about five minutes Whit Mosley climbed into a Ford Explorer and roared off. Stoney walked back into the foyer.

Alex put the gun on him. "A JP's a judge, right? Why's he here?"

"Probably to tell me my brother's body has been found," Stoney said. His voice sounded a lot more even.

"They'd call. And it wouldn't be a judge."

"I don't know and I don't care," Stoney said. "Put that gun down. I can't talk to you with it in my face."

"You're not in a position to make demands. You've lied to me. We agreed we'd rebury the treasure on the land you bought out at the Point. Discover it together as Laffite's treasure, make a mint, get famous," Alex said.

"You don't care about that, Alex," Stoney said. "Not about the fame. You just want the treasure. But we can both get what we want. We need to work together. Between the murders and now Danny everything's gone south. I'm making a drink and we can talk."

He turned and went back into the kitchen. Alex lowered the gun and followed him.

"Where's the courage coming from?" Alex asked. Stoney poured a thin film of bourbon into a glass, topped it off with ice water.

"From knowing I'm going to make a great deal with you."

"So. Deal." Alex never enjoyed killing but he thought he would really like killing Stoney, even if it was one bullet and quick, like snapping your fingers.

"First we have to find Danny. And find my brother."

"This whole kidnapping shtick's not a fake?"

"I swear, Alex, it isn't. You can't take the risk that it's not." He gulped at his drink. "Danny could screw us both over, end it for us easy. He's nuts. He's not going to behave like a normal human being."

Alex took a deep breath. "So we sit and wait?"

"I don't start calling around to Laffite Leaguers, showing an interest in him. They'd remember that later. So get patient. He's going to call. No way he's not going to see this through. We wait here, together. You can kill him when he shows up."

"Me? Why not you? It's your brother he took."

"Because you're good at offense. I'm better at defense." Stoney put down his drink. "And here's how we both stay happy. I'm willing to give you three-quarters of the gold and silver. You can melt it down or sell the coins on the market. I keep the rest and the Eye. That I rebury on the land, dig back up, have my glory."

"As the only discoverer of actual buried pirate treasure in history."

"We're both happy and we don't commit mutually assured destruction," Stoney said.

Alex tented his cheek with his tongue. "What about your brother and this cop girlfriend?"

"They'll have killed her. My brother, he can be reasoned with."

"Your brother might talk," Alex said.

"My brother will never have to work again if he doesn't want to," Stoney said. "You don't worry about him. Now. You can play tough, try to rough me up some more, and completely screw yourself over. Or you can crash here with me and see if Danny shows up tonight, and then we're home free. What's it gonna be?"

Alex crossed his arms. "I don't sleep on couches."

18

GOOCH THOUGHT THE Bayou Mee was appropriately named, as the two girls near its parking lot might say, *Buy. You. Me.* The Tulane Avenue open-court motel was grimy, the dive more residence than family fun stopover. It was a few blocks from the New Orleans Criminal Courts Building and nearby were several bail bond businesses, and Gooch wondered if maybe the Bayou Mee catered to those recently released from jail. He'd seen two women go from the darkened parking lot to rooms with new friends and return in a half hour, but they weren't shimmying hot-panted rears on the street corner; rather, the two looked more like regular girls, T-shirts and denim shorts, just hanging out in the motel lot, gossiping, and maybe if you knew the password, you'd get a date. Gooch spotted one police cruiser go by, not even tap on its brakes. Late Thursday night, the girls not too busy yet.

He'd paid for his room and said, "I'm looking for a friend of mine."

"What's her name?"

"Alex."

"Don't know an Alex."

"You know a man named Alex?" Gooch laid a fifty on the desk. "You know any Alex at all?"

"What's he look like?" The clerk was a bony kid, dirty-blond hair, sullen, his nose pierced with a thin hoop of gold. He scooped the bill into his jeans pocket.

"Alex was here about a month ago."

"But what's he look like? Names don't matter much here."

"He might have had some phone calls back to Texas on his bill. Does that ring a bell?"

"You a cop?"

"Do cops give money for answering questions?"

"Sure, sometimes."

"I'm not a cop. Or a PI."

"Alex don't ring a bell. Most of the guys here have classier names than Alex, like Bubba or Hoss. Or John." He laughed.

"Thanks," Gooch said. "Think about it."

He went back to his room, started watching the girls. A truck pulled in, the taller girl leaned down, chatted, laughed. The shorter girl walked over to a plastic crate two doors down from Gooch, sat, lit a cigarette.

Gooch opened the door, walked past her. She glanced at him, made a little frown. He fed coins into a decrepit Coke machine.

"It's broke," she called to him. His coins rattled in the machine.

"Works good enough to take money," he said. "My friend told me this was a real nice place to stay, and here you can't even get a sody pop." He glanced at her, grinned.

She grinned back. "Who's your friend?" she asked.

"You know Alex?"

"I don't believe I've had the pleasure." She flicked ash off her cigarette.

"How about a guy named Jimmy Bird?"

"Nope. You sure have a lot of friends," she said.

"Don't you?"

"I've always been popular because I see the best in people."

He stood near her. She glanced at his face, which wasn't ever going to make a girl smile. She looked at his worn jeans, his gray T-shirt, scuffed boots, trying to make if he was a cop.

"The Alex I'm looking for might be in Texas now."

"Better than here." She was looking down at the ashes at her feet, stubbing at them with her sandal.

"Any Alexes ever work here?"

"No," she said.

"Alex might have stayed here a month ago, for at least two days, maybe more."

"I said I don't know an Al—" But her voice broke off and she looked back up at him with fear and a bit of confusion, as though she'd just understood a joke. She stood.

"What's your name?" he asked.

"I got to go."

"Alex isn't a friend." He'd seen fear in her face now. "But I want to find him. Or her."

"Baby, I love chatting, but any more of my time, you pay."

"How much for an hour of your time?"

"Seventy-five."

"I just want to talk to you," Gooch said.

"Costs the same."

He nodded.

"We should go to my room. I got some Comfort there. I could use a drink."

Her room was on the opposite side of the court, the window missing, plywood up in its place. She said her name was Helen and she made them both drinks, Sprite and Southern Comfort, in little plastic cups. She didn't have ice cubes and the Sprite was a little warm.

"You're quite the hostess," Gooch said. He gave her the seventy-five bucks, all of it. She counted it and sat down.

"I said something that scared you," he said.

"Alex I don't know. But I know an Albert Exley. That was the name he used here. I called him Al 'cause I don't like Albert as a name. That's close to Alex, isn't it? He's here about a month ago."

"What's he look like?"

"Wiry. Way stronger than he looks. Wears glasses. Brown hair, about six one. I saw him come in here, I figured, all I need, another social worker trying to get me in a hair net at a chicken shack. Or a Jesus freak." Helen sipped from her cup. Gooch thought she couldn't be more than twenty-five, already faded, her skin pale and her hair a dark lank. "Yeah. He's a social worker like Hitler was."

"What did he do?"

"You a cop?"

"No. I'm a concerned citizen."

"Someone needs to concern Albert Exley off the street." She pointed at the plywood. "He put me through that window." She raised her arm and he could see a web of healing scar threaded along her skin. "Tore up my arms, my back, bad. And I'm practically his girlfriend."

"Explain."

"He's here for four or five days. I can't figure him out,

why a guy looks like a professor is here. He hires me a couple of times a day, like he's passing the time." She shrugged. "I kept feeling he wasn't just hanging out here, he was in New Orleans on important business of some sort. But I know better than to ask. Just keep my mouth shut. Well, open, but you know what I mean." She laughed.

Gooch wanted to give her a Greyhound ticket, say, *Just go somewhere else and start over and don't do this anymore*. She'd look at him like he was one of the Jesus freaks.

"We're getting along fine. One day he's gone most of the day, most of the night. Comes back in a bad mood. I think, he's been nice, I'll see if I can relax him. This was his room then, not mine, so I treat him how he likes and he gets in the shower. He says I can watch TV if I want, 'cause there's not a TV in my room, and he knows I'm not gonna bother his wallet. His cell phone rings when he shuts off the shower, and so I click it on, thinking I'll just hand it to Al, be cute, and a guy calling starts yelling, all panicked. I'm telling the guy to calm down and suddenly Albert yanks the phone out of my hand, listens, then throws me through the window. I'm lying there, naked, bleeding like nobody's business. He grabs his stuff, jumps in his car, he's gone." She shook her head. "Cops looked for him, but I guess not too hard. I don't pay taxes so I don't pay their salaries. Jerry, the owner, he makes me move in this room, says it was my fault the window got busted. Cheap bastard won't put in a new window yet, and it's too hot." Helen looked ready to cry.

"I'll speak with Jerry. You'll have a new window," Gooch said.

She stared up at him.

"The caller. What was he upset about?"

She shrugged. "I wasn't sure. I had trouble remembering real clear after I went through the window. I lost too much blood. But when I think about it, I think he was saying something like, 'You idiot, you got the wrong guy.'" She finished her drink. "You don't want to mess with Albert. He's nuts. He'd kill a person over answering the phone."

"When I find him," Gooch said, "I'll put him through a window for you."

"That's sweet. But you better grab him from behind," Helen said, and despite the sticky heat she gave a shiver. "Don't let that man see you coming. You don't get no second chance with him."

Whit left Copano Flats, driving through the soft, scrubby land, turning back onto the main highway as night took real hold, heading south again toward Black Jack Point. Stoney Vaughn was either shy or rude; Whit was sure someone was at home, the lights on in the house, the Porsche and the beige van in the driveway, just the sense he'd gotten of an eye behind the door. Maybe there'd been a girlfriend over. He'd try again in the morning.

He'd tried Gooch again while waiting to see if someone came to the door—no answer. *All problems for tomorrow,* he decided, too tired and jumpy to think. *Go to Lucy, have an honest talk about David's claims, go to sleep.*

When he walked into Patch's house, Lucy was sitting in a fat armchair, her knees pulled up to her chin. Suzanne Gilbert sat across from her, an empty wineglass at her elbow. Roy Krantz lounged on the couch.

"Hi," Suzanne said.

"Hi, Judge," Roy said. No warmth, not surprising.

"You took a while," Lucy said.

"I'm sorry. I had court business...what's wrong?"

"What isn't?" Lucy mopped at her face with her sleeve. "Suzanne and I are discussing the land. Selling it. I think it's a bit too early for that—Patch isn't even buried yet."

Oh, wow, he thought. *Lucy hasn't told them Patch cut out Suzanne.*

"Offers're gonna come in," Roy said. "We already got a call from a Houston developer."

"Who are these vultures?" Lucy said. "I hope they call me. I got a whistle right by the phone. They'll be deaf when they hang up."

"They're not vultures," Suzanne said. "They're businesspeople."

"Me, too, but I don't trade before funerals," Lucy said. "It's tacky."

"Tacky like exaggerating private loan amounts," Suzanne said.

Lucy ran a palm along the chair arm and didn't look at Suzanne.

"I love you, Lucy, and this pains me," Suzanne said.

"I love you, too," Lucy said. "But your vibe is all bent."

"We better go," Roy said. "Lucy, nobody meant to upset you." He stood. "C'mon, Suzanne."

Whit walked them out to their car.

"I forgive her," Suzanne said. "The innuendo. She wasn't thinking straight."

"Sure," Whit said.

"There's not going to be any more silly accusations, right?" Roy said. "We've got it straight now."

"That's between you and Lucy," Whit said to Suzanne, ignoring Roy.

They left.

He went back inside, sat on the arm of Lucy's chair, slid his arm behind her thin shoulders. She leaned into him, turned her face up for a kiss. One. Then another.

"The glue is gone," she said. "With Patch gone Suzy Q and I are not quite so sweet to each other."

"Did you argue with them?"

"No," she said. "But Suzanne feels betrayed. She doesn't understand why I mentioned her money troubles. But she didn't yell at me. I wish she would've thrown a vase at me."

"This will get better with time, Lucy." He sat on the ottoman at her feet, took both her hands in his. "Is there anything you want to tell me?"

"I'm not up for another firing squad tonight," Lucy said.

"I rode in to Corpus with David. For the autopsy reports."

"Oh." Her voice went small.

"He and I had a talk about you. Do you want to tell me anything?" Whit asked again, his voice soft.

"No. I'm too embarrassed."

"About your debt? Or the lawsuits? Lucy, I'm not mad but I sure wish you had told me."

She didn't move. "Do you bring your hearings home, Whit?"

"Not unless they're funny."

"Well, I keep my business separate from our time together, too. I knew I shouldn't have mentioned Suzanne's gambling. This is just bad karma piling up on me."

"How bad is your debt, Lucy?"

"I'm okay. Business picked up last month."

"How bad?"

"Fifty, sixty thousand. I can get a bridge loan. Phone entertainment is a growth industry."

"Have you really been sued?"

"David Power needs a doughnut in that mouth," she said. "Yes. A woman whose old mother called all the time. She was nutty, but she had a nice aura and so the girls helped her. No one was trying to take advantage of her, but I had to settle out of court. It's fine." She stared at him. "I'm sorry I didn't tell you but, Whit, you're a politician."

"Barely."

"You're still an elected official. I didn't want you to be embarrassed, dump me."

"Thanks for the vote of confidence," he said. He kept her hands in his. "David says you inherit everything."

"That's what he says." She shook her head.

"You don't know?"

"There's a message in there to call Patch's lawyer... but there's a ton of calls. I haven't called them back yet."

"Apparently Suzanne gets nothing."

"No. That can't be right."

"Patch probably didn't want his money gambled away. And he loved you, Lucy."

She made a noise in her throat, covered her face with her hands. "That makes me look worse, though, to the police."

"David's blowing smoke right now. You ever hear of a guy named Stoney Vaughn?"

She blinked. "The rich guy with the big house up the bay. I don't know him, just heard of him."

"Patch ever mention him?"

She blinked again. "I don't think so. Whit?"

"What?"

"You believe me, don't you? I didn't know about the will. Patch never said."

"I believe you, Lucy."

She leaned into his arm and they stayed that way, silent, for several minutes, the ticking of the den clock and the soft hum of Lucy's breathing the only sounds. "Could you make love to me?" she said in a quiet whisper. "I'm a wreck and you're all that makes me feel good right now. If you don't mind making love to wrecks."

He kissed her, slow, and she kissed him back, tentative at first, then harder, surer. They went up to the guest bedroom. Lucy stripped him first, opening his shirt, sliding off his pants, kissing his mouth, neck, shoulders, chest, pausing just long enough for him to ease her out of her T-shirt and shorts, her bra and little red panties. They slid onto the cool of the sheets and when he entered her she clung to him, fingers and mouth and nails and toes, with a fierceness that made his skin sing.

They rested in each other's arms for a while. Then she kissed him deeply, her fingertips exploring him, seeing if he might stir again.

"Whit?"

"Yeah?" he said in a thick voice, lying against the sheets.

"How much is the estate? Do you know? If showing an interest in the money doesn't make David Power indict me automatically."

"I don't know, Lucy."

"If it's enough, I think I'll shut down the Coastal Psychics Network," she said. "It's been nothing but a headache."

"So what will you do?"

"This all day." She straddled him and guided him into her. The second time was even better. They were less tense and they rode the wave together.

"Is that a job offer?" he said when he had his breath

back, laughing, liking the feel of her warm breath against his chest.

"I'm so the boss of you already," she said. "Love you."

"Love you."

"I'm safe with you, aren't I?"

"Always, babe."

Finally she slept. Whit stared at the ceiling, tired, spent, ashamed for the millisecond of doubt he'd allowed himself to feel. He drifted off into heavy sleep and it seemed two seconds later the phone rang.

Whit grabbed it, trying not to shift and wake Lucy. The digital clock on the bedside gleamed: 1:47.

"Hello?" Whit whispered.

"Judge Mosley?" David.

"Yeah?"

"We found Jimmy Bird. Dead."

PART TWO

HERE THERE BE DRAGONS

There are few things as powerful as treasure, once it fastens itself on the mind.

—JOSEPH CONRAD

19

THE RAW SMELL arose near a thick growth of oaks. Whit stood upwind of the grove. It was two-thirty Friday morning. A couple of summer-house kids, looking for a less crowded makeout spot, had found the battered winch truck nestled at the edge of the live oaks, just beyond the western city limits of Port Leo, away from the busyness of the beaches and the harbor. Jimmy Bird's body lay curled on the seat, the bullet hole in his temple surrounded by a direct-contact, mottled bruise from the gun. The gun—a .45-caliber—lay on the truck floor, below Jimmy's dangling hand. The DPS crime-scene crew pulled the body from the truck after their initial photographing and scene work. Whit filled out an authorization of autopsy form.

David finally came up to Whit to countersign the authorization.

"I suppose this wraps things up, Judge." David scribbled his name across the sheet below Whit's signature.

"Yeah," Whit said.

"Get the doubt out of your voice. There's a note in Jimmy's shirt pocket. Reads: 'I'm sorry for what I did Monday.' Broken shovel in the back of the pickup. And these were in his pants pocket." David pulled a plastic baggie from a paper bag, laid it flat on his palm, turned his flashlight onto his hand. A half dozen coins, roughly cut, clearly old, a shield capping one, a man's head crowned with laurels decorating another, one silver, the rest gold.

"These look old," Whit said. "I was right."

"Let's not jump to conclusions, Your Honor. Maybe Patch had a coin collection—we don't know. Jimmy might have stolen these from the house."

"Lucy never mentioned Patch collecting coins. Neither did he."

"Found cash and Patch's credit cards in the glove compartment. He's got to be the guy who did the break-in. This doesn't have to be complicated."

Whit leaned in, examined the coins through the plastic. "There's a date: 1818—see? This one's 1820. Wow."

"Yeah. And I know where you're going, back to this buried-treasure silliness."

Whit lowered his voice to a whisper. "David. Look. Don't think of this as buried treasure. See it from another angle. It's archaeology. If there were professors out on Black Jack Point doing a dig for artifacts, and they got killed and dumped there, you'd have to consider people stealing those artifacts as a possible motive. Right?"

David nodded.

"Well, maybe this was just a dig we didn't know about. That no one knew about."

David didn't nod, just shook his head.

"So, David, maybe Jimmy had accomplices. And if these coins are part of a treasure, where's the rest of it?"

David spat into the grass.

"Why are you resistant to this?"

"I'm not about to go in front of the press, or let Sheriff

Hollis go in front of the press, and say those people got murdered over buried treasure," David said. "If that wasn't the case, we'd be laughed out of town. No way are we going public with this. Let's just be real quiet about it right now, see what else we learn."

It was as much as Whit could hope for. "But we'll find out how much these coins are worth, right?"

"Yes, obviously."

"I suspect they may be worth quite a bit," Whit said. "Jimmy couldn't have been depressed over being broke. Maybe Dr. Parker's colleague, the one who identified the other relics—her name was Dominguez, right? She might know about coins."

"You let me worry about that. I want to confirm if Bird's tire tracks match the tracks we found on the Gilbert property, and I want to see if there's any extra fingerprints on that truck or gun. Let's go wake the widow, Judge." He shook his head. "Much as I don't like Linda Bird, I don't want to tell her that her husband's dead."

When he got back to Patch's, Lucy was awake, curled on the couch in a robe, watching the bargains unfold on the Home Shopping Network. He told her what had happened.

"But I don't think Jimmy Bird killed them," he said at the end.

She sat up. "You're unbelievable, Whit. David Power's been breathing down my neck. He finds the killer, and now you're going to debate him? What is it between you two?"

He told her about the coins in Jimmy's pocket. "They look old, very rare. Gold and silver. Why would he have those?"

Lucy folded her hands in her lap and said after a moment, "Patch had some old coins."

"You never mentioned that."

"Well, we don't usually discuss my uncle's heirlooms."

"I didn't know he was a coin collector."

"He wasn't. He got them from his dad, I think. I don't really remember. He said once they were valuable. He didn't keep them out in the change plate, Whit. He had them in a drawer in his study."

"How would Jimmy know where they were?"

"I have no idea. Maybe he made Patch tell him where they were. Maybe he knew from when he worked here before. I don't know." Her voice rose, got an edge.

"Okay, Lucy, okay. Did he have them insured?"

She stared. "I don't believe this, Whitman. You don't believe me."

"I do."

"I don't know if he had them insured. That Jimmy. I hate him. Uncle Patch never should have hired him in the first place." She got up, went into the kitchen. Whit followed her, watched her pour a glass of water, pick at a cookie from the many comfort plates on the kitchen table. "He killed them, then I'm glad he's dead."

"There's nothing more to be done tonight. Let's go back to bed."

"Fine. Okay." She gulped down her water.

In bed, he spooned next to her, his arm over her, listening to her breathe. He could hear she wasn't falling asleep.

"Whit?"

"Yeah?"

"I'm sorry I snapped at you. This has all been upsetting."

"I'm sorry, too."

"I thought finding out who did this to them would make me feel better."

"Probably not right away, hon."

"I just need you to not be trying to one-up David Power."

"It's not about a competition. I'm trying to help you."

"Do you think David sucks as an investigator?"

"No. I really don't. But I think he abuses his power. I think he's hurt about his life, he's mad at the world, and he's a spoiler. He knows how to push my buttons."

"Only works if you allow them to be pushed." She rose up on one elbow. "You've got a confession from a dead guy with a motive. Please stop pushing. Please? I can't take it anymore. I want this over and done."

"Okay."

"I can tell when you're not sincere, and it has nothing to do with vibes. I'm serious, Whit. I want you to stop."

"Okay."

She settled back into his arms, he didn't give an answer, and finally he heard her sleep. Only then did he close his eyes and let himself drift away, and in his sleep his breathing matched hers.

Lucy decided to put in a day at work and Whit, not due at court for two hours, followed her into Port Leo. Early Friday morning was not phone-jamming rush hour at Coastal Psychics Network. The little office was squeezed in between a grimy doughnut shop and a grimier liquor store in an old strip shopping center that had never seen better days. Two bored college students sat on duty at the phones, a woman reading a physics textbook, chewing on the end of her highlighter, and another woman watching *Today*.

"Hi, y'all. Slow night?" Lucy asked as they walked in.

"Yeah." The first woman looked up from her textbook. "People just don't have problems like they used to." She slipped a tarot card into her textbook, shut the book.

"It'll pick up," the other psychic said. "We're moving into the Bored Housewives hours." There was an embarrassed silence. "We're sorry about your uncle, Lucy."

"Thanks, Amanda."

"You don't want to talk," Amanda said. "It's okay. I sensed that in your aura. Let me know if you want a reading later." She glanced at Whit. "Oh, dear, isn't someone's aura a little thin today."

The two phone psychics looked at him, looked at each other, then back at Whit. "You're the disbelieving boyfriend," Amanda said.

"In more ways than one," Lucy said, but not sounding mad anymore.

"Man, ditch your negativity," the first woman said. "It's an anchor on your soul."

"I think I like being weighed down," Whit said.

"It's not insurmountable negativity," Amanda said. "You have a beautiful spirit. You just need a cleansing influence. Some healing crystal treatments should clear you up."

People pay a buck twenty-nine a minute to hear this? he thought. But he smiled and gave the peace sign. The two psychics frowned.

"C'mon back to my office, Whit," Lucy said. She hustled to the back, to a small office. She had a foil mobile hanging from the ceiling, an assortment of thick multicolored crystals and sculptures on a shelf above the desk, books on ESP, the tarot, and guerrilla marketing on a table. She shut the door. "Baby, after everything else, I don't need you upsetting the employees."

"They started it."

"They did not. They read you like a book. These are very sensitive, sweet girls and there you stand, thinking how stupid all this is. They can tell, you know."

"You didn't read my mind."

"I know you think this is hokum, but it isn't to me, to Amanda and Lachelle, to our customers. Okay?" She was being loud and for a minute he wondered if it was for the women's benefit.

"Okay." He took her in his arms. "I love you. Does my aura show that?"

"Yes, actually it does." She kissed his cheek. "I love you, too. Tons. Beyond tons." She hugged him hard. "This'll all be over soon, won't it?"

"Yes."

"Can we go away then? For a week, just us? Maybe Mexico. Hawaii. Disney World. I don't care."

"Sure, Lucy. You pick."

"No," she said. "You pick, and then I'll read it in the cards. I'll prove this works."

"Deal," he said. He left, letting her think he was headed to court.

20

———◆———

JASON SALINGER, at first glance, reminded Whit of a lawn gnome. He was short, bearded, with apple cheeks and fat pink lips surrounded by a thick beard. He wore a T-shirt that read FOOTNOTE FETISH.

Jason said, "Don't knock over any of my books."

Easier said than done. Whit followed Jason into a dingy living room converted into a library. Books tottered against a computer desk. More books covered the sofa and lay scattered across the floor.

"You're a big reader, then?" Whit stepped over a smaller stack of books and took a seat on the corner of Jason's sofa.

Jason looked at Whit as though he were mentally damaged. "Why, yes, I am."

Any books on social skills? Whit nearly asked but instead he smiled.

"Excuse him. He's a bear in the morning," Jason's wife said. Cute and plump, dressed in faded jeans and a blue T-shirt, she was as sweet as he was dour. "Aren't you, sugar pop?"

Jason made a strangled noise of agreement.

"Would you like some coffee, Judge Mosley?"

"No, ma'am, thank you. I've already filled the tank for the day," Whit said.

"I'll have a cup, please," Jason said.

"You know what the doctor said about you and caffeine." She patted Jason's shoulder, gave Whit a maternal wink, although he guessed she was six or seven years younger than he was. "I'll let you boys talk."

Then Whit noticed the headless pirate in the corner. Not headless. But an old tailor's mannequin, just the body's form, with a fancy blue coat, a red sash under the jacket, grayish pants. A sword and a revolver—they looked genuine—hung off the mannequin.

Jason swiveled a chair away from his computer desk and sat facing Whit. The Salingers' house was in an older, slightly untidy section of Port Leo. The lawn looked untended, the furniture in the house fresh from the consignment store. But the books in Jason's work area were fat, expensive hardbacks, lots of them, and his computer system was a top-of-the-line model.

"What can I help you with, Judge?"

"I understand you've done a lot of research on Jean Laffite."

"I do freelance magazine writing, substitute teaching, some book editing for a couple of very small presses."

"But Laffite's your own particular interest."

"Sure. Gonna go to grad school in another year or so, write the definitive book on Laffite one day. Probably get a doctorate with a focus on Gulf history. Be able to teach anywhere from Texas to Florida that way. I don't do cold winters well."

"I'm interested in the Laffite League."

"This has something to do with Patch Gilbert, right?"

"Why do you ask?"

"Well, he came to the last chapter meeting in Corpus in

May. I figured he was interested in joining. Sorry to hear about him getting killed."

"You knew Patch?"

"No. I just met him that one time at the meeting. He was a friendly guy, introduced himself to everyone. You don't forget a name like Patch."

"Let's talk about the League first. What exactly is it?"

"I can slice the Laffite League into three groups for you. The vast majority are people with a strong interest in history, perfectly nice and respectable. Then there are those who are interested in the legends of buried treasure, although there's never been anything other than old rumor to say Laffite buried his gold instead of spending it. But those folks have seen the movies, like *The Buccaneer,* and they think Laffite is Yul Brynner as a romance-novel swashbuckler." He swiveled on his chair. "Then there are the very small but fascinating subset of wackos. A few have claimed to be Laffite descendants, forged journals and documents to sell to the gullible or to try to live off the name."

"Dangerous wacko or amusing wacko?"

"Amusing. There's a guy who calls himself Danny Laffite—it's not his real name. Nutcase in Louisiana, says he's Laffite's great-great-great-great-grand whatever. But harmless. He tricked some guy in Houston into paying ten thousand for letters supposedly written by Laffite to Andrew Jackson. Fakes, obviously. He ended up giving the money back and avoided prosecution."

"He's in the Laffite League?"

"Was. They revoked his membership. Forgers don't make for trustworthy historians."

"What about all these legends of buried treasure?" Whit asked.

Jason shrugged. "There's no evidence Laffite buried an ounce of gold along the coast, but the rumors persist. Treasure means glamour. Adventure. Instant wealth attained in an interesting way, as opposed to the boredom of work."

"Romantic money."

"Sure. We all read or saw *Treasure Island* as kids. We all want to be Jim Hawkins, outwitting Long John Silver and finding the gold," Jason said. "Long John Silver. The only fictional murderer I can think of with a fast-food chain named after him."

"The truth is less romantic than the fiction," Whit said.

Jason jerked his head toward the mannequin. "Every year I dress up in that costume, pretend to be Laffite, go to the schools, and tell them the stories. The kids want to hear about Laffite being a movie-style pirate: storming ships, cutlass in hand, saving fair damsels on blood-soaked decks. That's all pretend. Laffite dodged taxes, sent out other captains to capture ships, dealt more in slaves and cotton than in gold. Was careful not to attack American shipping because that meant trouble. So he preyed on everyone else. More administrator than swashbuckler. And cold-blooded. A few months before he left Galveston a hurricane devastated the island. Not enough food for the thousand people living there. Laffite's solution was simple: round up every black on Galveston, slave and free, and sell them in the underground Louisiana slave market. Even the free black women who were married to Laffite's men. All hauled onto ships, the wives screaming for their husbands to save them. Laffite shot anyone who resisted. Fewer people to feed, fresh money in the coffers to rebuild after the storm. Simple and brutal."

"But you admire him."

"I admire his decisiveness," Jason Salinger said. "We're a much less decisive world now. We analyze. We agonize. We second-guess. Laffite never had that luxury. Maybe one day I'll write a book for business managers: *Business by Laffite*. You know, you find different avenues to make your money these days as an academic. Got to go mainstream."

"So where did Laffite keep all his money? There were no banks in Galveston then, and presumably a legitimate bank wouldn't touch him."

"He probably laundered money and gold back into the banks in New Orleans. He had the best lawyers in New Orleans working for him. And he and his brother, Pierre, filed bankruptcy, saying they had very little. But of course mobsters today have hidden under that same cloak."

"But any accounts would have always been in danger from the U.S. government? If they suspected an account was Laffite's, they'd've seized it, right?"

Jason frowned but nodded.

A large map of the Texas coast was pinned above the computer. Whit stood and studied it. "Indulge me. Let's just say, over the years, Laffite amasses a tidy fortune in gold. At least enough to get him started over if he abandons Galveston or his New Orleans accounts get seized. Or maybe he makes a few big captures right before he's forced out of Galveston. He can't go into port in New Orleans—he'll be arrested as a pirate if he steps on U.S. soil, right?"

"Yes," Jason said. "He'd have been arrested if he set foot in America. His forces had already annoyed the navy by attacking an American merchant ship, although he'd executed the captain responsible. What finally empowered the American government to kick him out of Galveston was the capture of one of his ships, *Le Brave,* during an attack on a Spanish ship. *Le Brave*'s captain had papers that outlined the division of booty, written in Laffite's hand, with his signature. It was the smoking gun the navy needed."

"So Laffite's on the run. He's got no place to go. If he's transporting gold he stands to lose it if he's stopped or attacked, right?"

"He was given a document guaranteeing safe passage by the U.S. Navy to leave the Gulf. They wouldn't have bothered him."

"But that wouldn't protect him from the Spanish, right, or any other country whose ships he attacked?"

Jason frowned. "No, it wouldn't. But pirates really didn't bury treasure very often. That's way more *Treasure Island* than common practice. I mean, it's accepted that Captain Kidd buried a treasure up in New England. But it's never been found."

"But maybe Laffite's got a better chance for long-term survival burying this treasure—just for a few weeks or months—than hauling it around a gulf sailed by navies who are pissed at him and risk losing everything. He's a man without a country. Put yourself in his shoes. Where would you bury it?"

Jason stared at him, as though wanting to ask a question, but didn't. He ran a finger along the curve of the coast on his wall map. "Not Galveston or Bolivar. Far too risky to be caught by an American patrol making sure he didn't return to the area to set up shop again. Maybe further south or north." His finger moved south along the map. "Laffite had camps up and down the coast. For sure in Matagorda Bay and on St. Joseph Island."

"Did he have a camp on St. Leo Bay?"

Jason glanced at him, then back at the map. "Legend says that he did, but no trace has ever been found."

"Maybe he wanted to erase the trace of himself here," Whit said. "If I had buried gold, I wouldn't have my name right over it in big letters."

"His camps weren't fancy. Just shelters if he or his men needed to get ashore, say in a storm, or to hide from other ships. Just four walls and a spare cannon, maybe."

"And one assumes if he buried the treasure he would mark it or come back for it quickly, if he could."

"Sure."

"So what happened to Laffite after he left Galveston?"

"No one knows. There were a variety of reports. He might have died, might have gone to Cuba or to Mexico. Recently it's been theorized he died in South America, as a freedom fighter." He smiled. "People are always trying to redeem pirates. We like them too much to remember they're murdering thieves."

"So—possibly—he could have been kept from retrieving a treasure. Killed. Or imprisoned."

"Possibly. Sure. We don't know with complete certainty what happened to him."

"Do the legends get specific about where this St. Leo Bay camp might be?" Whit asked.

"Some say Copano Flats, some say Black Jack Point. Obviously old Black Jack believed Laffite had been there."

"You know about him?"

"Just that he was a crazy old hermit, lived out on the Point from the Civil War until about 1890. I don't know if he was black or his name was Jack. I think the Point must've gotten its name from the blackjack oaks that grow there. And maybe the name stuck to him, too. He claimed he'd sailed with Laffite as a boy and Laffite was coming back to the Point, gonna kill everyone in Port Leo because they'd taken his gold. Loony. He sure thought there was a treasure—he dug up enough of the Point. I guess the Gilbert family—they've had that land forever—tolerated him. Sad, though. A whole life dedicated to greed."

"Wouldn't you say that was Laffite's life as well?"

"Yeah, you're right. Except for saving New Orleans, which was pretty cool." Jason raised an eyebrow again. "You going to tell me about why you're asking all these semiloaded questions?"

"I'm trying to get a feel for Patch's life in his final weeks. Everything we discuss, Jason, remains confidential. I'm conducting an official death inquest."

"I think you're believing these legends."

Whit shook his head. "We have no indication that Patch had found any antiquities or relics of any sort." That was true—Patch hadn't. Maybe others had. "I would hate for a bunch of rumors to get started. Have people stampeding around on that land like a bunch of Black Jacks when the Gilbert and Tran families are grieving."

"Of course not," Jason said. "I don't get off on rumors. I'll keep my mouth shut. But if there's a story . . ."

"There's not. I asked about treasure pretty much out of curiosity. It's what people first think of with Laffite and I knew Patch had this new interest in him. Nothing more." Jason didn't look convinced so Whit shifted gears again. "You know Stoney Vaughn?"

"Sure. He's the president of the Corpus chapter of the Laffite League."

"Friend of yours?"

"No. Cat litter has more brains than Stoney. He's all

into the treasure hunter mystique. He's financed treasure dives in the Florida Keys, where a lot of the Spanish galleons wrecked over the years. Tried to finance a partnership to dive on galleon wrecks down off Padre, but the state blocked him. The Texas Historical Commission, they hate treasure hunters. Any treasure in state waters or buried on public land is theirs by law, and they make sure you don't dive without their approval."

"He finances treasure hunts?" Whit kept his voice flat.

"Yeah, well, in Florida. Lot more wrecks there, in the shallows along the Keys. I think he might have been in the group that financed Barry Clifford diving on *Whydah,* up off Cape Cod. That's the only sunken pirate ship ever recovered. They got a load of gold, silver, and jewels off it. At least Stoney likes to talk big about it. He paid for a trip for about a dozen of the Leaguers last year to go to Yucatán, see the town where Laffite's brother died."

"Were Stoney and Patch buddies?"

"Don't think they knew each other, but they probably met at the meeting," Jason said. "Okay, now you got me hooked. You ask about Laffite's treasure and then you ask about a guy who does treasure hunts."

"If there's anything to say . . . I'll give you the exclusive story. But don't hold your breath. And if you say a thing too early, no story."

Jason raised an eyebrow. "Okay."

"Are there any other . . . treasure hunter types around here, or in the Laffite League?"

"Stoney did have a friend who came along on the Yucatán trip, a guy he knew from Florida. Allen Eck, I think his name was. Yeah. Looked like a professor. Comes across as very cool. But what an weird jerk. We were taking a tour of Mérida. The tour guide was telling about Laffite history, but got a couple of really minor details wrong. I mean, most people would never know. Allen told him he was wrong, very quietly, and the guide firmly said, no, he was right. Maybe just thinking Allen's some dumb tourist. I'll never forget the look Allen gave him, just beyond cold, like this poor stupid guide wasn't worth a roach's ass. But he didn't say anything more. Next day, they find the tour guide in an alleyway. Both arms broken, face a solid bruise, nose broken. Guy wouldn't say who attacked him—either he didn't see or he was too scared." Jason shook his head. "I know it's crazy, but I kept thinking maybe Allen beat up that man."

21

STONEY TOSSED ALL night, like he slept on rocks, lying on a blanket in front of the big French doors leading to the dock. He'd switched all the lights on along the dock, waiting. No boats came out of the night. Alex got comfortable at the dinner table, gun in front of him, reading a thick book on seventeenth-century Asian piracy he'd found on Stoney's shelves, making noises of agreement and disapproval as he scanned the pages.

Finally he'd fallen asleep. He awoke once to hear Alex talking quietly on a cell phone. He heard Alex say, "Fine. I agree." Then nothing more but the sound of Alex clicking off his phone. He played possum, felt Alex's gaze go along his back. Stoney didn't go to sleep again for a while, but the whiskey he'd drunk earlier caught up with him and he drifted off.

He awoke at seven, his tongue stuck to the roof of his mouth, his back a solid ache. Along the dock the lights still gleamed. No boat, no Danny, dead or alive. He got up, went into the kitchen. No Alex.

He should have felt relief. He knew Alex wanted to kill him last night. Wanted to burn his face. Instead he felt panic at Alex's absence. Where the hell was he? And if Danny or his gang showed up while Alex was gone...

He went to the phone. No messages. He called the satellite phone system on *Jupiter*. No answer. He turned on the television, watched the Friday morning local news. No reports of a millionaire's brother kidnapped at sea, nothing on a missing boat or Ben and Claudia's bodies washing ashore.

He heard the front door open, hurried to the foyer, saw Alex coming in, closing the door behind him.

"Where the hell have you been?"

"They show?"

"No. Where were you?"

"Attending to some business." Alex dusted his hands. "You can cook, right? Eggs. Bacon. Black coffee. I need some protein."

"What business, Alex?"

Alex's mood seemed ominously good. He patted Stoney's cheek. "They may not be coming. Danny and his friends must have lost their nerve. Or maybe Danny killed his buddies."

"Or he killed Ben," Stoney said. "He's got nothing to bargain with, except an accusation against me that won't hold up."

Alex went into the kitchen, washed his hands. "This girlfriend of Ben's. The cop?"

"Yes."

"Maybe she took them all out."

"She's one person. And a woman."

"A gun and the knowledge and will to use it are a great equalizer. Call your boat again."

"I already tried. There wasn't an answer."

"Danny Laffite, he has a boat? Presumably they had a boat to board *Jupiter* with."

"Yes."

"You remember the name?"

"*Miss Catherine.* After Catherine Villars."

Alex rolled his eyes. "Start hailing that boat on the radio. Maybe they're trying to figure out how to trick us. Maybe they're playing it safe. Maybe they didn't want to come in at night." He gave a wicked smile. "Maybe they found the Eye hidden on your boat and they've sailed off to China." The smile—wry, like he didn't care—stayed in place. It made Stoney's stomach sink.

"I got an extra marine radio in my office, high-end, long-range."

"Let's see if anyone wants to talk to us," Alex said.

Claudia awoke slowly because waking meant pain. Hard, throbbing pain that pulsed in her head like a heartbeat, each *pu-pump* a double shot of eye-clenching agony. The pain roared hard enough for her first cogent thought to be: *Don't move, because your brains will leak out your ears.*

She opened her eyes. Coldness—from air-conditioning—prickled her skin. Morning light, soft in color but a slap against her eyes. A slow awareness of the rest of her body—not welcome, everything hurt—crept along her nerves. She was tied again, hands behind her this time, wrists raw, foot a dull ache. A coppery, sour taste made her want to spit out her tongue. Bed sheets—smelling unwashed and of suntan lotion—lay greasy against her skin.

Tied up and tucked into bed.

"Danny?" Claudia called weakly. "Danny?"

The door cracked open, light hit her eyes like a fist.

"You're awake," Danny said. "You worried me. You wouldn't wake up before."

"What...what happened? I hurt..."

"You'll be fine." A pause. "It's good you didn't die, because then how could you help me?"

He sat by her on the bed, put a moist cloth dispenser next to her head, plucked a cloth free, gently wiped her face and her hands. "Moist towelettes help you stay clean. You should wash each day," he said, as if by rote. It sounded like a rule mentioned in a hospital, a mantra of nurses.

His tone was a little different today. She didn't like it.

She stayed still while he wiped her face, cleaning her skin and hair of dried extinguisher foam and her own spittle and blood. He brought her a glass of cold water. The water tasted bitter, but her mouth craved the wetness. He held her head up gently and she gulped the glass dry.

"Good girl," he said.

"Untie me."

"No."

"You...you hit me." Her mouth tasted like it was crammed full of wool.

"Just a little love tap," he said. "You'll be okay." His jaunty confidence made her skin crawl. He smiled, shook a finger in her face she wanted to bite to the bone. "Remember, we're going to Stoney's house."

"Ben..."

"I wouldn't worry about him anymore. They're gone."

"Gone where?"

"Sailed off. I'm certainly not looking for them now. He must've heard the gunshot, decided to take off. Zack—the redhead—he's basically a coward without Gar around. Probably dump Ben in the Gulf, ditch the boat close to shore, find a rock to hide under. Less likely he'd go to Stoney's house, cut a separate deal. But you just never know about people, do you?"

"You're a smart guy, Danny," she managed to say. "But you know the police are looking for me and Ben by now. And I need medical attention." She put the edge of a whine in her voice. "Please, you hit me hard in the head. I'm sick."

"How about some delicious Aspergum? I have regular and cherry flavors."

"I might have a fractured skull."

"You're blinking okay," Danny said. He frowned. "Gar called you *Officer*. Why?"

She stared at him. "I've no idea."

"I think you're a cop, Claudia."

"You think a lot of things, Danny, more than most people."

He laughed. "I suppose I do." He ran a thumb along her lip. "I wish we could be friends. Don't have a lot of those." He sounded regretful.

"We can be. Untie me."

"No. You'll nap for a while. I put a little of my meds into your water. I don't need 'em no more. I'm feeling awesome. I want you calm till we get to Stoney's house. I didn't want to go at night. I want to see clear. And let's say he's gotten his brother back from Zack. The brother being there, he'll make Stoney trade for you. Stoney wouldn't care about you on his own. If he hasn't gotten Ben back, then I tell him I've got Ben with you, down below. See?" He smiled at his own cleverness.

She closed her eyes.

"Because I'm gonna call him when we get in close to shore. Tell him he's got to meet us out on the dock with the Devil's Eye and the journal."

Claudia was silent.

"Then I'm gonna shoot him from the boat, make his head go boom like a ol' melon. Like Gar's did. Then I'm getting my stuff, 'cause he'll have it there at his house. I figured his house is big, he'll want the treasure where he can see it, know it's okay," Danny said with a smile. Touching his fingers to her throat, taking the measure of her breath, savoring the moment. Flush with success at having bested Gar. She saw suddenly that Danny probably hadn't had a lot of success in his life.

"If he doesn't have this emerald there, you're screwed."

"Okay. I'll shoot after he gives it to me or tells me where it is."

"The journal," she said. "Tell me again what it looks like, Danny. Maybe I saw it at Stoney's."

Danny studied her for a moment, touched her jaw—which ached still—with tenderness. Then he went to the cabinet in the stateroom's corner, unlocked it with a key from around his neck. From a drawer he pulled a piece of paper, bleary with photocopy streaks. He held the paper above her face.

She wriggled into position where she could see the page, written in the flowing scrawl that passed for nineteenth-century penmanship. Sorting the words was a struggle:

In late May 1820 a small force led by the schooner Lynx chased Laffite's little fleet (being two schooners and a brigantine) down the Texas coast. Feeling ran high that Laffite might simply move south onto other Texas islands and re-establish his pirating base. Captain Madison was ordered to ignore the safe passage that Commodore Patterson issued to Laffite, which made me uneasy. Our word in the Navy should matter. But in Vera Cruz Madison received reports of a Spanish ship, the Santa Barbara, carrying a trove of gold and jewels. SB vanished in the Western gulf—in fair weather—in the weeks before Laffite abandoned his privateering, and I suspect the government thought him involved. I fear no one informed Mr. Laffite of this change in the government's attitude.

We fired on Laffite's ships south of Matagorda Bay, but he turned into the maze of bays and shoals, guarded by the thin strips of barrier islands, and we could not give chase without running aground. We caught him coming out of St. Leo Bay the next morning. There was scant loot on his ship, some silks, Madeira, a few handfuls of coins at most— little enough for the great pirate. His crude, stupid men were hungry, and beaten. There was no sign of the Spanish treasure. Offers of immunity from prosecution won the crew over. We escorted Laffite's ship to Vera Cruz; I do not know what happened to him afterwards. We were all sworn—and paid in bonus—not to discuss this operation since it had disregarded a legal safe passage, and the navy wanted no embarrassment. I left Lynx in New Orleans, and tragically Lynx and all her hands were soon lost in a storm, on a cruise to Jamaica to fight piracy in the Caribbean. So I alone remain to give witness, but I cannot bear to dishonor Captain Madison's memory by confessing what the Navy did in public. Here I can write my thoughts without fear. For those who recall Laffite's heroic service to New Orleans—and to America—during our late War with the British, it seems particularly scandalous and unfair to have broken a promise, even one made to a pirate.

Ample discussion followed that Laffite had buried his booty along the coastline where he had evaded the task force and one of the younger pirates spoke of a nighttime expedition at Widows' Point in St. Leo Bay, where only Laffite, out of four men, returned. But this fellow Jack was both simple and a hopeless drunkard whose story changed with the level of rum in the bottle. I think that the idea makes an excellent story and my grandchildren enjoy it so at their bedtime. I record it here simply as a matter of interest.

"Who wrote this?" Claudia stared at Danny as he lowered the paper from her face.

"John B. Fanning, ship's surgeon aboard *Lynx*. He wrote this journal years later. I guess his descendants found it in a family trunk and they put it up on an on-line auction site, simply mentioning it talked about Laffite and navy operations in the 1820s. They had no idea of its value. So I bought it. Widows' Point, see. That's what they call Black Jack Point now."

Black Jack Point. Where those two old people had been murdered. David's case.

He didn't say anything for a minute, not looking at her, putting the copy back into the cabinet, locking it up. "You should understand why this is all mine. By inheritance. My last name is Laffite. Daniel Villars Laffite."

Claudia watched him. Finally she said, "You're descended from Jean Laffite?" She tried not to laugh.

"And Catherine Villars, his great love. So that money, that hidden gold, it's mine. Mine." His voice fell to a whispering mumble. He was used, she saw, to talking to himself, telling himself what he wanted to hear. "No. One. Else's. I got the best claim on it imaginable."

She gathered herself, tried to stay calm. At first she

thought his grudge against Stoney was a battle between one treasure hunter versus another. But this.

"You don't believe me," Danny said, a low rumble in his voice.

"Sure I do," she said. "Why wouldn't I?"

"People laugh at me. Not much longer though. Not much longer." His voice rose, spittle flying from his lips, hitting her cheek.

She didn't move, didn't react, put a gentle, calm smile on her face. "Danny, it was sweet of you to share your meds with me. Really. But maybe you should take them again. Just because you want to be at your best when—"

He leaned down and slapped her, hard. She stared past his shoulder. He rubbed her cheek, his fingertips smelling of the moist towelettes. "No. No more of those. Keep me from being me."

The radio beeped. She heard its call through a little speaker in the cabin. A hail for *Miss Catherine*. Maybe Stoney's voice? Hard to tell. Danny rushed out of the cabin without giving her another look. She heard his feet pound on the stairs.

She had to get loose, fight him, there had to be a way. The stateroom was dark now, with the door closed and the shades lowered, thin slices of light lying in lines on the bed, but she inched over. A bedside table stood on each side of the narrow bed. With her hands tied behind her, she pried open one drawer with her fingers, rolled around to see what was inside. A pair of reading glasses, stubby blue pencils, a notepad. She eased the drawer shut with her foot, wriggled to the other side of the bed, and slowly forced the other table drawer open. She rolled again. Inside lay a pack of gum. A ballpoint pen, missing its cap. A scattering of pennies, dimes, and quarters. A set of nail clippers.

Clippers.

She turned her back to the drawer, easing around, and carefully leaned backward, her fingers wiggling, trying to close around the little plastic case of the clippers. Her fingertips brushed the dimes, the foil of the gum pack. Her fingernails tapped the plastic…and she leaned back too far, her exhausted muscles in her back and arms cramping. She fell off the bed, the drawer smacking hard against her neck and shoulder. She hit the thin carpet hard, teeth jarring together, one of her fingers jamming and she cried out in pain.

She raised her feet, shut the drawer, her back straining, her muscles begging for mercy.

The door opened. He stood there, watching her, the Sig in hand, and she wondered, *Who's steering this boat?* He gently put her back on the bed, pulled the sheets over her like he was tucking her in for sleep.

"What were you doing?"

"Trying to stretch a little. I'm cramping everywhere. Please untie me."

"I just spoke with Stoney. He's agreed to the trade. He asked to speak to his brother but I said no. He thinks I got Ben." He grinned. "So this will be over soon."

And he shut the door behind him.

Her hand hurt like the devil; her head felt like it was full of sand. Tears of frustration stung her eyes. She blinked them back.

Not much time. She rolled back toward the drawer.

22

WHIT WAS GOING to be late for Friday morning juvenile court, but that hearing was his least favorite chore, lecturing kids who ought to know better while their impatient or embarrassed parents, arms crossed, stood there as the county doled out the discipline.

He pressed Stoney Vaughn's doorbell. The same cars—a Porsche and a beat-up van—were still parked in the oversize curve of the driveway.

He waited. No answer. He tried the doorbell again.

Still no answer. Whit walked around the front of the house, around a corner, across a lawn so manicured golf could have been played on it, and down to the sprawling home's back. A metal fence enclosed the back, fancy wrought-iron curlicues at the posts' tips, but the gate was unlocked. The back wasn't a yard so much as a multitiered deck. He climbed up wooden stairs. At the top he could see two more platforms below him, a nice long private dock with no boat in residence, lights still on like they'd been left on all night. A pool, set into the deck. Expensive patio furniture, a restaurant-style grill built into the brick.

The French doors opened behind him. A man—Whit knew he was Stoney Vaughn, recognized him from the pictures in the articles on the Internet—stepped outside. The guy looked like hell, rumpled clothes, unshaven, like he'd slept on the street. Lip split and puffy.

"Excuse me," Stoney said. "This is private property."

"I know," Whit said. "But you didn't answer your door."

"Yeah, I sure didn't, did I?"

"I'm Judge Whit Mosley. I'm the JP and county coroner. I'd like to talk to you about two recent homicides."

"Call my office. Make an appointment." Stoney shut his mouth, as though reconsidering this as an initial reaction.

"I'm here now. You don't appear to be busy."

"I had a late night working," Stoney said. "Sorry to be gruff." He shut the door behind him, came out onto the deck in full light, glancing toward the stretch of the bay. "And I'm afraid I have a business appointment in Corpus that I need to get ready for. I don't know how I can help you."

"You knew Patch Gilbert, though, didn't you?"

"The name's vaguely familiar..."

"You sent him a bottle of Glenfiddich after talking to him at a Laffite League meeting," Whit said.

Stoney shut his mouth, smiled, wiped his eyes. "Oh. Yeah. I do remember him. Charming guy."

"Was. You probably heard he got killed Monday night. Along with his girlfriend."

Stoney's eyes widened. "You're kidding me. Mr. Gilbert's dead?"

"You don't watch the news?"

A pause. "Not lately. And I'm deep in putting together a new business deal, so I've been working 24/7."

"More financing for treasure hunts?" Whit gave a look of angelic purity.

Stoney stared again. "Um, no, but you sure seem to know a lot about me, Mr. Mosley."

"Judge, please. I prefer the formal title." Whit folded his arms across today's shirt, lime-green with waltzing, bug-eyed pineapples.

"Uh, sorry, Judge. I'm out of the treasure-hunt game. Too expensive a hobby. May I ask how you know about me?"

"I'm conducting the inquest into Mr. Gilbert's death. I'm trying to get a picture of his life in the months before he died."

"Well, I met him the one time. We chatted." A pause. "I was interested in his land, asked him about selling. He said no."

"And the other Gilbert family members—you approached them?"

"Am I suspected of something here? Do I need a lawyer?"

"I don't know, do you?"

"Do you have some ID? Because you sure don't look like a judge."

Whit handed him a laminated card, showed his driver's license. "I don't have a lot of time either, Mr. Vaughn. But your name cropped up more than once and I wanted to know your connection to Mr. Gilbert."

"Vague at best, Judge." Now Stoney smiled. "Yes, I think I met another Gilbert—Suzanne, right?—and asked her about her land. She also declined to sell."

"Not everyone wants every inch of the coast developed."

"True enough," Stoney said. "Is there anything else? I'm sorry I couldn't be of more help—"

"Yes. Where were you Monday night?"

Stoney's smile faded, came back on. "Um, I was here at my house."

"Anyone with you?"

"My brother, Ben, lives here with me."

"I'd like to talk to him, if I may."

"He's not in at the moment."

"When do you expect him back?" Whit asked.

"You know, he's taken my boat out for some fishing and R and R, and I'm not sure when he's going to be back." The smile again. "I don't even have time to play with the toys, but my brother does."

"Okay." Whit glanced toward the French doors. He thought he'd seen someone behind the glass, but with the glare from the sun, maybe he was wrong. "Please ask him to give me a call."

"Is this really necessary, sir? Honestly, am I in some sort of trouble? I mean, the police haven't questioned me or contacted me."

"Thanks for your time," Whit said. "Oh. Since you're a treasure buff, maybe you can help me."

"Uh, sure."

"You got any books on old coins?"

The cutting was going slowly ... too slowly.

On Claudia's second try for the clippers, she'd managed to slide open the large file. She found after experimentation that she could hold the file in her right hand and saw at the knots binding her hands together. But the file was too dull, jabbing her wrist every third stroke, and the rope unyielding. Her hands and forearms cramped. She lay on her side, keeping the tedious cutting motion going, the ropes death-grip tight, no progress.

She stared at the ceiling, thirsty, hungry, trying to think straight.

Stoney hadn't—since yesterday—called the coast guard. Otherwise helicopters screaming out of Corpus Christi would have spotted *Miss Catherine* from the air, radioed her position and heading to cutters who would have intercepted Danny Laffite. She'd be off the boat by now, Danny in custody, wheeled in front of eager psychologists who could mine a dozen papers out of his obsessions.

Does a man like Stoney Vaughn—self-made, into millions—let a guy like Danny Laffite order him around? Did he tell Gar that you're a cop?

If police were with Stoney, helping him lure in Danny, they'd say, *Don't say anything about her, don't risk panicking him.*

Maybe it was a stupid mistake. Or maybe Stoney hoped Gar would kill you.

She had to get free. Because Danny was going to kill her if Stoney didn't have this emerald. And if there was one bit of truth to Danny's story, Stoney might not wish her well either. Claudia pulled herself along the bed, her feet and hands still bound. And the purr of the engines, the full throttle of *Miss Catherine* told her Danny had abandoned caution and now was in a hurry to get to Stoney's bayside house.

Danny was up on deck, leaving her below, but that might not last long.

She hopped across the floor. The closet door was a slider, one pane covered with a mirror. On the closet floor she found a pair of flip-flops, oversize for her feet. She put them on. The toe Gar broke was purpled and sore and she was about to make it feel worse. With her shoulder, she inched the closet door shut. She eased herself onto the floor, feet toward the mirror.

Now. *Either he'll hear you and come down and shoot you or the engines and the wind will mask the noise.* Time to find out. She thought of her mother and her gentle nagging for a moment, her father, so proud of her as a police officer. Her sisters and brothers, all good people that she loved dearly. David on their wedding day, smiling hugely. Whit, crazy, sweet Whit in a loud shirt and windblown hair that he'd forget to smooth down after he put on the judge's robe. The odd little twist he always put in her heart while knowing he wasn't really the one for her. Ben. Poor Ben, smiling at her, the nice boy grown into a better man. Probably dead now, thanks to Danny.

She aimed her feet and kicked hard against the mirrored door. It shook, wobbled in its cheap frame.

The engines still thrummed and hummed.

The glass webbed on the third hard smack, cracks in the mirror distorting her reflection. Her foot throbbed. She kicked again. Again.

Two big slivers of mirror fell out of the frame, one a crescent, the other a triangle. She stopped, breathing, listening to the engines. The roar stayed steady.

Now. The trick is to not lose a finger. Or all five.

Claudia turned, wriggled her back up against the bed, grabbed a corner of the cheap bedspread. On it dolphins and mermaids cavorted in tacky glee. But the fabric was thick and she covered her fingers and her palms with it. She took a deep breath, eased back toward the splinters, tried to lift the crescent of mirror. Her covered fingers closed around it. No grip. It shifted and fell from her hands.

Try again. Don't rush. Sweat dribbled along her ribs.

The third try, she got a hold on the sliver. She steadied with her right hand and slowly, slowly, gripped it until she was sure it wouldn't cut through the bedspread to her flesh. She leaned to one side, stretching, turning a sharp edge toward the ropes. There. She moved the glass, felt it slice into the meat of the rope.

Not too fast, and don't dare slip, or you'll cut your wrists open. That would be hysterical, yes. Lie here on the floor, tied up, bleeding out into the dingy carpet while Danny sailed them home.

She made a little noise in her throat as the first loop in the knot broke under the mirror's edge.

Slowly. Find the rhythm, feel the rope against you so you don't cut yourself. She sliced deeper into the big knot fashioned around her hands, forcing herself not to rush.

The knot began to unravel. She steadied her hand. Now the remaining rope was a thick strand right around her wrists, covering the tender lace of veins. Careful.

The deck began to pitch. Danny was in a hard turn, a sudden turn. The crescent slipped in her grip, an edge bit into her skin. She let the fragment go, rolled away from the closet. The deck pitched again, crazily.

Why wouldn't he steer like a maniac? He is a maniac.

The deck settled, the engines resumed their hum. A little ooze of blood tickled her palm. She pulled on the ropes and her left hand—uncut—came free. She pulled her right hand around to her front, saw a cut in the fleshy part of her palm, blood welling, odd that it didn't hurt much. Then as feeling crept into her numb hands, it stung like the devil. She unraveled the rope off her hand, grabbed the bedspread, stanched the bleeding. Not bad but worse than it looked.

Claudia cut through the ropes on her feet.

She wobbled as she stood, sensation ebbing back into

her feet, arms, hands, and the small of her back. She ached everywhere. She bandaged her hand with a T-shirt she found in the bureau, tearing off a sleeve and wrapping the fabric around twice.

She tried the door. Locked. A deadbolt, locked from outside, above the knob. She cussed under her breath, glanced around for a way to smash the door. Although Danny would hear that and come running, gun in hand.

The porthole. Salt and oily stains grimed over the glass. It was secured with four twisting locks. She began to undo them.

So what do you do? Bail out over the side and hope someone picks you up? You don't even know where in the Gulf you are. Maybe the cops are there at Stoney's house, waiting, and you're running away from a rescue.

But her gut said that wasn't the case. She couldn't be far from the bay; he couldn't have wandered or waited too far away.

She unscrewed the final lock, yanked the panel free from the porthole. Wind and cold spray hit her face. Salt stung her lips. She saw two sailboats in the far distance.

Go. Go.

She prayed Danny Laffite didn't see her launch herself into the water, didn't run over her and crush her or chop her into floating mincemeat with the prop. Or didn't stop to shoot her five times in the back as she tried to swim away. But he'd shoot her for sure, she thought, when he found her untied. Maybe she could take him, surprise him when he opened the door. But maybe not. Danny had the gun, his muscles weren't aching from having been tied for hours, and he had the strength of the crazy on his side. There were other boats on the water. Someone would see her, God, yes. And if she waited...she'd lost one chance before, aboard *Jupiter.* He could stop the boat at any time to come fetch her and she wouldn't be able to fight back. *Seize the moment,* she told herself.

She turned and dug through the closet. No life preserver jacket. Nothing flotational. And no flares. Nothing but musty clothing. She found a big pair of blue jeans and remembered a news story about a young American girl who survived hours in the sea after a ferry in the Philippines capsized and sank, by fashioning her blue jeans into a crude float. Fine. She pulled on the jeans over her shorts. She saw a bright red pillow on the bed, small. Easy to see. Claudia grabbed it, shoved it under her T-shirt.

Claudia pulled herself through the porthole. She threw herself into the deep green, pushing away from the boat with all the strength left in her legs.

She hit the water like a stone wall. Air smashed out of her lungs, water closed over her head like six feet of packed dirt. The roar of *Miss Catherine* slicing through the waves sounded above her, churning, like gods rolling dice.

She kicked down, down, down into the endless green. *Stay down. Don't let him see you.*

She felt the Gulf close its cold fist around her, and when she could no longer hold her breath, Claudia kicked hard again and broke the surface, a wave roiling into her chest, knocking her back down. She emerged; salt burning her hand, her face, her eyes. She coughed, keeping her head clear, turned toward the widening wake.

Miss Catherine roared away from her, Danny standing on the flying bridge, steering through the crests. Not stopping, not turning back. He hadn't seen her.

She shivered. A wave picked her up in its swell and

settled her back down. Her arms and legs ached like they'd been braided on a rack. Sharp, stinging pain hit in the hollow of her hand, and the T-shirt bandage she'd fashioned turned pink in the water. She thought of the silky sharks from yesterday, tearing through the chum. Drawn by the blood.

She tried to get her bearings from the sun, looked toward where she thought the shore would lie. *Second-guessing yourself already?* she thought. But she saw in the distance two sails unfurled, the dot of a cruiser cutting through the waves. *He's racing toward shore. You can't be that far out in the Gulf. You can't be. Right?*

Claudia pulled the bright red pillow from her shirt and began to wave it back and forth every ten seconds, facing the boats. Then she trod water. Wave. Tread. Repeat.

Repeat. Repeat. Repeat.

The boats headed away from her. As Claudia began to swim, the fatal heaviness of exhaustion began its terrible creep.

23

―――⊂◉⊃―――

I DON'T LIKE A JUDGE SNIFFING AROUND," Alex said.

"He was harmless." Stoney stood in front of the bay window.

"He's been here twice."

"He's talking to everyone who knew Patch Gilbert. It's not an issue."

"Not an issue."

"Look, he hardly asked me anything except where I'd met Patch. That was it. Said nothing about a land buy, nothing about Laffite, nothing. Okay? And I had to get rid of him. We couldn't have him around when Danny sailed up, or have him coming in and seeing you, could we?"

"No." Alex took his wire-rim glasses off, cleaned them on his shirt, put them back on. "If Danny's killed your brother, how are you going to explain the motive?"

"My boat's gone. He was on the boat. I won't have known what happened. Danny's a freaking nutcase. He finally snapped. He had a grudge against me no one could explain. Why do I have to explain anything?"

"You're a cold bastard, Stoney. I have to say."

"I didn't want my brother to get hurt."

"You didn't lift a finger to help him," Alex said. "Family doesn't matter to you?"

"You kill people and you lecture me about family?"

"I didn't have a thing against Gilbert and Mrs. Tran," Alex said. "Old, and they'd had good lives, probably. Jimmy was too dumb to live. I didn't want them messing up my life. But man, I wouldn't kill *family*."

"I didn't kill my brother."

"Sure you did. You stole from me. You probably let your brother die instead of parting with one red cent. You're a real honey." Alex unwrapped a stick of gum, offered the pack to Stoney, who shook his head. "Here's what happens when Danny gets here. We meet him down on the dock."

"If Ben and Claudia are still alive..."

"She's got to go, man. Sorry. The kidnappers and Danny are dead, too. Your brother...you think he can be trusted, then fine."

"You kill his girlfriend, he's not going to be happy."

"He'll be less happy dead."

"Don't kill him, Alex. Please." Stoney glanced out into the curve of the bay that fed the flats. "A boat's coming. Not mine. A sportfisher."

"Danny Boy," Alex said. "Let's go say hi." He tucked his gun into the back of his pants, closed a light jacket of Stoney's above it.

"You're wearing a jacket in summer? That looks suspicious."

"Would you like to go shoot him, Stoney?"

Stoney opened his mouth, closed it again. They headed down the deck stairs toward the dock.

The boat chugged along, kept correcting course, as

though the pilot was a bit unsure of his bearings. The morning had turned windy, the bay degrading into white choppiness.

"Stand behind me," Alex said. "Just a little."

"Are you going to shoot him right away?" Stoney whispered.

"No, I'm not," Alex said. "Just do what you're told."

The Bertram, in need of paint, hovered in close to the dock. But it didn't dock, staying about ten feet away. Stoney saw Danny—hair blown wild by wind and speed, standing in the shadow of the flying bridge. Holding a gun.

Alex raised both hands, palms out, showing they were empty.

The sportfisher cut its motors. "Who're you?" Danny called.

"I'm here to facilitate the transfer," Alex said.

"Stoney," Danny said. "This some thug you hide behind?"

"You mean like you're hiding behind my brother and his girlfriend?" Stoney said.

"Where's the journal and the Devil's Eye?" Danny asked.

"Inside the house. Where's my boat?" Stoney said.

"You ask about your boat before your brother," Danny said. "Nice."

"We want to see that Ben and Claudia are safe before the exchange," Alex said. "This is a business transaction."

"It's not quite like going to the ATM," Danny said. "You show me the Eye and the journal. You toss them to me on the boat. I pull out a little further. I let Ben and Claudia swim into the dock."

"No," Alex said. "You dock, and you show us that our friends are fine first."

"My way or no way," Danny said.

"Fine," Alex said. "Sail off into the sunset."

Danny frowned. "I'll call the cops, tell them what you did, Stoney. Here and in New Orleans."

"Call them," Alex said. "You're a kidnapper. And you don't have any proof. The guy who killed your cousin in New Orleans is dead. His name is Jimmy Bird. He shot himself earlier this week. He used us, he used you. Stoney didn't hurt your cousin."

Stoney couldn't even look at Alex.

Danny stared at Alex, shook his head. "I don't believe you."

"You got to work with me here, Danny, to get what you want. Otherwise you're going to lose."

"Who the hell *are* you?"

"I'm your only hope for getting what you want," Alex said. "Now. Dock. Or we walk away and you have nothing. Dock and you can have the Eye. We keep the rest of the treasure. Deal?"

Stoney could see it play out on Danny's face. The wanting. The obsession. The need to win, be right, not be the laughingstock anymore. "I'm supposed to check in with my associates on Stoney's boat in ten minutes. I don't, they kill Ben."

"You don't have Ben with you?" Stoney said. His voice rose.

"He's safe. I got Claudia."

"That's fine," Alex said. "See, we're willing to trust you. We don't want Ben or Claudia hurt. Jimmy Bird's the one who screwed you over. I can show it to you in the paper, Danny. We'll give you the Eye and trust you that you'll give us Ben." He slowly pulled out of his jacket pocket the fake emerald Stoney had left in the storage unit, let it glitter in the light. "See. Yours. Just give us Claudia and Ben."

Danny chewed his lip for a moment, then turned the wheel slowly in toward the dock. Alex kept the fat emerald aloft, holding it on his fingertips.

Danny hovered into position, pulled up against the dock. Stoney tossed bumpers against the dock to protect the boat, tossed a line onto *Miss Catherine*'s deck. Stoney quickly fed the rope around and through the dock cleat. Danny kept his gun trained on Alex.

"We don't have a gun on you," Alex said. "Put that down. Or I drop the Eye in the drink."

"Toss it up here," Danny said.

Alex smiled—Stoney saw it, thought, *Oh no, you're not*—tossed the fake Eye high, toward Danny's reaching hand.

Danny grabbed at the stone one-handed, his eyes widening, as Alex pulled his revolver from the back of his waist and fired once. Blood burst from Danny's shoulder, and he fell backward onto the deck, screaming.

Stoney climbed aboard, Alex following. Danny lay on his back, sobbing in pain. "You shot me." He sounded shocked.

"Go see if your brother and his girlfriend are aboard or not," Alex said. "I'll stay here with Danny." He knelt by Danny, steadied him by putting a hand on his chest. "It's okay, man. Calm down."

"Oh, please," Danny said. "Don't kill me."

"I won't," Alex said. He glanced up at Stoney. "What are you waiting on?"

"The guys that were with him…" Stoney said. "They might be below."

"Are they, Danny?" Alex asked.

"No...no..." Danny moaned. "They're gone."

"Go ahead, Stoney. Do some constructive work," Alex said. And he motioned with his gun.

Stoney swallowed and hurried belowdecks. He checked the galley, a small stateroom, an empty head.

"Ben buddy? Claudia?" Stoney called in a low voice at the stateroom. "It's okay. It's over."

He unlocked the door, pushed it open with his fingertips.

He saw the loops of cut rope, the broken mirror, the open porthole. Someone had been here, someone was gone now. He looked out the porthole to see if maybe Ben or Claudia was swimming away right now, but the water in the little cove was empty.

Stoney went back up to the deck. Blood still pulsed from Danny's shoulder, Alex kneeling by him.

"No one's there. Someone was tied up but they cut themselves loose and must've jumped ship."

"Claudia," Danny said. "I had...Claudia. I didn't hurt her."

"What did you tell her, Danny?" Alex asked.

Danny blinked. "Tell her...nothing. She doesn't know anything." He winced as he moved.

"Where's Ben?" Alex asked.

"Gar tried to rape Claudia. I shot him, dumped his body overboard. Zack...took off with the other boat. With Ben aboard."

"You know who he's talking about?" Alex asked.

"I don't know any Gar or Zack," Stoney said.

"Okay," Alex said. His voice went gentle. "Danny, who else knows about the treasure?"

"No...one. I didn't tell. Just wanted what was mine."

"That's why you didn't tell the cops who you thought murdered your cousin. You didn't want anything getting in the way of you getting the Eye. You were gonna dig up illegal, same as us."

"Where is my brother?" Stoney demanded.

"I don't know. After you wouldn't transfer the money, it all went south." Danny closed his eyes, opened them. "It hurts."

"I know."

"Please don't kill me," Danny said.

"I promised I wouldn't," Alex said. He stood, offered the gun to Stoney. "You do it."

"What?" Stoney said.

"Your turn. I've done all the risky work. You've stolen from me, lied to me. He's your problem."

"Um, really, no, that's okay. You do it." Stoney took a step back.

"If you don't shoot him, I'll shoot you."

Stoney gulped. "Then you won't get the Eye."

"I don't think it's on your boat, buddy. I think that's a little lie you cooked up so I'd stick around to clean up your mess. You wouldn't let your brother take off on your boat if the Eye was on board. I know you." He smiled. "Last night I evened the playing field. Moved the rest of the treasure while you slept."

Stoney stared. "You couldn't have."

"Oh, but I did," Alex said. "Shoot him."

"Please, no," Danny said. "You can't. I'm a Laffite."

"No, you're not," Alex said.

"I am!" Danny screamed.

"I won't," Stoney said.

Alex aimed. "Kidneys or heart? Your choice, Stoney. I'd pick heart if I were you."

"Shoot him," Danny said. "Not me."

Stoney took the gun from Alex—he thought it would be heavy, but it was light as air—and pointed it at Danny, who started to scream.

I can't, Stoney thought. Then the gun pulsed and the top of Danny's head blew off, sending a red spray across the deck.

Danny stared up at him, eyes full of dismay and surprise, drops of blood clouding the irises.

"There. Not so hard, was it?" Alex said, like he was giving back a test with a B plus when a failing grade had been expected.

Stoney thought, *Now shoot Alex. Do it. Just do it and all this is over.* But he thought of the rest of the treasure, the hundreds of silver and gold coins, and he handed the gun back to Alex without a word.

"Now. We got two problems. The girlfriend, maybe he killed her."

"I don't think so. I think she got away."

"So she's out in the water. Creates new risk, man. Changes everything. We gotta hurry. I need your help."

"I..." Stoney stared down at the body. "I just killed a man." He thought his knees would go weak, he'd vomit. Nothing. He waited for his hands to start shaking but now he felt pretty good. "If Claudia knows what Danny knew..."

"If she's out drowning in the Gulf, she may not be a problem," Alex said.

"My brother...maybe we should go look for him. Take Danny's boat and—"

"No. Not much we can do there. Ben's either dead by now or they'll contact us. We got to deal with the problem at hand. Help me below."

In ten minutes it was done. The deck hosed, the bilges partially opened, the pumps undone, the engines going full steam, *Miss Catherine* headed back into the bay. She'd be sunk in a few minutes, into the deeper reach of the bay, but probably not entirely submerged. But a mess, without a body.

They wrapped Danny Laffite in double-thick garbage bags, like a giant plastic burrito. Alex taped the ends closed, neat as Christmas wrapping. They put him in the back of the van, locked up the house, climbed into the car.

"Stoney?" Alex said. "Take a good look at Danny here. You try to screw me over, you're burrito boy, the sequel."

But I'm like you. I've killed a man now, Stoney thought, *and suddenly I'm not so scared of you. Because I have the Eye, the trump card, and maybe you're gonna be the next burrito.*

But he played safe. "I understand you completely, Alex."

"You got a good idea where to dump him?"

Stoney nodded. They both sat in the van and roared away from Copano Flats, down the dirt and oyster-shell road.

"Now," Alex said. "I got a new plan. Just in case this Claudia shows up."

Miss Catherine, never a proud ship, sputtered and gushed down into the muddy bottom of St. Leo Bay, in a fairly shallow twenty feet. Water poured in, flooding the belowdecks, covering the bed where Gar died, the shattered glass that Claudia used to cut herself free. *Miss Catherine* tilted hard to port as she sank and the back stateroom flooded entirely, including the armoire holding the photocopied excerpt of John Fanning's journal that Danny showed to Claudia. The seawater covered the paper as the armoire canted over, smashed through the closet doors, and rested on its side. Little spot croakers and hardhead catfish swam down the stairs and through the portholes and began exploring this new world.

24

W HIT," SAID GOOCH. "I'd like you to meet Helen Dupuy." Gooch, back earlier than Whit thought he'd be, by one in the afternoon on Friday, stood in Whit's courtroom as the last juvenile case wrapped up and a boy, chronically truant, and his embarrassed-to-the-bone parents left.

Whit still was in his robe, sitting at the bench. Gooch had an arm around a young woman, with a slight build, hair a little too frizzed, a hard, worn look to her, but pretty if maybe she ate a little more, slept a little more. Wearing faded jeans and an old blue T-shirt with a little rip in the shoulder that needed mending.

"Hello, Helen," Whit said. "I'm Whit Mosley." He shook her hand.

They were alone now in the courtroom, Gooch biting his lip, Helen looking like she didn't know why she was here.

"I brought Helen back with me from New Orleans," Gooch said.

"I see."

"We caught the first flight out this morning," Gooch said.

"You must've," Whit said. "You didn't tarry long in New Orleans."

"I felt we ought to be back here ASAP." He glanced at Helen. "Helen, I need to talk to His Honor private-like for a minute, if you don't mind." He gave her some change. "There's a Coke machine down the hallway—take a left. Get yourself something to drink and I'll be there in just a minute."

"Nice to have met you, sir," she said to Whit.

"You don't have to call me sir."

"I know better than to mouth off at a judge." Helen gave Gooch a smile, went out of the courtroom.

Whit waited until the door shut after her. "Who is she, Gooch?"

"She's a whore," Gooch said, "but not a crack whore."

"That's good," Whit said. "Why on earth did you bring this young woman back from New Orleans with you?"

"Albert Exley. Ring any bells?"

It did sound familiar. "It sounds like Allen Eck." Whit told Gooch about the crazy treasure hunter described by Jason Salinger of the Laffite League and that Jimmy Bird was dead.

"Albert Exley. Allen Eck. Alex," Gooch said. "His names seem to be shrinking."

"So who's Albert Exley?"

"The name used by the man who paid cash and stayed at the motel Jimmy Bird called and nearly killed that nice girl that just left." Gooch explained what Helen had told him. "If he's the same guy that Stoney Vaughn took to Mexico, then Stoney knows Allen/Albert/Alex. Triple A..."

"Triple A?"

"I ain't calling him by all his aliases," Gooch said. "Triple A was in touch with Jimmy. And Jimmy used to work for Patch. There's your connection."

"But no proof. Nothing to give to David. Albert Exley and Allen Eck could be two entirely different people."

"I don't think so," Gooch said. "Names too similar. One guy. Triple A."

"So why was he in New Orleans?"

"From that phone call Helen heard and got shoved through the glass for, I think he was there to kill someone. I'm gonna do some hunting today, get Helen to help me, see who all in New Orleans went missing or turned up dead during the time he was there. She's a quick learner."

"I'll bet."

"Don't you be that way, Whitman."

"Shouldn't you have stayed in New Orleans to do this?"

Gooch shook his head. "Triple A is here, man. *Here.* If he's this guy that Jimmy was in contact with, and he's the same treasure hunter Stoney knew, he's either been here or still here. Most of what I was going to look for is in newspaper archives. I can do all that via the Internet." He raised an eyebrow. "I sure as hell wasn't leaving you alone here, sniffing around. This guy's a freak."

"Why'd you bring Helen, Gooch?"

"I could use some help, and let's just say she's motivated to find this Alex. He hurt her pretty badly. And second, well, she needs a vacation. Whores don't get vacation time. Least not paid. And plus, she knows the guy. We don't have a picture. I thought maybe she could find an artist in town, describe this guy, get a sketch for us."

"Like a police sketch? Artists don't do that generally, Gooch. It's very specialized work."

"Whatever," Gooch said. "The key is finding this guy, Whit. If the three different guys are all one and the same... you got your man, I'm telling you."

"Take her to see Jason Salinger," Whit said. "Let them compare notes. That should help us know if Triple A is one person or not. Maybe he has a photo from Mexico."

"Then, maybe later," Gooch said, "I might take her to a movie. If we're not tracking down this loser."

"Gooch, you aren't sleeping with her, are you?"

"Yeah, we slept together last night. Didn't screw. Just slept."

"Just slept."

"Yeah. She snores a little. That doesn't bother me."

"I think, in short, you're screwed," Suzanne Gilbert said.

Whit had thought he was done with the juveniles, with teen court ended and Gooch gone, but Suzanne was waiting for him in his office, arms crossed, still wearing black shirt, black pants, despite the hazy heat that had broiled Port Leo. Pouting. Pissed as a spoiled teenager being told no.

"Don't you feel like a solar panel?" Whit said.

"Don't mess with me," she said. Her tone was still pleasant.

"I'm not. What's wrong?" He pulled the robe off, over his head. He hated wearing black, even in the air-conditioned comfort of the courthouse.

She watched him smooth out his lime shirt and hang up the robe.

"Shut the door. This conversation is private."

He did, gave her an indulgent smile, thought, *You have about five seconds to turn nice.*

"Lucy. She is apparently the sole heir of Patch's estate."

Legal news traveled fast. He wondered who told her. Maybe Lucy. Maybe the lawyers. Maybe David. "So I've heard. I haven't seen a will, though."

"And her lover is in charge of the inquest."

"Lover. I don't know if I've ever been called that before. Don't most people say boyfriend?" He sat behind his desk.

"It's going to make a nasty headline in the paper," Suzanne said. "You should recuse yourself from the case."

"Lucy is not officially under suspicion. And she's not a blood relative of mine or a relative by marriage. I don't have grounds to recuse myself."

"Of course she's not a suspect. Not with you working hand in hand with the police."

"David Power is not exactly president of my fan club," Whit said. "They don't listen to me as to who they suspect. They handle the evidence, they make the calls. Jimmy Bird is the guy they think did this, Suzanne, so why are you pitching a hissy fit?"

She was mad about all that land and money not coming to her, and whatever he said wasn't going to placate her.

"Jimmy Bird has a wife and family, and he just suddenly turns to burglary? I don't buy it," Suzanne said. "Lucy, somewhere, has her hand in this. That will's going to get a hard look, too. And for you abusing your position to protect her, I'll go to the papers—"

"You know, go and do what you please, Suzanne," Whit said quietly. "You're mad because Patch cut you out. You're a disgruntled relative. The papers will give you the tenth of an inch you deserve."

"Your career as a judge will be over."

"I've been threatened with that before," Whit said. "It'd work if I got caught screwing a goat. And even then it's only a maybe. I screw up, the judicial board'll spank me and I'll take it. You and the papers can try what you please."

He smiled. And he meant it. Before being elected, he'd run an ice cream shop, taken pictures for the newspaper, run a messenger service. All were decidedly less stressful than sitting on the bench and taking crap from this no-talent whiner. "Bet I'm more popular in town than you are."

"Don't make that bet, Whit." Her tone softened. "We can deal, can't we? I won't make a scene in the papers. I won't take your career down, which you seem to think is invincible but isn't. But we need to reach an agreement."

"On what?"

"Lucy can afford to be . . . generous to me. Share a little."

Whit stared. "You're unbelievable."

"I'm very believable."

"You'll make trouble and contest the will—unless you're paid off?" He shook his head. "Go paint your butt and roll yourself another bad mural."

"She's not worth it, Whit. Not worth your career. She's a phone psychic, for God's sake. Do you think she's, at heart, anything more than a con artist?"

"Con artist. That's good coming from you. You're better at working the cocktail party crowd than you are the canvas. It's the only way to explain why anyone would buy your garbage."

She stood. "My paintings hang in the houses of lots of really, really good lawyers around here, Whit. Tell Lucy I won't contest the will if you withdraw from the case and she's willing to share, oh, let's say thirty percent. I won't be greedy."

"You sure won't be, because you're not getting one red cent."

"Now that's up to Lucy to decide," Suzanne said. "Isn't it?"

*   *   *

The people Claudia Salazar had known in her life hovered around her, as though they could step on the waves and not dampen their feet. Her *abuelitas,* one stern, the other smiling. Her parents, her mother chiding her as though the boat she leapt from was the same as a good man: *Why would you leave a perfectly good boat, silly girl?* David reaching a hand down toward her, then vanishing. Whit, with his bad-boy smile he didn't know he had. Ben, sweet, folding his arms around her, letting her rest her head against his shoulder. She knew she was hallucinating, hunger and exhaustion and the salt water she couldn't keep from her mouth in the rolling waves working their toll. Her skin felt like it might slide off her organs, her bones. She had wearied long ago of alternating between treading water, swimming, and waving the electric-red pillow, of riding the waves up and then down again into the swells. The jeans—tied into knots of air pockets—didn't float and she finally let them sink into the emptiness below her. If she thought too long about the water beneath her—its depths, with bull sharks and jellyfish and the dissolved bones of sailors lost long ago—her breath caught in panic. She forced herself to stare at the sky, the vastness above, more comforting than the vastness below. The clouds could not hurt you.

She had tried to swim toward the coast, maintaining a steady pace, but it seemed to grow no closer. She wondered if the distant smudge of coast really was coast, or maybe a trick of the light and the water put there to tease her.

She swam, waved the red pillow, swam some more. She thought she saw a sailboat briefly in the distance but it seemed to vanish in the haze.

You can quit now, a voice she didn't recognize piped up. *It's okay. Just stop. Give up. Sink.*

"Shut up," she croaked through cracked lips.

No shame in lying down. The water is only cold for a while.

Some instinct made her stop for a moment in the chop, wave the little red pillow with leaden arms.

There are things worse than being dead. Better drown yourself before the sharks get ahold of you.

"I won't taste good," Claudia said. She swam again toward the smudge she thought was coast and wondered about Danny. About Ben, if Ben were alive or dead. The sky had been empty of planes and choppers and a cold ripple of grief in her belly, and between her shoulder blades, said, *No one is looking for you. They don't know where to look.*

She figured it was now past noon, and she used the sun as a guide to find west, to swim toward land. She wondered if this was the last time she'd see the sun, felt the hollowing sting in her eyes of having looked at it too much in trying to check her bearings. Maybe the next time the sun rose she would be lost forever under the waves. Bones never found, her flesh broken apart by the salt water, her atoms scattered by the tides over the next century or so. She'd get to Thailand, Australia, India, Sweden, all the places she'd dreamed of traveling, a little bit of her in the grains of sand, in the foaming curl of the surf. *Just let go. Let go. Let...*

"No!" Claudia screamed.

Between her and the ever-distant smudge was a dot, moving, with a crescent of sail. Getting bigger.

She screamed with all her might, rose up out of the water, waving the tattered, sodden red pillow. Waving, waving, waving and screaming her throat raw.

25

LUCY WAS GETTING ready to leave Patch's house, purse in hand, dressed in jeans, a plain white T-shirt, fat-lensed sunglasses, and a baseball cap. Whit pulled up, parked his Explorer to the side so she could move her Chevy out. She opened the car door, tossed in her purse, stood by the car, waiting.

"How was afternoon court?"

"Slow. Glad to finish a little early. Where you going?" he asked.

"A few errands," she said. "I haven't gotten a thing done since Patch died."

"I can do that for you."

She forced a smile. "It's okay. I'd rather go myself. I need to stay busy."

He told her about the conversation with Suzanne. Behind the sunglasses she gave no sign of emotion, but she crossed her arms, tapped her feet in anger.

"Well. What do you want to do?" she said.

"If I recuse myself, the press might make an issue of it. Think that you're more of a suspect than you are. But this is really your decision, Lucy. At least about the will."

"Mine. You mean ours." She gave him a smile, the thin kind that is barely meant. "We're a team, aren't we?"

"Yes."

"Then forget Suzanne. She crossed a line she's never going to be able to step back over."

"Okay."

She gave a sick little laugh. "I have no family left, Whit. Patch and Suzanne were it, and now... I'm not going to be able to forgive her."

"Never say never. She's upset. So are you."

"She's greedy. I hate greed in people. It's corrosive. Did you know that most of the callers at the psychic hotline want to know if they're going to get rich? Or win the lottery?" She shook her head. "They never ask if they're just going to be happy. Find love. That's not enough for people anymore."

"Forget the errands. Let's go inside, just be alone."

"No. It'll be good for me to get out. A little alone time."

"Okay, Lucy. I'll cook us some dinner."

"No need. The church ladies and Patch's friends brought a ton of food. Heat yourself up some dinner. There's salad, too. Open wine if you want. Don't wait on me. I may be out for a while."

He watched her pull out of the driveway. *I have no family left,* she'd said. *I'll be your family, Lucy,* and he nearly laughed, the odd way love kept sneaking up on you.

The fishing cottage was small, on a couple of private acres on the south edge of Laurel Point, fifteen minutes away from Port Leo. It was owned by one of Stoney's widowed clients who lived in San Antonio and rarely bothered with fishing. She'd given him a key a few months ago, asked him to get the real estate appraised, and he'd made and kept a copy for himself.

It was empty, of course, neat as a pin, decorated badly with nautical motifs: starfish light-switch plates, a mobile of crustaceans, fake compasses mounted on the walls like clocks. But very comfortable, a television in the corner, old bourbons and whiskeys in the bar.

"What good is a compass mounted on the wall?" Alex said.

"It's decorative," Stoney said.

"It must be nice to have a house you don't even need."

"The old woman who owns it, her husband invented an important valve on oil pumps. She's so rich she doesn't have to wipe her own nose if she doesn't want to."

Alex had inspected the cottage, took a deep breath, said, "It'll do." The cottage was isolated, quiet, not a place anyone would look for Stoney. Earlier, he'd outlined the plan.

"Sooner or later your brother and his girlfriend are going to be missed. People come looking for them, they want to talk to you. But you're gone. So's your boat. So you're presumed missing, too."

"Like I've been kidnapped?" Stoney said slowly.

"Yeah. At least until we see what's happened. They turn up alive, your brother might not be real thrilled with you since you wouldn't pay and told them to kill his girlfriend."

"I never said that—"

"Listen. But if the gang that kidnapped *them* had operatives that also kidnapped *you*…"

"To get the money they couldn't get before," Stoney said. "Yeah." So he thought for a moment, told Alex about the cottage, and they'd headed over after burying Danny's body in a thick grove of oaks, twelve miles inland. It had been hot, even in the shade, and both men were grimy and sweaty.

Alex washed his face off in the cottage's sink. "Now that I've done the thinking to save you, where's the Devil's Eye?"

"I told you. You can have the rest of the treasure, man. Take it and go with your share. You want to come back when I'm ready to stage the dig on the Gilbert land, help me fake it, that's cool, too. I trust you. And I'll pay you well." Cool confidence in his voice now. He'd killed a man and his hands weren't shaking, his stomach wasn't in knots.

"No. You're telling me now."

"Remember. Anything happens to me, your name surfaces. Immediately."

"Why should I believe that?"

"I managed to take down my investment firm's computer by remote control, Alex. I kept a virus executable file I could run on the servers, one the servers weren't protected against, in case I needed to freeze up my computers, if the Feds wanted to look too close at my records. I don't keep real backups. It's all insurance. I'm just a big believer in it."

"You are pissing me off."

"Tough," Stoney said, feeling tough himself. "I needed insurance you wouldn't off me like Jimmy Bird and I've been very careful about how I set it up. You want to leave with your share of the treasure? Go ahead. But the emerald, it's mine."

Alex stared. Stoney made himself not blink, not move. He thought Alex might say, *Well, screw the Eye,* and just shoot him. Stoney wondered what it would feel like to have the bullet tear into your skin, explode through organs, come out the back. He'd lie there dead until old Mrs. Mayweather in San Antonio decided to go fishing again and showed up at the cottage.

Alex's frown tightened, like he wanted to shoot Stoney but decided not to. Instead of going for his gun, Alex tucked his hands into his pockets.

"I've got some business to attend to," Alex said.

Stoney felt a little shock of pleased surprise; he thought Alex would stick to him like glue. He felt relief at the idea of being alone. Some business? He wondered what that was.

Alex said, "You need to stay out of sight, keep the lights off, don't attract attention here. You've been kidnapped, remember."

"That Whit Mosley saw me. He knows I wasn't kidnapped this morning."

"If he's a problem," Alex said, "I'll handle him."

"You can't go kill a judge..."

"Stoney. There's probably a good marathon on cable. Try the Cartoon Network. Knock yourself out."

After Alex left, Stoney made a phone call, poured a shot of Jack Daniel's, downed it like medicine, lay on the frou-frou pillows of the Mayweather couch, drowsily replaying in his mind killing Danny. It wasn't so bad. He hadn't liked Danny begging for his life; that bothered him, but what was done was done.

He decided he'd rather think about Danny than about Ben. They'd never been particularly close as brothers, especially since Stoney made his money. Not ones to sit and talk about life. He quit thinking about Ben, got comfortable, dozed.

The knock on the door woke him from his drowse, and for a second he thought, *Well, there's Ben, back from fishing.* No. He was in the cottage. Waiting for a friend. Stoney stood, opened the door.

"Come on in," he said.

Lucy Gilbert stepped inside, glanced around. "Are we alone?"

"Yeah," Stoney said. And as soon as he said it she pulled a gun from her purse, a big old revolver that must've been her uncle's, but cleaned and oiled, and she aimed it squarely at his chest.

"You bastard," Lucy said. "You killed them."

"What's this?" He tried to keep an easy tone in his voice. He hadn't expected sweet, ditzy Lucy to be armed.

"You killed Patch and Thuy."

"No, I didn't," he said. Wow, three times today he'd had a gun aimed at him and he nearly laughed, except Lucy looked a little ragged, and the third time might not be the charm. She was far more likely to shoot him. "I didn't kill anyone, Lucy. I called you because I wanted to be sure you were safe."

"I'm supposed to thank you? No one was supposed to get hurt. You were just supposed to dig up the stuff. I sell you my land, you rebury it, end of story."

"I didn't kill them," he said again, "but if you want the guy who did, I can give him to you. But just you. Not the police, though, that'd be a mess for both of us."

"I hate you," Lucy said and the barrel, trained right on his chest, steadied. "Do you know what you might cost me? What you've already taken from me?"

"If you feel so righteous, pick up the phone and call the police. I'll just sit on the couch while you explain to them how you knew who killed your uncle and his girlfriend and didn't lift a finger." He went and sat, crossed his legs.

"Don't think I won't," Lucy said.

"Phone's right there."

He waited; she waited. She lowered the gun, just a bit, down toward his crotch. "Tell me what happened."

Stoney did, quietly, saying how Alex had freaked when Thuy and Patch surprised them as they were finishing the dig, killed them both.

"And who killed Jimmy Bird?"

"Far as I know, he's a suicide." Stoney watched her lower the gun, the barrel pointing at the floor. "I'm not asking any more questions about it. Neither should you."

"This Alex," she said, "does he know about me?"

"He knows you're Patch's niece. He doesn't know we know each other." He cleared his throat. "I'm really sorry about your uncle and his friend, Lucy. Truly I am. No one was supposed to get hurt. If it's comforting, it was very, very quick. They might have been afraid for a moment but it was as painless as could be."

"Painless? He beat Patch's head in with a shovel."

"I know. First blow killed the poor guy. Alex just wanted to be . . . sure."

"That is not comforting to me in the least, Stoney," she said. She sat across from him in the heavy armchair. Closed her eyes. "I can't believe this has happened. This had a bad vibe from the beginning and I ignored it." She opened her eyes. "You've damaged up my aura, Stoney."

"You still have the emerald?"

"Yes."

"Where is it?"

"Safe."

"Alex wants it. He's not going to give up. I told him one lie about where it was, but he didn't buy it."

She gave a little shudder. "Why did you get involved with this guy?"

"A truly legit contract archaeologist wouldn't have agreed to do the dig. Alex did. And he'll do the redig on your land, make all the records and processes look clean." He paused. "You know your boyfriend came to see me."

"Oh, God."

"He knew I'd met Patch those couple of times."

"Oh, God."

"I said Patch was just an acquaintance. He believed me."

"I want you to stay away from Whit," she said.

He got up, sat on the armchair's arm next to her, put his arm around her. She felt good. He liked Lucy, her pert little nose, blue eyes, little barely visible freckles on her cheeks. He'd thought about what it'd be like to bed her, if she ever got over that judge and gave him a real glance.

"It's gonna be okay," he said, patting her. "I sure don't have a thing against him."

She stiffened under his hand. "So now what?"

"Alex might be a problem. Not just for me. For you. Or for your boyfriend," he said. He had to be careful, not panic her overmuch. She might crack and run to Whit or to the police, even if it cost her everything. He ran a thumb along her shoulder blade.

She shrugged his hand off.

"Sorry, just trying to be a help." He leaned back. "I know you're upset—you got every right."

"I don't want you to ever touch me, Stoney. You understand?"

"Sure, Lucy."

"I love Whit."

"I know you do. I'm sorry. I'm just trying to be a friend."

"You let Alex kill my uncle and Thuy and you want to be my friend?"

"I couldn't stop him," he said and then he had an idea, not a bad one at all, to solve his problems. It might work. "Lucy. That gun. You really know how to use it?"

She narrowed her gaze. "Why?"

"Like I said, Alex might be a problem."

"You said you need him for the fake dig."

"Sure. But he's gotten real unpredictable. Maybe if he doesn't want to do the fake dig on your land, just wants to take off, well, he might decide to hurt me. Or you, if he finds out someone else has the Devil's Eye. And he knows Whit talked to me. He might hurt Whit. I don't know."

She stared. "You want me to shoot Alex."

"I want us to be careful, sweetheart. We get through this, we both get what we want. You get your money, you get out of your debts, you get Whit."

"I don't know I want to sell you my land anymore, Stoney. And I think I have Whit—"

"Until he finds out about what you've done. Then he'll be gone, Lucy."

"I want out. This isn't what I signed on for, Stoney."

"Can't, Lucy. Train left the station." He went back to the couch, smiled at her, thinking, *And I will touch you when I please when all this is done.* "I'm not suggesting you kill Alex, Lucy. Clearly not. Just want you to be careful. I mean, he thinks Whit's a threat to him, he's going to come after him. We're kind of pretending that I've been kidnapped right now—"

"What?"

"Just calm down. I don't want to go into the why. But the last person who saw me was your boyfriend. Alex considers him a threat."

Lucy stared at the gun in her lap.

"You know how to use it?" he asked again.

"Patch showed me," she said. "When I was a lot younger."

"Alex is staying at a little motel on the outskirts of Port Leo. The Sandspot. You know it?"

"Yeah."

"Room 133."

She didn't say anything, looked down at her fingers closed around the gun.

"Well, now you know where he's at, sweetheart," Stoney said. "The rest is up to you."

26

---◈---

THE LITTLE PROSTITUTE was sitting on the flying bridge of *Don't Ask,* munching an apple, apparently enjoying the late-afternoon breeze and the shade.

"Where's Gooch?" Whit called as he came aboard.

"He said he had to hunt down someone," Helen Dupuy said.

Hunt down. Not a good sign. "Who?"

"I don't know. He said he'd call in a bit. He said it was okay for me to be here."

She had decided he was an enemy. He sat next to her, kicked his sandals off. "I'm sure it is. You're his guest."

She finished her apple, wiped her hands.

"Do you normally get on planes with men you barely know?"

"That's a really stupid question," she said. She seemed a little less intimidated by him out of the robe. "What do you think?"

"You're either very trusting or you're very naive or—"

"Or maybe I just want to help Gooch get the guy who hurt me."

"Okay."

"You think I'm not good enough to be his friend. I can

tell he told you what I do. You changed the way you look at me."

"Gooch has the widest range of friends of anyone I've ever known."

"He's nice. Really nice."

"When he wants to be. Don't get on his bad side."

"I bet I seen more bad sides than you have."

"So how long are you staying?"

"I don't know. I don't have to rush back."

"You don't have a pimp?"

"I have a manager. Gooch explained to him I had a civic duty to come help."

"Oh, Lord."

"I'm not a streetwalker," she said. She drank from a glass of water. "I got a regular clientele. Blue-collar guys. Most of 'em aren't even married. They just can't afford to spend a ton of money buying drinks for stuck-up girls who won't give 'em none."

"More civic duty."

"You want my help or should I just leave now?"

"I want your help, Helen."

"We talked with Jason Salinger. He didn't have a photo, but my description of Albert and his of Allen Eck are both pretty much dead-on, except for Albert having black hair and Allen having brown. Both of 'em got a little part-moon scar on the corner of their mouths."

"How did you explain to Jason what you wanted to know?"

"Just told him I was your secretary and you needed some more questions answered." And like she was his secretary, she handed him a file. "Here. Gooch and I got on his laptop and went into the back issues site for the *Times-Picayune*. We looked up all the crime stories from between June first and June fourth. And a couple of days each way past that. Gooch said you'd be interested in the top story."

As he started reading she gave him a summary. "Some rich guy up off St. Charles named Danny Mouton. But he goes by the name Danny Laffite, claims to be descended from Jean Laffite—got a history of mental problems, it says. Someone killed his cousin, who was staying at his house. Single shot through the forehead, close range. They don't say the caliber in the paper."

Like Thuy Tran.

"Was this Danny Laffite a suspect?" Jason Salinger had mentioned Danny Laffite, too, the supposed forger kicked out of the Laffite League.

"Nope. Visiting relatives in South Carolina at the time. Place was vandalized pretty heavily, apparently a TV, a VCR missing. A burglar. But Danny Laffite seems to have dropped out of sight afterward."

"No arrests made?" He scanned the rest of the article, and a brief follow-up that was more about the checkered career of Danny Laffite than about the poor cousin, whose name was Phillip Villars.

"No. We printed out all the stories about homicides—there's always more in the summer in New Orleans—but Gooch said he thought only this one mattered." She sipped her water. "Gooch says Alex—that's what I'm calling him now—is a treasure hunter, y'all think, and might have a connection to this Danny Laffite guy."

"Possibly a loose one. They have a mutual acquaintance named Stoney Vaughn."

"So that call Alex got, that he'd offed the wrong guy? Maybe Danny Laffite was supposed to get killed, not his cousin."

"Would you hand me the phone, please?" Whit said.

He dialed 411, asked for a New Orleans listing for Daniel Mouton on First Street. A message said the phone had been disconnected. He clicked off.

A hazy shape was starting to form. But with Jimmy Bird dead by his own hand, would David or anyone else give a crap?

"I'm going below and taking a nap," Helen said. "I had a long night and a long day and I'm tired."

"Helen, thank you." He hesitated. "I want you to know I don't have a thing in the world against you."

Helen Dupuy stood. "I'm real aware I'm not good enough for Gooch. I know it. He doesn't. Maybe you could let me have a couple of nice days before he sees it and gives me a plane ticket home." Then she went belowdecks.

Whit went back to his car and his cell phone rang in his pocket. He answered. Within a minute, he was roaring out of the marina parking lot, speeding toward the Port Leo hospital.

"You look good," Whit said, touching Claudia's hair. Lotion covered her skin, bandages wrapped her hands, an IV dripped into her arm. Her lips were swollen like jelly candies, her face blasted red with sunburn.

"You're the worst liar on the planet. I look like hell. I feel like I ran a marathon. On my knees."

She had spent nearly eight hours in the Gulf, treading water, waving as she told him, "a ridiculous red pillow," until a sailboat with a retired Michigan couple aboard spotted her and pulled her from the water. They'd hurried her into Port Aransas. Even before they reached Mustang Island, she was wrapped in heavy blankets and on the radio with the coast guard, telling them about the kidnapping, giving them details on *Jupiter* and *Miss Catherine,* and saying that Danny was headed to Stoney's house at Copano Flats, off the bay.

"Danny Laffite," Whit said.

"But his boat didn't make it. Apparently it sank earlier in the day, a bit off the Flats. No sign of Danny. And no one is at Stoney's house. They've sent people looking for him."

"I saw him today." Whit let go of her hand, sat on the edge of her bed. When he'd arrived she'd scooted her hovering parents out and asked a worried David to give them a moment's privacy, which had been granted with a frown but not an argument. She'd been talking with the coast guard command, the sheriff's office, and the FBI had been summoned in from the Corpus Christi satellite office.

"Why?" she asked.

He told her the complete story then, all of it, from the discovery of Patch's and Thuy's bodies, the links he kept finding between Stoney Vaughn and Patch, the connection to the Laffite League, Triple A, and Helen Dupuy, the murder a month ago at Danny Laffite's house, the suicide of Jimmy Bird and the coins found in his pocket, his theory about a treasure dig.

She told him Danny's story. Whit sat.

"It's David's case," he said. "I wasn't sure there was enough evidence about these connections...but based on what you've said—"

"We need to find Stoney Vaughn. Find Ben." She closed her eyes. "Danny and his thugs were demanding ransom for us right after the kidnapping. At least, as of this morning, Stoney thought Danny had his brother. Which suggests to me that Stoney paid no ransom or the redhead—Danny says his name is Zack—never picked up the ransom."

David stuck his head back into the room. "Pardon me, Whit, but we need to talk to her some more."

"Actually," Claudia said, "we all need to talk."

An hour later, Claudia said good-bye to Whit, gave a feeble wave.

David watched him go. "I mean, you and him, you can just take the case yourselves."

"David, no one could know that it was a much more involved case than anyone—" she started, but he was mad, his skin flushed.

"You're both gonna make me look like an utter fool. All this other stuff, it still doesn't change the fact that Jimmy Bird killed himself, left a suicide note pretty much admitting he killed Gilbert and Tran. The FBI's handling the kidnapping. They'll take it from me quick, and if all this is mixed up together, the Feds'll take that case from me, too. What the hell am I supposed to do, Claudia?" He stared at her, wobbled on his feet. "You could have been killed."

"I'm okay. I'm okay, David."

He sat down on the edge of the bed.

"Find Stoney. Find Ben. Stoney Vaughn seems to be the driving force of all this mess. Y'all find him—he's the key to this whole case."

He nodded. It was like they were still married, she thought. He knew what to do on a tough case but he had trouble delving to the heart of the matter, letting himself get distracted too easily. "Stoney Vaughn. Yes, you're right."

He went and poured them each a cup of ice water. He brought her hers; she wasn't so thirsty now, with the IV hydrating her, but she took a sip on her sore lips.

"I need some more information from you if we're to find

your...boyfriend." He said the last like he had a roach in his mouth.

"David," she said gently, "this clearly upsets you. Why don't you let me talk to another investigator?"

"It doesn't upset me."

She let it be.

He sat on the edge of the bed, had a notebook out but didn't open it.

"What else did you want to know?"

"Um..."

"Because I'm exhausted, David. I'm really, really exhausted. I'd like to get some sleep."

"Sure." He stood. "Sure. I'll be back soon. You rest." And awkwardly, he leaned down and kissed her forehead, quickly, chastely.

She watched him step out of the room.

Tomorrow. Tomorrow she'd be out of the hospital. She'd check herself out, help in the search for Ben and Stoney. The FBI, she knew, would be poring over the Vaughn house, looking for *Jupiter* up and down the Texas coast.

Maybe Ben still breathed. She'd find him if he did. And if he didn't, she'd find the bastards who'd killed him.

She fell asleep.

27

THE ELDERLY COUPLE had lived near Encina Pass for nearly seventy years, close to the bay, in an old, small house made of heavy cypress. When the knock came on the door both were nearly asleep, having dozed off during a particularly boring cable movie. The old woman nearly jumped out of her skin with fright, touched the rollers in her hair in case one had worked loose. The old man rose from his recliner, and answered the door.

The young man standing on the front stoop was sopping wet, with a heavy bruise marring his nose and cheekbones, like he'd been in a crash, smelling of the bay, shivering in the night heat, a broken pair of handcuffs dangling from his wrist. One finger was purpled, clearly broken.

"Could you—could you please call the police?" the young man stammered. "My name is Ben Vaughn and I was kidnapped by some crazy people. I think they killed my girlfriend."

Alex Black returned to his motel room Friday night, tired, frazzled, in need of a shower. He stood in the shower's hot spray for nearly twenty minutes until the water began to cool. He scrubbed soap hard into his skin and scalp until his body tingled. Then he toweled off with a vengeance, put on shorts and a T-shirt.

His cell phone rang. He picked it up, glanced at the readout. His father, calling from south Florida. At least it wasn't that idiot Stoney, him he couldn't deal with any more tonight.

"Hello?"

"Hey, son, how are you?" Big Bert's voice was dry with cancer, but optimistic, like always.

"You chasing the ladies tonight? Taking a breather to call me?" It was an old game between them, pretending an active romantic life was barreling ahead at full steam. Suddenly Alex's throat felt thick.

"I chase 'em but they run faster'n me these days." A pause. "Sure would like to see you soon."

"Probably another few days," he said. "I'll be there soon."

"Dig keeping you busy?"

"Client's a big pain, but it's okay."

A dry click in his father's throat. "Find anything interesting?"

"Well, not as interesting as gold," Alex said, trying to cheer the old man up.

"What you getting?" Big Bert asked.

"Pottery shards, bones, arrowheads."

"Not much junk to keep you from your old man."

Alex didn't like his tone. Not telling something, skirting an issue. "You feeling okay?"

His father gave a soft burp and Alex figured one of Big Bert's friends had sneaked him beer into the hospice again. "Don't you get thrown out of All Saints, having a party."

"That was from a Pepsi, thank you kindly."

"I'm glad you're feeling okay," Alex said.

"I never said I was."

"Well. Okay. I got to go, Dad. I got an early, early morning."

"Yeah. You got pottery shards calling your name."

"Okay then. I'm gonna be there soon. Promise."

"Don't take too long."

What did that mean? "Dad. Are you worse?"

"I just want to see you soon. Good-bye, son. I love you."

"Yeah, back at you." He did not want to think of his father wasting away in a hospice bed, the cancer he'd ignored for too long seeping through his body like rot. Big Bert belonged on a boat, diving for galleon treasure, hauling up lost Spanish coins. But always just to have Florida bureaucrats snatch them out of his hands. Bureaucrats had ruined him slowly with promises while breaking him on the rack of their antiquity laws. *Here, go get yourself an ice cream,* Big Bert would say to Alex as a little boy, handing him a piece of eight from 1690 or a doubloon from 1712. *Knock yourself out with a double scoop.* Funny, yes, but then the state government would take most of the gold, the IRS would sniff around Big Bert's boat, squatters would try to maneuver their boats over his dive spots, the treasure would be nibbled away by a thousand grasping hands more clever than good-natured Big Bert's.

His way was better, Alex knew, but he didn't want to discuss it with Big Bert. Let his father think he still scrabbled through the loam for pottery and beads and junk. He'd sell much of the treasure quick. He'd go to that hospice—such a nice crisp word for a death place—grab Big Bert, fly off to Costa Rica. Let him die in blue splendor under a bright, forgiving sun. Die happy.

*Every day you waste with Stoney is a day you don't have
with your dad.* Tomorrow he'd get it sorted out. Find the
Eye, eliminate Stoney. Screw Stoney's threats of posthu-
mous exposure. He was tired of this game. He needed his
money, he needed it now. He'd made new identities before,
he could do it again. No one in Costa Rica would bother
him. And he could stay there forever.

Alex clicked on the television, waited for the ten o'clock
news out of Corpus Christi. First story was a dramatic hostage standoff at a church in Dallas, two people killed. Then
the news was all Port Leo: a boat wreck in St. Leo Bay, a
Port Leo police officer rescued from out in the Gulf, Ben
Vaughn's face on the screen as a kidnapping victim. Then
Stoney's face, also described as possibly missing. At the
least the authorities wanted to ensure he was well, considering his brother had been kidnapped.

Claudia Salazar was alive. But there were no other
details offered, no mention of a connection to the deaths
at Black Jack Point. At the end of the newscast the pearl-
toothed anchor broke in to say that Ben Vaughn had been
found in Encina Pass, alive and well, no details yet on his
missing brother, financier Stoney Vaughn.

He picked up his cell phone, called Stoney at the fishing
cottage.

"Your brother's alive," Alex said. "Congratulations."

"I just saw on the news." Stoney's voice sounded a little
funny. Like he was surprised to hear from him. "Where
you at?"

He suddenly didn't like the question. "Just around.
Keeping a close eye on you."

"So how long do I need to lie low? I can't stay holed up
here forever."

"I suppose that depends on what your brother says," Alex said. "He accuses you of anything, you're screwed."

"Ben would never do that to me."

"You just screwed him over royally, Stoney. You might have lost that old brotherly love."

"Ben's not like that."

"You mean he's a better person than you," Alex said. "I think you want to stay there a couple more days, Stoney. Let them get good and worried about you. Maybe we'll make a fake ransom demand to your brother, just for show. Then you can crop up, no worse for wear." *Yeah, right, dream on.* "I'll call you tomorrow. Stay low."

"I will."

Alex got up, packed his bag. He liked knowing where Stoney was but didn't like Stoney knowing where he was. He checked out of the Sandspot, drove across town to a smaller motel, the Surfside—did every coastal hotel have to have an S in the title?—checked in, got settled.

On the way over Alex didn't notice the little Chevy, gold and violet and amber crystals dangling from the rearview mirror, following him.

28

WHIT AWOKE EARLY Saturday morning, Lucy shaking his shoulder. She still hadn't been home when he returned from the hospital, but he was exhausted. So he ate a sandwich, curled in under the sheets, felt her arrive next to him and spoon into him, felt her kiss on the back of his neck, and fell back asleep.

"Phone call," she whispered into his ear. He hadn't even heard the phone ring. "Guy sounds like he's squeezing coal into diamonds using his ass."

Whit picked up the phone, listened, said, "Uh-huh" and "Okay" a couple of times, hung up, rolled under the covers.

"Who was that?"

"The FBI."

"The FBI?" Lucy's voice rose an octave.

"Hoover doesn't run it anymore. You don't have to be afraid." He wriggled his face deeper into the pillow. "They want to talk to me about Stoney Vaughn. I guess I really was one of the last to see him before he vanished, or took off, or whatever." He told her a highly abbreviated—and edited—version of Claudia's kidnapping. He sighed as she ran her hand along his back.

"What do they think happened to this guy?"

"I don't know. Maybe the kidnappers that took his brother went after him." He didn't want to talk about Danny Laffite or Gooch's trip or any of the rest of it with her. Lucy couldn't keep her mouth shut, he thought, and all of it might upset her needlessly. He rolled over onto his back.

"So was this Stoney guy involved in Patch's murder or what, Whit?" She was whispering into his ear, running a hand along the flat of his belly. "I thought it was Jimmy Bird."

"Stoney knew your uncle. That was the only reason I went to see him. His brother's kidnapping, it may have nothing to do with your uncle's death."

She ran fingernails along his ribs; he loved that. He wriggled and smiled. "No time, babe. I got to get showered for the Feds."

"Okay," she said.

He opened an eye, looked at her. "You okay?"

"Yes, I'm fine. Tired."

"Your errands took a long time."

"No, I got back and you were gone. So I ate a quick dinner and then went back over to my apartment, to get some fresh clothes."

"Okay." He got up from the bed, started up the shower.

"Whit?" Lucy stood in the doorway, in a T-shirt and thin little white panties.

"Yeah, babe?"

"You're doing an inquest, what, next week?"

"Tuesday."

"Why, if it was Jimmy Bird? He's dead."

"It's just a formality, I guess. And maybe by Tuesday we'll know more. But I don't think he acted alone. That might be where David and I differ."

"David's the cop, though, hon."

"That he is." Whit shucked his boxers, stepped into the hot spray. "An inquest is just a format for determining if one person caused the death of the other. If I put it on Jimmy, it still doesn't explain the why of what happened."

She kept standing in the bathroom, watching him shower.

"You find any insurance on those coins?" he asked.

"I haven't had time to look," she said, and as he shampooed, he heard a brief flash of anger in her voice. "Maybe they weren't Patch's. I really don't know. Could I look at the coins?"

"I'll see what I can arrange. I didn't mean to piss you off."

"Conflict is bad for your aura, Whit. You're basically a peaceable guy. I get a bad vibe from you as long as this investigation is going on."

Whit rinsed his hair.

"You're not saying anything smart back to me," Lucy said.

"You said conflict was bad for me, baby."

"I know you don't believe in my psychic powers. That's okay. You're scientific in nature and we don't have the imaging technologies to show auras like I wish we did. You could get it done like getting a CAT scan."

"Lucy, if you say you're psychic, I believe you. Because I love you. End of story."

She said nothing and he finished washing and when he turned off the water she was standing there, sobbing quietly.

"Baby," he said.

"I'm such a big fake. I don't see auras. I don't see the future. I get hunches, like any other person, and that's it."

"Well, I never get a hunch, so you're ahead of me."

"But I'm a fake. How can you love a fake? I don't say it's the Intuitive Hunch Hotline." She pulled toilet paper off the roll, dabbed her eyes, blew her nose.

"Lucy." Whit wrapped a towel around his waist. "You're not a fake. You're like, well, a counselor without a license. Like I'm a judge without a law degree."

"You were elected. You don't need one."

"People elect to call you, get a little tarot, get a little advice." He pulled her close, gave her a warm peck on the mouth.

"I want to get out of the hotline business," she said. "I want to make you proud."

"I'm proud of you," he said. "Love you just as you are."

"You're not proud of me, Whit," she said.

"I am."

"No."

"Trust me, I am," he said, toweling off, rummaging in the little duffel bag he'd brought. He found boxers, stepped into them, found a shirt, electric-yellow with sashaying red crabs dancing across it. Pulled on khakis and stepped into his sandals.

"Don't wear that to meet the FBI," she said. "Wear a suit."

"You're putting me in a crabby mood," he said with a smile.

"Whit. Don't joke. I'm serious. I don't want to be an embarrassment to you."

"Is this about Suzanne?"

"No. Me."

"Whatever you want to do, I'll support. You want to keep the psychic hotline? Great. You don't want to do it anymore? Great. But you could never be an embarrassment to me." He waved the shirt in front of her, slipped it on, began to button it. "Way more likely I'll embarrass you."

"I think you're wrong," Lucy said quietly.

They kept him waiting twenty minutes, and as far as he could see—from the chair in Stoney Vaughn's expansive living room—the two federal agents were just sitting and talking, drinking Stoney Vaughn's coffee and not offering him a cup, making incessant short calls on their cell phones. He wondered—no, he knew. David had already talked to these men, painted an unkind picture of Whit, and that was why he was thumb-twiddling.

When one started a refill Whit got up and stood in the kitchen. "Excuse me. Saturday may be your day to suck down hazelnut, but I have work to do. Either y'all talk to me now or make an appointment with my office."

They both looked at him like he had a big streak of piss down his pants but one smiled and the other one pulled out a chair at Stoney Vaughn's kitchen table. Whit thought maybe Lucy was right that he should have worn the suit, and that made him even madder. But he sat.

They both had G names: Grimes and Gordell. Whit immediately dubbed them the G Men. Grimes was muscular and spare, all throat and shoulders and arm muscles with skin the color of teak. Gordell was chunkier, not fat, wide-set and blocky. Grimes had a Southern drawl; Gordell spoke with the nasal clip of New England. The G Men wore suits, nice, summer-weight blends, still far too hot for the Texas coast in July. Whit's shirt seemed to irritate Agent Gordell like a thumbtack in his seat; he kept glancing at it in disbelief.

"Judge Mosley," Grimes said in his slow, friendly cadence, "you visited Mr. Vaughn yesterday?"

They always had to waste time asking what they already knew. "Yes. In conducting an inquest into a double homicide this past week I found that there was a slight connection between Stoney Vaughn and one of the victims. I wanted to ask Mr. Vaughn about it, so I came out here yesterday morning about eight-thirty. Mr. Vaughn looked like death warmed over, like he'd slept in his clothes, and I could smell whiskey on him. His lip looked split."

"Like maybe he'd had a stressful evening?"

"He certainly didn't mention his brother and Claudia had been kidnapped. He knew, didn't he?"

"We're not at liberty to discuss that. Judge." Grimes added the title with an embarrassed smile, like it was an afterthought. Like they even knew for sure.

"Claudia Salazar's an old friend of mine. We work homicides together. I wouldn't take it well if Stoney knew she was in danger and didn't help her."

The G Men smiled politely. What he took well mattered not a bit.

"But there had already been a suspect identified in this double homicide, right?" Gordell said. "A suicide."

"As coroner, I haven't officially ruled that death a suicide yet," Whit said.

"And you just decided, what, the sheriff's office was wrong and you'd keep pressing other angles?" Gordell said. "A little presumptuous, wouldn't you say?"

David must have poured on the charm. "I don't believe I have to justify my actions to you, sir," Whit said politely.

"Excuse me?" Gordell said. Grimes glanced up from jotting on a legal pad, his face blank.

"Excuse me . . . Your Honor," Whit corrected. He smiled.

"Your Honor," Gordell amended. He didn't look repen-
tant for one second. "No offense meant."

"Meant. Taken. Whatever," Whit said. "If I feel addi-
tional information is warranted for an inquest, I go get that
information."

"You're not a lawyer, are you? I mean, you're not one of
those judges that's required to be formally trained in the
law," Gordell said with polite snideness.

"No, I'm not a lawyer. I'm an elected official."

An unpleasant light glinted in the back of Gordell's eyes.
"I'm sure the voters might take offense at you not cooperating with the FBI."

"How have I not cooperated?"

"Cocky. You don't see that much in politicians," Gordell
said.

"Jim," Grimes said, a little weary.

"You didn't answer my question," Whit said.

"Let's not get into a turf war, Judge Mosley. You'll lose
and lose badly. We ask the questions. You answer them."

Whit counted to ten. "It's good I came here yesterday,
as I can tell you Stoney Vaughn was alive and well then. If
he's been kidnapped since then, or he's run off, at least I've
narrowed the time frame considerably for you."

"Thank you," Grimes said.

"What I'd like to know is why," Whit said.

"Why what?" Gordell said.

"Why were Ben and Claudia kidnapped?"

"Mr. Vaughn is a wealthy man."

"Mr. Stoney Vaughn is. Mr. Ben Vaughn isn't."

"They thought Stoney was aboard."

"Why did they think that? They knew his schedule?"

"We don't know yet, Judge." Grimes cleared his throat.

"Quite possible the perps have been watching the house, waiting for his boat to go out. Maybe they just assumed his boat's out, he's out on it."

"So. Stoney Vaughn has a vague connection to my murder case, and he gets smack-dab in the middle of a kidnapping. Now he's gone. It just doesn't seem coincidence to me."

"You're the one on this buried treasure kick, right?" Gordell said.

"I prefer to think of it as archaeological relics," Whit said. "This whacked-out supposed treasure hunter, Albert Exley or Allen Eck or Alex, I want y'all to find out who this guy is."

Grimes's lips tightened. "We're appreciative of the information you gave Officer Salazar and to the other local authorities. But please understand, these various threads that may tie to a case, those are for us to sort out and prioritize, Your Honor."

"Let me tell you why this matters. This Alex, this certifiable nutcase, was in New Orleans when Danny Laffite's cousin got murdered. He put a poor woman through a window because she might have heard someone telling him he 'got' the wrong guy. I think Danny Laffite had been in touch with Stoney Vaughn in the weeks before, trying to cut a deal to finance a dig for this treasure. But Stoney got greedy and sent Alex to steal Danny's evidence about the treasure and to kill Danny. Only Alex killed the wrong person at Danny's house. Danny must have phoned Stoney after the New Orleans break-in, and Stoney freaked at the thought Danny was still alive." He stopped, looked at the two agents. "So if I were you, I'd be looking really hard at Stoney Vaughn's phone records. See if he called the Bayou Mee Motel in New Orleans. See if he had incoming calls from New Orleans or from South Carolina, where Danny Laffite was when his cousin got killed."

"We've heard this is your style," Gordell said. "Not sticking to your judicial duties." But Grimes was looking at him, head tilted slightly, with interest.

"You shouldn't listen to rumors," Whit said. "Has there been a ransom demand made for Stoney?"

"Thank you for coming by, Judge Mosley." Gordell stood, didn't offer a hand to shake.

"I'm thinking Stoney didn't want to pay five million. Did he not have it? Maybe y'all are checking his finances, finding some holes . . . I could see him taking off."

"Judge—" Grimes blinked at him, like he couldn't believe the words.

"I wouldn't buy a single share of a penny stock from that guy. And he had someone in the house here with him, I'm pretty sure."

"Did you see someone?" Gordell asked.

"No. But I felt watched. Stoney didn't want me in the house. I asked him to lend me a book and he said no, he didn't have one, looked back three times at the windows in a twenty-second period."

"But you didn't see anyone."

"No, I didn't. But there was a beige van here that's not here anymore. A Chrysler, I think. I didn't notice the license plates." And that made him feel stupid, that if he'd been so suspicious he should have made a note of it. "I don't think Stoney Vaughn has acted alone in this, and I think this Alex guy may be helping him. We have a description of him. We want people to be looking for him, too."

"That's fine," Grimes said. "Give us the info, we'll see if there's anything to it."

"Thank you, Judge," Gordell said. "We'll call you if—"

"Since I've answered your questions while you've looked at me like I was a urine sample," Whit said, "maybe you'll defrost slightly and help me. I'd like to speak with Ben Vaughn, and I'm guessing he's under your protection at the moment."

"Speak with him why?"

"For the inquest into the Gilbert/Tran murders."

"He's recuperating. Probably not up to questioning," Gordell said. He stood, signaling the interview was complete. "And we have certainly not treated you like a urine sample, sir." He gave Grimes a glance: *This is a judge?*

"I just need five minutes with him."

"We'll ask him for you," Grimes said after a moment's hesitation.

"Thank you," Whit said and stood.

"Judge Mosley," Gordell said, "I understand you're a big fish in a little pond here. But we think for a second you're interfering or messing around with us, you'll be the small-town magistrate in front of a federal magistrate. You understand me, sir?"

"I understand you, sir," Whit said. "And if you don't take me seriously and follow up on this Alex guy, I'm going to call every television station in Corpus Christi, Houston, and San Antonio and tell them that the FBI is purposely ignoring findings presented by the Encina County coroner. Me." Whit smiled. "It may only be news for a few minutes. But it'll be news."

Gordell's mouth worked like he had a bee lodged in his gums.

29

CLAUDIA SAW BEN Saturday morning, after the FBI and the police had questioned him further. A guard stood outside his door, watching the nurses. She came into his room and he opened his eyes. He looked pale, a thick bruise on his face, his dark hair little-boy tousled on the pillow.

"Thank God," Ben said and she came to the bed, crawled in next to him, hugged him. He hugged back, winced a little.

"Are you hurt? They said you were okay . . ."

"The ribs, a little, but not bad." His voice was throaty. "Face hurts. I'm glad you're okay. Gar said he was going to—"

"He didn't. Danny shot him."

"That's what your ex told me."

"You spoke with David?" She sat up.

"Yeah," Ben said. "I mean, he questioned me last night. For about an hour, around three in the morning or so, once they really couldn't find Stoney anywhere."

"Please be kidding. He didn't."

"Sure. Claudia, it's fine. If it helps them find my brother."

"Did David behave?"

"Perfect gentleman."

"That's somehow worse." She touched his chest. "Tell me what happened. Everything."

"Gar...was furious about not getting the money. He said he was going to rape you. The other guy—"

"His name is Zack," she said.

"Zack, then. He freaked. I wanted to reason with him, tell him to call Gar off, but he belted me across the face with his gun." He touched at the livid bruise on his battered nose, his cheek. "When I woke up he had me tied and handcuffed in the forward cabin's head."

"Where did he take you?"

"I think in circles. He didn't know much about boats, sweetie," Ben said. "Then he panicked, tried to call Danny on his boat, didn't get an answer."

"Danny never mentioned that. He told me Zack would probably kill you."

"The moron probably couldn't operate the radio right. Asking on the wrong channels. But he did figure out the phone. I heard him make a call, asking someone to come and get him, he was stuck out on the Gulf in a big boat he couldn't drive with a hostage. Crying about his boyfriend, cussing Stoney for not being on the boat and it all going down wrong. You would've thought his car had broken down and he was calling roadside assistance."

"But Zack left Gar. He cut the lines."

"I don't think so, Claudia. From what I heard, I think Gar cut those. To keep his boyfriend from interfering with him going after you."

Claudia let out a long breath. "So someone came and rescued him?"

"Not exactly. He told me he'd gotten the boat in close to shore and he didn't know how to drop the anchor but he was gonna swim in. Said all this to me through the closed door of the head. I kept thinking, he's gonna open it up, shoot me. Then he says he doesn't want to face a murder charge. Says he'll let me be if I just say Gar and Danny were behind it all, maybe do him a favor, not mention him. I'm saying, sure, not a problem. Thinking he's just going to shoot me when it comes time for him to leave. But then he was gone. I didn't hear another boat draw close, and I started hoping, he didn't set the anchor, we might be drifting into the Intracoastal. I was hoping to be a threat to navigation. It'd mean people found me."

"How'd you get out of the handcuffs?"

"I found a little wrench under the sink. Had to pull it to me with my toes. Stoney probably left it there the last time he fixed a faucet. He never puts up his stuff. So I used it to hammer the lock, finally broke it, and while I'm trying, *Jupiter* went aground. I'm sweating bullets. I'm thinking, am I sinking? I smash the cuffs, get out, see that I've run aground on a little oyster-shell beach, on a little strip of island not far off the Intracoastal. I could see a freighter in the distance, heading down toward Corpus. Zack tore all the wires out of the satellite phone and the radio. I was so ready to be off that boat, thinking maybe you could still be rescued. I just got into the water and swam. Halfway to shore I'm thinking, maybe I could have stayed on the boat, set off a flare. I was just mental. Reached Encina Pass." He squeezed her. "Claudia. I thought for sure…"

"I know." She kissed him then, and he was gentle, like he couldn't quite believe she was there.

He let the kiss linger and then said, "My brother."

"They'll find him." She sat up. "I want to talk to you about your brother."

"Zack. Or his friends. They must have gone after Stoney for the money."

"Your brother knew we had been kidnapped, Ben. He didn't call the police. He didn't tell anyone."

"They said they would kill us, Claudia."

"Did he or did he not refuse to pay ransom?"

Ben's mouth worked. "My brother wouldn't do that to us."

"Danny said the next morning that Stoney had agreed to a trade, thinking you were with Danny and me. So I'm assuming he hadn't paid a ransom the day before."

"Stoney said his computer systems were down, he couldn't do the transfer. Claudia, my brother's not some cold-blooded monster. You can't believe this of him."

"I know you love your brother, Ben…"

"You heard him, didn't you? You heard him repeat back the account numbers for the transfer, Claud. But he didn't have this imaginary emerald that Danny wanted. Danny was nuts, you know that."

"Yes," she said softly. "But your brother didn't call the police. At any point."

"The kidnappers took him before he could."

"A judge—my friend Whit Mosley—saw him Friday morning at his house. Looking like hell. What if there's no virus, Ben? He didn't want to move the five million…"

"No. He couldn't move the money. He must've been waiting to hear from the kidnappers again. Zack's friends grabbed him. It's the best explanation. You don't believe what Danny said, do you?"

"I honestly don't know what to think about Stoney."

"My brother—" Ben's voice broke.

"If I'm wrong, I'm sorry. I hope I'm wrong."

"Stoney loves me."

She said nothing.

"He was afraid they would hurt us if he called the police." Trying to convince himself, convince her.

"Ben, Gar knew I was a cop. He called me *Officer*."

Ben stared down at the sheets covering his lap.

"Did you tell them I was a cop?"

"No."

"Did your brother?"

"I don't want to talk about this anymore, please. My brother isn't a bad guy, Claudia. We don't know the truth yet." He moved slightly away from her on the bed.

He was too deep in denial. "I care about you," she said. "I don't want you hurt." He didn't look at her and she felt the little gap grow. "Ben..."

He let go of her hand; she took his hand in answer, squeezed hard.

"Don't say these things about my brother."

"Okay," she said. "You need your rest." She kissed his forehead. "I'm going to go for a while so you can sleep, all right? You need sleep."

Ben said nothing and she went to the door.

"Claudia?" Ben's voice, small, low.

"Yeah?"

"If he didn't refuse to pay the ransom...they came and took him, didn't they? They just don't give up on five million, not when there's another option to get it."

"I hope not, Ben."

"I mean, did he not think we were worth five million? He could have made it back in a few years, the way he worked, the deals he cut. I mean, I'm his brother."

"Maybe they took him, Ben." Odd, her tone of hoping

that a guy got kidnapped, that it could be a remotely positive thing.

"But if he can't get to his money," Ben said, "won't they kill him?"

Ben was staying at the hospital, at least through the day. Claudia, tired but hating the sterile walls and wanting her own bed, checked herself out around noon. Her mother, Tina, accompanied her home, fussing the whole way, fluffing pillows, fixing a pan of chicken enchiladas and a plate of chocolate chip cookies that Claudia uncharacteristically had no appetite for. Claudia went to go lie down on her bed, trying not to think about how Stoney could betray Ben so completely. She was still exhausted and she catnapped, loving the feel of her own pillows, sheets, the solidity of the bed. She didn't like thinking about the water, with nothing but the depths beneath her feet.

A knock on the door woke her; Tina entered with a thick envelope. "Something from work. The officer said you asked for it. Sweetie, I don't want you working, tiring yourself out."

"That's okay, Mama." Claudia sat up. "Put it on the bed. I'll look at it in a minute."

Her mother did, doused the lights again.

Claudia waited. Mama was exhausted, worn out from staying up most of the night fretting over her. Fifteen minutes later she glanced into the small den. Tina Salazar lay on the couch, snoring softly. Claudia covered her with a light blanket, went back to her room, and opened the file. She'd asked the Port Leo PD to get her what they could find from the New Orleans PD on Danny Laffite and his suspected associates in the kidnapping. She began to read.

*   *   *

Alex had stayed away from Stoney for the morning, sleeping a little later in his new, no-better motel room, dreaming
of his dad, the two of them diving for treasure in the shallow waters off the Keys. He hadn't slept well; someone had
knocked on his door at some point near midnight, waking
him instantly, and he'd crept to the door with his gun in
hand, finally peering through the peephole. No one there.
He could hear teenagers laughing down the hall—probably
just kids. But it unsettled his sleep and he didn't go back for
a while, wondering how to best get his sick father to Costa
Rica without attracting too much attention.

He got up, showered, dressed, turned on the local Saturday morning TV news. All Stoney—the missing financier.
Nothing on Danny Laffite, though, nothing on the murders
at Black Jack Point. But still. He needed to get moving.
And he needed to take some precautions.

He drove the van over to the big grocery near the Port
Leo harbor. It was a chain superstore, an H-E-B, the mega-
chain in Texas, and the store was pink. Coral pink, the
whole building, like all they sold was Pepto-Bismol. He
slipped on sunglasses and a Marlins cap and went inside—
it was busy, full of retirees and young babies, families,
Mexicans, Vietnamese, Anglos, sunburned Yankees asking where the juice was in their nasal whines. He bought
some doughnuts, a coffee, a small milk, and a box of hair
coloring. Time for a change. Go punkish blond, cut the
hair short, dump the van at the Corpus airport. The cashier
looked a little funny at him, a guy buying blond hair coloring, but bagged it up with the food and took his money.

Alex was halfway across the parking lot when he saw
Helen Dupuy.

She was walking toward the store just out of a truck—
an old beat-up red truck, walking with a monster of a guy.
Big-built, freak-ugly face, military burr of dark hair. And
he thought she might have seen him, just two rows over, if
she hadn't been looking up all goggle-eyed at this freak.

Can't be Helen, he thought, and he took a hard left,
heading away from his car, stepping behind an SUV, peering at her. Maybe not Helen. It couldn't be her. The two
of them walked into the grocery, now forty feet ahead of
him, and he turned and followed them, thinking, *No way
it's her, no way.*

He kept his sunglasses and his cap on as he entered the
store, scanned the register lines, the crowd of shoppers
going their separate ways into the aisles. Didn't see them.
He looked to his left, over at the bakery section clogged
with morning pastry buyers, and saw them, the guy pulling
Helen through the maze of carts and screaming kids and
tables of pies and doughnuts. He followed, hanging back,
trying to keep at an angle where the woman couldn't see
him. It *was* Helen. She was wearing a halter, a plain blue
one, not slutty—it was a hot morning. Above the top of the
halter on her back was a discolored hatch of lines, the scars
he must've put on her skin when he flung her through the
glass window.

Big Ugly and Helen stopped, a round-faced man greeting Big Ugly with a call of "Gooch!" Big Ugly starting to
chat, introducing Helen to the old man. Now ten feet away,
Helen's back still to him, Alex stood at the corner of the
aisle where the bakery fed into the beer-and-wine section,
trying to hear.

The old man must've been part deaf or just one of those
old guys who likes to talk loud. Alex heard him say: "You

take me out next week. I got two buddies from Dallas want
to come down and get tight lines. You open on Wednesday
morning?"

"Might be busy, let me check." Big Ugly had a low rumble of a voice.

Two kids arguing over a chocolate doughnut passed,
their mother chiding them, and he missed what was said
but then Big Ugly—Gooch?—said, "I got a hot spot for red
drum, over on the south side of the bay. I'll take you there,
but you got to keep it secret, Fred."

Fred roared. "Yeah, I'm your man for keeping secret
fishing spots. I call you tomorrow, we set it up? And think
about where maybe we land some big tarpon?"

"Fine," Big Ugly said.

A fishing guide, Alex thought. He heard the conversation
end, held his breath, glued to the floor, waiting for Helen
and this Gooch to turn into the beer-and-wine section and
see him. Ten seconds. He risked a glance around the corner. They had moved past the baked goods, Helen holding a
big bag of bagels, moving off into the milk and dairy, sticking close to Gooch, turning to smile up at him. He knew
the line of her jaw, the slant of her smile. Her.

What to do? Suddenly the huge grocery store felt
cramped as a cell. He moved past the registers, out into the
lot. He hurried back to his car, scrambled inside.

How? Think it through. Someone made a connection to Helen Dupuy and brought her to Port Leo, how,
who...Jimmy Bird. Jimmy had called him twice at that
motel when he was in New Orleans, in his room, nervous
about the several nights they planned to spend on Patch's
land, searching with the metal detectors to find the buried
cache. Giving him the motel number in New Orleans was

a mistake. Jimmy dead, his phone records must have been searched for some reason. Found the calls to his room at the Bayou Mee. Why would a fishing guide bring Helen to Port Leo?

He fumbled for his cell phone, dialed Stoney at the fishing cottage. "There's a whore I met in New Orleans here. At the freaking grocery, Stoney."

"So?"

"So I met her when I was taking care of Danny. She knows what I look like."

"Get rid of her."

"She's got a six-six musclebound bodyguard with her. I think he's a local fishing guide."

"You must've made a mistake."

"She slept with me nine times in four days," Alex said. "I know what she looks like, man."

"What exactly do you want me to do about it, Alex?"

"Don't take that tone with me."

"I got my own problems. They have got my picture all over the news this morning. What Ben must think of me."

"Like you care."

"He's my brother."

"But he was too heavy, wasn't he, Stoney?"

"You're not funny," Stoney said.

"If I were your brother I'd shoot you in the knees for what you did," Alex said. "I'm coming over there. I got a couple things I need to do, but I'll be there soon."

He hung up, weighed the options. Run. The mess had gotten deeper; it was now time to get out of the entire situation. He thought about following this Gooch and Helen—and risk she'd see him? She might be even more dangerous than Stoney. No, it was too much right now; he needed to act but go on the defensive. He waited, saw them return to the truck, holding cups of coffee and a small plastic bag. They pulled out of the lot, drove down the street past the harbor to the curve of Port Leo Beach. He followed, four cars behind. Big Ugly's truck turned in, parked. Alex drove by, did a U-turn, drove by again. Big Ugly and Helen walked to one of the picnic tables near the beach, sat down, pulled bagels out of the bag, a little plastic knife, cream cheese. A breakfast picnic by the bay.

He couldn't get closer without parking near them, and he couldn't risk it. He turned and drove off from the park, scared now for the first time and feeling mad. Stupid Stoney. Stupid Jimmy Bird. Alex went back to the motel, scarfed down his breakfast without tasting it. He went through the Encina County phone book, going through the yellow pages for the fishing guides. Most had pictures of sun-squinting men smiling next to gargantuan fish. No picture of Big Ugly. But one ad, small in the corner, was for Don't Ask Fishing Services, just listed a phone number, and in little quotes below read: *Go with Gooch.* Alex dialed the number. A machine answered, "You've reached Leonard Guchinski and Don't Ask Fishing. I'm probably booked, but leave a message and I'll give you a call back." Alex hung up.

Leonard Guchinski. Now he had a name.

Alex applied the blond hair coloring, forcing himself to be consistent and careful, and while he waited twenty minutes to shower it off before finishing the treatment, he checked and rechecked the clips in his gun. He suspected he would need several. It was just shaping up to be that kind of day.

*   *   *

"I got some business to tend to today," Gooch said. "Whit's arranged for you to meet a guy who does criminal sketches. Describe Alex to him. He's driving in from Corpus. Then the folks on the boat next to us, they invited you to sail with them while I'm gone." He slathered cream cheese on his bagel. "They're friends of Whit's, too."

"Business. About Alex?"

"Maybe," Gooch said.

"Do you know where Alex is?"

"Nope."

"But you know something, Gooch." She frowned.

It was a little crazy. This girl could read him easier than most people, whom he presented the blank page to, and he'd only known her a couple of days. "I just think you'll have fun with Duff and Trudy on their boat for a few hours."

"Duff? Trudy?"

"Don't hold their names against them. They're bankers. They got to have names like that. FDIC requirement."

"Did Whit tell them what I am?"

"What are you, Helen?"

"I'm a…" She stopped, as though the word had gotten harder to say.

"See. It's a blank. Fill it in with what you like."

"Do you not want to have sex with me because you think you're gonna fix me?"

"I haven't known you long enough to have sex with you," he said.

She shook her head. "You're a strange man, Gooch."

"You're not the first to notice."

30

———◉———

THIS FAKE KIDNAPPING isn't going to work, Stoney thought.

He had hardly slept, and he picked up the phone once, to call home, to talk to Ben. But then he thought the phones might be tapped. And maybe Ben was at the hospital.

Facing the walls of the cottage, he wondered if prison would be so very different. He thought of his friends, the little social-climbing debs he got to bed, his house. He was a deal maker—it was how he made his money—and the long night made him think that perhaps he should cut a deal. The odds were shifting. Lucy was unstable. Alex was cracking. And if there was a woman in town who knew Alex from the time in New Orleans, well. He thought Alex was jumping at shadows.

He tried to construct a series of lies that would protect him more thoroughly, but could stitch nothing credible together that left him clean enough. He picked up the phone to call the police; no, he couldn't do it. Not the police, they weren't deal makers. A lawyer, yes. A lawyer to negotiate the deal. A high-powered lawyer.

He paced back and forth, trying to work up the courage. The worst was Danny. If he could convince people Alex

had killed Danny, well, then... but the thought of not having the gold, the Eye, made his chest hurt. Take it for the
value, maybe, just leave the country and—

The knock at the door made him jump. Alex. The door
had no peephole, and the small windows meant you couldn't
easily peek out of the curtains without giving yourself away.

So Stoney Vaughn opened the door. Not Alex. A big,
ugly hulk of a guy stood there and he belted Stoney hard in
the chest, landing him on his back on the floor. Breathing
was a memory. He stared up at the ugly guy.

"Mr. Vaughn? How you doing? No, don't get up. Don't
talk." The man closed the door behind him. "Catch your
breath. You gonna puke? That's a nice rug. Let me find a
bucket. No? You okay?"

He picked Stoney up by the neck, like a schoolboy
hauled by the scruff to the principal's office, dumped him
on the couch, pulled a wicked, fat black foreign gun out of
the back of his pants and let Stoney see it.

"Puh... puh..."

"Please? I admire politeness. Are you asking me to
please not shoot you?"

Stoney managed a nod.

"I won't. At least not yet. Not for the next two minutes.
But we're gonna talk—you understand me?" The ugly man
leaned down close. "My name's Gooch. I think you're trying to mess around with friends of mine. You see this gun?
That kills you in a second. Easy. You see this fist?" Gooch
held up a big, thick-fingered, closed hand that looked more
like an oversize hammer than a fist. "That kills you slow.
It takes its time. After about, oh, twenty or thirty punches,
when the bones are all broken up and starting to stick out
the skin, and I'm still pounding on you and my knuckles

get abraded and I get in a foul mood." Gooch smiled. "You don't want the old fist of death, do you?"

Stoney shook his head, got the force of his breath back with a shudder. "How...how..."

"Did I find you? That's what I want to talk about. You and Lucy Gilbert."

Stoney's mouth moved.

"And why you're holed up in a cottage when lots and lots of folks are missing you right now."

"I...I didn't do anything wrong," he managed.

"Who knows you're here?"

"Lucy...that's all."

"How about a guy who likes first names beginning with A?"

"What?"

"Alex. Albert. Allen. What's his name this week?"

"I don't know what you're talking about—"

Gooch cocked the gun, jammed it into Stoney's temple. "This is a Soviet-made Shootyadickov-69. Very sensitive. It misfires a lot." He pressed it harder, as if trying to reach Stoney's brains. "Are you willing to put that much trust in Soviet engineering?"

"Alex! His name is Alex Black." Stoney's eyes bugged.

"Is the treasure here?"

"No."

"Where is it?"

"I...I don't know. Alex has it."

"Where's Alex?"

"He moves around a lot," Stoney said. "I don't know where he is."

"I don't believe you, Stoney. The Shootyadickov doesn't believe you."

"I don't have it—please, mister."

Gooch studied him, seemed to think about it. He dragged Stoney over to the phone, placed a call, waited, hung up, called another number, waited, said, "It's Gooch, call me," hung up. He pushed Stoney back to the couch.

"C'mon, we're leaving."

"You...can't kidnap me..."

"Don't whine. You're already kidnapped, right?"

Gooch hauled up Stoney, pushed him through the door. He pulled him away from the cottage, into a dense grove of twisted live oaks beyond the thick grasses above the beach. A beaten red pickup, a big Ford, was parked there.

"This is how it is," Gooch said. "I have absolutely no compunction about shooting you. You bug me, I'm firing. You're going to sit on the floor, hands where I can see them. You behave, you're going to be fine. I'm kind of the opinion you're not the big bad shark in the sea, is that right?"

"Alex...Alex is bad," Stoney said. "He'll kill you." He wanted to say, *Yeah, well, I killed a man,* but suddenly saw it wouldn't intimidate this guy. Wouldn't make him blink.

Gooch shoved him into the truck, revved the engine, tore out of the grove of oaks onto the road. He was a quarter mile from the highway when a beige van turned in hard, headed toward them.

"What does Alex drive?" Gooch asked Stoney, still crouched on the floor.

"Beige van," Stoney said.

"Hello there," Gooch said. He leaned out the window, opened fire. Gravel and crushed shell exploded from the road near the tires, sparks flew from the end of the van.

Stoney screamed.

Gooch floored the truck and despite its beaten appearance

the engine roared into sweet, precise power. The road was rough—part of the rustic charm—and Gooch left the highway, tearing through a grassy field, taking a hard right, careening down a rocky swath of weed and stone and roaring out onto a thin strip of beach itself.

"Did you know it's legal to drive on the beach in Texas?" Gooch said. "Fascinating. Against the law most places."

"Yes," Stoney managed. He wondered if he could grab the steering wheel, wrench it, stop this guy long enough for Alex to shoot him.

Gooch gave him a long glance. "I can smell stupid thoughts, man. Don't do it. I'll kill you."

Stoney stayed put, his face buried in the worn upholstery of the truck, feeling it rumble off the beach, back onto grassland, then back onto the smooth road.

The van couldn't navigate down the long spill of rock to the sandy wet of the beach, and Alex drove back to the road, the van heaving like a horse, and peeled back toward the main highway—his only hope of cutting the guy off.

Gooch in that same red truck, leaving Stoney's hideaway, shooting at him, the gun in the hand rock-steady. He worked his own gun out, kept it in his left hand, steered right-handed.

The van rumbled onto the main highway, narrowly missing a Mercedes with an older couple. The driver laid on the horn. The woman lifted a manicured middle finger in salute and Alex nearly shot it off. Instead he swerved around them, bolted south to where the beach came closer to the main road. He kept glancing at the rearview mirror, thinking the red truck might burst from the trees or from another feeder road.

He drove all the way down to where a curve of beach came close to the road—no sign of the truck. He patrolled up and down the stretch of highway for a half hour but the only red truck he saw was new and had two women in it, pulling a horse trailer.

Finally he returned to the fishing cottage. Front door closed but unlocked. No sign of Stoney. No sign of a struggle.

So—Stoney had been kidnapped for real? Maybe Gooch was a partner Danny Laffite had that no one knew about. Or maybe Stoney had switched sides, decided to get out from under Alex's thumb, gotten himself a new partner to take care of Alex. He swore. Screw worrying about getting the emerald, he should have killed Stoney the moment he figured out Stoney betrayed him. He felt the sting of his own greed.

Where do I start looking for them?

He tried to calm his thoughts. Say Stoney decided to bolt, decided to hire muscle to cut out Alex. He'd have to call. Did Stoney have a cell with him? Alex went to the cordless phone in the cottage. There was a redial button. He pressed it. An answering machine clicked on, a low, comfortable drawl: "Hi, you've reached the office of Justice of the Peace Whitman Mosley. Office hours are nine a.m...."

Alex clicked off. Whit Mosley. That young judge in the loud shirt who came looking for Stoney to ask about the murdered old people.

So what the hell did a gun-happy Gooch have to do with a judge? He paced the floor for a minute. Maybe Stoney cracked. Decided to cut a deal and called the judge.

No. Police cars and sirens and Miranda rights would

have been involved. Judges didn't hire mercenaries to kidnap people.

But maybe it was even worse...maybe they knew about the emerald, the treasure. Maybe the judge and Gooch were just chasing it for themselves. Alex could see it: Stoney, babbling that he knew where a fat emerald was and knew a guy who'd hid millions in rare coins and could they help him cut a deal? Maybe a cop or a judge would think, *Well, I'd like me some of that.* Even assuming Stoney hadn't cracked, Gooch had already found Stoney here at the cottage. They must know enough. And nothing on the news yet about the treasure. No one else knew.

But they had Stoney, who had the Eye, and could completely ruin Alex.

PART THREE

THE EDGE OF THE WORLD

"For thirty years," he said, "I've sailed the seas and seen good and bad, better and worse, fair weather and foul, provisions running out, knives going, and what not. Well, now I tell you, I never seen good come o' goodness yet. Him as strikes first is my fancy; dead men don't bite; them's my views—amen, so be it."

—THE LIFE PHILOSOPHY OF ISRAEL HANDS, PIRATE, IN ROBERT LOUIS STEVENSON'S *TREASURE ISLAND*

31

━━━◆━━━

THE LUNCHTIME HEAT wasn't unbearable, the breeze a cool comfort. Whit met Dr. Parker and a bookish, attractive woman on the waterfront dock of a small restaurant at the Port Leo harbor for Saturday lunch. Dr. Parker introduced the woman as Dr. Iris Dominguez with Texas A&M-Corpus Christi. Pronounced her name the Spanish way, *Ee-res*.

"The bones from the dig are in Iris's car trunk," Dr. Parker said. "I can sign custody of them back over to you after lunch if you like."

Whit saw the waitress approaching for the drink order keep her smile frozen in place at the mention of bones.

"He's really not a maniac," Whit told her.

"The day is young," Iris Dominguez said. She had a beautiful voice, soft but forceful, and a cool, unfussy elegance. Whit liked her immediately. They ordered hamburgers and onion rings, Parker asking for a Salty Dog, Iris and Whit ordering beers.

"So you want to know about the coins and you're bribing us with lunch." Parker scooped a tortilla chip with salsa and popped it into his mouth.

"Yes, sir."

"Why not just ask the sheriff's office?"

"I could. But I'm not popular with law enforcement right now. I just insulted the FBI."

Iris Dominguez raised an eyebrow.

Parker laughed. "And why did you think that was productive?"

"I'll see if it gets the results I want," Whit said. "Plus, I wanted to thank you and Dr. Dominguez for your help." He smiled at Iris. "You identified the relics. That was extremely helpful to me."

"You're welcome. You've made my weekend interesting."

The waitress arrived with their drinks; Parker licked the salt from the glass rim, sucked down half the grapefruit juice and vodka in a hard swallow.

Dr. Dominguez waited until the waitress had departed. "Okay. What do you know about coins?"

"They don't stay in my pocket long enough," Whit said.

"Let me give you a quick primer. These kinds of coins weren't treated like how we treat quarters and pennies and dimes. They were created to make it easy to move massive amounts of wealth from Mexico to Spain. They might be struck in Mexico, shipped, and then immediately melted down in Europe." She sipped at her beer. "These are called milled bust coins, the last produced Spanish colonial coins. The gold coins come in denominations of eight, four, two, and one escudo. The silvers are reales. Obviously the gold coins are worth more." She dug in her purse, pulled out a file of photos. "I took some pictures of the coins, nice big blowups so I can show you why these coins are particularly unusual." She spread the photos out, one group to one side, the other by Parker's dwindling cocktail.

"These all have a typical reverse side," she said. "See the pillars and shield? Typical of many Spanish colonial coins. And these have double rosettes under the pillars. Very unusual." She pulled the other section of photos into the center of the table. "The obverse sides of the coins often have either a monarch's shield—like British paper money having the queen on it—or a design of the emperor's head, which you can see these have. Most of these are Ferdinand VII. Don't you think he had a weak chin?" She pointed with a pencil tip.

"Yes," Whit said.

Iris flipped the picture back over to the pillars, to the letters encircling the design. "You see the *Mo*? That means Monteblanco. Next, that's the denomination—this is an eight escudo; and next are the initials of the assayer. Here that's ET, Esteban Torres, the official of the Monteblanco mint. The other side has a date...Here, this coin was minted in 1819. Monteblanco was at that time the newest Mexican mint. Just opened. Freshly minted, you could say."

"Iris doesn't get out enough," Parker said. "Does it show?"

"I think you're brilliant," Whit said.

She smiled and Parker said, "Hey."

Just friends, Whit thought, *right.*

Iris tapped the photos with her fingernail. "So I dove into the historical archives, called a professor friend of mine in Mexico City to run some local checks down there for me. A large cache of the original silver and gold coins minted at Monteblanco—with this unusual double-rosette design— was being shipped to Spain right after being minted, aboard a schooner called *Santa Barbara*. But according to the records, *Santa Barbara* was lost at sea in March of 1820, somewhere south of Cuba."

"I see," Whit said again. Eighteen twenty. Jean Laffite's time. His heart neared his throat. This would make Jason Salinger's day.

"But the records of the time indicate that the weather was fair throughout that time in the Caribbean. So *Santa Barbara* probably didn't fall victim to a Gulf storm."

Whit cleared his throat. "I will embarrass myself a little now. But what if the coins were buried, as part of a treasure?"

"Yeah, I didn't tell Iris that part," Parker said. "I didn't want to influence her data."

"You couldn't have," Iris said dryly. "You're talking about the locks. The latches I identified. They're from the same period as the coins. You think the coins were originally buried with those relics and skeletons?"

Whit lowered his voice, leaned forward. "Yes, I do. I think Jean Laffite took *Santa Barbara* as his last prize, and he had no time to take and bank it under a false name in New Orleans. He was forced out of Galveston in the spring of 1820. Navies from Britain, Spain, and the U.S. would have been hunting him in the Gulf. He had no base to hide, nowhere to run."

"So you think he buried the *Santa Barbara* stash, hoping to reestablish later," Iris said.

"He just never got reestablished," Whit said. "Is this too big of a jump?"

Iris Dominguez sipped at her beer. "The coins have to have been somewhere for the past one hundred eighty years. They're worn but not from human handling."

He thought of Lucy, her claim the coins were Patch's. "You don't think they've been in a collection all these years?"

"No, Judge, considering what else you've discovered, I don't think so." She closed her eyes. "The historical significance. Enormous. An actual buried pirate treasure."

Whit's throat felt dry. "More valuable than the monetary significance?"

"I don't know. I'll see if I can locate a copy of the manifest from *Santa Barbara* from the archives. See how much gold and silver it carried—but even manifests didn't always represent an accurate count. There was a lot of corruption, theft in the financial system then. Sometimes up to forty percent of the treasure on a ship wouldn't even be on the manifest, to minimize taxes. And the Monteblanco mint was destroyed in a peasant uprising in 1822. Coins from Monteblanco are exceedingly rare."

"It could be quite large, then."

"It could be millions, Whit. The accounts of *Santa Barbara* I found also mentioned that the ship carried a noted Colombian emerald. No emeralds in Mexico—it's not a gem-rich geography—but lots of incredible emeralds out of Colombia. This one was particularly noteworthy. The Catholic priests nicknamed it the Devil's Eye."

"Oh, Lord," Whit said. He thought of Claudia's story of Danny Laffite's demands. "The archives in Mexico. Do they have any information on this emerald they could send to me?"

"I'll ask," Dr. Dominguez said.

"Judge, what is it? What's wrong?" Dr. Parker asked.

"You don't happen to know the value of the emerald, do you?"

"I should imagine it to be worth a few million. And of course, if it's become Laffite's treasure, and it's provable, then the value probably triples," Dr. Dominguez said.

"Iris," Whit said, "can you help me find out how some-one might try to sell this Devil's Eye? Or these coins?"

"Sure." She shook her head in pleased amazement. "Actual pirate treasure."

"Actual pirates," Parker said. "Can I keep those bones for a while? They just got way more interesting to me. They must have been the unlucky guys who helped Laffite bury the treasure, then got killed for their trouble. Dead men tell no tales and so on."

"So you're the famous Whit." Ben Vaughn sat on the edge of the hospital bed, dressed in loose khakis and a T-shirt.

"I didn't know I was famous."

"To Claudia and the FBI. Claudia thinks the world of you." He didn't say what the FBI thought.

"I think a lot of her, too," Whit said, and it didn't quite come out right and Ben glanced up toward him. "Thanks for agreeing to see me."

"What did you want to talk about?"

Whit sat on the edge of the room's institutional recliner. "Your brother. I saw him."

"So I heard." Ben sat up. "The FBI told me."

"Where's he at, Ben?"

"I think the same gang that was after us took him. He was the initial target."

"So Danny Laffite kidnapped your brother and sank his own boat?"

"I don't know."

"Maybe Stoney hid so this same gang couldn't find him."

"Maybe." Ben sounded less sure.

"But he . . . what, leaves you and Claudia to die? Not very brotherly."

Ben said nothing. The bruise on his cheek had gotten nastier with the passing hours, turning black and lemon-yellow. "I told Claudia he wouldn't abandon us."

"He just didn't want to tell the police."

"He didn't want to endanger our lives."

Whit sat next to him. "I have five older brothers. Two of them I'm extremely close to. Two I'm not so close to but I love them very much. One I practically hate but I still love him at the same time. He's a prime-grade jerk but he's still, and always will be, my brother. He matters to me."

Ben said nothing.

"You're not helping him, Ben. If you know where he might be, tell us. We all need some answers from him."

"Listen, Stoney was in a panic. For all the swagger, he's not good with situations he's not firmly in control of or can't get control of."

"All his brokerage firm's computer systems were down."

"Well, see..."

"But Stoney took them down, Ben. He sabotaged his own network from his home PC. I just saw the computer forensics report; the Corpus police sent copies to the sheriff's office here. He broke the systems so he couldn't transfer the ransom funds."

Ben stared at his bare feet. "That still doesn't mean he hasn't been kidnapped."

"Your brother financed treasure dives in Florida. I'd like to know more about those."

"And you're here exactly in what capacity?" Ben said.

"Tuesday I'm conducting a formal inquest—a hearing—into the murders of Patch Gilbert and Thuy Tran. You heard about that?"

"Yeah."

"The guy who's the number-one suspect and who apparently killed himself had some rather rare and valuable gold coins in his pocket. They've been identified as being from the same time period as Jean Laffite's pirating." Ben's eyes widened. "I don't think Danny Laffite sounds quite so crazy now, do you?"

"Listen, Danny Laffite was a nutcase. Ask any of Stoney's friends who are in this Laffite League. Stoney was the big fish in that pond, lot of money, well-known, popular. He was the leader and that's who a loser like Danny gloms on to. I think, if there's any truth to this, Danny Laffite had some delusion about Stoney knowing where this treasure was and thinking Stoney wouldn't tell him." He stood, a little shaky. Whit steadied him.

"I'm fine." Ben flinched slightly at Whit's touch on his elbow.

"Sorry. I know you've been through an ordeal. I—"

"I know my brother a lot better than you do, Judge. You're Claudia's friend, and I know you both mean well. But you're wrong. My brother wouldn't risk my life like you say." He walked into the bathroom, splashed cold water on his face.

"Did you ever hear Danny or Gar or Zack mention a guy named Alex?"

"No."

"How about Albert Exley?"

"No."

"Allen Eck?"

"No." Ben dried his face. "I think, y'all find out who the other two kidnappers are, you're not going to find they got any kind of treasure or archaeological connection. They didn't give a lick about what Danny raved about. They used him, thought he was nuts. He had the boat and he'd given them a good target in my brother. They just wanted cash, pure and simple, and they thought they had a low-risk way to get it." He paused. "Maybe Danny Laffite killed those people on the Point, with the dead guy you mentioned. What a freak."

"Your brother's lucky. Having a defender like you."

Whit wondered just what Ben knew, how far he would go to protect his brother.

Ben tilted his head. "Thank you."

"I'll let you rest," Whit said.

"Judge?"

"Yeah?"

"You and Claudia. Was there ever anything there?"

The question surprised Whit. "No. We're just friends."

"Good," Ben said.

32

CLAUDIA THOUGHT A good police file on a major case should not only contain the pertinent data, but read like a well-crafted short story or novel. The motivations, the fears, the human failings should all be subtly suggested between the lines of forensic data and witness statements. David thought her attitude nuts when they were married, told her if she wanted that from a file she needed to take a creative writing course.

The New Orleans police made a guess that the redhead called Zack was one Zachary James Simard, so the investigators thoughtfully sent his record along. The photo was indeed Zack, sallow face, pouty lips, calculating glare. Degree in finance from LSU, from a family from Lake Charles. Suspected of handling money and accounts for a drug-and-prostitution-fueled crime ring based in New Orleans that stretched eastward to Pensacola and over to Beaumont. Five years ago he'd done two years in a state pen in Louisiana on a marijuana-possession charge. He'd stayed clean since, or at least clean enough to avoid charges thus far and therefore avoid the pressure to testify, to make a deal with the Feds. He had dropped out of sight two weeks ago.

Gar Johnson, aka Gary Paul Jackson, born Gerald Paul Jones. Suspected of being a hired gun; suspected in a slaying in Biloxi and a double homicide in New Orleans. The victims were all drug dealers who, the police suspected, skimmed profits. The pair in New Orleans had been a young married couple, both mediocre jazz pianists tapping a living out of the second-tier club scene, dealing coke to the well-heeled on the side. Every finger on the couple's hands had been broken before they were shot; both the man and the woman had been raped and then their bodies dumped in a ditch in Algiers. Claudia's stomach roiled.

Gar had served two stretches, one for armed robbery, and he'd been at Angola prison during Zack Simard's time there. They had been released within a month of each other and both headed for New Orleans. Maybe they'd been sweeties in prison.

She turned the page.

Daniel Villars Mouton. From an old-money family, he was the last of the Moutons, living in a grand house in the Garden District. But Danny had a record. Petty theft, shoplifting history books from a bookstore. Then the charge of forgery she knew about that had been dropped. A brief stint in a pricey mental clinic in Metairie, apparently checked in and then checked out by his only cousin. The Villars middle name was real, a family name handed down with pride, and Danny's reading about the great love of Laffite's life apparently fueled the delusion he was descended from the pirate. One diagnosis of schizophrenia, another diagnosis of bipolar disorder. A charge of marijuana possession that had been plea-bargained into nothing. Maybe the drug connection was how he'd met Gar and Zack.

Beneath these papers were notes and reports compiled

from the investigation into the murder of Danny's cousin. Less than a month ago the man had died in a burglary gone wrong. A back window had been forced. Phillip Villars, age fifty and a widowed antiques dealer in the French Quarter, staying at his cousin Daniel's house during the remodeling of his own home, had apparently surprised an intruder and been killed with a single gunshot to the forehead. Left dead in a downstairs hallway. His cousin, Daniel Villars Mouton, found the body later that evening after returning from a trip and phoned police. Danny was questioned extensively, given his background, but he had an ironclad alibi—visiting friends in Charleston, South Carolina, for the past week, every hour accounted for—and neighbors and friends said for all his eccentricities Danny got along well with his cousin, the last two members of a faded family. Note on the file that the New Orleans police had no further leads. Just a report that Danny Mouton quickly dropped out of sight after his cousin's funeral.

He'd gone into hiding, she thought. Running and hiding from Stoney, maybe.

Not everything Danny had said was a lie. She covered her face, thought of his odd mix of earnestness, gallantry—he had saved her life when he could have let Gar rape and murder her—and absolute craziness. There might have been a decent person in there, someone who wanted to accomplish much, derailed by psychosis and drugs. A wasted life. She closed the folder.

Fingers tapped at the bedroom door; Claudia's mother stuck her head in. "David's here," she said. "Brought brownies. Your favorite." Tina retained a great fondness for David.

"Thanks." Claudia followed her mother into her little living room. David stood there, in full-dress uniform, sweaty patches under his arms, his Stetson in his big freckled hands. Tina Salazar disappeared into the kitchen with the brownies, where she could still hear but pretend not to.

"I just wanted to see if you were okay," David said.

"You phoned this morning, David. I'm still the same."

"But still. You had such a horrible ordeal, hon."

Hon. Like they were still married, still tethered to each other. He hadn't wanted the divorce. At times she had wondered if parting was the right thing, if perhaps she had sold him short. Maddening one minute, sweet the next, and she finally tired of the inconsistencies.

"They're still searching the bay for Danny Laffite's body," David said. "Assuming he's dead in the first place or that he drowned when his boat sank. But nothing."

"Have they raised Danny's boat yet?"

"Probably tomorrow. Where do you think he is?"

"I don't think Danny would give up," she said. "It's entirely possible he killed Stoney Vaughn. He might have killed him, dumped the body somewhere. But he thinks this jewel and gold are in Port Leo, he won't be leaving." She turned back to David. "I absolutely don't see him sinking his boat for any reason, though. I guess I think he's dead." She wondered for a moment, *And if he's not, you think maybe he might try to find you?* "Maybe he grabbed Stoney, the boat wrecked, and their bodies are in the bay."

"Maybe," David said, glancing at Tina.

"I'm going for a walk," Tina Salazar announced. "Just down to the store for some milk to go with the brownies." She kissed Claudia's cheek, patted David's shoulder, scurried out of the apartment.

"She wants us to be alone," David said.

"I think you might be overanalyzing," she said, although she knew he was right.

"Can I ask you how long you've been seeing Ben Vaughn?"

She owed him no answers but since he was involved in the case there was no point in arguing. She wished, though, he'd sent another investigator to talk to her. Of course, he wouldn't. "Not long. A couple of weeks. Very casually."

"Is he nice to you?"

"Very nice and pleasant. Did you expect he would be a loser?"

"His brother sounds like a prime one."

"I only met Stoney once," she said, "except for maybe back in high school."

"I think Stoney Vaughn got scared and he ran to protect his money, and now he can't surface. I also think your boyfriend's protecting him. If he blocks this investigation in any way, he's going to be in serious trouble."

"Wouldn't that just be perfect? How disappointing for you it wouldn't be your case."

"Stoney Vaughn's house is in county jurisdiction. Just might be mine." He sat down in the reading chair next to the sofa.

"So what does that mean, David? You're going to make trouble for Ben?"

"You could help us, Claudia. Find the brother. Get Ben to talk."

She said nothing.

"Oh, gee, would that ruin your shiny new relationship if you helped us out?"

"Don't be this way."

"I really hope you're not protecting Ben yourself, Claud. Know anything about your boyfriend's brother you're not sharing? Places he might go, resources he might have?"

"Absolutely not." She stood. "I told you, the FBI, everything Danny Laffite told me."

"And that's being followed up on," David said. "Especially whatever grudge Danny had against Stoney Vaughn. Danny Laffite did have a cousin murdered in New Orleans last month. He was telling you the truth. We're determining if Stoney Vaughn was in New Orleans those days."

Oh, don't let this be true, she thought. *It will kill Ben.*

"If your boyfriend"—the term said like he had mud in his mouth—"knew anything about his brother committing a murder, he's an accessory."

"You're correct," she said quietly. "But if you start an unfounded witch-hunt against Ben, I'm going to have your badge for it. Promise you, David."

"Whoa. Passion. Haven't seen that from you in a while."

"Don't bait me. I won't bite."

He hesitated. "The last thing in the world I want is to see you hurt."

"Unless you can do the hurting."

"I'm going to tell you something no one knows. It's not to make you mad or to try to win sympathy or to gain advantage." He crossed his arms. "I still love you."

Claudia said nothing.

"So I don't want you hurt. By anyone, including me." He stood. "I get around you, my mouth starts running because I'm mad still. I'm trying my best not to be. Enjoy the brownies. I'll call you if we hear anything about Vaughn or Danny Laffite."

"All right." She didn't know what else to say.

She watched from the window as David went down the stairs, putting his Stetson back on, heading to his sheriff's department cruiser. She watched him pull out of the parking lot. She picked up the phone, wanting to hear Ben's voice, but knowing he needed his rest.

Instead, she went back to the bedroom and opened the file from New Orleans.

Phillip Villars, the wrong place, the wrong time. Single bullet in the middle of the forehead. Thuy Tran died in a similar way.

If Stoney had been involved, where was this journal now, the one Phillip Villars had been killed for? If Danny was right, Stoney had it. Or knew where it was.

She had access to the house, to Ben, that might help her. And she could do it to protect Ben.

Yes, do that. Find the evidence against his brother and Ben may hate you.

Her mother came back with the milk, and out of duty Claudia ate two brownies.

"Nice of David to bring these," Tina said.

"Yes," Claudia said. "He says he still loves me."

Tina stopped a brownie halfway to her mouth.

"He's full of crap," Claudia said. She told her what David said.

"David's all angry and hopeful at the same time," Tina said. "Maybe he loves you. But he wants you to squirm a bit, sweetie, feel as torn as he does. And if he can get you to sabotage your relationship with Ben, better for him, he thinks."

"You're not taking his side?" This was a change.

"Today I'm taking your side," Tina said, rolling her eyes. "Enjoy the moment."

"But David's right," she said. "I could get to Ben faster than anyone else could, if he's holding back."

"You cops. You can never let anything be." Tina ate her brownie.

Claudia kissed her mother's cheek. "I think I'll go by the hospital, see Ben."

But she didn't. Instead, Claudia drove to Copano Flats, toward the big Vaughn house.

33

I DON'T THINK Lucy's very interesting as a suspect any-more," David said. He'd run into Whit at the Coke machine in the courthouse hallway, Whit in the office to use the faster Internet connection than what he had at home, David doing whatever he did on a Saturday he had duty.

"You got a new mouse to play with?" Whit could guess where this was going.

"Jimmy Bird killed those old folks. No question. His tire tracks match the tracks found on the Gilbert land, same gun killed him as killed Mrs. Tran. I just made your inquest real easy."

"Thank you."

"Now. What's interesting to me is your theory about how maybe Stoney Vaughn had a connection to old Jimmy."

Whit fed quarters into the machine, selected root beer, waited for the can to drop. "Or, wow, even better if Ben Vaughn did. Now wouldn't that get your nipples hard?"

"Be grateful for small mercies. I'm leaving your girl-friend alone." He handed Whit the Saturday edition of the *Port Leo Mariner,* the semiweekly local paper. "Nasty letter to the editor in there about you. You pissed off the other half of the Gilbert family. Bring that back when you're done, would you? I got a new puppy I'm training."

Whit didn't open the paper, wouldn't give David the satisfaction.

David got a Coke from the machine. "Given what's in that paper, you might have a crowd at your inquest. With a recall petition."

"David, may I give you a friendly word of advice?"

"What?"

"You're never getting her back," Whit said. "Ever. And I don't think it'd make you happy anyway. So you might as well get over being mad at Claudia and all her friends you have to work with. You want to be sheriff? It's never going to happen, as long as you keep pissing on people." He turned and walked off. "I'll bring your paper back when I'm done."

Whit took the paper back to his office, shut the door. He'd been searching for information on the Devil's Eye emerald and *Santa Barbara* on the Internet, impatient to wait on what Iris Dominguez and her colleagues might find. He'd found one site devoted to famous lost jewels that included a description of the Devil's Eye. There was no photo, of course, and the actual existence of the Eye was questioned by the article. The emerald's supposed weight—estimated by modern standards to be just shy of two kilograms—was listed, its story told as part of the billions in mineral and gemological wealth mined from the New World and dispatched to fill the Spanish treasury. Estimated value of the Devil's Eye—named by a disapproving priest of the viceroy who claimed the weak-willed stared at it, as though hypnotized—ranged from a million to four million U.S. dollars. Having been lost for so long, its legend and value had grown.

His phone rang. "Whit Mosley."

"It's Iris. Listen, I talked with the gemologists in Mexico. You asked how you might sell an emerald like the Devil's Eye."

"Not in a pawnshop, right?"

"Don't joke. My friends say there is an underground market for emeralds, and it's controlled by emerald traders in Colombia. You know Colombia suffers much violence and corruption. Prominent emerald traders there have been accused of sponsoring right-wing paramilitary groups. These are dangerous men."

"And these men would be the buyers for the Devil's Eye?"

"If one wished to get the maximum amount of profit, yes. For a stone like the Devil's Eye, there'd be much competition."

"So our seller has to have the nerve to deal with rich Colombian extremists. How reassuring."

"I thought you should know. I'll let you know what else I learn, as soon as I hear anything."

He thanked her, hung up the phone. His stomach felt a little unsettled. He'd tried to imagine disposing of a treasure—how exactly would you go about doing this? The coins could be melted down or sold in small batches to collectors. But the emerald, if it was as grand as he thought it must be . . . Colombian extremists. How many guns, bombs, bribes could the Devil's Eye buy? That the case could move into international crime rings and violent politics made his throat go dry. He thought, *I bet Triple A and Stoney are gone. They got that emerald and took off to Bogotá and we'll never get them.*

He opened the newspaper to the letters to the editor.

Suzanne Gilbert was a better painter than writer. But the letter still stung. The rant was adverb heavy. Accused Judge Mosley of malfeasance in ignoring the beneficiary of Patch Gilbert's death and asked for an investigation into Judge Mosley's inquest and finances, perhaps suggesting a bribe had been paid. He glanced at his phone: The message light blinked, no doubt the outraged voters of Encina County calling for his head. Maybe. He clicked the phone on: one hang-up, four messages from voters asking for an explanation about Suzanne's letter, not angry, but now curious.

His cell phone beeped and he answered it, hoping it wasn't another voter wanting a one-on-one explanation.

"You're not going to be happy with me," Gooch said.

"I'm afraid to ask."

"Could you get me a legal definition of kidnapping? Because I don't think I technically kidnapped Stoney Vaughn. I prefer to think of it as protective custody."

Whit's mouth opened, then closed. "You what?"

"That other guy, Triple A—although since I shot at him, I'm thinking we're on a first-name basis—this Alex guy, he drives a beige Chrysler van, by the way. I think he might have meant harm to poor Stoney here. I found Stoney at a fishing cottage in Laurel Point. We've moved on."

"How did you know Stoney was at this fishing cottage?"

"That will upset you."

"Like I'm not already upset."

"I followed Lucy."

"I absolutely do not understand."

"I. Followed. Lucy."

Whit's stomach lurched. "Why, Gooch?"

"I've never trusted her. Sorry."

"Where are you?"

"If I tell, you're in trouble with the law, and I think I should keep you free and clear."

"I'm already an accessory to kidnapping if I don't report you."

"Stoney went with me willingly. He's sure willing now. Aren't you, Stoney? Hey, Stoney!" Calling to him, loud, an echo in the room. "Yeah, he's nodding big-time. He's a happy guy."

"Gooch. Where are you?"

"See, you can't always take the direct approach, Judge. Stoney and I are going to have an extensive chat here shortly. We're going to find out who exactly Alex is, what he knows, where he's at, and then how Lucy's involved in all this. Find out what he knows about poor Patch and Thuy. It's gonna be fun and educational."

"Gooch, don't—"

"Then I'll call you and fill you in. I won't say it's me. Then you do what you think best. Consider it an extended anonymous tip."

"Gooch, don't do this—"

"Helen's out boating with Duff and Trudy Smith, so she should be out of harm's way. Take care of her, okay? She's a good kid. She can stay on my boat long as she wants. 'Bye, Whitman. Don't turn your back on Lucy." He hung up.

Whit dialed Gooch's cell phone. No answer. He called the marina where Gooch docked *Don't Ask*. The marina master said yeah, Gooch's boat was there, just fine—did he want to leave a message?

At least Gooch wasn't out on the water, conducting a floating inquisition.

He cursed Gooch. He cursed Stoney Vaughn. No idea where they could be...but there had been that brief echo when Gooch called to Stoney. So a big space. Covered roof. A big space but private so Gooch could have his extended, perhaps violent chat with Stoney.

Now where might that be?

Could be the old high school gym, awaiting a tear-down in a month or so. There was a soundstage at an old television studio, now empty and for sale, on the edge of town. Possibly. Or...there was a marina on the north edge of the county, past the Flats, abandoned since part of the docks burned a year ago—but the big metal covering and high roof of the old marina were still there. No one used it, and Gooch had talked about buying it from the uninterested, unmotivated owners in Houston.

Whit grabbed his car keys. He had to stop this, find a way to reason with Gooch. The thought was nearly alien.

The FBI had the Vaughn house, but the agents knew who Claudia was and let her in.

"I'm getting the house ready for Ben to come home from the hospital," she said, and the two agents nodded and went back to their phones and laptops.

She searched carefully and as inconspicuously as she could, ignoring the nagging feeling that said she had no right to do this. First Stoney's bedroom. She found nothing of interest except a wad of a thousand dollars in cash, tucked in the back of the underwear drawer. She left the cash alone. The bathroom produced nothing but a daunting cache of toilet paper, fourteen different scents of high-dollar cologne, a nearly empty box of condoms, and expired cold medications.

She went to the top of the staircase and glanced downstairs; she could hear the drift of the agents' voices from the kitchen, talking on their phones, discussing the coordinated search for Stoney Vaughn. There had been a sighting in San Antonio, a couple of hours away, of a man who looked like Stoney. The most promising lead thus far.

She went to the study at the end of the hallway. Books lined the shelves. Stoney had not struck her as a book person, and many of the books looked too pristine to have been read—lots of recent hardcover bestsellers, crime fiction, investing, and finance. Biographies of business leaders. But one whole wall on the history of piracy, on archaeology and nautical salvage, on Jean Laffite and Texas history.

She browsed through them but decided as a hiding place it was too obvious. He wouldn't hide the journal here. Maybe a safe-deposit box—see if the FBI had access to that. Or Ben, if he could be convinced.

There was a PC on Stoney's desk, shoved to one side. The desk was in disarray—she suspected the FBI had sat down and copied the hard disk to see if there were any clues as to who had Stoney or where he might have gone. Easier than going through the rigmarole of getting actual custody of the hard drive.

Claudia sat down, powered up the PC, and opened Stoney's e-mail application.

"What are you doing?" Ben said from the doorway.

"What are you doing out of the hospital?" she said.

"I couldn't stay there. Not with my brother missing. I checked myself out. I'm okay." He leaned against the doorway. "What are you doing on Stoney's computer?"

She took her hands off the keyboard.

"Sending an e-mail," she said coolly, with a smile. "Is that okay?" She had wanted to see if there had been an e-mail from Danny Laffite, or other Laffite Leaguers, or

Patch Gilbert, or anyone connected to the case. Maybe Stoney made on-line reservations to go somewhere, maybe his browser had a history suggesting travel sites he'd visited.

"Sending an e-mail from here?"

"I just remembered something from when I was on Danny's boat," she said. "It's better to get it down in writing than give a statement." She stood, turning off the system as if sending the e-mail was no big deal.

"Claudia. You were spying."

"No. It's not my case. I don't have a warrant. I really was just logging on." *Okay, the first lie to him. How does it taste in your mouth?*

He turned and walked away. She followed him to his bedroom, watched him lie down on the bed, put his arm over his eyes.

"I'm sorry, Ben."

"It's in your nature to pry."

"*Pry* is an ugly word. I'm trying to help you and I'm trying to find your brother."

"Please don't get involved in this."

"You know where he's at."

"Not with certainty," he said in a low voice. "You think they've bugged my room?"

"Of course not, Ben."

"So I'm supposed to tell you and betray my brother?"

"He betrayed you."

"Innocent till proven guilty."

"The authorities find that Stoney's involved in any crime, and they think you're protecting him, they're going to come after you whole-hog. Your life could be ruined, babe."

He closed his eyes, opened them. "If I think I know where he's at . . . and I tell you, you'll tell them."

She made the decision. "No. I won't."

"Right, Claudia. You're a cop. You have to."

"Why's he hiding?"

"I think he's ashamed of not paying. Maybe he doesn't have the five million to pay. So he's humiliated and he ran."

"Then he didn't commit a crime. So this is a private matter between the two of you. I'll take you to him, Ben, if you know where he's at. You can work it out. Then he can come forward."

"Would you let a guy who wouldn't pay his brother's ransom handle your finances, Claudia? That's what he's afraid of. The public response. His clients will dump him. He'll be ruined. He'll lose this house, everything."

"It's not the public's business."

"He sabotaged his own computer systems to keep his money safe," Ben said. "It'll get out. He'll be ruined because he panicked."

"Ben, finding him is the only way to help him. He can't hide forever. Where do you think he is?"

"Let me sleep on it," he said. "I'll give him another day."

"So you've given up this he-was-kidnapped thing."

"We would have heard a ransom demand by now," Ben said. "Don't you think?"

34

———◆◉◆———

"AS A KIDNAPPER GOES, YOU'RE OKAY," Stoney said. "At least the food's tasty." He had his nerve back once he saw that Gooch wasn't going to take a pair of pliers to his mouth or a blowtorch to his feet. Right now they were eating Chinese takeout, sitting at a metal desk in the back of the warehouse.

After they had driven out of Port Leo, the truck ambling along, Stoney still crouched on the floorboards, Gooch had said, "Your choices are two. You either help me, or you end up dead in the Gulf."

"Tough call. I'll help you," Stoney said from the floorboard of the car.

"I expect complete honesty. I don't get it, you're dead. You understand?"

"Yes."

"First chance for honesty. Did you kill Patch Gilbert and Thuy Tran?"

"No. I didn't." He could say that and be honest.

"Do you know who did?"

"Yeah. Alex." A pause. "No one could have stopped him."

"A person of conscience would have stopped him, but

we won't judge you on your obvious deficiencies," Gooch said.

"You're right. I didn't. But it wasn't planned. They weren't supposed to be there." *Give a little ground,* he thought. Dealing with Gooch was a negotiation, not so different from the deals he'd cut when he worked in venture capital. He thought suddenly that, yes, he could handle this.

"How comforting. How deep in is Lucy Gilbert?"

"She knew we were getting the treasure off Patch's land because he refused to sell to me. I offered him too much for his land; he checked on me, found out I was into treasure hunting and he started wondering if maybe there was something valuable hidden on his land, what with me offering a price I thought he'd never say no to. He made the connection about Laffite, although he didn't have any proof. It just dug his heels in that he wouldn't sell. We'd used metal detectors to find the cache on his land. But there was no dealing with him, so I found out Lucy Gilbert needed money, approached her. She was going to sell her acreage to us and let us rebury it on her land."

"Alex wanted to rebury it?"

"Not anymore. Maybe he never did. He gets a cut. I get the rest."

"You," said Gooch, "are a piece of work, man."

"It seemed like a good idea at the time. Everyone would have been happy, no one hurt."

"Yeah, if Patch got his hundred thou together and conducted a legitimate dig, you or Alex would have had to kill him anyway, right?"

"No," Stoney said quietly. "No."

"Jimmy Bird?"

"He helped us. Alex shut him up." He prayed Gooch

wouldn't ask if he'd killed Danny Laffite. Maybe he would just assume Alex did.

"You need a new hobby," Gooch said. "Where's a place you and me can go and not be bothered?"

"What, I get to pick my place of execution?"

"I'm not killing you. I want a place where you and I can go and call Alex, set up a negotiation with him so I can kill him."

"You're going to kill him?"

"The chances are fairly good," Gooch said. "I don't like him."

"Why don't you just call the police?"

"They like courtrooms. Those take time. I'm taking a simple, blunt approach to a complicated situation. It's a public service."

Stoney took a deep breath. Maybe this would work. Get Gooch to lure in Alex someplace private. Gooch could kill Alex. Then he could cut a deal with Gooch. Or maybe get rid of Gooch. He was afraid of Gooch but there was a bit too much cockiness in the big guy, and maybe he underestimated Stoney.

He thought of blowing off Danny's head and his confidence returned.

"You afraid of this Alex?" Gooch asked.

Stoney was silent.

"You say he's got the treasure."

"He says he does. Or he's lied and it's still in the storage unit over in Laurel Point. But knowing Alex, he's definitely moved it. So he and I are at a stalemate."

"Where's the Devil's Eye?"

Stoney took a deep breath. Now he needed to lie; he was going to lie because that emerald wasn't up for negotiation;

it was his. "I hid it on my property. Buried it deep in a flower bed, where the earth was already turned. It's safe. Alex wants it bad."

"We'll use that as our bait then."

"If you want a good place to talk to him," Stoney said, "I got one. I own a couple of warehouses down at the port in Corpus Christi. It's quiet down there. Alex could meet us there."

"Stoney?"

"Yeah?"

"No tricks. It's a death sentence."

"So what happens to me after you kill Alex?"

"How much are you worth, Stoney?" Gooch said.

Finally. Money. The universal language. Gooch could be bought; this was a sudden, warm comfort. "About two million, I guess."

"I can think of any number of local charities who need about a two-million-dollar donation."

His gut tightened. "That's extortion."

"Fund-raising. You can rebuild your fortune. But you let people die. There's a price to pay for that. You can pick: prison, poverty, or pine."

"Pine?"

"As in box, buddy."

"I would pick poverty, then," Stoney said carefully.

And so they had crossed the high Harbor Bridge in Corpus, the port to their right, the retired battleship USS *Lexington* docked to their left, grabbed takeout Chinese in downtown Corpus. The warehouse, in the heart of the port of Corpus Christi, was quiet on a Saturday. Stoney unlocked the door with an electronic code. The warehouse was big but cluttered, a maze of tall boxes and crates and wrapped pallets. And now they sat, finishing the Chinese at a metal desk.

"What do you keep here?" Gooch asked around a mouthful of garlic chicken.

"One of my companies buys up furniture and equipment from failed businesses, sells it at discount." Stoney shoveled in moo shu pork; he wasn't sure when he'd get to eat again.

"You're just a full-time vulture, aren't you?"

"I am sorry about your friends. I am."

"Don't worry. You will be."

Stoney ignored him. Eating the last of his moo shu, he searched his memory for any weapons that might be in the warehouse. He couldn't remember whether the old foreman kept a gun in the desk. He slid the metal drawer open a bit; the drawer was loose, came out too quick. No gun, just pencils and Post-it notes and a thin little flask of Crown Royal. He pushed the drawer back but it didn't quite want to go.

That drawer would come right out in your hands, Stoney thought. *Heavy. Metal. What do you know?* He nudged the drawer back into place.

Gooch stood a ways off, talking on a cell phone, calling to Stoney if he were happy. *Yeah, I'm delirious with joy,* he wanted to answer but he played along, said he was happy, nodded. The room echoed slightly with their voices.

Gooch said, "Let's discuss how we get your friend Alex."

A freaking useless wild-goose chase, Alex thought.

He had been following the Honorable Whit Mosley from the courthouse square. Alex earlier ditched the beige van in the Port Leo Wal-Mart parking lot, and walked along the rows of cars until he saw keys dangling in a Ford Taurus, windows slightly lowered to dissipate the midday heat. A bumper sticker announced CARPENTERS HAVE BETTER WOOD. He drove the Taurus to a quiet apartment complex, quickly but calmly switched license plates with a lonely little red Hyundai at the back of the lot, tore off the offending bumper sticker, and drove to a Dairy Queen for a soda and a burger. There he found Whit's address in a local phone book and headed straight for the big Victorian house, thinking, *I'll just take him here. His buddy took Stoney. I'll take him.*

The woman who answered the door was blond and pretty in a melt-your-knees way and Alex thought, *Or I'll just take you, honey.*

"Hi, I'm looking for Judge Mosley."

"His place is out back. The guest house," the woman said. She looked to be a little younger than Whit, blue eyes wide enough to drown in, and her noticeable accent sounded funny. Russian, maybe. "But he's not here right now. I'm his stepmother, Irina. May I help you?"

Stepmother? Wow. He wished his dad had bothered to remarry. "Well, um, ma'am, I had information for him on a case. It's kind of private."

"Ah. He was here but went to the courthouse. His office is on the first floor. If the building's not open you could knock on his window. Fifth window on the left from the entrance. If he's not there he's probably with his girlfriend."

"Thank you, ma'am." Alex let Irina Mosley live and headed for the courthouse. He waited for forty minutes, running the AC in the Taurus until he saw Whit Mosley come out of the courthouse, run—in this heat, running—to a white Ford Explorer and get in and roar off. He pulled out after him, staying two cars back, blending in with the busy summer weekend traffic.

The judge had driven past the old marina, an old, for-sale television studio, the high school auditorium. Like he was checking out real estate to buy. Following him was becoming more difficult if not impossible. He was looking for something and he wasn't getting out of his car where Alex could grab him and run. He was hanging so far back he was not always keeping Whit Mosley in sight, worried he would be noticed, and finally the judge turned around and drove through Port Leo and north toward Black Jack Point. Alex followed.

Next to him on the car seat, his cell phone rang. Alex kept his eye on Whit's car. "Hello?"

"Hello, Mr. Treasure Hunter," Gooch said. "Want to deal?"

35

———◆———

WE NEED TO TALK," Whit said. Lucy lay across Patch's fat leather couch, a cool cloth on her forehead, a bottle of aspirin and an opened can of ginger ale on the floor.

"Okay." She didn't open her eyes.

"About you and Stoney Vaughn."

She didn't open her eyes, but she folded her hands across her stomach.

"Lucy, look at me."

She opened her eyes, turned her head.

"You know him." He kept his voice steady.

"Yeah."

"You knew Stoney was hiding at a fishing cottage."

A long silence. "Did he turn himself in?"

"No. Gooch has him."

Now she sat up. "Has him?"

"Stashed somewhere," he said. "Gooch grabbed him. He's using him to get at the guy who killed Patch and Thuy. Gooch found him by following you."

"Hell's bells," Lucy said.

"This Alex guy. Do you know him, know his real name?" She hesitated and Whit said quietly, "Answer me, Lucy, right now." *Who are you?* he thought.

She raised her chin. "Don't speak to me that way."

"You knew who killed Patch. And you said nothing."

"No, baby, I didn't know. Not when it happened. I found out later."

"You sure know how to keep a secret," he said. "That's a new one."

"I did it to protect you," she said. Now she tossed the washcloth on the floor.

"Protect me. You're one great shield, Lucy. You've just destroyed my career. Everything your cousin said about me in the paper today is going to be considered holy writ. You lied to me, to the police." Whit stopped, sat down. "Forget being a judge. I could care less. You've destroyed *us*. We're done. That's a thousand times worse."

She reached for him; he moved away from her, as though her touch might scald. "I said nothing because I didn't know for sure. And I knew if I came forward I'd lose you."

"You've lost me. You thought I'd stay with you?"

"So much for true love." Her jaw quivered but her eyes were dry. "I love you, Whit. That's why I did this. Stoney came to me when Patch wouldn't sell the land to him. Said he'd buy my land. I didn't even know about the treasure he wanted to move. But before the dig, he told me. Wanted me to be sure Patch was out of town. I was scared he'd do something to me if I said anything."

"Right."

"I gave Thuy and Patch that trip to Port Aransas to get them gone. Baby, I didn't know he'd changed his will. I swear. I swear, Whitman."

"This isn't a courtroom."

"Yes, it is. It's the court of Whit and you're judge, jury, and executioner."

"Who killed them?"

She swallowed. "Stoney says Alex."

"Jimmy Bird?"

"Alex, probably."

"The coins in Jimmy's pocket?"

"They're not Patch's. I guess they're from the dig. I guess Jimmy swiped them and Alex didn't know it."

"Where is Alex?"

"Stoney...he told me where he was hiding. I went to the cottage with Patch's gun. Ready to kill him for what he'd done. But I couldn't just shoot him, not even him, in cold blood. He asked me to shoot Alex. Alex knows about you, was there when you came to Stoney's house. I followed Alex to the Surfside Motel. He's staying there, at least he was." She stared at him. "I thought of killing him. Make it look like a random shooting. I even knocked on his door in the night, just shoot him and run. Nothing to connect me with him. Because he might hurt you. But I chickened out. I'm...scared."

He saw she was: rough, tough Lucy, breaking under the weight. He wanted to hold her, wanted to scream at her. His chest felt like it might explode. "Where is this gun?"

"In my purse."

He went to the purse, pulled out the gun with a tissue, checked the bullets, put on the safety, stuck it into the back of his pants.

"You running around with a gun." He shook his head. "Is there anything else I should know, Lucy?"

"I love you."

He covered his eyes with his hands.

"I love you, too. I did...why did you do this?"

"I thought I was doing the right thing."

"For you. Screw Patch. Screw Thuy."

"If I turned on Stoney, I was afraid of what would happen to you." She crossed her arms. "Tell me something, Whit, you being all high and mighty. You say Gooch grabbed Stoney. Have you called the police?"

"No. I have reason to think Stoney went voluntarily with him."

"Reason to think." Her voice went low, angry. "Stoney wouldn't. Don't tell me that lunatic Gooch gets a free pass and I don't?"

"This isn't a double standard."

"The hell it's not. You lecture me, you tell me that we're done, that loving each other doesn't make a difference, but Gooch commits a kidnapping and you don't turn him in?"

"Fine. I'll call the police right now." He picked up the phone. "I'll tell them about you, too. This'll make David Power's day for the next year. Then I'll resign and—"

She grabbed the phone from his hand. "Listen. I did this because I needed to make a lot of money, fast. I got debts, Whit, a lot of them. I didn't want you to know—"

"Just like David said."

"I didn't want to beg for help, but I didn't know all this would happen. I swear. Please." She put the phone back in its cradle; he let her. "Okay. Stoney might have gone with Gooch voluntarily. Stoney's scared of Alex. I don't want Gooch in trouble just because you're mad at me."

"Mad at you. The understatement of the year. Mad doesn't quite cover what I feel."

She swallowed, reached for him again. He stepped away and a hard, hurt light came into her eyes.

"Where is this treasure, Lucy?"

"Stoney had it, but he said Alex took it from him. Most of it is coins."

"Most of it?"

"There's a big emerald—"

"The Devil's Eye."

She took a deep breath. "I'll make a deal with you—"

"No deals."

"Let me finish my sentence, please." She sat down. "Let's say Gooch goes after Alex. But Gooch doesn't win. Maybe Alex comes after you or me. I don't know if he knows about me or not."

"I'm thinking he doesn't. Otherwise you would be dead."

"Okay," she said, a little shudder in her voice. "So Alex doesn't know about me. I know where he's at. We just call the police with an anonymous tip about Alex. Just say he killed Patch and Thuy and Jimmy. Give them the room number."

"And what, hope he's got evidence hanging around?"

"Maybe he does. Maybe he can be tied back to the crime scenes. But it takes him out. Stoney won't say anything if Gooch has saved him from Alex. Then we're home free."

"Home free. What about Patch and Thuy?"

"Alex killed them," she said. "He's the one who pays."

"It works until Alex points at Stoney, and Stoney points at you," Whit said. "I don't care about free and clear. And pardon me if I don't believe Stoney Vaughn. He could have killed them—you see that?"

"He's not lying."

"Because why, Lucy? You sense his aura?" His voice rose.

"That's exactly why I wanted to sell the land," she said. "Because you sneer at me. You think running a psychic hotline is tacky, borderline dishonest. Even when I'm just trying to help people. I'm never quite good enough for you, am I?"

"I loved you like no one else, Lucy, and it still wasn't enough for you. Your self-esteem problem is in your head, not mine."

Lucy opened and closed her mouth. She went and sat on the couch. "So go. Turn me in. I don't care."

He resisted the urge to hold her, to make her care again. His throat ached, his hands trembled. It couldn't be over but it was. *If you love her, truly, you forgive her, right?* He steadied his voice. "Right now we need to find Stoney and Gooch."

"What about turning me in? Isn't that at the top of your to-do list?"

"I'm giving you a chance to cooperate, Lucy. Where is this cottage Stoney hid out at?"

"Why?"

"Because I want to see it. I want to see if there's a sign of struggle. If Gooch really kidnapped him, then my path is clear. Will you show me?"

"Yes," she said, and he saw the hope flash in her eyes.

It had taken guts to hang up, but Alex did it as soon as he heard Guchinski's voice and figured out who other than Stoney would be calling him. Let Gooch wait.

He stayed in his car, parked a bit down the highway from the turnoff to Black Jack Point. The phone rang again. Alex clicked it on.

"Do you want to deal or not?" Gooch again.

"I'm busy at the moment. Give me a number to call you back on."

"Don't think so."

"Then you call me back in ten minutes, Mr. Guchinski." And clicked off. Let him sweat that Alex knew his name.

But deal? How was he supposed to deal? The only leverage he had left was the treasure and maybe Gooch didn't care about that. What did Gooch want? The treasure? In exchange for Stoney? Fat chance.

Just go. Go get the stash, rent a truck, get away from the coast, feel out your buyers, get the money, go get your dad. Go to that big blue sky in Costa Rica, sit on the beach, pretend he's not dying for a while. Forget the emerald.

But no emerald—the biggest prize, the one worth millions in one fell swoop after he made carefully placed calls to Bogotá—and all these loose ends. Helen. Guchinski. That judge. And Stoney, insufferable Stoney, getting the better of him. Claudia. Ben. And he'd spend the rest of his life looking over his shoulder? No way. He rubbed his face and when he brought his hands down headlights flashed in his mirror, a car turning and heading south. Whit Mosley's Explorer.

If you don't have leverage, grab it and take it. Alex shifted into gear and tore out after him.

The cottage was dark, no lights spilling along the beach or along the small private road. The sun retreated below the horizon. Whit kept his headlights pointed at the cottage's small door. It was closed.

"Not hanging off its hinges," Lucy said. "That's a good sign."

Whit said nothing.

"So I'm getting the silent treatment?"

"No. I just have nothing to say. Stay here." He got out

of the car, she followed. He tried the door. It opened. He flicked on the lights.

The room was a mess.

"Not good," she said.

"No. It's not from a fight. It's been searched. Or robbed."

"Isn't this trespassing? Oops, you broke a law."

"Lucy, shut up."

"Do you think I don't have guilt that's eating me alive? But I didn't kill them. I tried to protect them."

"I'm not blaming you for their deaths. Although it seems to me you could have warned Patch about them stealing the treasure off his land."

She shook her head. "I hope you're never afraid."

"Danny Laffite. Is he dead? Did Stoney or this Alex kill him?"

"I have no idea."

"He blamed Stoney for a murder and for stealing an antique journal from him. Do you know where that's at?"

"No."

"I just can't figure…Stoney didn't know his brother and Claudia were going to be kidnapped. And that he would need to go hide himself. That old journal's the key to everything, if he wanted to rebury the treasure, right? It validates that Jean Laffite was involved, makes the treasure more valuable for Stoney's purposes."

"Yeah."

"So he has to pick a place to hide. Quickly. Why not where he had already hidden what was of great value to him? Alex doesn't care about the journal. Stoney has access and no one would suspect him putting it here. His house, yeah, maybe a safe-deposit box. But not a client's house. Maybe the journal is what someone was looking for." Alex? Maybe, to close a loose end. Gooch? No. Or Danny Laffite? How?

"Or maybe Alex was looking for the Eye. That's what Alex wants." She straightened a couch cushion. "It's not here, though. I hid it well, Whit. You'd be proud of me."

He turned to stare at her. "You have the emerald?"

"Stoney gave it to me for safekeeping." Her tone went defiant.

"Tell me where it is."

"No," she said. "It was on Patch's private property. They stole it. Now it's mine again. According to his will it and the rest of the treasure should have been mine all along. Stoney was never quite smart enough to look at it from that angle." She gave him a smile, but not a warm one. "So the Eye's my property and I don't have to tell you a thing about it."

"I swear I don't know you." He shook his head.

"But you don't want to know me, Whit. We're finished. You don't love me, so why shouldn't I say whatever crosses my mind? Do you want to look for this journal or do you want to call the police and turn in Gooch?"

"Let's look for the journal."

"You and your double standard."

He didn't argue with her and they began to comb through the house. The cottage was small but elaborate and Whit went upstairs to look through the two bedrooms. They were small but had been searched thoroughly and he decided this was pointless. If anything was to have been found, it had been taken already.

He had just opened a closet door when he heard Lucy cry out, "No—"

"Lucy?" he called.

No answer for a moment, then a crash and she screamed, "Whit!" Another crash. Silence.

Whit moved quietly, down the stairs, pulling Patch's old gun he'd taken from her purse, cocking it, stopping just above the corner where the stairs met the kitchen.

"Judge Mosley?" A man's voice called. Gentle, calm. "You need to step down with your hands up."

"I'm armed," Whit called. "And if you hurt her, I'll kill you."

The answer was a single shot.

Whit froze.

"She's unconscious," the voice called, "so she didn't feel that. But I just shot off a couple of fingers on her left hand. You have five seconds to come out. Moving the gun to her forehead now—"

"No!" Whit stepped out of the stairwell, hands up, gun held between forefinger and thumb.

A man knelt by Lucy, a 9mm Glock in his hand, aimed squarely at Whit. He was rangy, tall, hair dyed cheap blond, round wire-rim glasses. He looked like a professor turned punk rocker.

"Drop it," the man said.

Whit did.

"On your knees, hands on your head."

Whit obeyed. He could see Lucy's hand...all five fingers, there, not shot.

"I lied," Alex Black said. "I really hate messes."

36

———◉———

BEN HAD KICKED the FBI out. Or rather, Claudia thought, he had asked them to leave. He politely told them that he appreciated their help, he felt safe with Claudia around—she blushed at that—but he wanted to be alone and have some time to recover. And there was no proof, after all, that Stoney had committed a crime or actually become the victim of a crime. The phones were tapped in case Stoney or Danny Laffite or the boogeyman called.

The agents gave him thin smiles in answer, but they left, and from the window Claudia watched their cars cut through the Flats. After Agents Grimes and Gordell left, the house seemed too quiet. Ghost empty. She wondered if David might drive by on the pretense of checking on Ben. But the road stayed empty.

Ben clicked on the stereo. Soft Vivaldi filled the room, a whisper of violins and flutes. She stood by the fireplace, studying a nautical map, drawn in an ancient's hand, that hung above the mantel.

He came up behind her, put his hands on her shoulders. "I'm glad you're here, Claudia. I'd be nuts in this house alone."

"I like this old map," she said.

"It's a reproduction, although if Stoney has too much to drink he tells people it's an original. Long ago a big chunk of the world was unknown. See, there's Europe, badly drawn—they didn't see the known world like it really was. You leave it, you reach the middle"—he pointed at a giant serpent in the waves, its head thrown back and tongue extending like fire—"they say, 'Here there be dragons.' If that doesn't scare you off, go all the way and you sail past the edge of the world. Lost forever. The point of no return."

"I think this map is more accurate than a real map."

He kissed her neck. "Would you like some wine? Or some beer? You want me to fix you a michelada?"

"A michelada sounds good."

He went into the kitchen, filled two tall glasses with ice, a dash of Tabasco and Worcestershire, a bit of tomato juice, a sprinkle of pepper, and a dollop of lime juice. Then he poured a cold Dos Equis lager into each glass. He brought a glass to her and they sat down on the Mexican tile floor, watching the sunlight die over the bay. They sat side by side, their shoulders barely touching. Claudia sipped. The michelada tasted like a perfect steak, but cold and smooth.

"When will they bring *Jupiter* back?" she asked. The FBI had it, treating it as a crime scene.

"I don't care. Not sure I ever want to set foot aboard that boat again. I suppose if something's happened to Stoney the boat is mine."

She said nothing; he seemed mildly surprised at the thought.

"You hungry? I can grill up some amberjack," he said.

They finished their micheladas and then he cooked them dinner, pouring cold sauvignon blanc and fixing salad, fish scented with herbs, risotto, sliced kiwis, deftly moving from pan to pan. She could see he was making a strenuous effort to shove the darkness of the past few days behind them. They ate, her appetite suddenly ravenous. She drank two fat glasses of the New Zealand white and mellowness tiptoed over her.

He was opening a fresh bottle when she began to shake, standing by the counter. She set the wineglass down, suddenly afraid it would break between her fingers. She felt cold as ice.

"Hey. Hey now." Ben took her in his arms, held her close. Her breathing grew ragged.

"Something's wrong," she said. "De—de—delayed shock. I don't know."

He steered her toward the couch, sat with her, warmed her with his arms. He said nothing, kissed her jaw, her throat, gently. She held him tight.

"It's okay, 's'okay." A few moments later, the shivers subsided.

"Well, what was that?" she said, embarrassed. "Aren't I the big baby?"

"You know how much braver you are than I am?" he said. He tipped her jaw, looked into her eyes. "I cried. Locked up on that boat. Afraid of what they'd done to you. Afraid of what he was going to do to me."

She took his face in between her palms and she kissed him. First on his giant bruise, gentle as a feather, then on his lips. He kissed back, a little tentative, like she might still be shaky. She wasn't. After five long kisses Ben eased open the buttons on her blouse, touched the lacy edge of her bra, nuzzled the top of her breasts.

"I want you," he whispered.

He took her hands, led her upstairs to his bedroom. She

undressed him; he undressed her, from head to feet, kissing the wrap that bound her broken toe, the bandages on her hands. She kissed the horrid bruise on his face again, the broken finger.

He kissed her in her middle and they moved the sheets into a slow tangle, Claudia finally surrounding him with her heat.

"Our first time in what, thirteen years?" she whispered.

"Lucky thirteen." He laughed. He was confident with her, more sure of his touch; she was more relaxed.

"Worth waiting for," she said, eager for the touch of his skin against hers.

"I always cared for you, Claudia. Always," he said, closing his lips over her throat, his hands cupping her breasts. She felt the life in his mouth, his hands, and suddenly life seemed far sweeter than she had known, thinking of lying on that boat, bobbing in the waves, the sun a glaring, remorseless eye.

"Now," she gasped. "Now."

Afterward, his breath warmed the back of her neck, and she fell asleep.

She didn't hear him rise from the bed.

"Doesn't hurt too bad, does it?" Alex leaned down, patted Whit on the cheek. He'd taken four steps toward Whit after Whit laid down the gun, smashed the butt of his Glock twice across Whit's face, knocking him nearly cold, opening his cheek. Whit sat, half-propped against the refrigerator, blood splattered all over his dancing pineapples shirt.

Lucy was still out, breathing shallowly, a trickle of blood oozing from her hairline and meandering down her forehead.

Alex Black squatted down in front of Whit, the gun aimed at Whit's stomach. "Your friend Guchinski," he said. "Where's he at?"

"I don't know." Whit's face felt broken. The cheekbone might be fractured. It hurt. His voice sounded thick and dopey.

Alex cocked the gun, aimed it at Lucy's head. "Try again."

"It's the truth. Please don't hurt her. I don't know where he is right now."

"So what's his angle?"

"I don't know."

"Rethink your answers, Your Honor. Can I call you that? Your Honor. I feel so privileged."

"I didn't know he was grabbing Stoney. I didn't know he even knew where Stoney was."

"How'd he find out Stoney was here?"

Whit paused. No way he'd point to Lucy. "He must have followed you out here."

"No, I don't think so," Alex said. He closed his hand— fingers hard from digging, Whit thought; they felt like steel springs—around Whit's windpipe. Alex wormed the gun in between Whit's legs, pressed the barrel against his testicles. Whit quit breathing.

"Here's my theory, Your Honor. Stoney wanted to get rid of me. He got himself a new partner. He gave the Devil's Eye to new partner, who has a guard dog mentality. I think new partner was Guchinski, and he's cutting you in, too."

Whit risked a very small, shallow breath. The barrel didn't ease its pressure.

"Now Guchinski has gotten Stoney hidden away and is calling me, wanting to deal. But I smell a trap. What do you smell?"

"Gooch doesn't have the Eye."

"Who does?"

"Stoney. You think he's gonna trust anyone with a multimillion-dollar emerald?" Whit breathed again, cleared his throat. *Let this lie work.* "I can't believe you fell for what he said. Giving it to someone else."

"So you've chatted with Stoney."

"Just that once. When you were hiding in the house."

Alex smashed his fist across Whit's face. Whit tried hard not to cry out, to groan.

"I wasn't hiding." Alex shook his head, ran his tongue along the little scar at his mouth's corner, gave a little annoyed laugh. "I give you this, Judge: You got balls. Big ones. I pull the trigger here, there's gonna be, what, sixty percent of your balls left?"

"If you kill me or Lucy, you don't get the Eye," Whit said. "Gooch has Stoney under his thumb, and he'll never give it to you. Gooch'll hunt you down and kill you. An inch at a time."

Alex picked up a cell phone from the kitchen counter. He keyed in a number, dialed. "Mr. Guchinski, you answering Stoney's phone now?"

Whit could not hear Gooch's reply. Alex stood, let the gun slide along Whit's bruised face, took a step back. On the floor Lucy stirred, moaned Whit's name.

"No. You listen. I got my own trump cards, idiot." He held the phone close to Whit's mouth. "Speak to him. Say hello. Say more than hello and I kill the woman."

"Hello," Whit said.

Alex yanked the phone back. "I got the judge's woman, too. So you got Stoney, man. I don't care. Get rid of him now—he's nothing but trouble." A pause. "You want these two, you're gonna give me the Eye." He glanced at Whit.

Whit thought: *He believed me. Or I just confirmed what he already thought, that Stoney has the Eye.*

Alex listened, winked at Whit. "Give me directions," he said. "Okay. We'll meet there. In an hour or so." Pause. "We make the trade then." He clicked off. "People are so predictable."

"What?" Whit asked.

Alex stared at Whit. "Tell me, how come a judge is friends with a crook like Gooch?"

"We have a lot in common."

"Yeah," Alex said. "Lots of judges in Florida are crooked, too. Trust me." Whit saw a shift in his face, amusement hardening into contempt. He cocked the gun, kept it aimed at Whit, and stood over Lucy. She was trying to surface back to consciousness. The amber necklace around her throat was broken, the jewel loose on the floor. He wanted to reach over, fix it for her, hold her, tell her it was okay.

Her eyes fluttered open, looking at him but not quite registering him. Whit could see two little trails of blood from her hairline where Alex had pistol-whipped her, her right ear bloodied.

"I don't think she's in any condition to travel, do you?" Alex said with a crooked smile.

"What?" Whit said again. *Okay, I can be the hostage—*

"We don't need her." The grin widened, the gun moved to Lucy.

"No, please—" Whit yelled.

"Devotion. That's nice," Alex said. Then he fired three times.

37

━━━◉━━━

CLAUDIA AWOKE IN complete darkness. The night surrounding her felt as solid as glass, and panic tightened her stomach, thrummed between her shoulder blades. She felt tied. Danny. Danny still had her, Gar waiting nearby, the tattooed arms ready to force the life out of her, hungry to force himself inside her. She sat up in bed, blinking, easing out of the snarl of sheets.

No Danny. No Gar.

No Ben in bed.

She glanced at the digital clock. Ten-forty-six p.m. She'd drunk too much, the michelada and the wine too early in the evening; she wasn't used to it. She had a little headache, not bad. She got up, went to the bedroom balcony that faced onto the bay. The heavy curtains were pulled closed and she parted them an inch. St. Leo Bay lay calm in the night, the moon a wafer in the wash of the Milky Way.

She closed the curtains, found her clothes on the floor. She stepped into panties, pulled her khaki slacks up over her legs. She groped for her bra and blouse and put them on.

She started down the stairs, toward the spill of light in

the kitchen, heard Ben say, "All right, I'll be there." When she entered the kitchen he was standing by the granite-top counter, a cell phone in his hand. He set it down on the counter.

"Ben?"

"That was my brother, babe. He's alive."

"Where is he?"

"In Corpus Christi. He wants me to come see him. Right now."

"He decided to come out from under his rock?"

He didn't react to her sarcasm. "He's ashamed. Embarrassed that he panicked. But he's alive." He took Claudia into his arms. "He's at a warehouse he owns down by the port. You know a guy named Leonard Guchinski?"

"Yeah. He's nuts. How is he involved?"

"Stoney's with this Guchinski guy, and I'm not quite sure why."

"So what are you going to do, Ben?"

"I should call the police," Ben said in a tone that said he actually didn't want to do that. "Let them know he at least is all right."

"You want to wait until you talk to him?"

"I kind of think I should." He tucked the cell phone into his front pants pocket. "You want to go with me?"

"Maybe this should be a private meeting," Claudia said.

"I'd like it a lot if you came. He owes you an apology and an explanation. Maybe you can help us figure out how to deal with the authorities, help him avoid embarrassment. He's probably going to need a lawyer, too."

"He's going to need a PR firm," Claudia said. She wasn't worried about Stoney's embarrassment. "Let me run upstairs, get my purse, and we'll go."

*   *   *

The trunk was dark, so dark that when Whit shut his eyes he could not tell the world had gone darker. The rattle and bump of the Taurus shook him back to full consciousness as they sped down the highway.

I'm going to kill you, he thought.

If he simply lay here, prone with grief, Alex won. He had no doubt Alex's goal was to kill him, Gooch, Stoney, whoever got in his way. A clean sweep. If he thought too much about Lucy a sickening paralysis crept into him.

He had hardly moved since Alex punched him again for good measure and dumped him into the trunk. He felt in his pocket for his cell phone. Gone. He groped in the dark, trying to find anything that could be used as a weapon. Alex had been at Stoney's when Whit stopped by, but this car hadn't been. So either a rental or maybe stolen. Maybe Alex hadn't paid enough attention to what was in here if it was stolen, and the trunk seemed cluttered with junk.

His fingers found the rim of the spare. Soft material that felt like silk, maybe some clothes destined for the dry cleaner's. A small wrench, probably left out for the lugs of the spare. A book, a wilting paperback. A cool plane of metal, with three hinges on the side.

Tool box.

Whit slowly turned the toolbox around, found its opening. Closed, but not locked. He managed to open it, heard the clatter of metal tools as the car hit a bump in the highway. Waited for the car to slow, pull over to the side. If he made too much noise—if Alex thought he were anything but grief-stricken and broken now—Alex would kill him.

Taking his time, forcing himself to be calm, Whit let his fingers explore the tools. A tape measure. A hammer, which would be great to swing at Alex's face. A baggie, with what felt like an assortment of screws, nails, and lug nuts inside. A small ball of twine. Pliers. His fingers found a bar in the space above the tools. A handle. The tool box had a lift-out tray, with another compartment beneath.

He eased the top compartment out. His fingers fumbled inside the deeper well of the box. More baggies with nails or hooks. Screwdrivers with hard plastic handles, two or three. A ball peen hammer, the better to break Alex's teeth with if he got a chance. Masking tape, a roll thinned from use. Electrical wire. He pricked his finger on a long V of sharp metal, with wicked little teeth on each side, a carved wooden handle. He gently explored the tool with his fingertips. A wallboard saw, the kind used to slice through Sheetrock, to make cutouts for light switches and electrical outlets. But with that nice pointed blade for plunge cuts into walls.

All it takes is one mistake, Whit thought, *and, you murdering bastard, you just made it.*

"You're gonna sit here real quiet," Gooch said. "You mess this up so that Whit or Lucy gets hurt, you're the mess."

"And I thought we'd gotten to be friends," Stoney said.

"Yeah, I'm going to be godfather to your kids."

"So what, I sit here and you negotiate with Alex?"

"No. You sit here and I get rid of him if I have to," Gooch said. "Then I give you to the judge and he figures out what to do with you."

Talking to him like he was a kid. "Be nice, Gooch. Or I'll press charges and you'll go to prison."

"Are you quite so eager to get more in the public eye that way, Stoney? Sit down," Gooch said, and Stoney said nothing. He eased down into the chair behind the desk and Gooch turned to douse out the lights.

Now, Stoney thought. He grabbed the handle of the desk drawer, gave it a heavy yank.

The drawer slid out, fast, and Stoney swung it as he bolted around the desk, connecting with Gooch's skull as he turned. Gooch went down. Stoney brought the drawer down again.

Gooch's eyes went white. "Fuuu—"

Stoney took the heavy end of the drawer and smacked it down hard on Gooch's head again, twice. Gooch sprawled across the concrete floor.

That was fast, Stoney thought. He picked up the gun, groped Gooch's thick neck for a pulse. After a moment he found it. But Gooch seemed to be out cold. Stoney considered whether or not to shoot him. Easier than shooting Danny. At least he wasn't looking at him with a wet face and a horrible, blubbering pleading look. He pressed the gun against the back of Gooch's head.

But then headlights gleamed against the shuttered warehouse windows, a car turning in, and Stoney Vaughn threw a tarp over Gooch, took the gun, doused the last light, and stepped back into the shadows, into the maze of unopened crates and equipment in the clutter.

Stoney knelt down by a section of crates in the back. He checked Gooch's gun by flashlight, a full clip. He sat back, raised the flashlight, its little circle of light spilling along the crates five feet in front of him.

He froze. "That bastard," he whispered.

38

———⊷◉⊶———

WHIT FELT THE car come to a stop, heard the engine turn off. He had reloaded the toolbox, closed it, tucked the wallboard saw into the waist of his khakis, tightened his belt. He hoped he could pull the blade out fast without slicing himself open. He closed his eyes, thought of Lucy.

Her asking, *I'm safe with you, aren't I?* And him saying, *Always, babe.* She'd wanted reassurance—she'd wanted to know he loved her no matter what.

He was crouched, shoulders against the trunk's lid.

C'mon, c'mon, he thought. *I want you.*

The driver's door slammed; he heard footsteps against concrete.

"Judge?" Alex's voice called, low, quiet. Even gentle.

"Yes?"

"I want you to lie facedown, hands laced on your head. You yell for help, you kick the trunk or me, you fart too loud, I empty this clip into you. You understand me?"

"Yeah," Whit said. He lay down as Alex ordered, the little wicked saw sharp against his hip.

A key slid into the lock, the trunk door opened. The muzzle of a gun pressed into the back of Whit's neck.

"Up. Slowly. Not a sound."

"You'll be in hell in less than ten minutes," Whit said. "You don't have a prayer against Gooch." He got up, felt the saw stay in its place against his leg.

"You got in over your head, Your Honor. I don't hold greed against you. But you took on too much."

He didn't want Gooch to kill Alex. He wanted to do it himself.

He stepped out of the trunk, the gun still firmly at the back of his head, and the two men walked to the warehouse door. An electronic keypad was by the door and Alex entered in a code. The electronic locks on the door clicked open.

"You first, Judge," Alex said.

Whit stepped inside the darkness.

"Guchinski?" Alex called. "Put the lights on. Now. Or the judge dies."

"Chill, Alex. It's all right." Stoney Vaughn, a little rasp of voice in the blackness.

"Where's your new buddy?" Alex called.

"Barely breathing on the concrete floor. I bashed his head in."

Alex waited. "I don't believe you."

"Come in and see." Stoney's voice shook.

Fear? Anger? Whit wondered.

"What are you mad about? He kidnaps you. I try to save you—" Alex said.

"You're quite the hero," Stoney said from the dark. "You coming in or not?"

"Do you have the Eye, Stoney?" Alex said.

"Right here in my pocket."

"Okay, we're cool, right? I'm coming in now." And Alex did, pushing Whit along in front of him, not closing the door after him in case he had to barrel out fast. No light on in the warehouse, just the smell of dust and machinery, and oddly enough, the reek of greasy Chinese food.

"Alex," Stoney's voice called. "Shut the door."

"Turn on the lights. What's with this darkness act?" Alex's hands fumbled for the switches, couldn't find them.

The lights clanged on, Stoney standing ten feet away, a gleaming pistol in his hand.

"Nice gun," Alex said.

"It's a Shootyadickov," Stoney said. "I got it from Gooch. Hello, Judge. Sorry about this. Wow, Alex, you beat the snot out of him."

Whit's heart sank. The wallboard saw was a stupid, stupid idea. Gooch down. Him stuck between these two jerks, each with a gun. He kept his hands down by his untucked shirt. "He shot Lucy," he said.

Stoney's lips—clenched together in a tough-guy sneer—parted. "What?"

"She's dead," Alex said. "I didn't want to bring them both."

"That . . . wasn't necessary. I . . ." Stoney said.

"You what?" Alex said. "You need her land to rebury the gold so you can discover it and, what, get your picture on the cover of *National Geographic*? Man, give it up."

"I liked Lucy," Stoney said.

"Yeah, she seemed real nice. A shame. I hate what I have to do sometimes. Where's the Eye?"

Whit kept waiting for Alex to say, *Well, Gooch is out of the game—don't need you* and shoot him dead. But instead Alex kept Whit in front of him, still a shield.

"Don't worry about the Eye," Stoney said. "I promised you could keep most of the coins. I'd get thirty percent and the Eye. That's more than fair. Let's just settle our accounts now, Alex."

"I can get the coins for you tomorrow. I kind of had my hands full tonight."

"You'll get them tonight." Stoney's face reddened.

"I can't," Alex said.

"Sure you can. They're just about thirty feet away, in crates over there," Stoney said. "What I want to know, Alex buddy, is how you got the treasure into my own warehouse."

"Don't know what you mean."

"The coins. They are all over there in that corner, crated, just as we left them in the storage unit," Stoney said.

The silence hung in the air. *Now,* Whit thought.

"Alex," Whit said. "Stoney doesn't have the Eye. He's lying. He said it was in his pocket. Make him show the Eye to you."

"Stoney. That's not a bad idea. I've missed seeing the Eye over the past couple of days," Alex said. "But slowly."

"I was not speaking literally when I said it was in my pocket," Stoney said.

"That means he lied," Whit said. "You were right. He gave it to Gooch. But now he's betrayed Gooch. You think he's gonna play clean with you?"

Alex took a step toward Stoney, keeping Whit close in front. Whit took a step forward in response, moaned, as though the pain of the beating had caught up with him. He closed his hand over his shirttail and around the handle of the wallboard saw.

"I didn't give it to Gooch," Stoney said. "He kidnapped me, Alex."

"You seem to have suffered mightily."

"We have to stick together," Stoney said.

"Do we?" Alex said.

*   *   *

Late-night traffic was light heading into Corpus Christi. Claudia drove, finished a cup of hot coffee, the warm effect of the wine fading. Ben said he was too nervous to drive so they took her pickup truck.

"I think I would feel better if he'd actually apologized," Ben said. "On the phone. He sounded so cryptic."

"Give it time. Maybe he thinks he didn't do a thing wrong."

"How could that thought even live in his brain?"

"You've gotten angrier during the drive," she said.

"Knowing he's okay, I'm finally feeling mad. I don't let myself get mad enough."

"Not me," said Claudia. "I'm sort of comfortable with getting pissed off. You're way too even-keeled."

The port area was aglow with lights as they reached the Harbor Bridge, arching two hundred thirty-five feet above where the Nueces and Corpus Christi bays joined. Claudia saw the blue lights centered on the USS *Lexington*, retired in the calm of Corpus Christi Bay, the Texas State Aquarium, the soft glow of downtown ahead of her. She barreled onto the Harbor Bridge, the traffic in front of her thin.

Ben squirmed in his seat, as though trying to get comfortable, and suddenly she felt rather than saw the gun hovering close to her head.

"What—"

"It'll help if you're even-keeled right now. I'm sorry."

Her breath caught and Ben said, "Just keep driving, okay? You're losing speed. Pick it up."

"Tell me what you're doing or I'm going to drive the car off the bridge," she said.

"No, you won't," he said. "I know you." His voice quiet now, bled of the earlier anger.

"Ben...this isn't the way to help your brother."

"He can rot in hell for all I care," Ben said. "He would have gotten us both killed. You think I care about him now?" His tone softened. "You, I'm sorry about. I couldn't help myself. Never quite got over you. If we hadn't been kidnapped...if you hadn't learned about all this...I wish you weren't a cop." The lights of the bridge flashed by them. His voice toughened. "Take the port exit. Then a hard right, then two more lefts until we get where we're going."

Hadn't learned about all this... "Are you saying you know where this treasure is?"

"Just be quiet. Talking is only going to make it worse."

"What, you're going to kill your brother? And me?"

"I'm not going to kill Stoney," Ben said. "Even now, I'm not sure I could. My partner will take care of that."

"Partner," she said. "Ben, no. Please. Don't do this."

"Take the exit," he said. "Or I'll shoot you, and I'll shoot whoever's in the first car that stops."

The bridge began its downward slope, toward Corpus Christi Beach and the port, and Claudia took the Port Street exit. It was a very short exit, forcing a hard right turn, and she thought of letting the car just go straight, crash, although she couldn't risk the life of anyone else who might stop to help.

"I really respect that you're not crying right now. Or calling me names."

"I'm waiting for an explanation, Ben. Money? Jealousy of your brother?"

"Money. You know what it's like to be ten times smarter than Stoney and not have a hundredth of what he does?" He sighed. "I wish you could come with me. But that's not possible. Turn left here. Then the next left." She turned onto a side street dominated by one large warehouse, the lot by it empty except for a battered red pickup—she recognized it as Gooch's—and a nondescript Ford Taurus. She parked on the other side of the truck, away from the Taurus.

"Turn off your headlights."

Claudia thumbed the switch and the little lot went dark.

"Now what?" she said. Her own service revolver was in the compartment between them. She couldn't possibly reach it without him blowing her head off. He opened the compartment, fished out her gun, put it in his lap.

"You know," Ben said, "I'm grateful we made love. Truly. We're going inside."

"So no one will hear you kill me?"

He started to reply, but gunshots sounded inside the warehouse, three of them in rapid fire. "Damn."

The gun wavered for a second and Claudia flung open the door, threw herself out onto the asphalt, the driver's-side window exploding above her. She crabbed under the car as Ben scrambled out of the truck.

39

‑‑‑◦◉◦‑‑‑

As ALEX FIRED, his arm outstretched past Whit, Whit slammed hard into his arm, pinning him into the wall and trying to pull the gun from his hand. He got his fingers around the grip, gouged Alex's wrists, but Alex grabbed the back of his head, smashed it hard into the concrete wall.

Whit went down thinking, *Stupid, stupid.*

Alex pressed down on him, knee in his back, and Whit saw Stoney lying on the floor, bone and blood and shredded jaw showing.

"That was stupid," Alex said. "You missing your girl? You want to see her?"

"I know where Gooch hid the Eye, idiot. Shoot me and you'll never get it."

"Liar!" he screamed. "You would have told me to save Lucy."

"I didn't think you'd really shoot her." His right hand closed over his shirttail and the hidden saw's handle. But he couldn't pull it free, not with Alex's weight on him. "Let me up and I'll tell you."

"You'll tell me now." Alex grabbed Whit's left hand, flattened it on the concrete. Jammed the hot barrel of the gun against the back of Whit's hand.

"I'll show you," Whit said.

"Show." Alex froze. "It's here?"

"Let me up and I'll show it to you. Don't shoot off my hand." Whit let out a scream, a sob. "Just don't shoot off my hand, man, please. I'll show you. Please?" He began to mumble and cry.

Alex hesitated for two seconds. "Okay." He eased up into a squat by Whit. "Get up." His voice was thick with contempt.

Whit got to both knees, holding his side, lips quivering, fresh blood smearing his broken cheek. Then, slowly, to his feet, his hand under the tail of his shirt, like his side ached.

"Please...please..." Whit said, unsteady on his feet, like standing was an ordeal. "Please, I'll show you..."

And then in one swift motion he slashed out at Alex with the little wicked blade.

Claudia had counted on Ben running around the car to finish her, hoping he'd think she'd try to put distance between her and his gun. So instead she rolled under the car. She heard his feet pound around the truck's back, trying to get a sight on her, seeing if she was hit or running. She saw his feet—tennis shoes bright white in the dark—she let him race past her, peering into the dark of the lot and the loading docks, listening for her running feet and looking for her moving shadow. She rolled out from under the truck as he started to curse, the broken glass crunching under her shoulders. Ben turned and she barreled toward him in a flying tackle. His gun blazed and she felt the devilish whisper of a bullet sear past her head. She slammed hard into him, smashing her forearm into his throat, driving her knee into his groin.

He went down heavy, his head cracking against the pavement. She piled on top of him, one hand yanking his hair back and the other hunting his eyes. He screamed and elbowed her hard, shoved her down onto her back.

It was dark, a dim gleam of lights from the warehouse and the port blocks away, and she saw faint shine on a gun's barrel—he'd had both guns; he must've dropped one when she kicked his feet out from him. The shine was a half foot from her hand and she seized the gun, prayed the safety was off, swung it toward his face and fired.

Missed.

He stumbled to his feet, turning and running for the warehouse. "Freeze! Ben!" He didn't freeze and she fired twice in the dark. She heard the wet-meat sound of a bullet striking him, heard him sprawl along the steps leading to the warehouse.

She ran to where Ben lay. In the thin light from the shuttered windows she saw the wound in the lower part of his back, blood a black spurt. He breathed in sharp hitches, groaning.

Gunshots inside, and she'd just shot a man. Gooch in there, maybe in trouble. She ran back to her truck, fumbled for the cell phone.

Missed, Whit thought in that split second.

The blade missed and Alex would shoot him before he could stab again. But then Alex's eyes went wide, shocked, his hand went to his throat and the blood fountained. Alex trying to scream and nothing coming but blood.

Alex's eyes flashed with rage and fear and horror and he brought the gun back up toward Whit but then he dropped it, the other hand going to his throat to stem the flood. He fell to his knees. Whit grabbed the gun, stood there.

"How does it feel?" Whit said, his voice breaking. "How does it—"

And he saw Alex's lips forming the word *please*.

The organic coppery smell of rupture filled the air, overpowered the scent of gunfire.

"Gooch?" Claudia's voice called.

Whit saw her coming through the still-open front door, her service pistol out, in a firing stance. He tried to speak, as silent as Alex.

Claudia ran to him, seeing Alex bleed out his life, toppling to the floor, grabbing at Whit's shoes. She gasped at the sight of Stoney's body.

Whit didn't let go of the saw; its handle felt burned to his hand.

Claudia tore Alex's shirt off him, pushing the fabric around his throat, trying to stanch the flow of blood, apply useless pressure, telling him help was on the way.

Whit said, without looking at her, "Gooch is here. Help him."

"Whit . . ." Claudia started.

Whit set Alex's gun on a table. He dropped the saw on the floor.

"Let him die, Claudia. Just let him die."

Alex paled, stared up at him, then through him.

"I'm going to find Gooch." Whit's voice didn't sound quite right.

"Whit," Claudia said. "Whit."

40

---◄●●►---

CLAUDIA WENT WITH Whit to the Coastal Psychics Network on Sunday afternoon, not having slept that night. He had a spare key Lucy had given him two weeks ago and he opened the doors. The business was closed, the psychics mourning at home.

"I didn't think straight. Didn't think about where she'd hide it," he said.

"We don't have to do this now, Whit," Claudia said.

"She loved this place. And I don't want it here," Whit said. "If I'm right. Her office is this way."

Jean Laffite's treasure was finally confirmed to consist of twenty thousand dollars' worth of gold bars, ten thousand in silver bars, and a cache of rare 1820-minted Monteblanco coins worth, in numismatic and historical value, five million dollars. Scattered among the coins and bars in the crates used by Alex and Stoney were fragments of bone and soil from the Gilbert dig site, including a finger bone. The Corpus Christi police kept the treasure in the warehouse under heavy guard while they processed the shooting scene and called the Texas Historical Commission. But the Devil's Eye was yet to be found.

In her office, Whit glanced at the small foil mobile, the

scattered books on ESP and phone marketing, still with their little neon Post-its as bookmarks, worn from her thumbing. On the mantel above her desk were the crystals, amber and yellow and clear and green and red. Arranged just so for the healing powers they emitted. He didn't feel healed.

"There," he said.

"Oh, Whit," Claudia said. "I don't think so. These are too small."

"No. Look," he said. He inspected several, then ran his finger along the largest green one. It was the muddy green of a riverbed. He scraped paint off the stone with a thumbnail and the soft green glow came through, the color of time. The seductive green of envy.

"It's really sort of ugly." He handed it to her. "Iris Dominguez can tell us if this is it. Or a gemologist. Right now I don't know where else to look. Hiding it here is classic Lucy. Plain sight. She—" He stopped.

"Whit..."

"I never want to see it again, okay, Claudia?"

"Okay," she said. "Listen. I'm worried about you. We need to talk."

He stared at her. "The way you shot your boyfriend. I meant to say that was well done, what with it being so dark."

A day later four gemologists said the Devil's Eye was worthless: the right size, but not the valuable emerald. A nicely done copy, not worth millions, not worth anything at all. At some time—either by a thief in Mexico before *Santa Barbara* sailed or by Jean Laffite or by Stoney—the Eye was replaced with a worthless hunk of green crystal.

Claudia stopped by his house and told Whit about the report. He was silent. She wondered if he had slept.

"Whit?" she said after the silence grew too long.

Finally he said, "People will keep looking for it, won't they?"

"I suppose they will, after all the news coverage. Dig up Stoney Vaughn's yard, or the rest of Black Jack Point. David's mentioned they've already chased some folks off Stoney's land. Thinking he hid some of the treasure there."

He turned away from her.

"Whit?"

"I figured out the person who snooped through my house was Lucy. She knew where my key was, under the fern on the porch. I guess she wanted to know if I had notes on the murders, if there was any way she could be implicated. Or if Stoney was implicated. Whatever might lead back to her."

"Maybe Lucy came here, waited for you to come home, wanted to tell you the whole truth. Then she lost her nerve, left."

"It's nice to think that," he said, "isn't it?"

When Claudia got home David was waiting there in shorts and a T-shirt. He sat on the stairs leading to her apartment with a cold twelve-pack of Shiner Bock.

"What's this?" she said.

"I think we should get drunk," David said. "I'm more likely to apologize when I'm drunk."

"That's a good reason."

"Someone finally put you through more hell than I did," David said. "That sucks. I'm sorry, Claudia."

She let him in and they drank the beer, her sitting on the couch, him on the floor. She drank the first one fast, too fast, and made herself promise to take longer for the second.

"So Ben was in it with Alex Black from the beginning?"

"I wasn't the only seduction in Ben's life," Claudia said.

David raised an eyebrow.

"Ben got seduced himself. Living with a wealthy brother who was living on the edge of the law in more ways than one and wasn't paying a price for it. Of course Ben is not talking and he's using Stoney's money to hire some fancy defense lawyer from Houston." She sipped her beer. "I won't get a chance to say this on the stand at Ben's trial unless we find evidence, but I think Ben found out about Stoney's plan to steal treasure from Patch Gilbert's land and fake an archaeological dig on Lucy's land. And if he'd gotten to know Alex Black through Stoney, he would have seen that Alex was more interested in the treasure's financial value than in the fame of discovery. Ben didn't have Stoney's blind spot for glory. So he must have cut a separate deal with Alex. They would have grabbed the treasure and then Alex would have eliminated Stoney. But then they didn't plan on Patch and Thuy Tran showing up and having a double murder complicate their whole deal. And they sure didn't count on Danny Laffite coming after them with a gang and a vengeance."

She finished her beer. David handed her another. "You know what pisses me off?" she asked.

"What, honey?"

"That jerk," she said. "He abandoned me with Danny and Gar, maybe he even cut a deal with Zack Simard to get him to leave us behind on the other boat. He knew Gar would kill me, kill Danny. I'm sure he killed Zack Simard at some point, dumped the body, ran the boat aground. He looked like the poor little victim. The whole time he was in with Alex Black. I'm pretty sure Stoney never called Ben that night, asking him to come to the warehouse. That was Alex and Ben's plan: get rid of Stoney, get rid of me since I was pushing on Ben to help the cops, leave the country with the treasure."

"He should have stuck with teaching."

"Ben molding young minds—I may puke." She downed more beer, wiped her mouth with the back of her hand. "I don't think it would surprise me if he and Alex had planned on getting rid of each other, in the end. Greedy bastards."

"Claudia, it's not your fault." David rested his chin on his knees, gave her a sad smile.

"What?"

"I know you. You're mad at yourself for not having seen through this guy. Listen, his own brother didn't see through him."

"I'm smarter than Stoney Vaughn ever was, please." She shook her head. "I think my career at the PD just flatlined. He's ruined a couple of major league pleasant high school memories for me."

"Memories?"

"He was my first, David, back when we were in high school."

He opened another beer. "You mean I wasn't?"

"I never told you you were. You were my second."

"Well," said David, "you weren't my first either."

"I think I'll wear a red dress to Ben's trial," she said, a little drunk. "That loser."

"I'm sorry," David said. "For you. For Whit."

"You can't stand Whit."

"I'm gonna try to stand him, Claud."

She smiled for the first time. "Now you're drunk."

They drank too much, both of them, and they ended up kissing but she wasn't drunk enough to sleep with him. She wouldn't let him drive, so David slept on her couch and at one point in the night, dehydrated and hungover, she got up for water and she watched him sleep and to her surprise a little part of her missed him.

Then she went back to bed, hoping it was just the beer.

41

———◈———

LUCY WAS BURIED next to Patch, in Port Leo's big, grand Catholic cemetery. Afterward, Whit felt as hollow as though his bones had been plucked from beneath his skin. He took a month off from court, got a retired county judge to fill in for him. He did not have to rule on Lucy's cause of death or see the autopsy papers. He let Gooch take him out on the waters each day after the funeral, the summer roaring into its hottest days, sat and stared at the flat of the bay, watching the waves live and die in their brief existence.

The third week Gooch invited Claudia and she sat with Whit on the stern of the boat, in chairs designed for deep-sea fishing. Gooch stood on the flying bridge, steering out into the Gulf. Helen Dupuy had gotten work in Port Leo, cleaning at a bed-and-breakfast, and could not join them. Whit drank a Coke, not talking much, only saying how the Astros were bound to disappoint again this summer.

"Lucy enjoyed baseball, didn't she?" Claudia said.

Whit didn't look at her. "Yeah."

She touched his hand. "I didn't love Ben—I hadn't quite gotten past the infatuation point. We hadn't been together very long. But you loved Lucy."

"Yes, Dr. Claudia, I did." Sounding a little irritated with her now.

"But you haven't grieved for her."

"Of course I have."

"Tell me, did killing Alex make you feel better, Whit?"

He stared at her, turned away. "This is going to be a damn long day fishing."

"It was self-defense. But you killed him. You even told me to let him die. Not that anything could have saved him then." Her words—unsaid in the long quiet of the past weeks—came in a rush.

"Claudia, let it go."

"Are you worried you're like him in some way? He killed Lucy, you killed him—you think you're on his level?"

"No," he said after a pause. "I don't feel anything about killing him yet. That bothers me." He looked away. "But Lucy. I…yelled at her. I ended it with her. I said terrible things to her."

"You had every right to be mad at her, at what she'd done. You can be mad at someone you love."

"That only works if you get to say you're sorry, Claud."

"She knows, Whit. She knows." She laced her fingers with his.

Gooch stopped the boat, dropped anchor, called down that it was time to fish.

"Let's go swimming first," she said.

"You want to get in the water? After you nearly died out here?"

"Not the water's fault. What am I supposed to do, avoid the Gulf for the rest of my life?" Claudia stood, took off her T-shirt, dropped her shorts. She had a swimsuit underneath, a navy two-piece, not cut too brief.

"Is that a police-issue bikini?" Gooch called.

She shot him the finger, dove over the edge. She surfaced. "Come on, it feels great," she called to Whit, who stood at the rail.

He didn't move.

"Whit, come on."

Whit shucked off his shirt, cannonballed over the railing like he thought he'd better before he changed his mind. Broke to the surface, let the gentle wave swell pick him up, settle him back down. Claudia kicked away from him, giving him space.

"It feels okay," he said.

She watched him dive down, surface, again and again, swimming through the waves, and if there were any tears on his face she could not tell.

They swam, they fished, Gooch saying no more than two sentences about what a good job his Washington lawyer had done in keeping his record clean. They talked instead of baseball, of books, of perhaps a trip to Austin for a long weekend to hear Lyle Lovett play. The day was warm and sleepy, the water fine and greenish-blue, the sky smooth as pearl. On the way back in through the bay Whit watched Claudia doze in her chair and he wanted to reach out and touch her hand and say, *I know how bad Ben hurt you. I know, and still you worry about me and I can't believe how you care. But I'll be okay. Given time, I'll be okay. I will choose to be okay.*

But Whit didn't say any of these things. He just closed his eyes and let the sun warm him. Knowing that here, with these two people sacred to him on this boat, he had a wealth to outshine rare gold or the most precious gem. More than he could ever need.

NOTES AND
ACKNOWLEDGMENTS

The lore about Jean Laffite—and his buried treasures—
is rich along the coasts of Texas and Louisiana. For this
novel, I have drawn on sources both historical and legendary. Laffite, the great hero of the Battle of New
Orleans and privateer, left New Orleans to continue his
pirating operations on Galveston Island. Laffite was
ordered out of Galveston in 1820 (also often cited as 1821)
by the United States Navy. He burned Galveston to the
ground, most of his pirates dispersed, and Laffite sailed
off into the Gulf; after that point, history blurs the line
between fact and romanticized fiction. Did he die of fever
in the Yucatán? Or did he die in a sea battle or in a Cuban
prison after committing more piracy in the Caribbean? Did
he die in a battle off the coast of Cartagena, Colombia?
Did he retire to South America and a generally peaceful
old age? As of this writing, we do not know with absolute
certainty.

I have drawn on legends local to Aransas and Matagorda
bays in Texas: that Laffite buried a large treasure there

after abandoning Galveston, since he was facing pressure from both the American and British navies and did not want to be captured with his remaining booty aboard his vessel. But my "end history" for Laffite is entirely of my own imagining, although Dr. John Fanning and *Lynx* were real. And since Port Leo, Black Jack Point, St. Leo Bay, and Encina County are fictional places, Laffite's presence there is of course fictional. The supposed descendants of Jean Laffite and Catherine Villars—did she exist or not?—who are described herein are entirely fictional. There was no Monteblanco mint in Colonial Mexico.

In researching and writing this book, I am indebted to the following:

- My wife and children, for their extraordinary support and patience.
- Genny Ostertag and Peter Ginsberg, for insight and support in finding the heart of the book.
- Mitch Hoffman, Emi Battaglia, Beth de Guzman, Siobhan Padgett, Lindsey Rose, Barbara Slavin, Andrew Duncan, Jane Lee, Sonya Cheuse, and the entire Grand Central team.
- Joe Stanfield, for coastal hospitality and unfailing generosity.
- Sue Hastings Taylor, author and preeminent historian of Aransas County, who shared lore about Laffite in the Texas Coastal Bend and took me to probable treasure dump sites in the maze of offshore islands and inlets.
- The Honorable Nancy Pomykal, Justice of the Peace, Calhoun County, Texas, and the Honorable Patrick Daly, Justice of the Peace, Aransas County, Texas.

- Sheriff Mark Gilliam of Aransas County and Rockport, Texas, Police Chief Tim Jayroe, for answering questions with great courtesy, patience, and humor.
- Mark and Pam Kohler. Mark is a friend since early childhood and an extraordinarily gifted painter, and both he and Pam provided information on art.
- Mindy Reed, for research assistance.
- Dr. David Glassman, forensic anthropologist at Southwest Texas State University, who kindly walked me through the burial and recovery scenario.
- Casey Edward Green and the staff of the Historical Center at Rosenberg Library in Galveston, for access to their famous Laffite archive and assisting me in my research.
- Robert C. Vogel, Jean C. Epperson, Reginald Wilson, and Jeff Modzeleski, Laffite scholars extraordinaire, who answered questions on Laffite's history and related subjects with patience, good humor, and thoughtfulness.
- Patricia Mercado-Allinger, state archaeologist, Texas Historical Commission.
- Malcolm Shuman, fellow author and contract archaeologist, for sharing his thoughts on his everyday working world.
- David Lambert, for investments information.
- John Bauer, attorney, for information on probate law and proceedings.
- Scott Curren, who provided access to his sportfishing boat, the model for the *Miss Catherine*.
- Horace Green, who provided information on metal detecting.
- The Laffite Society, Galveston, Texas, for warmly welcoming me and then not stringing me up for playing

goombah with their favorite historical persona. Need-less to say, the Laffite Society consists of people far more polite, intelligent, friendly, and charming than certain members of the Laffite League, which is an entirely fictitious invention. The Laffite Society can be found at www.thelaffitesociety.com.

Of course, any errors are my responsibility, not theirs.

When his best customer—and friend—is killed outside his Miami bar, ex-CIA agent Sam Capra goes undercover to bring down a criminal family unlike any he's seen before...

Please turn this page
for a sneak peek at

INSIDE MAN

0

The car tumbled off the cliff, hurtling toward the distant blue shimmer of the water.

The first, instinctive reaction is to draw in, brace yourself for the impact. Brace, never mind, *survive* the impact.

Next was the peculiar itch in my daredevil's brain, figuring gravity's pull at 9.8 meters per second squared, thinking, *We have five seconds before we hit*.

In the second of those seconds I felt the gun's cool barrel press harder against my temple, realized my passenger was aiming right at my head in case the crash or the water didn't end me.

That is attention to detail. That is commitment.

Three: The water rushed toward us. I moved forward, reaching, the cool steel barrel staying on me, my fingers along the floorboard groping for my one chance.

The sky, the water, my last breath, everything blue.

Four: The gun fired.

1

———◆◆◆———

FOUR WEEKS EARLIER

YOU'RE SOMETHING, aren't you, Sam?"

"I'm just a guy who owns a bar." I slid Steve another draft beer. Someone had left an abandoned checkers game on the bar and I moved the glass around the game. The guys who'd left it might be back tomorrow to finish it. It was that kind of bar.

"But you used to be something."

"A bar owner is being something." Why is there no one-word term in American English for being a bar owner? Publican sounds too English and formal. Barkeep isn't enough. I glanced through the windows. A young couple still sat on the outside couch, a dog at their feet, and I could tell from the angle of their beer bottles as they sipped that they were nearly done. The covered patio of the bar was otherwise empty, a slow Sunday night headed toward empty. I had to close at midnight, and that was twenty minutes away.

"But you used to be *something.*" And I couldn't miss the prying hint in Steve's voice.

"We all used to be something," I said. "You too, Steve."

Steve smiled. "The way you move. The way you eyed

that jerk who bothered that young woman in here last night. You didn't even have to raise a fist, threaten to call the cops. Or even boot him. Just the look you gave him."

I shrugged. "Looks are cheap."

"The way you study every person who comes in here, Sam. One glance of assessment. That's a habit of being in tough situations."

"I just don't want trouble and it's better to see it coming than be surprised."

"So the something you were," he said. "I think if you were ex-military or an ex-cop, you'd claim it right away. Proud of it. But you don't."

I shrugged again. Bartenders are supposed to listen more than they talk, anyway. We're not the ones paying. I wiped the bar. Every night was too slow. My other bars around the world were high-end joints but Stormy's wasn't, it was a certified dive. It had been open for years, sliding through an assortment of owners until it came into my possession. The other nearby bars in Coconut Grove were a bit higher end than Stormy's. Scarred bar, couches under a crooked TV, games such as checkers and Connect Four on the little tables. No fancy drinks; beer, wine, and your basic hard liquor. If I told people I owned a bar in Miami they'd automatically assume I owned some uber-trendy nightclub in South Beach, women pouring out of limos in tiny skirts and huge heels. Many of my customers walked to Stormy's from the surrounding neighborhoods in Coconut Grove. We were not a tourist draw.

I wondered why I was bothering to keep this joint open. It was just me and the couple on the patio and Steve and two older guys watching a west coast basketball game on the corner TV; they'd already finished a pitcher. Miami wasn't playing so there wasn't a crowd.

"So. Since you won't claim what you used to be, maybe you can't." Steve kept playing at Sherlock. He could play all day. I don't talk about my past, not my real past, and for sure not to a guy who drinks too much. Even if he was my best friend in Miami.

"You mean like I was in jail?" I said. I didn't smile. I had been in a prison once, but not the kind he thought. A CIA prison is a different proposition.

Steve laughed. "No. Maybe you were working in something you can't talk about."

"Maybe you're just underestimating the skills involved in running a bar." I didn't have a manager in place here, which was why I'd spent two weeks in Miami. Maybe I could offer Steve a job. But that would mean being honest with him about what I did, what I'd done in my previous life, and asking him to stay silent. I wasn't sure he could stay quiet.

I would wonder, later, if it would have all been different if I'd offered him work during the past two weeks. I needed someone to run the bar, and to keep the secrets associated with it, and Steve needed a purpose. If I'd let myself say, *Here's an old friend who could handle the secrets, the tough situations.* If I'd let myself trust him. But I was worried he'd tell my parents. If I had trusted him…then it might all have been different for him, and for me. He might not have kept the job that he did.

"I know what I see," Steve said, suddenly not smiling, serious. "You know how to handle yourself, Sam. I could use some help, maybe."

"Help how?"

"Well, you know I used to work in freelance security." I'd first met Steve when I was fifteen years old. He'd worked a security detail attached to my parents' relief workers team in central Africa. He'd saved my family's lives during a chaotic evacuation from a war-torn nation, pulling my parents and my brother and me from a wrecked vehicle and getting us to an airport to board the final military flight before the rebels bombed the runways. He'd stayed in steady touch over the years: sending us Christmas cards from distant corners of the world, a pen and pencil set for my high school graduation, flowers and a thoughtful note when my brother Danny, a relief worker in Afghanistan, was kidnapped and executed. When I'd come to Miami two weeks ago to address the nagging problems of my bar here, he'd showed up and claimed a barstool the next day. I first assumed my parents had sent him to spy on me; after years of estrangement they'd decided to take an interest in my life. But Steve was living in his parents' house in Coral Gables and was already a semi-regular at this bar. He hadn't done security work overseas in a while. He seemed happy to guard the bar against any potential danger.

But he saw something of himself in me right now. It was unnerving that he could read my past in my movements, my attitude. I thought I had mellowed more.

Part of me just wanted to tell him to forget it, that he was entirely wrong, and hope he'd let it drop. But spies, even former ones, are curious people. We want to know things. Even when we're not spies anymore. I was twenty-six and had spent three years with a secret division in the CIA. I guess it showed. Or did Steve know more about me than he was willing to admit?

"You're wrong about me, but what is the job?"

He looked at me as though he could recognize my little white lie and shook his head. "Am I wrong? Maybe I can tempt you. I could use an inside man." He gave me a smile. I shrugged like I didn't know what the term meant and went to the guys watching the basketball game to see if they wanted anything, which was an unusual level of service here at Stormy's. But I wanted Steve to change the subject. Inside man. To be a spy again. When the guys wanted nothing more, I returned to the bar and resumed tidying.

Steve lowered his voice. "So. I'm meeting a friend here tonight."

I frowned. If I was trying to impress a woman, Stormy's was not my choice of venue, and I owned the damned place. "Uh, you know we're closing in a bit?"

"I just need to talk to her for a bit. You don't have to serve us. It'd be a big favor. You'll be here anyway." That was true. I lived in an apartment above the bar; every one of my bars around the world, they all had living quarters above them. There was a reason for that, and it was the reason I didn't think I could offer my talkative friend a job. But Steve was here every night when I shut down the bar, and we'd hung out and chatted after I turned off the OPEN neon sign.

"I should charge you rent," I said, joking. The couple on the patio left; the two guys watching basketball got up and left. I left Steve for a moment to collect their tips and their empties. I didn't have a server on duty, the one I'd hired hadn't bothered to show up. The staff, the location, the rundown look of the place, the long lack of a manager, all were problems. I owned over thirty bars around the world and so far Stormy's was the divey-est. I didn't live here in Miami and the place was dying of neglect. Hence my past two weeks, trying to decide whether or not I'd sell. If I did, I'd have to buy another bar in Miami to replace this one. I

have very secret bosses—who gave me the bars to run—
and because this place doubled as a safe house for their
operations, I could not sell it and then not replace it. Miami
was a town where they would too often need a safe house.

I dumped the glasses and slid the money into the cash
register.

"I could pay you, Sam."

"What, your tab? I thought you had a friend coming..."

"No, dummy. To help me with this security job I got."
He was trying again.

"Thanks for the offer," I said. "But like I said, I'm not
anything. Just a bartender."

Steve studied me. He was older than me, in his mid-
forties, burr haircut going silver, a man who had once
been handsome and still could be but there had been too
much beer and too many fights. He looked worn and beaten
down. "You sure? I still think I'm right about you."

"My brother always told me to stay on my guard. I think
that's what you see."

"You know how sorry I am about Danny."

"I know."

The thing was—I don't think I'd talked to another guy as
much as I had to Steve since my brother Danny died. Most
hours that the bar was open, I was here and Steve was here,
drinking sodas during the day, tapping at his laptop or reading or watching the TV. My closest friend from my days in
the hidden Special Projects branch at the CIA was a guy
named August Holdwine, and August and I no longer talked
much. We didn't have reason to; and as much as I liked him,
he felt like a part of my past I didn't care to revisit. And as far
as my friends from my Harvard days went, to them I was a
mystery. I graduated, went to work for a London consulting

firm that was secretly a CIA front, and had now ended up owning bars. I had fallen out of the drawn lines for what was acceptable success. And I wasn't on social media, posting pictures of my child, recording what I'd eaten for lunch, or talking about my favorite football team.

But every day for the two weeks I'd struggled with getting the bar on its feet again, Steve had been here. So we'd spent those past fourteen days and nights talking for hours, everything from basketball to women to books to movies. I hadn't had a friend in a while. I hadn't had the time for one. And he was someone who had once helped my family during a dark hour. I owed him. Maybe I should listen to his offer, help him. I felt torn.

"When's your friend coming?"

He glanced at his watch. "Any minute now."

Then the woman walked in. Even in the dim light you could see she was striking. Long dark hair, a curvy figure. She wore a scarf around her neck that blocked some of her face and as she unwound the length of red cloth I could see her mouth, lipsticked, set in a determined frown.

She was my age, mid-twenties, and I thought: She's not really his friend. But then, I was his friend, and I figured it was none of my business.

She seemed to give Steve a look of polite surprise. Like she couldn't believe she was here. It was close to midnight and we were in a cheap bar. Who meets at a bar so close to closing?

"Hello," she said, shaking his hand. "Let's sit over on the couches, where we can talk."

She clearly wanted to be away from me. But Steve, ever the gregarious one, said, "This is my good buddy Sam. He owns this dump. I just keep it in business."

The woman offered her hand, and I shook it. She had a confident grip. She didn't tell me her name, though, and I couldn't tell if she simply forgot or she didn't want me to know. Steve didn't introduce her. This was odd; this was off. Something else was going on here. "Hello. What may I get you to drink? We're about to close, but you're welcome to stay and talk."

"I don't want to inconvenience you . . ."

"Sam lives above the bar; he can't be inconvenienced," Steve said. "This is a very private place. Like you asked."

She glanced at Steve's empty beer. "Well. All right. That's kind of you, Sam." And her lovely eyes met mine. "Could I please have a club soda? With lime?" And her voice was low and slightly loping in how she spoke, and heating you while you stood there.

"Of course. I'll bring it to you." I muted the post-basket-ball game analysis that was playing so they could hear each other more easily.

The woman gave me a grateful smile. "Thank you, Sam; you're kind." That molten voice, like warmed honey.

They headed for the couches and I got her a club soda. I wished our bar glasses were better crystal. I saw her glance at the walls: the vintage Miami Dolphins posters, worn signs from local breweries, a framed photo of the bar's original owner—a famously irascible woman named Stormy who had died a few years back—and Ernest Hemingway from the 1950s. A message blackboard where anyone could write a morsel of wisdom. This evening it announced, in blue chalk: SPECIAL TONIGHT, BUY TWO DRINKS, PAY FOR THEM BOTH. I hoped she'd think the bar was retro cool instead of outdated lame.

I brought her the club soda, with the nicest looking lime

slice in the whole bar, in time to hear Steve talking about his service in working security overseas. He shut up— nothing could get Steve to shut up normally—when I set down the drink. I left them alone, feeling vaguely uneasy. I wondered what kind of job he'd needed help with where he'd need an inside man—someone to go undercover. I knew he owned a security firm and that he'd handled body- guard duties for celebrities when they came for big awards events, although he hadn't seemed at all busy the past two weeks. He had a house close by, and I wondered why he wasn't meeting his lovely friend there. They spoke in low voices, too low for me to hear, like lovers.

I turned off the OPEN sign, locked the door, retreated back to the bar. I wiped the already spotless counter, work- ing around the checkerboard, and did a quick inventory. Short on wine and beer. I'd have to reorder, eating up the scant profits. And then I'd have to decide if I was going to go home next weekend, to New Orleans, and see my son Daniel. The weekend would be the busiest time, and the bar couldn't easily afford for me to be gone. No one could manage it; the current staff had no stars I could groom. And given that the bar had its own secrets in the apartment above it, I needed a manager I could trust entirely. I could maybe recruit one of the managers from my other bars: Gigi from Las Vegas, Kenneth from London, Ariane from Brussels...The Europeans might particularly enjoy a stay in Miami.

I saw Steve lean back suddenly from his friend. They'd become huddled, her talking so softly that I couldn't even hear the murmur of that honey river of a voice of hers.

I glanced at the clock. Ten past midnight.

He studied a small piece of paper and then handed it to

her and she tucked it into her purse. I heard him say, "Considering what they sent me, you have to treat this seriously."

She said, clearly, "I don't know what they want. I don't understand it." Then she glanced at me, as if realizing that she might have spoken too loud.

And then his voice dropped back down again.

I opened up a laptop I kept under the bar for the extra slow times like this. Keyed it on. Typed in a website and then there was a video feed of my son Daniel, asleep in his crib. His sleep was so deep that for a moment I got worried, and nearly called Leonie, his nanny (of sorts—she used to be a forger and I saved her from her life of crime, long story). She'd set up the feed for me, the traveling dad who had to be away too often.

Then he stirred, that magical breath of life, and I watched my baby sleep.

This is why I can't help you with your security job, whatever it is, Steve, I thought. *I need to stay out of that world.*

"Sam," Steve's voice broke my concentration and I closed the laptop.

"You all want something else?" I asked. The woman was still sitting on the couch.

"I'm going to go get her car and bring it around, then I'm going to follow her home on my motorcycle." Steve lived only a few blocks away, in a nice lush corner of Coconut Grove, near the landmark Plymouth Congregational Church. When he didn't walk to the bar, he rode his motorcycle. "Will you stay in here with her, please?"

"Sure. Has someone threatened your friend?"

"Just keep an eye on her." He turned to go.

"Steve? Seriously, is there a problem?" I raised my voice.

He cracked a smile. "Just keeping her safe. You sure you didn't used to be somebody?"

"Just a bartender," I said, automatically.

He paused, as though wishing I'd finally given him another answer. He headed out the door. Most of the parking for the bars in this part of Coconut Grove is either valet (with several restaurants sharing the service) or individual paid lots of banks or other early-closing businesses scattered through the neighborhood. Stormy's was between a valet station for a couple of nice restaurants, closed by now, and a paid lot three blocks away.

Something was wrong. I walked to her table. "Is there a problem?"

She glanced up at me. "You're a lot younger than Steve is."

"So?"

"Don't you have friends your own age?"

"Yes. Steve seems concerned."

She said nothing.

The spy in me. "Are you in some kind of trouble? Are you his client?"

She didn't answer me. She glanced around. "It's not what you'd call a nice bar, but I like it," she said. "I like that you have left that checkers game untouched. That's some customer service, there." She tried out a smile. It was lovely.

I shrugged. "Every game should be played until there's a winner."

"I agree completely." She stood and watched for him at the window. Steve's motorcycle was parked out front, and he'd left his jacket and his helmet on the bar. I moved them down to the end of the bar and I could hear his bike's keys jingle in the jacket pocket.

I joined her at the window. A block down was another

bar, with no one sitting outside. A moderate rain had started, chasing the Sunday night drinkers inside. Rain was a fact of life in Miami; some days it felt like the humidity never eased. But traffic had thinned, a light mist coming with midnight. The street was empty. "I'll be fine waiting for him."

"He asked me to stay with you," I said.

"That's my car," she said. I wondered why on earth he would have insisted that he bring her car around rather than just walk her to it if he was concerned for her safety. Steve was Steve. It was an older Jaguar, in mint condition. I saw Steve at the wheel, turning onto the street from the prepaid lot, three blocks from us.

He pulled up. He stepped out onto the bricked sidewalk.

Then from the opposite direction, from the road Steve took to his house, a heavy SUV roared down the street, slowed when it reached Steve. He turned to look at it.

I heard a single shot, muffled.

Steve fell. The SUV roared past us.

The woman screamed.

ABOUT THE AUTHOR

Jeff Abbott is the *New York Times* bestselling, award-winning author of fourteen novels. His books include the Sam Capra thrillers *Adrenaline*, *The Last Minute*, and *Downfall*, as well as the standalone novels *Panic*, *Fear*, *Collision*, and *Trust Me*. *The Last Minute* won an International Thriller Writers award, and Jeff is also a three-time nominee for the Edgar award. He lives in Austin with his family. You can visit his website at www.jeffabbott.com.

LOOK FOR EVEN MORE
JEFF ABBOTT THRILLERS

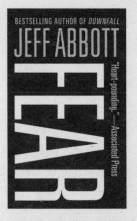

Available now